THE BLADE KINGS SERIES

FULL TILT

RUTH STILLING

To the queens who fix crowns behind closed doors.
Keep reigning.

Want to stay in the loop on all things Ruth Stilling?

Join my **newsletter** for release updates, book news, and more.
Sign up using the QR code below.

For exclusive first looks, art reveals, and the only place to see NSFW art, come join me on **Patreon**.
Join Patreon by scanning the QR code below.

TRIGGER/CONTENT WARNINGS

Dear reader,

Thank you so much for choosing to read *Full Tilt*, the fourth book in The Blade Kings series.

While this book is a contemporary fictional romance and, of course, has a happily ever after, I want to bring to your attention certain themes featured within this story so that you can make an informed decision about whether or not to continue reading. Please be aware that the following information does contain spoilers; however, I want to offer all my readers the opportunity to be fully versed in all potentially triggering scenarios prior to reading.

Full Tilt contains sexually explicit content and strong language throughout the entire story. It is also an enemies-to-lovers story, where both main characters set about creating scenarios where they can sabotage and humiliate each other. This does include **perceived** *other woman* drama.

In addition, you will find discussion of parental neglect, including on-page verbal abuse and manipulation from a parent. Also, while the actual event does not take place, there is an on-page scene where the main female character encounters someone who could potentially sexually attack her. There is also discussion around this topic thereafter. Finally, this book has on-page discussion of conception and struggling to conceive—not involving the main characters.

With all that said, when Tommy falls, he really does fall hard, and tension gives way to adorable, swoonworthy moments!

I hope, after digesting these warnings, you feel comfortable to continue with reading this book.

Enjoy Jenna and Tommy's story!

Lots of love,

Ruth

PROLOGUE
TOMMY

There's nothing more dangerous than misplaced faith in other human beings.

Take this doorman, for example. With a phone to one ear, he speaks with a guy I've recently learned might be my dad, wearing an expression like I just rolled in dog shit before I entered this fancy building.

I can actually see my face in the white floor tiles.

I already know how this is going to go down—I'll be turned away in the next thirty seconds and told never to come back. It's not just my face that doesn't fit around these parts of New York; my clothes don't either. Not a designer label in sight. I mean, my white sneakers are Nike, if you can look past three years' worth of grime, which makes them more of a gray color.

Truthfully, I don't know why the fuck I thought this was a good idea. I used a whole month's wages from the burger joint to fund my flight here, and I can already tell I'll be kicking my heels for twenty-four hours while I wait for my return flight home.

Alex Schneider doesn't want to talk to me. He's had seventeen years to reach out to his estranged son—if I am, in fact, his blood.

Helen, my mom, might've spun me a ton of lies about my father being in the special forces and killed in action after they had a one-night thing. But that story would only carry her so far, and she knew it. I've been asking questions for a while about the NHL player who looks like me and shares the same skating style.

All I want is answers from someone. Anyone at this point. Is the former Blades defenseman my dad, or am I just grasping at straws, hoping he wasn't blown up in a military operation?

You know what? Fuck this. I'll see myself out. The pretentious brow floating around in the doorman's hairline tells me everything I need to know.

"Excuse me. Mr. Williams?"

I spin a full one-eighty on my heel and lock eyes with the doorman as he replaces the handset and points toward the elevator on the far side of the pristine lobby.

"Mr. Schneider has approved your visit. You can head up to the fourth floor and take a right. His apartment—number 41—is at the end of the hallway."

It's a full three minutes later when I hit the smart doorbell and take a step back from the glossy black double doors, swallowing down my nerves and ignoring the latest phone call from Mom. I've got an inbox full of apologies and pleas—begging me to come back home and not jump to conclusions based on the fact that we look alike. But just like the messages in my voicemail, I don't want to hear what she has to say. I know she's been lying to me for seventeen years; I can feel it in my gut. Why should today be any different?

Perhaps I shouldn't be shocked when the first face I see is some random blonde as she flies out the apartment and pushes past me, half-dressed and red-faced, carrying the rest of her clothes in one hand and a purse in the other.

You'd need to be living under a rock not to know the reputation Alex Schneider carries both on and off the ice—he's the one warming the penalty box during games and women's beds straight afterward. At least, he was, until he nearly killed Scorpions defenseman, Zach Evans, last season in a brutal hit that left him a free agent.

"You just gonna stand in the doorway and stare or actually cross the threshold?"

An aggravated voice that I know belongs to my potential dad has me stepping inside and closing the door behind me.

"Leave your sneakers on."

I pause my right hand, hovering it above my lace as I look up.

Alex comes into view, adjusting himself on the large gray corner couch set in the center of his sleek living space. When I see him in the flesh, I might as well be looking into a mirror.

At first, I think he's going to switch off the flat-screen TV set on the wall opposite him. Instead, he snatches the PlayStation controller from the coffee table and resumes the game of GTA he previously had on pause.

"Take a seat." He points to the far end of the couch, swiping a bottle of Bud from the side table next to him. He takes two large pulls before setting it back down.

I perch on the corner of the couch while his GTA character loots a store and holds up the owner.

A nervous twitch pulls at my throat as I watch Alex play without giving me a second glance.

Does this guy even know who I am? Surely, he can see the resemblance as clearly as I can.

"The store owner has a ton of cash in his safe. It's kept behind a shelving unit in the back room." I don't recognize my own voice when I finally speak.

The side-eye he offers is the first time he's looked at me since I arrived. "I know. I've played this map more times than

years you've been on this earth. I was bored and needed something to do."

I try not to let the fact that he's still gaming despite my presence affect my confidence and push on with what I came to say.

"Did the doorman tell you who I was?" I ask, probing for
more information.

Putting a bullet straight between the store owner's eyes, Alex
flicks his stony gaze to mine. "That's literally the point of his
job, Tommy. I don't allow nameless people up to this apartment.
I get enough with the desperate puck bunnies trying to sneak in
at all hours."

"Did you just kick that blonde girl out of your apartment?" I
know that my question sounds like an accusation, and the second
it leaves my mouth, I realize the monumental mistake I just
made.

Hitting pause on the game, Alex tosses the controller onto
the glass coffee table with a clatter.

Arms folded across his chest, he sits back on the couch and
narrows his eyes in my direction, leaving me in no doubt over
his thoughts.

He hates me.

"Tell me something, Tommy."

My stomach roils at the cutting edge in his voice.

"Did your mom send you here? Did she run out of money, or
is she freaking out that the child support payments will stop in a
couple of months when you turn eighteen?"

I might as well be the fictional store owner with a gaping
hole in my head.

"What?" I croak out, my suspicions finally confirmed. "No
... I caught a flight here from Minneapolis. I wanted to meet you
since you're—"

"Since I'm what?" He laughs darkly, downing the rest of
his Bud and rolling the empty bottle between his palms on a
smirk. "Since I'm your dad? And you thought you could just

4

show up at my place and all would play out like some fucking fairy tale? I don't do family. I told your mom that enough times."

I'd reply if I wasn't stunned into silence by his brutality.

"Last I heard from Helen Williams, she told me she'd spun some bullshit about how your dad died in service out in Afghanistan. Apparently, you've been asking questions about who your real dad is for years." He pushes his head back into the couch and laughs toward the ceiling. "The way she wanted to get married and live happily ever after when she found out she was pregnant. Naive little girl. As if I wanted to settle down at twenty. My hockey career was just getting started. I never wanted kids, and nothing has changed."

Bile rises up my throat as reality sinks deep within my bones. I'm getting the answers I came for, just not the ending I convinced myself wasn't required. I was determined I didn't need a father figure in my life. I'd come this far without him, and I could live the rest of my life in his absence. All I thought I wanted was answers.

Faith has a funny way of fooling you, persuading you it isn't there while it waits in the wings for the crushing truth to take ahold of your hopes. Pushing you to spend your last dime and board a three-hour flight, believing you'll be met with your father's open arms.

Alex is staring at me as I lift my head and look at him, blinking twice to rid the wetness as it coats my vision.

"Your mom told you that story because I made it really fucking clear I wanted nothing to do with the baby. After she proved you were mine with a paternity test, she agreed to sign an NDA in exchange for above-mandatory child support payments." His laugh is dark. "I bet she's freaking out right now, worrying I'll come after her for breaking our agreement."

He drops his eyes to my sneakers, disgust screwing up his face. "I've no fucking idea where that money went, but it sure as shit wasn't on your wardrobe. Maybe it was on your budding hockey career."

Rolling his lips together, he attempts to suppress his obvious amusement. "I hope you aren't expecting to get drafted. I've seen you play, and I find it hard to believe that you share my DNA, even if your mom proved it to me."

He kicks his feet onto the table in front of him as his dark laughter reemerges. "That said, word is the Detroit Sting have eyes on you." He scoffs. "They haven't lifted the Cup since I can remember. If I wasn't so embarrassed by those sneakers you're wearing, I'd be fully cringing at the projection of your hockey career."

Words stick in my esophagus. I'm desperate to tell him what a fucking prick I think he is and that I'm not surprised the Blades didn't renew his contract. Although nothing materializes, and I remain silent, feeling smaller and smaller with every passing second.

Eventually, my "dad" rises from the couch and makes for the kitchen on the far side of the open plan space, pulling a single beer from the fridge and snapping off the cap.

"I would offer you one, but you're still a baby." He downs the beer and tosses the glass bottle into an open trash can, and it smashes into pieces.

Everything this guy does is barbaric.

Despite everything I've learned in the past ten minutes, I can't deny what we share beyond our DNA.

The way he lives his life with such reckless abandon, the way he handles objects, his words, and people with such brutality. I can feel that deep in my gut—an anger that simmers just below the surface, threatening to spill over each time someone pisses me off. Or walks all over my feelings like it's a crime to have them in the first place.

Maybe it is. Maybe that's how you get ahead in life—not

giving anyone an inch to prove that you're not a fool who harbors faith in the first place.

The cold tiles seep through the soles of my sneakers as icy truths meander through my mind. *If your own parents can lie to you and reject you so seamlessly, why should any other fucker treat you better?*

The back pocket of my jeans vibrates again.

Another lie from Mom.

I shove my hands into the front pocket of my hoodie and look around at the kind of lavish apartment I know I'll be living in just as soon as I turn pro. Which I will.

My dad might not want anything to do with me, but he can sure watch me become the most remembered Schneider in the NHL. Every time a hockey fan utters the Schneider name, I'll make sure the only player they're referring to is me. All this guy cares about is himself and his ego, and this is the perfect way to hurt both.

ONE

TOMMY

More Than Six Years Later

September

"What's the significance behind this one?"

No matter how many times I get a tattoo, the pain never feels any easier. Especially not when the area getting inked is your neck.

Lying on my side, I shift to get more comfortable on the black leather bench, trying not to let my discomfort show, along with my irritation at the incessant questioning I've endured for the past four hours. My usual tattoo artist moved out to California six months ago, and now I'm stuck with his apprentice, who he assured me was just as good, although I highly doubt that —I don't see how anyone can maintain a high level of concentration when all they do is fucking talk. Oxygen is needed to power the brain as well as the mouth.

"No significance," I answer bluntly.

Aside from confirming the final design I wanted, I've barely said ten words since I climbed onto the bed and he got to work.

"Oh, right," he replies, wiping down my raw skin for the thousandth time. "It's just that most people only get a neck tattoo of something significant. I guess because it's hard to hide it on this area of the body."

On a sigh that is designed to convey my irritation, I remind myself that he's nearly done and then I'm free to escape. I fucking hate small talk. "Yeah, well, I'm not most people, and this isn't exactly my first rodeo."

"I'll say." He chuckles. "How many have you got now?"

Why *the fuck* are some people so fucking cheerful? They could be having the worst day or have the grumpiest client, yet their bright persona never fades.

It's fucking annoying as hell.

"Lost count at number twenty-five."

He blows out a long breath. "Of them all, I think this king cobra is my favorite. And not because it's my work. It's the way it snakes up your spine. The idea is right on."

What I just said isn't strictly true—the tattoo does have meaning, as does a lot of the ink on my skin.

The first tattoo I got—a pair of scissors cutting through a thread—was done right across the street from my dad's apartment. They had walk-in appointments available, and I had twenty hours to kill before my flight home. I used my fake ID, and they inked me there and then. It's still my favorite tattoo to this day.

"I would ask if you planned to stop after this one, but everyone knows that once you get one tattoo, the addiction takes hold."

Lifting my hands up, I twist my wrists around so my palms are facing him. "Aside from my face and feet, the only blank canvases I have left are these, and I heard they are the most painful and difficult area to get done."

The artist—who gave me his name when I arrived, but I can't remember it since I plan to erase him from my memory as soon as I leave—sucks a sharp breath through his teeth.

"Yeah. Palm tattoos generally fade quickly or fail altogether. You have to go really deep to achieve any kind of longevity."

I shrug. "That doesn't bother me. I welcome the pain."

He huffs out a laugh, and I'm ready to take the ink gun he's holding and shove it up his ass. One false move, and he's fucked this tattoo.

"No kidding. You literally just had your spine and neck tattooed in two sessions, and I didn't feel you flinch once. Most clients—no matter how experienced they are—would be crying like a baby and begging me to stop by now."

"Showing pain is a sign of weakness, and I already told you, I'm not most people."

Wiping the nape of my neck again, he sets down the gun, and I inwardly breathe a sigh of relief.

Fuck, that one was tough.

"Okay, I think we're done."

He slides his small roller stool across to a metal chest of drawers, and I stand from the bench, already making my way over to the full-length mirror.

"So, I went with a shading technique called stippling to create the intricate details you can see on the scales."

The artist holds the mirror he grabbed from the drawer unit and brings it closer to my fresh tattoo.

Jesus, it's good. I underestimated this guy.

Not that I plan on telling him that.

"You missed a bit," I bite out.

Like he just found out his puppy died, the guy flares his eyes wide before carefully examining each section of the snake.

I turn to face him, a usual smirk overtaking my expression. "I'm just fucking with you. It's a good piece."

He wipes above his brow, genuine perspiration emerging. "Holy shit, you sounded serious. Like, deadass pissed."

"Nah. You'll know when I'm pissed. That was my friendly voice," I reply, taking a seat back on the bench so he can wrap the tattoo.

He doesn't respond as he begins treating and bandaging.

"I gotta admit ..." To my surprise, he begins talking. Again. "I was a bit taken aback when you booked in for September. Don't you guys have preseason now? I thought getting tatted was only allowed in the offseason?"

I can't help the groan as it leaves my throat. Tipping my chin over my shoulder, I raise a brow in his direction. "Tell me you don't watch hockey without telling me you don't watch hockey."

He snaps a piece of medical tape from its holder. "I don't follow."

My smirk returns, even though he can't see it clearly. "Because if you watched the game, you'd know I'm not the kind of player who follows the rules."

He snorts, securing the wrap against my skin. "Oh, I don't need to watch it to know that. The second my new boss found out who we had booked, he told me to watch my mouth."

I like this guy's new boss, and I haven't even met him.

"He also told me your dad liked getting under people's skin when he played too." He laughs again at a thought. "I tattoo people, and you punch them. Looks like we share something in common."

When he finishes up on the dressing, I grab my shirt from the back of a chair and throw it on, ignoring his comment about my dad. Aside from confirming to the media that I was his son when I started playing under his last name, I haven't publicly talked about him since. The aim isn't to perpetuate his legacy, but to bury it under mine.

"Hockey fights are a standard part of every game; the crowd feeds off them, and despite what people claim, the age of the enforcer isn't dead," I reply.

The guy shakes his head and makes for the counter, ready to ring up my bill. I grab my bag and follow him.

"I'd make a shit enforcer. I never let people wind me up," he says, taking my Amex and processing the payment. "I'm so laid-back; I'm practically horizontal."

I balk. "Who said anything about letting people wind you up?" I point at my chest when I take my credit card back. "I'm the antagonist, not the other way around."

He quirks a brow at me, green eyes looking doubtful. "I don't know, man. You sound like you're getting wound up right about now."

I grin. "That's what I allow people to think. I'm always in control. *Always.* If they have a pulse, they're eating out of my bare palms."

He snorts again. "Everyone has an Achilles' heel. Even Superman."

"And like I told you twice already—"

"Yeah, yeah." He waves a hand in front of him. "You're not like most people."

"Exactly." I tap my temple twice, masking the real truth behind a self-assured expression. Because, in reality, I do have one weakness—or thorn in my side.

With dark brown hair and deep blue eyes, all five feet eight of her crawls around in my brain, taking up space she doesn't deserve. In the past six years, no one has gotten to me like she does—and especially not someone I've only spoken to a handful of times.

No woman has ever turned down an advance from me, but Jenna Miller did. I swear to God she only said no because her pretentious girlfriends—whose husbands happen to be my team-mates—hate my guts.

The New York Storm soccer team barely registers on the sports radar, and their goalie should've been honored—no, begging—to have the Blades best defenseman show her even an ounce of interest. Instead, she blew the only chance she'd ever get with me.

"You look like something—*or someone*—might be getting to you."

I come to, completely forgetting my surroundings and who's standing in front of me as I let Jenna fucking Miller and her perfect face invade my mind once again.

On a headshake, I reach into my pocket and toss a couple of hundred-dollar bills onto the counter. "Nah, just working out how much tip your work deserves. Two hundred should do it, right?"

His eyes grow wide as he blurts out, "Y-yeah, that works for me."

I slide them toward him and lean in a little closer. "I lied earlier, about the tattoo. It does have meaning."

He takes the cash and pockets it quickly, keeping his eyes on mine, waiting for me to elaborate.

"King cobras are generally acknowledged to be the smartest of their species. They are apex hunters, meaning they can adapt to their surroundings and prey. They're always one step ahead of their next victim, planning their next move. They rarely make the same mistake twice." I tap my knuckle on the counter. "That's what makes a superior predator. Once bitten, twice shy."

TWO

JENNA

"Is that good for you, baby?"

It would be if he was actually massaging my clit and not my pubic bone.

"Yes," I reply in my best faux moan, one I've perfected over the past few months. Initially, I would be honest because I'm nothing if not truthful, but I quickly learned that telling a guy he hadn't made me come was more trouble than it was worth.

I can't deal with the barrage of responses like: "What's wrong with you? I've never had a girl struggle to climax with me before." And, "Why don't you relax? You're so uptight."

Yes, Casanova, it has to be all my fault, doesn't it? It couldn't possibly be the fact that you're rubbing a numb area, and now I only feel sore from the way you've prodded at me for the past hour rather than turned on.

"Come for me, Jenna," he—the guy hovering above me, whose name I can't remember—rasps into my ear as he slowly pumps in and out of me, his fingers still way off the mark.

How can my labia even remotely resemble a clit?

"Are you close?"

Since I've given up on talking and subtly helping him with a lesson in female anatomy, I nod my head once and pray he finishes soon.

"I'm not coming until you do, Jenna."

Well, shit, now this *really is* awkward. Nameless Guy knows my name and wants to look after my needs in bed. There's no way I'm going to climax. Not genuinely anyway.

On the next stroke of his dick, I release a whimper that sounds borderline passable as an orgasm and then another when he slides into me again.

Lord above, please let this be over soon. I promise not to sleep with another guy ever again.

I'll become a nun and be a well-behaved girl for the rest of my life.

"I'm gonna come. I'm right there."

Thank Christ for small mercies.

"Do it," I tell him, gritting out the words and trying to sound as into this as he is.

The attraction I felt for this guy a few hours ago when I agreed to head back to his place might've all but dissipated, but I'm not a complete hard-nosed bitch. He clearly wanted to look after me tonight, and that's one up from the guys I usually get with.

It's just a shame his bed game didn't quite match up to all the promises he'd repeated in the bar.

On a groan that vibrates in my eardrum, he finally finishes and pulls out, sitting back on his heels as he snaps the condom off and tosses it into a trash can by his bed.

He turns back to face me, a smirk pulling at his top lip. I've seen that look before—one that leaves no doubt that he's already thinking about round two.

I sit up and pull the duvet over my body, trying to send a message that I'm done. In fact, I'm likely leaving in the next thirty minutes.

He drops his head between his shoulders and shakes it

slowly. "I was going to ask if you wanted to stay the night ..." His smirk is gone when he lifts his head, running a hand through disheveled sandy-blond hair. "But by the way you just recoiled up the bed, I'm guessing a repeat performance is out of the question."

At least he's perceptive.

I look over at my bag and clothes hanging from a chair on the far side of his bedroom. I've got no idea who I went home with. All I know is, he drives a fast car and owns his own legal practice. He reminded me often enough. For all I know, he could be a serial killer with a dozen women locked in his basement.

I push down the thoughts and smile sweetly. "Staying over isn't my usual MO. Plus, I have practice first thing in the morning."

His blue eyes flare wide, and now I'm internally scolding myself for giving away information. I never offer guys more than my first name. It's easy to stay under the radar since female soccer players aren't exactly famous.

"Now it all makes sense."

He points to my covered body, and I quirk a brow.

"What do you mean?"

He edges closer, and I'd back away further if I wouldn't fall off the bed.

"Your body is so tight. Toned to fuck. Your muscle-to-fat ratio is basically zero. Since you wouldn't tell me anything about yourself earlier, I figured you just worked out a lot, but you being an athlete makes way more sense."

My raised brow rises further. "I only said that I had practice. I could be a musician."

His confident headshake isn't buying it. "Nah. What sport do you play?"

"I'm a swimmer," I blurt out a little too quickly.

He shrugs and joins me under the duvet, resting an arm along the headboard behind me. He's getting comfortable, and I just want to get out of here.

Why is it so fucking hard to find a boyfriend in this town? I'm twenty-seven, hardly retired. My last boyfriend, Lee, started off so promisingly until the relationship fizzled to nothing.

I just want a man to make me feel alive. Excited.

"You don't have the build of a swimmer." His eyes scan me beneath the duvet again. "You've got the height, but your shoulders aren't screaming swimmer to me."

I fight back an eye roll. "For a lawyer, you sure as shit seem to know a lot about physiology."

Shame you didn't pay closer attention in sex ed.

"My ex-girlfriend was a physical trainer. You remind me of her a lot actually."

Annnd get me out of here immediately.

"Lovely," I deadpan. "I play ice hockey."

He pulls back, examining my face for a lie. "You have the feisty attitude. What position?"

"Goalie." At least that part is truthful.

Nodding once, he reaches over and passes me a glass of water. I study it for a few beats, checking for any residue at the bottom.

"You can sniff it, too, if you'd like. I promise I haven't spiked it." He chuckles. "I spend my life prosecuting criminals. I don't plan on becoming one."

I set the glass on the nightstand beside me, not bothering to risk it. I've hooked up plenty of times since Lee and I split, and I've never felt so unsure as I do now. Perhaps the magic of one-night stands is wearing off. Not that they're all they're cracked up to be anyway.

"I'm a big hockey fan," he continues, pushing some hair away from my face. "I genuinely thought the Blades were going to lift the Cup last season." In the soft glow of the room, his easy face turns harder. "We need to offload Tommy Schneider—and fast. All the guy does is warm the penalty box. That powerplay deep in the third of the final game last season cost us everything."

Every inch of my body tenses, including my jaw.

"You're a big fan of him too, I see?"

He drops his arm from the headboard and rests it around my shoulders. I hate it, but I'm too distracted by the face of the one person I hate more to shrug off his advances.

"He's a prick," I bite out, unable to hide my disdain.

"Shouldn't you be defending his honor since he's a fellow player?"

A single bubble of my sarcastic laughter fills the room. "No! I happen to agree with you. The Blades general manager made a huge mistake when he signed Schneider, and he absolutely cost us the Cup. If veteran defenseman, Emmett Richards, hadn't busted his knee, there's no doubt that he would've been on the ice and not serving major penalty time like Tommy."

He shrugs, not looking as sure as he did before. "I guess the Flames guy did have it com—"

"Their winger did nothing wrong," I say, cutting him off. "Tommy is looking for a fight every time he enters the rink, and he's a fucking liability. You know his dad nearly killed a Scorpions defenseman, right?"

He nods along, already looking bored with the conversation. I continue anyway, hatred turning into word vomit. I know it looks like my anger appears unjustified, but really, it isn't.

"He's a dangerous thug, and he needs taking out of the game."

Retracting his arm, my hookup pulls back the duvet and rises from the bed. "Sounds to me like I touched a nerve. Did you sleep with him and now there's bad blood?"

I scoff. "I would rather eat myself."

On a light chuckle, he pulls on a pair of boxers and heads for the en suite. "I'm going to grab a shower; I'll be back in a second."

When he closes the door, I flip back the duvet and stalk across the room toward my bag, pulling out my cell to see multiple messages from my girls.

> **KENDRA**
>
> $100 says Jenna went home with Jason.
>
> **COLLINS**
>
> I see your bet and raise you another $100.
>
> **DARCY**
>
> I didn't think she was into blond dudes, but he's a lawyer, and he drives a Maserati.

Oh, so that's his name.

I type out a quick text with one hand as I begin getting dressed.

> **ME**
>
> I did, in fact, go home with him. Although I am now leaving. He's in the shower.
>
> **COLLINS**
>
> It sounds like I'm the only one winning from tonight. He was that bad that you're already sneaking out? It's only eleven p.m.
>
> **KENDRA**
>
> She needs to leave now; we have practice in the morning.

Kendra Hart, otherwise known as the most committed center back I have ever played with. Also my best friend and the wife of Jack Morgan, newly appointed captain of the New York Blades.

COLLINS

> Eh, who needs sleep? Sawyer keeps me up all
> night, and I'm good to go for work the
> next day.

Collins Bryce, all-round bad-ass biker girl with a Harley-Davidson empire. Recently married to Sawyer Bryce, former captain and veteran Blades defenseman, playing out his final season in the NHL.

DARCY

> I feel like we need another girls' night to
> discuss Jenna's Jason experience in more
> detail. Archer and Emily are inseparable, and I
> plan to take full advantage.

Darcy Moore—mom to baby Emily, wife to the Blades goalie, Archer Moore, and an all-round British queen—completes my favorite trio, formed of women I couldn't live without.

ME

> I'm down for that. Although there isn't much to
> tell. The sex was meh, and he thinks I'm a
> hockey player.

KENDRA

> Ha! Now he's going to be showing up at the
> rink, hoping to catch a glimpse of you.

ME

> We all know there's zero chance of that
> happening. I don't go to the rink anymore,
> remember?

COLLINS

> Girl, you can't avoid Tommy Schneider forever.
> It's been eight months since he punched your
> brother.

Rage builds inside me again as I slip my feet into my boots and zip them up one at a time.

ME

> He nearly broke Holt's jaw! He's lucky Holt agreed not to press charges and he didn't go to the press. He only kept quiet because he didn't want a bar fight tainting his own rugby career. It was uncalled for, and he's a dick. Plain and simple.

KENDRA

> Just ignore him. You don't need to even acknowledge his existence. I miss going to the Blades games as a group.

DARCY

> I get why you're mad, but I agree with Collins. You can't avoid him forever. It's the first game of the season next week. Why don't you just come? He probably won't even dare look at you, never mind speak to you, after what happened.

ME

> You sure about that? He lives to piss me off. He was doing that well enough before he hit my brother. All because he couldn't handle that I'd turned him down. I wouldn't pee on Tommy if he was on fire, let alone sleep with him.

COLLINS

> *snort* I can't believe you told him that. Way to dent a guy's ego.

ME

> Yeah, well, the truth hurts. And I'll tell him that again if he even so much as looks in my direction.

KENDRA

I think Tommy got the message the first time around, babe. Plus, I'm ninety-nine percent sure Holt will board a flight from France if he goes near you again.

ME

True. I'll think about the game. Right now, I need to get out of here, undetected. The shower just stopped.

Snatching my bag up from the chair, I creep across the bedroom, a small sense of guilt settling inside me as I pull the door open and close it quietly behind me. Jason doesn't deserve to be abandoned, but I'm calling time on tonight.

I take the stairs quickly and breathe a sigh of relief when the front door opens. Bringing my finger to my lips, I quickly shush his cute Westie dog and silently step out into the Brooklyn night air.

Heading up the sidewalk to flag down a taxi, I type out a final message to the group.

ME

Mission accomplished. I'm out and free. A quick roundup of the night: two drinks, a cute Westie dog that I'd honestly rather have snuggled than his owner. Zero orgasms were achieved, and I'm ten out of ten grabbing Chick-fil-A on my way home. Screw the nutritional plan. I need junk food.

THREE

TOMMY

After a zero to two loss in the opening game of the regular season, I'm minding my own business and listening to Black Sabbath during cooldown when a hand reaches across the treadmill and hits the red Emergency Stop button.

Fucking rude.

Slowly, I pull off my headset and lock eyes with Archer Moore. With his arms planted across his chest, he stands at the end of my treadmill.

"I don't know how many times Coach needs to say it, but he doesn't like us listening to personal music during gym time."

We both know that isn't what's really eating at him. Still, I'm not about to broach the subject. He can man up and tell me tonight's loss was my fault. And then I'll explain why it wasn't.

"Why do you care?" I say, scrubbing a hand across my jaw. "You hardly ever talk to me anyway." I pause and consider leaving my retort there, but holding back isn't my style. "Unless you want me to save your ass in practice or games, that is. Then it's more of an incessant plea."

Archer Moore has been the Blades goalie since before I left college, and he's widely considered to be one of the best of a generation. He annihilated his own shutout record last season, and truthfully, he's the best I've ever worked with. Not that he needs to know that. I'm not lying when I say I've saved his ass a time or two. In part, his excellent performance last season— where we narrowly missed out on the Cup—was down to my speed on the ice, especially traveling backward.

He just smirks, and there's nothing remotely friendly about it. "That major penalty you picked up tonight, it cost us the game."

Ah, so now we're getting down to the crux of the matter.

"We were already a goal down when I got handed time in the penalty box. We had one shot all game, and that came from a turnover I'd created in the second period. Coach has come into this season fresh out of ideas, and the entire team looks lethargic and unmotivated." I motion around the empty gym, noting that we're the only players in here. "Aside from me, that is."

When Archer opens his mouth to reply, it's not his voice that materializes.

"How about you repeat that in my office?" Coach Morgan's harsh tone rips through the music I can still hear through the headphones that rest around my neck.

All my goalie does is grin.

I turn around to face a fuming Coach as he stands at the other end of my treadmill. "I mean, I can repeat what I said," I reply to him. "But I'm pretty sure you heard me the first time."

I'm a certified idiot to wind this guy up. Other than the GM —who, for some reason, seems to like me—Coach holds the strings to my career, and let's just say, I haven't exactly gotten on his good side since I walked onto the team last season.

"My office in five minutes," he grits out before heading straight for the exit, the gym door crashing against the jamb when he leaves.

"Don't worry about being late to Lloyd's tonight." I don't bother to look at Archer as he speaks, and I snatch up my towel and water bottle from the treadmill. "It wasn't like the team would've saved you a seat anyway."

"Sit," is all I get when I push into Coach's office fifteen minutes later.

I took my sweet time in the shower and then getting dressed. Like hell was I going to sit in my postgame sweat while he reamed me out for speaking nothing but the truth.

Flopping down and adjusting my tie, I unbutton the top button on my dress shirt. "Jesus, Coach, why do you always have to run it so hot in here?"

His jaw tightens, and he pushes away a few papers on the desk in front of him, clearing the space between us. "More to the point, *why* are you always in here?"

I shrug like a petulant teenager, unable to stop myself. It's like I'm daring to see how far I can push this guy before he snaps. But I know he needs me on the team just as much as I need my position. With Sawyer Bryce playing out his final season and Emmett Richards on the slow path to recovery, following a serious knee injury, he has very few options. That, and the GM seems to back me each time Coach and I come to blows. I'm aware my trade to the Blades last season was unpopular at best, driven solely by the guy at the top, calling the shots.

"Because you always summon me here like some kind of principal or something," I reply, gazing around the room.

A picture of his wife, Felicity Morgan, sits in an emerald frame on the corner of his desk. She's got her arm wrapped around her daughter, Darcy Moore. Last season, Archer was the bad guy in town for secretly hooking up with their golden girl. Although that was quickly forgotten when he made a bunch of declarations about promising to love her for eternity or some shit like that. The fact that he had gotten her knocked up didn't seem to matter.

I wonder if I start fucking a teammate's sister, will I suddenly enter the magic circle of trust?

Coach sits back in his black leather chair, despondency flowing off him. "Why is it that your main priority is to piss off everyone around you? At this point, I'm wondering why you chose to play a team sport like hockey."

It's a fair question, one I can answer easily. I focus back on him and away from the image of his family. "Because I don't like people and because I'm really fucking good at hockey."

"Is that genuinely your full answer?" He sounds more desperate now.

I shake my head and lean my elbows on the desk. "Listen, if this is your version of a pep talk to get me to see reason or want to start making friends around here, then I'd save your breath. I'm here to play hockey and earn money." I drop my palms to the desk, and as I lean back into my chair, I slide my hands until they fall off the edge and slap against my thighs. "Being liked is overrated."

"I'll agree with you on two points." Coach holds up a couple of fingers. "One, you're right. You are a good hockey player. I can see it beneath the layers of unnecessary bravado you bring to the ice. You're the fastest I've ever seen going backward, and you're advancing game is some of the best out there."

I agree with that.

"Two, being liked is most definitely overrated. But proactively trying to make everyone hate you is worse. You call yourself a serious player, but all I see is a kid throwing his weight around, both in the locker room and in the rink." He leans forward, lips pressed into a thin line. "I mean, why? *Why* did you drop your gloves today? We could've been looking at a draw tonight instead of a loss since we were beginning to turn the screw on them. Instead, Philly is thinking their

27

Christmas just came early since we were odds on to clinch the W."

I clear my throat as I think of a valid excuse. I don't have one. Their center had been in my ear all game, and for the first time since I can remember, I didn't know how to handle it.

"Why, Tommy?" Coach repeats.

I look up at him then, surprised at the use of my first name. I don't like his coaxing tone, even less the understanding edge it carries.

"Gentry had it coming," is all I can manage. "The opposition can't be allowed to believe that they can talk shit when they play on our home ice. Someone has to put the hammer down, and that someone is me. Bryce is past his best with one eye on retirement, and no one else has the build or the balls to bring the intimidating role our GM asked me to fulfill when I was brought on board. I'm doing my job, simple as that."

Satisfied with my response, I sit back and rest one leg over my knee.

Coach doesn't seem to share the same opinion as he drums his fingers on the tabletop. "I hate to burst your bubble, kid, but even Adrian is growing tired of your antics. Our GM only has so much patience, and he's part of the reason why you're in here tonight."

A kernel of discomfort blooms in the pit of my stomach.

"That's not the impression he gave me," I argue. "I only spoke with him last week. He wanted to see more of the same this season."

"Yeah, well …" Coach blows out a low breath. "Opinions change, and I gotta be honest with you …" He pauses, looking me dead in the eyes. "Tonight's hit stunk of your father."

The slight unease I was feeling earlier morphs into something way worse as cold shivers trickle down the length of my freshly tattooed spine.

"It was a clean hit," I insist. "He had the puck, and I was the obvious player to tackle him. The penalty was unjustified and only because the ref panicked. The entire league is turning soft."

Coach quirks a brow. "The hit was questionable, but Gentry has a bad concussion and a twisted knee. He'll be out for multiple games."

I lift a single shoulder. "And?"

"And you just lost us the fucking game! Moreover, I don't want this team to go back to what it was when I was playing. The Blades were nothing but animals. As an opposing player, the aim was to leave the rink with all your limbs still attached. That was considered to be a win when you traveled to Brooklyn."

I make a face akin to pride. "Sounds like a great way to run an NHL team."

When he pushes a hand through his silky brown hair, I can tell Coach's patience is wearing thin.

"Is that what you want? To follow in your dad's footsteps? To have your career cut short because no team wants to sign you?"

Shortly after I turned eighteen and changed my last name to Schneider, I didn't hesitate in confirming my relation to my dad. What I didn't tell the world was that my father wanted nothing to do with me. Naturally, he wasn't going to publicly denounce that I was his son since that would make him look like a grade-A asshole—and even he's not that stupid. In truth, I don't want the world to know about how I got rejected either. That's not something I particularly want splashed across the internet. All I care about is being the better Schneider—the one who hit harder, secured more shutouts, was feared the most and talked about in bars after each game. Call it poetic justice.

"That won't happen," I reply, feeling less assured than I sound.

I'd never outwardly admit it, but the first seasons of my pro career have been harder than I thought they would be. At one point, I didn't think I'd make it out of Detroit's farm team, having been sent there as punishment for fighting in my first NHL season. Then came a trade option to New York, and my agent took it with both hands, reminding me this was a second chance to get my career back on track.

Trouble is, I don't know any other way of playing. Brute force is what my game is centered around. It's who I am and what I do.

"I know where the line is," I tell Coach.

He twists his lips in thought. "Do you? Gentry might say different tonight. Your teammates might say different too. You've got an anger problem. I don't know why, but I'm pretty sure I know where it comes from."

Unease gives way to rage, only proving his point right.

"I don't have an anger problem!" I yell, earning a smug smirk from Coach. "I …" I grip the back of my neck so hard that I regret it as my healing skin stings beneath the pressure. "I'm not going the same route as my dad. Although I'm not about to switch up my game because you tell me I need to start taking it easy on fuckers like Gentry, who like to get in my face every ten seconds. At least my punches are open and honest, unlike his snide comments."

Coach's brows pull together. I know he used to play with my dad in college, so if anyone can compare our games, it's him. That's not what he's thinking about right now though.

"What did Gentry say to you?" he asks, care threatening to bleed into the conversation again.

"Nothing." I shut down the question quickly.

"What did he say, Tommy? That's a fucking order."

I can feel the flush of embarrassment as it heats my cheeks.

Fuck me, she's a fucking menace. Even when she isn't trying to be.

"Jenna Miller," is all I say.

Coach scratches at his chin, understandably lost.

I puff out a single laugh and stare at the photo of Coach's

wife, avoiding all eye contact. "Gentry seems to think I have a thing for Jenna Miller, the New York Storm goalie who hangs out with—"

He holds up a hand, cutting me off. "Yes, I know who she is and that she's tight with Darcy and a number of the guys' wives. What I want to know is, what the fuck does she have to do with the five minutes you spent in tonight's penalty box?"

I might be a questionable thug on the ice, but I'm sure as shit not a liar.

Puffing out my chest, I continue, "Like I said, apparently, he caught wind that I'd made a move on Jenna last season and she turned me down." I clench my jaw so fucking hard that the tendons ache. "Allegedly, he banged her when the Storm traveled to Philly earlier this season. They were laughing about me and the way she'd burned me out. He said I'd missed out because she was phenomenal."

Coach clears his throat as his eyes track around the room.

"This is probably none of my business, but do you have a thing for her? Is that what got under your skin?"

I scoff, more heat pooling throughout my body. "Jenna Miller is talking shit. We don't get along—we never have. If anything, I was the one who blew her off last season, and she couldn't handle the rejection, so she decided to play petty games and make shit up."

Okay, maybe I am a little liberal with the truth when I need to be.

Like he's done with the conversation, Coach stands from his chair, gathering the paperwork he pushed away earlier.

"Somehow, I doubt you'll ever take advice from me, and personally, I think that will be your downfall, Tommy." He slides a single sheet of paper across the desk, and I read the first line.

Tommy Schneider: first formal written warning.

The letter is one page long with the GM's signature at the

bottom. I don't bother to read its contents; I've seen this kind of thing before.

"But from a guy who knew your father and has witnessed enough shit go down between players over girls to last him a fucking lifetime, let me tell you this. You are quite literally skating on thin ice. One more misconduct like we saw tonight, and you'll be benched, fined, and maybe even sent to the farm team in Connecticut. I don't know if you have a thing for Jenna Miller, and quite frankly, I don't give a fuck."

He towers over me as I drop the written warning back onto the table.

"Get your head screwed on straight and drop the fucking act. It doesn't impress anyone, not even Adrian any longer. You have the bones to be one of the greats, better than most I've coached and played with, but your attitude stinks, and I'm tired of dealing with your bullshit. Your job as a professional is to hold your tongue and keep your fucking head when players like Gentry try and mess with it."

I want to scream at him that I do. The only exception to that rule is Jenna Miller.

Fucking bitch.

My mouth opens, but he shuts me down quickly, pointing at the door.

"Now get out and go spend your evening thinking over what I just told and handed to you."

I push my chair back as I rise to my feet and slide the letter back across to him. "I'll think about it."

Coach nods once, anger contorting his face. "You do that, Tommy … oh, and one last thing."

I look over my shoulder as I make for the door.

"Stay away from Jenna Miller. Whether or not you two have a checkered history is inconsequential, as are your feelings toward her. Get your head out of your ass before it gets shipped off to Connecticut."

FOUR

JENNA

I rarely let anyone talk me into doing something I don't want to.

Apart from when it comes to my girlfriends. They say jump, and I'll ask them how high. And tonight, they wanted me to go to the game and then come out, just like old times.

Standing at the bar with Darcy, Collins, and Kendra, I check over my shoulder once more, wishing I were anywhere but here. Any second now, the entire Blades team is going to waltz into the private area of Lloyd's—their usual postgame hideout—and at least three of their players will descend onto our group, reuniting with their wives and licking the wounds from their first game of the regular season, which ended in a humiliating loss.

My issue tonight isn't with the team or even their woeful performance. It's with one player who I wish would vanish from existence. And by the way he carried on tonight in the game, I'm positive I'm not the only one praying Tommy Schneider will put in for a trade, preferably to the Outer Hebrides or somewhere equally as remote.

I turn back to my friends just as the first set of players starts arriving and Collins and Darcy break off to join their husbands.

"You need to relax." Kendra hands me a drink just as a thick forearm wraps around her neck.

Automatically, she smiles and looks up at Jack Morgan.

"Hey, Kitten." Jack rests his chin on top of Kendra's head, closing his eyes as he does.

What I wouldn't give to feel a love like that.

"I need a beer and a double lobotomy after that game." Jack shakes his head slowly, now looping both arms around my best friend's waist. "Nothing came off. We felt sluggish and clueless out there. I'm hoping it was a onetime thing. Way to kick off my captaincy." He groans in his British American accent.

Kendra swivels in his arms, setting a chaste kiss against his lips. "You have nothing to feel guilty over." She points behind her, motioning in the rough direction of the hockey arena, her blonde hair sparkling beneath the twinkling lights. She's absolutely stunning. "Bad games happen, and you and the guys left it all out there tonight. We could see that, couldn't we, Jen?"

Kendra invites me into the conversation, and I nod a couple of times, taking a sip of soda. She isn't wrong. The Blades were a length behind, but their work ethic was never in doubt.

"I've had games where everything I touched turned to gold and other times where all I wanted was for the ninety minutes to end so I could take a shower, head home, and search for a new day job."

Kendra snorts a laugh, burying her face into Jack's dress shirt.

"The only place where fingers need to be pointed," I continue, taking another sip of sweet soda until it turns sour at the thought of him, "is at number fifty-five. He needs to go."

I expect Kendra and Jack to instantly agree with me, like they always do over Tommy. Literally no one likes him. Instead, Kendra looks up at Jack, and he stares straight ahead.

"Well, that's super disappointing to hear." Tommy's unmistakably gruff voice shifts the fine hairs atop of my head, and a tall, shadowy figure looms over me. "And here I was, thinking you were my biggest fan."

I'd roll my eyes if that wouldn't grant this guy way too much of my effort, especially given that my back is to him and my disdain would go to waste.

"Fuck off, Tommy," I grind out, swirling what's left of the ice cubes in my drink.

The shadow doesn't disappear, not that it's necessary for me to sense his presence. Unfortunately for me, Tommy Schneider is exactly my type. The *classic tall, dark, and handsome meets tattoos* look has always been my downfall, especially when they extend to his neck and knuckles. I've never seen him topless since he declined participation in the annual Blades charity calendar—unsurprising, given his mean nature—but I'd like to bet his torso is inked too.

He might think I'm keeping my back to him because I can't stand the sight of his face, and for the most part, he'd be right. But hiding my physical attraction to this guy is a challenge, even though I hate the person lurking beneath his delicious exterior.

"No can do, I'm afraid. I only just got here, and I'm not even halfway through my beer," he eventually replies.

I look across at Kendra when she turns back to me. Without words, we share the same thought: *Why can't this guy take a hint?*

I spin around on my heel, practically spilling my soda in the process. "Literally no one wants you here." I motion around the private bar, pointing at the various booths, which are now full of Blades players and their partners. "Archer doesn't want you here, Sawyer doesn't want you here, their wives don't want you here." I move on to Kendra and Jack. "Not even your own captain welcomes your presence."

He just continues to smirk down at me like I'm talking in a foreign language he doesn't understand. Maybe he doesn't since he seems pretty fucking dumb.

I decide to make the message even clearer, pointing to my chest.

He drops his eyes, an appreciative glaze forming at my low-cut black sweater, which only ignites my anger further.

"And *I definitely* don't want you here. Of all the people in this bar, you couldn't have picked a bigger hater."

His face doesn't change, and neither does the position of his eyes.

"Stop staring at my fucking tits!" I yell, garnering attention from a number of people standing around us.

Tommy only finds my outburst amusing, a small tip of his top lip confirming his glee.

He doesn't move, eventually lifting his glass and eyes in perfect synchronization before he takes a large pull of his beer, downing the whole lot in one go.

I know there are people all around us, bearing witness to the way I can't help but watch the column of his tattooed throat work. He's styled his sleek, dark hair to the side, like he always does, and he left a short scruff along his jawline. I shouldn't be watching; I should still be yelling at him to get away from me.

Better still, I should return the favor on behalf of my brother and punch him straight in the face.

Instead, I do nothing.

On a deep swallow, Tommy peers down into his glass. "I guess I'm ready for another beer." His deep brown eyes find mine. "Can I buy you a drink, Jenna?"

With the way I grind my molars, I'm mentally dialing my dentist to ask for an emergency appointment.

"No."

He casually shrugs and reaches across to the bar top, setting his empty down. "That's a shame because I need to talk to you. Alone." He casts a brief glance at Kendra and Jack.

"I'm not leaving my friend alone with you." Kendra quickly comes to my aid, not that I need her to. I can handle Tommy.

"Not going to happen," I reply to Tommy.

Before I get a chance to protest further, Tommy snatches my glass and quickly sets it down next to his.

"What the fu—"

"That wasn't a request," he cuts me off, expression turning more serious. "Do you really think I want to be within a hundred feet of you either?" He scoffs, and for the first time, I'm not ashamed to admit that I'm a little intimidated by his dominance. "You know exactly why I'm here, enjoying the pleasure of your charming company."

My eyes flick to Kendra's, and I offer her a reassuring nod. I hoped the fight that broke out between the Philly center, Patrick Gentry, and Tommy was because of the game and nothing to do with me running my mouth on an away series, but Tommy's glare tells me it wasn't.

I owe this guy nothing, least of all my respect, after what he did to my brother. Still, curiosity gets the better of me as I ask Kendra and Jack to give us a minute, and they make for the booths behind us. If Tommy thinks I'm about to apologize for what I told Patrick, he's in for a nasty surprise.

When we're left alone, Tommy takes a couple of steps back into a quieter—and darker—part of the bar, and I reluctantly follow.

The throbbing music does nothing to alleviate the tension as it builds between us, not that it affects Tommy, his sharp gaze cutting straight through me.

"You've got sixty seconds," I tell him. "And then I'm retrieving my drink and joining my friends."

He ignores my comment—or at least doesn't acknowledge it. "Tell me something, Jenna."

My thighs shouldn't clench each time he says my name.

"Tell me something, Jenna ..." he repeats, casting his gaze down my body and pausing on my thighs. "Were you dropped on your head as a child?"

I balk. "Excuse me?"

He taps his temple twice, smugness oozing from every pore. "Your mental comprehension must be affected. That's the only explanation I can reach when I try and figure out why you told Patrick Gentry that I made a pass at you the first night we met."

My cheeks flame so red that even the dim lighting offers zero camouflage. "Ah, now it's all starting to make sense."

Folding my arms over my chest, I'm fully aware what I just did to my bust, and I dare him to take another look.

Annoyingly, he doesn't.

"What's making sense, Jenna?" His tone drips with sarcasm.

"English isn't your first language, is it?" I smile sweetly. "Schneider is a German last name, right?"

Tommy shifts from one foot to the next, and for the first time, I see a seed of uncertainty, the faintest chink in his otherwise steely armor.

I seize the moment and dig the knife a little deeper.

"Did Daddy not explain to you that asking a girl to leave and head to another bar alone amounts to flirting on this side of the Atlantic Ocean? Or is this just a case of your ego being too bruised to accept the truth that I did, in fact, turn you down last season?"

Tommy looks off to the side, pinning his plump lip between his teeth.

"I don't get with immature little boys." I add, "Particularly ones who act like the world owes them something."

He hates what I said—that much is obvious as he refuses to give me eye contact.

For a split second, I worry that I'll become another victim of his short fuse. Images of Tommy turning aggressive flash through my head as the hit he landed on Holt for defending me back in January come roaring back. Asshole or not, Tommy is one of the biggest hockey players I've ever seen, and I know a lot about the sport, having grown up in a hockey madhouse.

"You're a fucking bitch—you know that?" His eyes are almost black when he finally shows me them again.

He opens his mouth to add something more but quickly closes it, and I breathe an internal sigh of relief. I don't know what he was about to say, but apparently, Tommy Schneider does have lines he won't cross.

"You say that like you think it'll hurt my feelings."

Reaching out, I pat his shoulder mockingly, and he pulls back. I wouldn't describe the action as a recoil, more like I electrocuted him.

It doesn't track. Tommy has built a career steeped in animosity, and there was nothing friendly about my gesture. A condescending tap on the shoulder shouldn't even register, let alone elicit that kind of response from him.

I push past the doubt and solidify the upper hand I've got.

"Did Patrick tell you that I banged him?" I smirk just like he always does at me. "He was pretty good actually. So good that I lost all my inhibitions. Anyway ..." I wave away the details of that night, which was less than memorable. "One thing led to the next, and he started talking about New York and my soccer career, and then we got onto the Blades, yada yada. He agreed with me that he thought you were a subpar player at best, and *that's* when I pointed out that your flirting game wasn't much better. I'm sorry that what I said upset you."

There's no sincerity to my empty apology, and he knows it.

The entire time I talked, Tommy's grin only grew wider. He leans one thick forearm—white shirtsleeves rolled up to the elbows—against the wall next to us. He crosses his legs over at the ankles—and, goddamn, if it isn't hotter than hell.

"How many times did he make you come?"

If I still had my soda, I'd throw it in his face.

The audacity of this guy.

"I beg your pardon?!"

He runs his tongue across his bottom lip. "Orgasms, Jenna.

39

How many did he pull from you? You described the sex as good enough to lose your inhibitions, so I figure that he fucked your brains out."

My eyes narrow at him. "I lost count."

Roughly translated: I didn't come once.

He taps his knuckles against the wall, clicking his tongue once. "I'm surprised Gentry can still get it up, to be honest. He's gotta be at least thirty-four."

My brain fights to keep my eyes on Tommy's face and not drop them to his crotch. "I tend to find older guys are better. More experienced and confident."

Tommy nods like he's agreeing, leaving me confused. "That's what older women say when they reach a certain age and no longer interest younger guys." He leans forward, and his breath has a minty edge to it. "*I'm* not interested in you, Jenna."

Something unwelcome shoots through me, pooling in my eyes. Rapidly, I blink away the wetness. Of all the turns this conversation could've taken, it had to head down my one vulnerable route.

At twenty-seven, I fear being left on the shelf while I watch all my friends happily marry and have babies. It's probably my biggest fear, full stop.

Truthfully, I don't know how I see my future, but I do know I don't want to spend it alone.

My dad was an asshole to my mom, constantly cheating on her when he worked out of town. For a while after their divorce, I was determined never to get married or settle down and risk being torn apart in the same way Dad did to my mom. I think the turning point was my split from Lee almost two years ago. I liked having someone in my life, all I needed was for it to be the right person, and now, it feels like I'm fighting against time before I'm left out in the cold.

Given my failure to hide my upset, I'm certain that Tommy can tell he's rattled me or at least touched a raw nerve. His face doesn't change though, not an ounce of empathy entering his expression.

I fucking *hate* him. Before Holt returned to France, he told me to never speak to Tommy again. That he was bad news and out for petty revenge. I wish I'd listened to his advice.

"You are a cold and callous asshole, and I wish Holt had buried you that day."

When he shrugs nonchalantly, it's only my soccer career that holds me back from doing what my brother should have. All Holt asked Tommy to do that night was repeat what he had said under his breath when he walked by us.

I never found out what Tommy had said, not that I particularly care. I know it wasn't a compliment.

He'd called me a stuck-up princess the day I told him I didn't want to leave and go to another bar with him. We both know he was trying to get me into bed. Unfortunately for the Blades bad boy, I'd already figured he was an asshole who would likely fuck me and kick me out the first chance he got.

I'm the one who leaves a man's bed. Always on my terms.

For a split second, I think Tommy's going to kiss me when he leans in closer, and I hate the conflict that stirs low in my belly.

Everything about him should disgust me. He's cruel and just like his father on the ice. He doesn't respect the opposition, only seeking to cause as much collateral damage in his quest to be the tough guy. Hell, I'm not even sure he cares about his own teammates or the loss they endured tonight. He isn't a professional, and he doesn't deserve to earn big money while I play and practice with athletes who make a tenth of his salary and possess more talent and integrity than he ever will.

He stops an inch from my lips, enunciating each word as he speaks. "Talk shit and try and humiliate me again, and you really will wish your brother had retaliated that night. I can make your life hell, and I promise you I will. Don't play this game with me, Jenna. You will lose."

FIVE

TOMMY

"Listen, I know we only just started talking, but why don't we get out of here? There are quieter bars only a couple of blocks away."

Jenna's sleek, dark hair shone as she flicked it over her shoulder, and I tracked the movement, enraptured and way too fucking attracted to someone I'd only briefly laid eyes on once before. I wanted her, and for the first time since I could remember, I decided to make the first move. I could tell she wanted me too. I was exactly her type—apparent by the way she checked me out every time she thought I wasn't watching. I'd been warned by my teammates to stay away from her, not that I had any intention of following their advice.

She stared down into her half-empty glass, bottom lip pinned between her teeth as she considered my proposal.

I knew she was single and liked a good time. I'd overheard conversations with her girlfriends about her latest conquests.

"I'm sorry, but I can't accept your offer." Her eyes found mine on the final few words.

There was still conflict in them, like she didn't truly believe *what she was saying. Regardless, she'd still blown me off, and that went down like a lead fucking balloon.*

I'd never had a girl reject me before. Ever.

I stood up straighter, attempting to ease the tension as it built between my shoulder blades. "Don't tell me you have a guy on the scene or some other terrible excuse like that. I know you don't."

She smiled, and I hated that I liked it more than her frown. "No. I just don't think us hooking up would be a good idea. Plus …" She paused for a second as her gaze roved the room until it landed on Collins, Kendra, and Darcy on the far side of the bar. "I'm flattered and everything, but you aren't really my type."

I scoffed, disappointment overtaken by bitterness. This girl was full of bullshit.

As I inched closer, Jenna's Angel perfume drove me wild. "Is it because your petty little girlfriends and their husbands don't like me?"

Keeping her gaze averted, she rolled her eyes. "Your comment insinuates that I can't make decisions for myself and that I'm easily led by others. I'm not into you, and I'm also not into leading people on when I don't find them attractive."

The temptation to pull away was strong, but I maintained our close proximity just so I could relish in the way the hairs on her neck stood up each time my breath fanned her face. This girl was hot as hell, but she was also sorely mistaken if she thought she'd get another chance with me when her friends weren't around to witness us leaving together.

I didn't do second chances. My parents could vouch for that.

"I didn't have you pinned as a stuck-up little princess, more a down-to-earth girl with her head screwed on straight."

This time, I did pull away, and she immediately turned to look at me. It could've just been my imagination, but I swore I saw a hint of regret in those deep blue eyes.

Shame.

"*Stuck-up princess?*" *She cocked her head to one side, annoyance evident.* "*I guess I shouldn't be surprised by your immature response to being turned down. You're barely out of diapers.*"

My hand gripped my pint glass so hard that it was one squeeze away from shattering all over the floor. "*I'm far from immature, Jenna.*"

I smirked down at her. She was at least five feet eight, but I still towered over her, and I liked that I did. It would be so easy to throw her around the bedroom, and I knew she was into that kind of thing—I could sense it.

"*Not that you'll ever get a chance to find that out.*"

She only found my response amusing when she swiped her glass from the table in front of us and started for her friends who hadn't noticed us talking at the back of the room.

I should've let her walk off, but instinct had me wrapping my hand around her upper arm; her soft skin was smooth against my callous palm. I was determined to have the final word. "*No one is to know about this conversation, Jenna. You already made one mistake, blowing me off tonight; don't make another and gossip to your pathetic little friends.*"

Even though she didn't respond, I could tell she'd gotten the message just fine, and I released her with a cocky grin that doubled as a warning. With that, she gave me one last glance before she disappeared and joined the rest of our group.

I CRANK THE HEAT HIGHER ON THE SHOWER UNTIL THE HOT streams of water threaten to scold my skin.

Another day, another unwelcome flashback of a night I should've forgotten fucking months ago. I might as well get a transcript of the conversation inked into my body since my mind refuses to let it go.

It's been a week since I snatched Jenna's drink and pulled her to the side in Lloyd's Bar, warning how I could make her life hell. At the time, I was convinced her smug smile was to hide the way I intimidated her, but now—as I lean against the shower wall in the locker room—I'm starting to think the only person suffering is me. Maybe I did a bad job at hiding my attraction to her and she could tell.

My dick bobs just below my navel, determined to remind me that despite my hatred for Jenna Miller, I would still destroy her body, given half a chance.

Her voice annoys the shit out of me, chipping away at my patience with its high-pitched tone. I could silence her so easily, make her gag as I pushed right to the back of her throat. Words would fail her when I slammed her against a wall and buried my cock deep inside her needy pussy, ripping the air clean from her lungs.

"Fuck me. Are you trying to have a shower or a fucking sauna in here?" Jack's voice permeates my thoughts, quickly followed by a hard knock against my shower stall door.

"Easing my aching muscles after an intense practice. You should try it sometime." I reach over the door and grab my towel, wrapping it around my waist as—mercifully—my dick softens. "Working hard, that is … although a shower would probably help you too." I pull the door open and find my captain standing on the other side.

Fully dressed, he folds his arms across his chest, his lips pressed into a thin line. He's trying to rise above my gibes and failing miserably.

I release a laugh on his behalf and push past him.

"I'm not here by choice," Jack calls after me, and I stop before exiting the room. "I need to talk to you about the upcoming away series in Boston."

I motion down my dripping wet body. "What part of my current state makes you think this is an ideal time to go through our schedule? I have it all on email anyway."

Jack steps toward me, trying to keep his temper. He's hated my guts since the day I walked onto this team, determined not to give me a chance. My best guess is, his initial issue had to do with the hit my dad had put on Zach Evans way before either of us was playing pro hockey. At least now—in my second season with the Blades—I've given him a more valid reason to curse the ice I skate on. I'm a way better player than he thought I would be when I got traded, and that realization eats away at him. I might be on a warning with the GM, but I'm still picked to start most games, and today, I killed it in practice.

All the guys on this team want a happy little hockey family with no issues, where they can crawl up each other's asses. If your face fits in the locker room, then they're willing to accept mediocrity on the ice. Half the guys on this team are yes men who should be in the AHL.

I'm the opposite of that, and my golden retriever captain hates it.

"I couldn't give a fuck about your current state, Tommy. I want to go home to my wife. I'm not about to wait for you to finish up on your unnecessarily long shower while you chew over your average practice session."

I smirk at him and his bullshit.

"Why the lies, Jack? I thought being captain meant encouraging *all* your players."

He deadpans, "Only the guys I actually want on the team. Anyway …" He pushes a hand through his showered hair. "The Boston away series next week—you're sharing a hotel room with me. Rookies usually share with their captain."

I decide to ignore his subtle attempt to goad me. We both know I'm far from a rookie. "You usually share with Archer or Sawyer."

He shrugs, not looking at all happy about the situation. "Coach Morgan's orders. He wants you to make an effort and integrate into the team. He figured you sharing a room with me would be the best way to go about that."

All I want to do is argue my case, but I'm already on a warning, and I don't want to make life any more difficult for myself.

"Sure, sounds like fun. I'll bring Twister; you bring Battleship."

Jack's lips twitch, and I'm not sure if it's to fight back amusement or contempt.

"You should know something else too." He brushes off my invite to get cozy with a couple of family-favorite games. "The hotel we're staying in … it's the same hotel the New York Storm uses since it's a popular choice for a lot of sports teams when they travel to Boston."

I open my towel and rewrap it, finding my own behavior entertaining. Jack keeps his eyes pinned on my face and away from my crotch.

"And that concerns me how exactly?" I reply, already bored with the conversation.

"Because our series overlaps with the Storm's, meaning both teams will be staying in the same hotel at the same time."

I can't deny the shot of excitement as it pulses through my body. Jenna and I will be under the same roof.

Shrugging, I add a faux yawn. "I'm still struggling to see why this is relevant to me or our roommate status."

Jack releases a frustrated groan. "In addition to helping you integrate into the team, you're staying with me so I can make sure you don't start hounding the Storm's first-choice goalkeeper." He steps closer until he's in my face. "Last week, when Jenna joined our group after you spoke to her in Lloyd's, she had tears in her eyes. I don't know what you'd said to her because she refused to repeat it, even to Kendra. But know this: she's my wife's best friend, and she hasn't got a bad bone in her body. I don't like it when good people are upset, especially ones I care about. Keep away from Jenna."

Another yawn emerges, this one genuine.

"She isn't the angel you make her out to be, and that's likely the reason she held off on telling you why she was upset. What I said, she had it coming ..."

Jack's stoic face hardens further.

"But," I continue, "before you go and get your panties all in a twist over a twenty-seven-year-old crybaby who should be able to look after herself, I promise to be on my best behavior. If she keeps out of my way, I'll keep out of hers."

He looks placated by my response.

"To sweeten the deal," I add for good measure, "I'll even read you a bedtime story. Let me know which one Archer and Sawyer use when you room with them, and I'll be sure to give it my best shot."

Jack's lip twitch returns, and this time, I'm sure it's to hide his anger. "While you're avoiding Jenna, make sure you keep out of my way too, Tommy. If you manage that very simple task, then we won't have a problem."

SIX

JENNA

"Kendra, if you want the burger, have the goddamn burger."

My best friend eyes me over her menu, brown eyes dancing with excitement. "I guess I could ask them to hold the cheese and add an extra slice of fresh tomato."

I drop my shoulders as the server approaches us in the hotel restaurant we've dined at more times than I can count when we play away in Boston. Each time, we have the same conversation.

"I'll take the surf 'n' turf with everything," I quickly tell the server. "And my friend here will take the cheeseburger, fully loaded."

"You got it!" the server replies, taking our menus and heading straight off to key in our order.

Kendra's mouth hangs open, and I pick up my Diet Coke, taking a sip through the straw.

"Are you kidding me?" she squawks. "I'm already battling with my nutritional plan. Just because you can eat and not pile on the pounds doesn't mean I can."

I lift a shoulder and continue to sip on my drink. "Okay, I'll eat yours too then."

She raises an unimpressed brow. "No way. I have postgame hunger pains. I'm nailing that burger, along with the fries. Just don't tell anyone." She sits up in our corner booth, checking to ensure no one we know is around to witness her nutritional treachery.

Life has gotten busy for us both, especially since Kendra met Jack, so it's been a while since we talked like this, one-on-one. It's one of the reasons why I've always loved an away series—it gives me a chance to share a room and hoard my best friend's attention.

"What's the score with … you know …" I drop my eyes to her stomach.

Jack and Kendra started trying for a baby a while back, but with no luck so far. I know she's getting anxious as more time passes without her getting pregnant. She doesn't talk much about it and I sense that's more because the topic is so painful for her, and it breaks my fucking heart to think of her hurting. I think that she can also sense my growing anxiety over still being single, and why I'm the only one in our group who still hasn't found someone.

I just wish she wouldn't avoid the subjects with me; I want my friend to know that we can talk about anything. Nothing is off-limits between us. Just because our journeys look very different doesn't mean our individual path is any easier than the other one's.

Kendra releases a long, forlorn sigh, and my heart drops a little.

"Talk to me," I say softly.

She pushes away her water, eyes glued to the table in front of us. "It doesn't matter how hard we try or how many times we do it, nothing seems to work."

Finally, when she looks at me, I see the tears threatening to break free, and I reach across and interlace our fingers.

"I feel like I'm letting him down because I know how

desperate Jack is to start a family." Her words are more of a sniffle.

"You're aware that's bullshit, right?" My voice is a touch incredulous, although I don't mean it to sound harsh; the last thing I want is for Kendra to start blaming herself.

She nods slowly. "I know, but it doesn't make the feelings any easier. Take last weekend—Archer and Darcy brought Emily to see us, and Jack spent the entire afternoon playing with her, whizzing about the place with her on his shoulders. His face was a picture of happiness, and I want to give him a baby so badly."

"Kendra …" I attempt to soothe.

"And then last night, while you were sleeping, I was lying awake, tracking my ovulation cycle for the hundredth time. Yesterday was my most fertile day of the month, and we were apart, so now I'm feeling guilty because of my career."

The bullshit spewing from this girl's mouth is only getting worse.

"Do you really believe that?" I say, rubbing my thumb across the top of her hand.

One tear escapes her lashes, running a track down her cheek. "No, not really. I'm just an expert at beating myself up."

I chew on the corner of my lip, desperate to find ways to help. Anything I say will feel empty because, realistically, all I can do is remind her I'm here, and she already knows that.

"What about if we break a few more rules beyond ordering a cheeseburger and fries?" I suggest.

She snorts a wet laugh. "What do you mean?"

I click my tongue, dropping my voice a little lower. "So, I know, technically, we shouldn't start shifting rooms, but what if I make myself scarce tonight and Jack stays with you? The boys arrive later, don't they?"

Kendra might try to hide it, but I see the way her face lights up at my proposal. "You know Jack is sharing a room with Tommy, don't you?"

That's the last person I'd have expected him to be rooming with.

"And you know I'm not insinuating a room swap. I'll ask the hotel if they have a vacant room and come up with an excuse for Coach. Like you snore really badly and I can't get the rest I need for games."

Her face changes to unamused.

"You do actually snore, Kendra."

She looks like she wants to argue just as our food is set down in front of us. "I know I do. Jack once recorded it to prove I did."

Leaning across, I steal a fry from her plate even though I have a ton with my surf 'n' turf. "That boy loves you immensely, and you need him tonight, not just his dick."

"Who needs dick?"

I immediately halt chewing at the one voice I never want to hear again.

"I thought you had strict instructions to leave us alone?" Kendra snaps at Tommy as he pulls up a spare chair from the empty table next to us and steals a fry from my plate, smiling at me around his mouthful.

"I did, but I also have the right to eat where I want. I just got off the flight, and I'm hungry."

He flexes his biceps in the black Dri-FIT top he's wearing, and my mouth waters for a whole different reason than the surf 'n' turf in front of me.

"This body needs feeding," he finishes.

Kendra doesn't even look at Tommy, picking up her burger and taking a huge bite.

His eyes cast down to my plate. "Not hungry, Jenna?"

"Someone arrived, and I lost my appetite," I reply with a sweet smile.

Clasping his hands under his chin, he runs his tongue across his bottom lip, not caring who witnesses the act. "I thought you loved meat?"

Shock paints my face.

"Don't go all coy on me," he goads, and I know exactly what's coming next. "I thought a good porking meant you lost your inhibitions?"

My cheeks flame as my stomach twists, and Kendra shakes her head at the Blades defenseman.

"That terminology hasn't been used since the '80s. You're so fucking strange." I sound disgusted.

My best friend slides out of the booth and eyes me carefully. "Are you going to be okay if I use the restroom, or do you want me to have him thrown out?"

Tommy doesn't even react as he pins me in place with a stare.

I look up at Kendra, desperate for Tommy to leave but more determined to show him he doesn't bother me. "Go ahead. I heard the hotel takes the trash out at this time anyway."

His face doesn't flinch when he rises from his stool and sits in Kendra's place opposite me, sliding her food away and pulling mine toward him. "Look at us two, getting all cozy on a date."

I pull my plate back. "Fuck off, Tommy."

He just chuckles, picking up a shrimp and devouring it in a couple of bites.

"I watched the highlights of your game today on YouTube." He swallows his mouthful and winces. "Well, I did until I got bored. Christ, you played like shit. That one-timer from their center forward ... she scuffed the shot, and it was like watching the goal in slow motion as it trickled underneath you. I had to double-check I hadn't switched the play back to slow motion."

Mary Rosen's finish was unstoppable, and he knows it.

I pick up my Diet Coke and take a careful sip before calmly setting the glass back down.

"You know, when you started playing, I had to check that you were, in fact, Alex Schneider's son since aside from looking similar, I could hardly believe you'd inherited his hockey DNA."

I lean forward as his lips start to tremble. "You're like Bambi on ice."

Maybe now he regrets disturbing our dinner. I hope so. Nothing hurts this guy more than a blow to his precious ego.

I decide to go in for the kill, picking up a fry and chewing it slowly. "Tell me, since my brother plays rugby in Europe and I didn't get to feel the full benefit of my family giving me a head start, what's it like, launching your career off the back of Daddy's and still failing to make waves in the sport?"

I've seen many different smiles from the boy sitting in front of me, but never this particular one. It's marred with anger—rage, in fact.

"I told you not to play this game with me, Jenna."

I shrug. "I'm not the one who interrupted your dinner and proceeded to insult your latest performance. I'm not playing any game, merely defending myself. I don't take well to being bullied."

Tommy looks off to the side, his same smile still evident as he runs a hand across his jaw and releases a slow, insidious laugh.

He stands from the booth and moves the chair back to the table next to us. "Enjoy your dinner, Hellion."

As he walks past and slides my surf 'n' turf straight off the table, warmth lands in my lap—fries, steak, and shrimp all soaking into my light-gray leggings.

Okay, now I'm fucking playing.

SEVEN

TOMMY

"What the fuck is that smell?" I bolt up in bed and rip back the duvet.

"Jack?!" I yell, searching for the light switch in a pitch-black room. "I told you a week ago to take a shower."

When I finally find the light, my captain is nowhere to be seen, and his bed is still made with not a wrinkle in the sheets.

Did he not come back last night?

The smell hits me again and I gag and stalk toward the source. If there's one thing I can't stand, it's any kind of filth. I keep my place pristine, and I expect the same when I travel and stay in hotels.

Apparently, the same cannot be said for other guests.

When I take a final step toward our hotel room door, ready to ream someone out for leaving their half-eaten food in the hallway, my foot squashes down into something cold and slippery.

"What the fuck?!" I retch when I flick on the main light to find ... a fucking shrimp stuck to my foot with congealed ketchup.

Jenna fucking Miller.

My fingers tremble with fury as I peel the half-eaten seafood from my foot, the ketchup squelched between my toes.

Beside the plate I just stood on, there's a handwritten note. Despite never seeing Jenna's writing before, I know it's hers. Only she's capable of a sick, immature prank like this.

TOMMY,
YOU WANTED TO PLAY.
BEST GET A GOOD MEAL DOWN BEFORE WE DO.
—HELLION

I fist the note, considering the best way to respond. It's the middle of the night, and I've no idea which room she's staying in. Hell, I've no idea how she snuck leftover food into my room, unannounced.

Still, regardless of my rage and the sticky sauce coating the base of my foot, I can't help but feel a smidgen of delight at the way she signed off the letter.

Hellion.

She heard what I called her and obviously embraced it. Never has there ever been a more appropriate nickname for someone.

"MR. SCHNEIDER, HOW CAN I BE OF ASSISTANCE?" THE FRONT-desk clerk covering the night shift stands to attention as I waltz into the lobby, having pulled on a pair of sweats I wore early in the day although not bothering to grab a shirt.

For a brief moment, my mind wanders back to the time when I showed up unannounced at my dad's apartment building. Back then, I was fully dressed and polite, yet I was looked at like I was a nobody—a far cry from the reception I'm receiving today.

That only enrages me further as I stalk toward the front desk.

"I need to know which room Jenna Miller is staying in," I bite out, not really caring about maintaining a friendly exterior.

Whether or not the Blades use this hotel again next time we play Boston really isn't at the top of my current agenda.

Finding Jenna is.

The young blond clerk shakes his head, eyes wide and a little frantic. "I'm sorry, sir, but I can't disclose that in—"

I lean forward on the desk, holding the guy—who can't be any older than me—hostage with my glare. "Do I look like I'm about to accept an *I can't* from you?" I circle my face for effect. "Moreover, I'm a famous hockey player who is worried about a friend. Do you really want that on your conscience tomorrow morning when I splash your lack of compliance all over the internet?"

His eyes grow even wider as they dart around the lobby, and mine fall to his name badge.

"Listen … Chad. You have a simple choice—Jenna Miller's room number or your job. You decide which one you'd rather give up."

His wide eyes fall to the keyboard, and he types in a couple of words, twisting the screen around to face me. Perhaps he feels less accountable by not reading the number aloud.

Either way, I have it. Room 612.

I tap him lightly on the shoulder, and he visibly deflates. "Good man. You and your paycheck live to fight another day."

Two minutes later, I'm on the sixth floor—two floors above my own—stalking the hallway until I pull up outside Jenna's room.

My knuckles hover over the door, and I swallow thickly. I know I'm overstepping by doing this. The feud between us is entering into dangerous water that could get us both reprimanded by our teams.

I knock anyway and step to the side so she can't view me through the peephole and refuse to open the door.

Nothing, not even a sound echoes from inside the room, and I begin to question if Chad values his job as much as I thought he did.

I knock again, louder this time.

"Who is it?" a sleepy Jenna asks on a yawn.

I smile and move aside again, summoning my best fake voice. "My name is Chad. I'm working reception tonight, and I have a message that I didn't think could wait until tomorrow."

Her voice gets louder as she moves toward the door. "A message from who? And why didn't you just call me?"

I ignore her reasonable question. "From your brother, Holt. He was injured in a rugby incident and—"

The door swings open before I can finish my sentence, and I'm inside before she gets a chance to scream or react. I slam the door behind me, and the room is flooded in soft lighting from her bedside lamp.

She's alone. Good.

"Tommy!" she yells.

I step forward and pin her against the bedroom wall, one palm over her mouth, the other flat above her head.

"Don't even think about yelling, Hellion," I grit out, my heart pounding clean through my chest. "You entered my room without consent earlier to deliver room service, and I'm merely returning the favor."

Her pretty eyes are wide with shock immediately before she narrows them and bites the inside of my palm. Hard.

I pull my hand away, certain she's drawn blood.

"Fucking Jesus," I announce, surprised to see she didn't break the skin. "I've got a hockey game in the morning. You nearly fucked the entire thing with that move."

The blood racing to my palm diverts to my dick when I take

her in, seeing she's dressed in silky black sleep shorts and a tiny black bralette.

"You're a sick man—you know that?" She crosses her arms over her chest, her full breasts squeezing together as she taps a manicured foot against the plush carpet. "Forcing entry into a woman's hotel room and then proceeding to ogle her. I thought you'd already had your fill with the surf 'n' turf I hand-delivered to your room earlier."

A growl emanates from my chest, and I press her against the wall again. "Why are you such a silly little girl?" I desperately want to wrap my hand around her throat just to see how well her neck would fit into the space between my thumb and forefinger.

She'd do anything I asked if I held her like that. Completely at my mercy, just how I'd like her.

"Get away from me, Tommy," Jenna spits.

"Not until I have answers," I reply, forming a fist against the wall above her head. "How did you gain access to my room? Was my captain in on your pathetic prank?"

She scoffs. "Jack's too busy with Kendra to care about humiliating you."

She drops her eyes to the floor, and I track her line of vision, more humiliation rippling through me when I notice the smear of ketchup across the bridge of my foot.

"Oh. My. God." She howls with laughter. "You did, didn't you?" A hand covers her mouth. "You stepped in my dinner!" Jenna shakes her head, struggling to believe her plan actually worked out. "This couldn't have gone any better."

"You owe me an explanation," I demand again.

With one strong arm, typical of an athlete capable of distributing a soccer ball halfway up a pitch, she pushes me back and gets into my face.

"And you owe me a new pair of Lululemon leggings! They don't come cheap, and I don't earn an exorbitant hockey-player salary."

I smirk and pull my cell from my pocket.

Unlocking the phone, I spin it around to face her. "Go ahead. Order some."

Initially, she hesitates, but then seems to clear her doubts, snatching the phone from my hand. "One pair of train high-rise in the same color you ruined." She taps the screen once, and I peer over the top, watching her add them to the cart. She then scrolls to a different color and adds those too. "Another pair for the dinner you wasted, which I then had to replace."

I chuckle and cross my arms, certain where this shopping trip is headed.

She backs out of that page and finds another—more expensive—collection of leggings. "Another pair to make up for being an asshole." She clicks the cart and then keeps scrolling. "No, wait. One pair couldn't possibly make up for your attitude." She clicks on a pair of dark green cropped leggings that will hug her fine ass perfectly. "I've always wanted these, so they're going in the basket too."

She adds a black and then a cream version of the same style before she looks up at me, eyes narrowed to slits.

"Finished?" I ask.

"Not even close." She twists the phone back around, the total coming to just over seven hundred dollars. "My next spree will have to wait because I'm tired and I want you out of my room so I can sleep."

I hit Purchase on the cart and use Apple Pay.

"You do realize they will be delivered to my place, so you'll have to come and collect them."

She shrugs. "Ask your posh doorman to leave the package at reception, and I'll pick it up when I'm available."

I raise a brow. "Or you could just give me your address and cell number, and I'll have the package redirected to your place. Traveling across town to my apartment would be a waste of money for an athlete earning semi-pro wages."

Her face turns beet red as she grinds out, "I'm a full-time professional."

I wince. "Ope. My bad. With the YouTube video earlier and then your comment about earning a low salary, I figured you must struggle to get by." I flip my phone around to her again. "Do you need anything else while I'm here and feeling charitable? Groceries, new cleats … Tampax?"

Letting her temper get the better of her, Jenna smacks the phone from my hand, and it flies across the room, hitting the wall with a crack.

I don't flinch or even look away from her. "Did you just break my new iPhone?"

She cocks her head to the side, a devilish attitude rolling off her in waves. "Perhaps. A little like you almost broke my brother's jaw."

I roll my eyes. "Are we still arguing over that? It was a light tap and warranted. He stuck his nose in where it wasn't needed."

"He was defending me, and he'd do it again if he were here right now." Her voice shakes a fraction—a show of similar vulnerability I saw that night in Lloyd's when I told her that she was past her best.

"You're tight with your brother?" I ask. It's a genuine question without any malice.

"Why do you care?" she snaps.

I shrug, shoving both hands into my pockets. "Because you seem like you miss him and the hit I landed still bothers you over nine months later."

"Yes, I'm tight with my brother," she replies, her voice still hard as stone.

"What about your parents?" I ask with no idea why. The question tumbles from me before I can register what I'm saying.

Jenna's defenses are back up, and she steps away from me, snatching her own phone from the nightstand and unlocking the screen. "I don't divulge details about my family to assholes. The most I'll give you is my address and number so you can have the leggings mailed to me directly. Beyond that, I never want to speak to you again."

Without responding, I head to my phone and pick it up.

"You can input the details yourself if you can make out the screen." I hand my cell to her, and for a brief moment, her eyes soften, guilt flashing through them as she takes in the large crack straight down the center.

She begins entering her contact details. "After delivery, I want this to be deleted."

"Why?" I ask, watching her type out a cell number.

She finishes up her zip code and passes my mangled phone back. "Because I don't trust you and I don't like you. Not one bit."

"But you'd still let me buy you leggings? That seems a bit hypocritical, don't you think?"

When she presses her finger into the center of my bare chest, her eyes drop to the scissors and thread inked over my heart. "In case you weren't listening earlier, you owe me at least two pairs due to the dinner you slid into my lap. The other pairs are to make up for you generally being an asshole."

"So, we're even?" I ask.

Jenna twists her lips to the side. "I'm willing to drop our feud if you can promise to leave me alone and delete my deets."

Unable to stop myself, I lean over her again. Our lips are almost touching, but not nearly close enough. "Deal," I whisper. "I don't keep women's contact details on my phone. They contact me."

She looks doubtful. "Aside from your mommy's?"

I can smell her vanilla perfume, reminding me of the time she turned down my offer to have fun.

Once bitten, twice shy.

"Maybe I do have my mom's details saved; maybe I don't," I

muse. "Not that it's any of your business, Hellion. I don't divulge details about my family to assholes."

EIGHT

JENNA

I had such high hopes for this hookup.

Not in terms of being my happily ever after because—let's be honest—that's not in the cards for me. My hopes were more centered around orgasms and this guy's confidence that he could deliver them.

But here's the thing: despite what my mom always told me, I don't see sex as a sacred act I should only share with that one special person in my life. If I did, then I'd still be a virgin at twenty-seven, and no one wants that.

And while I'm not expecting fireworks to explode in the night sky behind us, I would like to at least bury my face in the duvet, preventing any neighbors from overhearing my rip-roaring high. If Mr. Right isn't out there for me, then the rest can at least bring the goods in his absence. The trouble with one-night stands is, they're rarely exciting, mostly awkward, and the more of them I have, the clearer that harsh reality is becoming.

Trying not to wake the guy whose name I can't recall—even though he promised me I'd be screaming it nonstop last night—I slowly peel out of his bed and grab my bag and clothes, which I slung over the end of the frame, and make my escape.

After our major win last night, we have three more games before the end of the regular season wraps up in November. Keeping a clean sheet against our rivals, Pittsburg, was fundamental in our pursuit to lift the shield this season—something our club has never done and sits right at the top of my career bucket list.

With that in mind, along with our four to zero win, I figured I'd stay out with a couple of my single teammates—since the vast majority of the team has partners and families to return home to—and celebrate my best performance of the season so far.

When will you learn that when it comes to their talents in bed, men are liars, Jenna?

As I speed through my hookup's living room, pulling on my jeans and sweatshirt as I go, I catch a glimpse of myself in the ridiculously large mirror he has hanging above the side table next to his front door.

I look like shit and deserve to be hungover even though I was as sober as a judge the entire night. With hair sticking out of my day-old ponytail, a smudge of mascara under one eye, and a stain right in the center of my sky-blue top, any semblance of guilt for leaving yet another guy to wake up alone soon diminishes.

No one can see me like this.

Thankfully, my knee-high boots are right by the front door and not in the bedroom, and I slip them on and slowly do up the zips.

Sliding the dead bolt, I carefully twist the lock and pull the door open, checking to make sure I haven't left anything behind when my cell starts ringing, and I quickly hit Accept on Holt's call, closing the front door gently.

"Talk about timing," I whisper-hiss.

"Do I even want to know why you sound like you're hiding?" My brother's gruff voice acts like a warm blanket around me.

I wouldn't exactly describe my childhood as lonely, but I would argue there were better parents out there, ones who didn't favor one sibling over another. Ones who didn't sacrifice their kid's needs in pursuit of their own. Ones who didn't operate like they were still living in the 1920s.

Unfortunately for me, I wasn't my parents' favorite. That honor was bestowed on my thirty-something-year-old brother. Aside from my girls, he's the greatest friend I've ever had, and he's also my hero.

When I was twelve and Dad left my mom, disappearing into the sunset with a younger woman, Holt stepped up to help care for me since Mom lost her shit entirely, finding daily solace in local casinos.

Holt had only just turned eighteen and got himself a job at a local restaurant, waiting tables in between rugby practices and games. He declined a dream scholarship at a prestigious English university, and instead, entered the draft system at a local college no more than an hour's drive from home. All because he couldn't leave his baby sister.

He drove me to soccer practice and helped Mom pay for my kit. He beat up the bullies I had in high school because I wasn't one of the cool kids with the latest Nike sneakers or iPhone.

He protected me.

He advocated for me.

He knows everything about me—past, present, and future.

I only wish he still lived close to me. As soon as I was old enough to attend college, Holt moved to Europe to pursue the dreams he'd put off for my benefit, and he's been there for the past nine years.

I won't lie and say it's been easy. Being without him has been the hardest time, and these past nine months since he was last in the US have somehow felt almost as long as the whole time we've been separated across different continents.

Money has always been an issue for us since neither sport

pays super-high wages, meaning expensive international flights are hard to afford. Holt makes way more than I do, but trying to find the time in a ten-month-long rugby season to travel halfway across the world brings a whole new set of challenges.

I'm down the steps of my hookup's brownstone and heading for one of my favorite bakeries, Rise Up, when I finally answer my brother, chewing over what version of the truth to give him this time.

"I wasn't ... at home."

I can visualize his eye roll right now. When it comes to the opposite sex, Holt and I couldn't be more different. I can count on one hand the number of women he's slept with—two of them long-term girlfriends.

"You scare the shit out of me, Jenna. Please tell me you knew this one before you went home with him?"

Now only a block away from Rise Up, I round the corner just as my stomach rumbles, hungry for raisin toast and caffeine.

All a part of my nutritional plan.

"I mean, partially," I reply, crossing the road opposite Rise Up. "But my question to you is this, would you be so concerned about where I was last night if I were a dude?"

Holt releases a sigh. "I'm putting you on speaker so I can continue cooking, but fair warning, Ryan is sitting right behind me, and he can hear all you're saying."

Like a freaking schoolgirl, I release a small giggle.

Ryan is Holt's hot British teammate and also roommate, who I've met on a couple of occasions when I visited my brother in France. Unfortunately for most of Europe, he also isn't single.

Lucky bitch.

"For the record," Holt continues while he loudly chops food and I pull the phone away from my ear as I push into Rise Up and wave to the owner, Ed, "yes, I would be saying the same thing to you if your name were Jeremy and not Jenna."

"Jeremy?!" I squawk. "That would not be my name if I were a male."

When the chopping stops, sizzling begins, and my stomach protests again. Holt's the best cook I know.

"I hate to burst your bubble, sis, but Jeremy is the exact name you'd have been given. Mom told me once."

"I agree with Jenna," Ryan yells in his posh accent. "Jeremy would not suit her at all."

I nod along with Ryan and tap the glass in front of me, ordering two slices of raisin toast and a cappuccino to go.

"Did Mom tell you what you would've been named if you were a girl?" I ask, a small knot forming in my stomach.

I rarely have conversations with my mom, let alone this kind. She's always wished for a girl who was cutesier and less tomboy. Even today, we barely speak, and I seldom go home for the holidays. I can't remember the last time I saw or spoke to my dad. I'm not even sure I'd recognize him if he were sitting in this café.

"Madalyn," he replies.

"See!" I say, then mouth, *Thanks*, to the server before spinning around with a brown takeout bag and coffee, my phone pinned between my shoulder and ear. "That's a much nicer na …" I trail off.

"What's up?" Holt eventually asks, figuring out I'm likely not going to finish my sentence.

"Nothing," I reply quickly, staring up at a towering Tommy, who smells freshly showered with wet hair styled in his usual way, wearing gray sweats and a dark blue Blades hoodie. "I actually have to go," I tell Holt.

He grumbles something inaudible before clearing his throat. "I'm thinking of coming home for Christmas this year and spending a week with you in Brooklyn. What do you think?" he asks.

"Sounds great," I say, still staring up at Tommy.

He smirks at me, brown eyes moving to my phone as Holt continues speaking about dates and flight prices. I don't know if Tommy can tell it's my brother, but he can probably hear it's a male voice, even over the low music playing in the café.

"You didn't take any of that in, did you?" Holt asks.

"December 23 through the 28." I repeat the dates Holt just confirmed back to him. "Return flight prices are good right now."

My brother chuckles. "All right, cool. I gotta go as well, to be honest. This bourguignon won't finish itself."

"Okay, speak later," I reply brightly, trying not to sound like the guy who landed a punch on him earlier this year is standing right in front of me, looking all delectable.

"Your brother?" Tommy wastes no time asking as soon as I disconnect the call.

I pocket my phone in my jeans. "If you must know, yes."

He scratches at the back of his neck as people move around us in the café. "I thought we were declaring a truce?"

"We are," I reply, pointing to the door. "But I only stopped by for breakfast, and I really need to go."

Tommy folds his arms across his chest, leaning down to my height. "So, your bratty attitude is your default personality and not something you reserve especially for me?"

I deadpan, "Would it make you feel more special if I told you it was just for you?"

He nods and points to a table set behind him. "Yes, it would. I also just ordered breakfast. Why don't you come join me? I was actually on my way over to your place anyway."

I sound surprised as I respond, "Why?"

He looks perplexed, a crease forming between his brows. "Your leggings. They arrived, and I was going to stop by with them, but since you're here"—he reaches behind him, tapping the training bag on his back—"I might as well give you your gift over breakfast."

Despite his permanent cocky, self-assured smirk, I can tell he's making an effort to be friendly, and I wonder how many people he does that with.

I drop my gaze to my coffee and takeout bag.

"Unless you really do need to leave and it wasn't the bullshit excuse I think it is?" Tommy adds, cocky smile morphing to a grin.

I tip my chin at the table. "All right. Five minutes."

Ten minutes later, I'm the proud owner of multiple new pairs of Lululemon leggings, watching Tommy inhale eggs on toast.

He swallows his latest mouthful, chasing it down with a sip of water. "At the risk of being a flirt, you look like shit." He circles his fork at my hair. "Did you wake up this morning and decide to make even less effort than you usually do?"

I wrap my hands around my to-go mug, trying to work out if he's being serious since I do, in fact, look terrible.

"Maybe I did. Did you abandon your sense of humor too?" I feign a light-bulb moment. "Oh wait, for that, you'd actually have to have one in the first place."

He laughs into his eggs, taking a final bite before wiping his mouth and throwing the napkin onto the plate in front of him.

Leaning back in his chair, Tommy stretches both arms above his head, and I can't help but sneak a little glance at his lower torso when his hoodie rides up with the motion.

He has a deep V, one that's been replaying in my mind since he pushed his way into my Boston hotel room wearing only sweatpants.

My entire body heats, threatening to warm the rapidly cooling coffee still nestled between my palms.

"No, seriously …" he says on a yawn, finding my eyes when I flick them from his body to his face. He grins as he catches me, and I flush a little more. "Did you have a rough night last night?"

I clear my throat, shifting slightly on my seat. "I guess you could say that."

Tommy's grin falls, replaced with mild concern. "Did something happen?"

I shake my head. "Yes—well, no. Nothing bad or anything like that."

Picking up his water glass, he pauses with it to his lips. "Were you finally caught sneaking into another guy's room and depositing last night's food by his door?"

I half wince, half laugh at the memory. Kendra and I were in hysterics when we snuck Jack's room key from his overnight bag and slipped my ruined surf 'n' turf inside the hotel room. It must've really stunk.

"You're halfway to the truth. I was inside another guy's room last night. Only I wasn't playing any pranks." I lift a quick shoulder. "I guess you caught me doing the walk of shame." I straighten in my chair. "Not that I have anything to be ashamed about."

When I look across at Tommy, his jaw is clenched, eyes boring into the table beneath us.

"Did I say something wrong?" I ask, giggling away as I take a sip of coffee.

Tommy remains motionless until, suddenly, he pushes back his chair, the screech turning heads from a few of the other customers.

Shocked, I leap to my feet, grabbing my handbag and leggings. "Tommy, what the fuck is wrong?"

Without another word or glance at me, he grabs his bag and makes for the door, practically pulling it off its hinges as he exits.

I follow after him into the chilly fall air. "Tommy," I yell.

"All right then, just ignore me." I try one final time.

Tommy stops in his tracks, turning on one heel to face me. He's around twenty feet away, although it feels like he has me pressed into the wall, like he did that time in Boston.

Pulling at the back of his neck, he tips his face toward the sky before centering his focus back on me. His gaze is intense, and I can't deny it; it's sexy as hell.

"You're nothing but a fucking tease," he spits.

I balk at his tone and take a couple of steps toward him. "Excuse me?" Memories of the fight we had in Lloyd's come racing back. "What did you just call me?"

He closes the rest of the distance between us. "I said ... you're nothing but a tease."

"What?" I scoff. "How could you possibly reach that conclusion?"

His gaze descends my body, and despite the menacing way he's looking at me, I can't suppress the attraction I feel to him. It's like a pull I can't get away from. No matter how hard I want to.

"Don't play dumb with me, Jenna ... or should I say, Hellion?" He rolls his shoulders back, both thumbs hooked under the straps of his backpack. "You blow me off in the bar that time, then proceed to flirt and check me out on the regular, and now I find out you're hooking up with random guys again?"

My mind is spinning with thoughts and possible responses. I'm so taken aback by his reaction that I don't know what to say first.

"Where the fuck is all of this coming from, Tommy?" Keeping my attention on him, I fling an arm out behind me, Brooklyn traffic speeds past us as we square up to each other. "You literally told me you weren't interested, and now you're calling me a tease?!"

I don't miss the pink briefly staining his prominent cheekbones.

"So, why don't you fill me in here and tell me what's really going on, huh?" I bite out, anger levels quickly rising.

Just like in Lloyd's that time, when he inches closer, I contemplate if he's going to kiss me. I wouldn't stop him if he did, but at the same time, I'd hate myself for allowing his mouth on mine.

He speaks very low but with purpose. "Back when we were in Lloyd's, I told you I wasn't interested. And I wasn't. I'm still not interested." He squeezes his eyes shut and then looks at me. "I just need to fuck your brains out."

I shake my head at him. "You're talking in riddles."

Tommy pulls his thumbs from underneath the straps of his backpack, letting both palms slap against his thighs. Over my shoulder, he gazes off into the distance. "Although we can't stand the ground each other walks on, it's undeniable there's this magnetic force pulling us back together, and it's charged as hell. You want to hate-fuck as much as I do, and you know it."

He's right. I'd only be fooling myself if I tried to refute it.

Still, I'd never go there with him. Not after everything that's gone down and *especially* not after the incident with Holt. They say to keep your enemies close, but having him in my bed would be taking it way too far.

I glare up at him. "I'd rather become celibate."

He releases a single puff of air into the small space between us, his brown eyes burning to amber. "Careful what you wish for, Jen. With an attitude like that, I'm betting you'll die old and lonely too."

I'm determined not to reveal how deep his callous remark cuts.

"Maybe you should take a hint then. When an aging woman way past her prime won't even hate-fuck you, I'd probably call time on trying to woo the opposite sex."

I can tell he loves this. The toxicity feeds him, and I quickly conclude that getting at people, male or female, is how he lives his life.

His sad, pathetic life.

"Oh, I wasn't planning to woo you." He laughs darkly. "I was planning to fuck you and then toss you to the side. Think of it as an itch I wanted to scratch. Or a brother I wanted to piss off."

Fire burns through me, and I'm ready to bite back when he spins back around and stalks off into the crowd, waving a sarcastic, tattooed hand above his head.

"Have a nice life, Hellion."

NINE

TOMMY

Games against the Scorpions are always heated, but tonight, it wouldn't matter who the opposition was because I'm on the warpath.

It's been three days since I saw Jenna at Rise Up, and I'm no calmer, even now.

At this point, I'm not sure who I'm madder at—her for turning me down again when we both know she wants me or at myself for giving in to my need and opening myself up to more of her rejection.

Jenna Miller is the exact reason I don't give second chances. I barely answer the phone when my mom calls any longer because I don't believe a word she has to say to me anymore.

People lie, and Jenna is no exception to that rule. She's lying to herself right now if she can't feel the burning tension between us each time we're in the same room.

When Jessie Callaghan—the Scorpions winger—picks up a turnover at center ice, realistically, the only player capable of stopping him is me.

He's fast and agile, and he has the smartest brain in the game.

But while he has all that on his side, I have weight and power on mine.

He tracks my every movement as he bolts toward me, the Scorpions center racing to keep up with him. I chew on the corner of my mouth shield, trying to read which way he's going to go.

Callaghan has one of the best dekes, but while his center could double as a decoy, he frequently likes to go it alone.

He lives for scoring, and he's damn good at it too.

In a split second, I call it, making the decision to stand my ground. He's going solo and taking Archer on himself.

I'm skating backward toward our goal, giving myself time and space to maneuver and adapt as I need.

He isn't getting past me. We're one-to-one deep in the third period, and like hell are we suffering another loss. Not on my watch anyway.

The arena crowd is loud, only growing louder as Callaghan edges closer, but all I can hear are his blades as they cut through the ice. Faster, sharper, ready to skip around me at the final second.

With one last glance at his center, I'm all in on Callaghan as he fakes to pass off to his teammate, but it doesn't have the desired effect when I don't commit.

But when he pulls the puck back between his legs in a move I haven't seen him pull off in game tape, I'm left stranded, wondering if he's going to dive down my left or right side.

The fucker does neither, pulling the puck back for a second time and laying it off to his center in a last-minute pass right before he collides with me.

They score, and Archer drops to his knees in front of the goal, shaking his head at the crease. Our goalie coach, Jensen Jones, stands on the other side of the plexiglass, directly behind the goal, with his jaw agape, trying to process what he just witnessed.

It was likely one of the best moves this season—if not in modern-day hockey—but that's not enough to stop my frustration from bubbling over into rage. It feels like the whole arena is mocking me when the lamp continues flashing for what feels like way longer than normal. Callaghan and his teammates all bump fists along the benches as they draw out their celebrations just to rub salt into the wound.

With my hands propped firmly on my hips, I skate back to center ice just as one of their rookie wingers passes by me.

"Nice assist, Schneider. Did your dad teach you how to be a fool? Because you sure have the knack."

I see red. Like a curtain dropping on a performance—or possibly even my career—I skate after the rookie who just signed his own death warrant, pulling off my gloves and thrusting them onto the ice.

I've never spoken with Curtis Freeman before since this is his first pro season.

Never too young for a rude awakening.

I crunch my elbow into his ribs, and I spin around to face him. I already know I'm destined for the penalty box. Might as well go the whole way.

"I'm sorry, but you'll have to speak up. My bullshit filter is on its highest setting today." I cup my hand around my ear, cheers from the crowd reverberating around the arena.

They want a fight, and they're going to get one.

Ordinarily, I'd probably let the first or second gibe from a player slide and bank it as ammunition for later in the game or season. Unfortunately for Freeman, he caught me on a bad day with the worst possible reference he could make.

His eyes dart around the rink before he drops his gloves in front of me.

"Zach Evans already retired." I grin at him. "And the rest of your teammates aren't going to save you."

I'm vibrating, firing off like a coiled spring when I land a punch into his ribs.

He wraps his right arm around my neck, gripping on to me on a choked cough.

"Repeat what you just said to me," I spit. "I want to hear your mouth talk smart while it swallows my fist."

I pull out from his body and land an uppercut on the underside of his jaw, one reminiscent of the hit I put on Jenna's brother.

It feels good. Cathartic even. Purging pure rage.

The rookie escapes my grasp and takes a wild swing for me, which practically sends him crashing to the ice. I stand with my hands on my hips as I circle him, laughing and enjoying the show.

Blood drips from his chin, and I know we only have seconds before the ref breaks us up.

Plenty of time to land another hit.

I give him a matching bruise on the other side of his rib cage right before the ref pulls me from him, ushering me to the penalty box beside the Blades bench and Freeman off the ice to get medical treatment, along with the stitches he's definitely going to need.

"You're brutal, Schneider," the ref grits out beneath his breath. "Major penalty for the glove drop, plus another two minutes for being the instigator."

He slams the box door as I step in, and I beat my stick against the plexiglass like a rabid bull. "He fucking started it!" I point at the bent-over rookie as he leaves the ice. "He showed unsportsmanlike conduct!"

I'm still going wild when our veteran defenseman, Sawyer Bryce, skates past the penalty box, pulling up in front of me.

I've lost complete control of my emotions, probably humiliating myself more than Jenna ever could.

He shakes his head at me, disappointment in his eyes.

Sawyer has always been the guy everyone turns to on the team, the levelheaded single dad who's seen it all, on and off the ice.

"What?!" I yell, earning a few jeers from our traveling fans.

Like I give a fuck that I'm laying into their golden boy.

Sawyer just watches as I take a seat on the bench behind me, throwing my stick down in the process.

Above the arena noise and behind the glass, it's virtually impossible to hear him, although that doesn't mean I can't make out what he's saying.

You're going to fuck your career, he mouths at me.

I throw out a hand, my confidence giving way to self-pity. I'm so fucking done with people and trying to prove myself.

So fucking done with hockey and trying to be a team player when, clearly, I'm not made for it.

So fucking done with Jenna Miller.

"So fucking what?!" I volley back at my former captain. "Maybe I already did." I pull at my jersey, practically ripping it at the seams. "Once a Schneider, always a Schneider, no?!"

TEN

JENNA

I thought I'd seen it all when it came to Tommy Schneider.

But nothing could've prepared me—or anyone else who watched the Blades away series against the Scorpions a few nights ago—for that crazy display of pure rage from Tommy.

The fight, the way he lost his shit in the penalty box, smashing his stick until it cracked from brute force.

He's an animal with zero sense of remorse, beating that poor rookie to an absolute pulp.

And why?

Because Tommy Schneider is little more than a thug, using hockey as an excuse to vent his rage.

The media is speculating that his career will be over well before his dad's was, and I personally can't foresee an outcome where it isn't. He's on a slippery slope to nowhere.

I witnessed the way he spoke to Sawyer. And when the crowd jeered at his actions, Tommy seemed to feed off it.

The Blades just played Ohio at home and secured an emphatic win. I don't know if he'll show at Lloyd's tonight, but if he does, I plan to ignore him. The last time Tommy saw me, he told me to have a nice life, and I should definitely do that. Push past his existence and get on with my soccer career.

Life without the Blades bad boy in it will be way less complicated and stressful. He reminds me of my bullies from high school—constantly searching for the next opportunity to goad and back me into a corner. He brings the worst out of me, makes me say things I don't mean.

But above all else, he doesn't make me proud of my actions. Just being in his presence pushes me to the very brink of my patience as I permanently bite my tongue. I'm not a mean or scornful person. I'm a kind and caring friend to my girls, a loving sister to my brother.

I'm not the kind of girl who gets involved with brutes like Tommy Schneider.

"You're searching for him, aren't you?" Darcy clinks her cocktail glass against mine.

I didn't plan to have alcohol tonight, especially since I have a game the day after tomorrow, but sometimes, it's needed.

I smile at my friend while she examines my expression. "I'm more concerned about the Scorpions rookie, Curtis Freeman; he isn't on their roster tonight." I point at the TV above the bar, which is showing the Scorpions game live.

Darcy shrugs like she isn't surprised. She's Coach Morgan's stepdaughter, and her family has a history with the Schneider last name. "I give it a few weeks, and he'll be on the trade list. The difficulty will be shipping him off. I can't imagine any team wanting to take him on. He's the ultimate disruptor."

I open my mouth to agree when she continues.

"Trouble is ..." She twists her lips to the side. "If he dropped the bravado, he'd actually be a pretty decent player."

"Oh, it's more than just bravado," I scoff as Archer arrives and pulls her into his side in an act of pure possession.

I try not to melt and wish I had the same.

"When I left to head here, Tommy was being summoned to

Coach's office. Postgame meetings like that usually mean only one thing." Archer slides the edge of his hand across his throat. "He played like shit tonight, and I'm pretty sure he's finished."

My stomach flips. "You think he'll be forced into the farm team?"

Archer just shrugs, not seeming bothered either way. "I mean, if he is, then it'll probably be for the best. Not a single guy on the team likes him."

A hint of sadness on Tommy's behalf creeps into my conscience, and I quickly push it away, remembering the way he spoke to me outside Rise Up.

He deserves everything coming to him, I remind myself, downing the rest of my cosmo.

Darcy takes my empty glass and sets it on the bar behind her.

I decide to switch subjects, a gnawing discomfort settling into my bones each time I think of Tommy.

"Does your mom have Emily tonight?" I ask her, plastering on a faux bright smile.

She sees straight through it, but doesn't call me out. "Yeah …" She chuckles. "For saying she didn't want to be called a grandma, she sure has taken to the role like a duck to water."

Archer loops his arms around his wife's waist, setting a kiss into her hair. "I think we should have more babies. We can sneak off, and I'll put one inside you right now, if you'd like?"

Another pang of discomfort hits me straight in the chest, knocking the wind right out of me.

Darcy swivels in his arms, swatting him on the shoulder. "Archer, I swear to God, if you've tampered with my birth control, I'll never forgive you."

He just smirks at her; it's cocky, but it doesn't carry the same edge as Tommy's, and I find myself scanning the bar for him once again.

Archer's strong hand wraps around my upper arm. "Are you okay, Jen? You seem … off?"

It's times like this when alcohol can come in very handy, although it's not a luxury pro athletes can afford to indulge in. I'm barely clinging on to my nutritional plan, let alone introducing a hangover into the mix. Another cosmo would not be a good move.

I motion to the restroom on the far side of the bar. "I need to use the bathroom and maybe get some air. I'll be back in a bit."

Leaning forward, I swipe my purse from the back of the barstool in front of me and catch Darcy's attention. "I'm fine," I reassure her. "I just need a minute."

I push through the door into the women's restroom, and the relative silence provides a welcome relief as the door clicks behind me, blocking the thumping music ringing through the main bar area.

I set my purse down, flattening my palms against the countertop and inviting the cold marble to cool my clammy skin.

At first, I figure I'm alone in here, but at the sound of a soft whimper echoing from one of the stalls, I realize I'm not, and it's possible someone else is having an even worse night than I am.

Another soft whimper, and I turn to face the stalls.

"Is everything okay?" My voice is clear as it echoes in the quiet restroom, although it doesn't receive a response.

A shadow shifts in the middle stall, followed by another whimper, only this time, it's muffled, and it sounds more amused than upset.

I shake my head to no one and turn back around to my purse, pulling out my lip gloss and applying a fresh coat. I'm done with playing games. If whoever's in there needed my help, they would've made it clear.

A few seconds later, when I'm snapping my purse shut, the dead bolt slides across the door, but again, no one materializes.

Way too curious to ignore it, I pick up my purse and walk the few steps toward the stall door, tentatively pushing it open with one hand.

"Hellion. Fancy seeing you here."

Now the whimpers and muffled noises all make sense as I lock eyes with Tommy, his head tipped over his shoulder to take in my reaction. With his back to me, he thrusts one hand into some random blonde girl's hair, his postgame pants pooling around his ankles, and he pulls her head closer to his crotch.

I want to puke right here on the gross tiled floor. Instead, I force myself to look at him.

This is deliberate and all for effect. This is to get back at me for sleeping with that guy and telling him about it. This is a move designed to reject me in the way I rejected him.

It has to be.

I can't be sure how Tommy knew I'd catch him. Maybe he just banked on me using the bathroom at some point during the night and hoped I'd be alone when I did. Not that the how or why matters because he's already accomplished what he set out to achieve.

I hate him even more than I did thirty seconds ago.

When his jaw hangs open, I know she just brought him to the point of no return, and I slam the stall door shut, stalking out of the bathroom with tears in my eyes that I'm certain he noticed.

I'm halfway to the bar exit when I swear I hear him calling my name.

Or maybe that's just my imagination. I don't know, and I don't care. Tommy can call after me all he wants, but he'll never get an answer. He'll never get to see the whites of my eyes ever again.

When the freezing air hits my bare skin, I realize I left my jacket in the bar. I keep walking, not caring and with no intention of heading back to retrieve it.

"Jenna!" a gruff voice I know to be Tommy's calls after me again, and I pick up my pace, convinced I'm capable of outrunning him in my sneakers.

Another few steps, and a thick forearm wraps around my waist, spinning me around to look at him.

His eyes are remorseful, the complete opposite of the Tommy who beat up Curtis Freeman. Still, I won't be fooled. I know what lurks behind those pretty irises.

"Get off me!" I yell, but he pulls us both into a darkened side street.

I momentarily break free before he recaptures my arm and pins me against a filthy brick wall.

Every cell in my body thrums at his proximity, but not in the good way, like before in the Boston hotel. This time, I genuinely want him to leave me alone.

More tears threaten to spill free, and I will them away as Tommy towers over me, brushing a few strands of hair away from my face.

He doesn't get to be gentle with me. He doesn't get to show that he cares.

With two hands against his chest, I push him out and into the center of the street. He could have probably fought back or held on tighter if he wanted, but something tells me he got the message loud and clear.

It feels like my eyeballs are busting from their sockets as I raise a single finger in front of me. "Never. *EVER.* Come near me again. Don't ever look in my direction." I barely recognize my own voice or the words that cut at him.

He opens his mouth but quickly clamps it shut, and I start to tremble in the cold night air, a mixture of the chilling fall breeze and adrenaline taking hold deep within my bones.

"You make me sick," I spit at him. "*You* are fucking sick."

A tear runs down my cheek, and I swipe it away, more infuriated with myself and the display of unwanted emotion.

He doesn't get to see my upset.

"She never touched me in that way, Jenna." His tone is soft but unsure as he takes a cautious step toward me.

I raise my finger again in warning, and he stops dead.

While Tommy's body completely blocked my view of what was happening, I don't need to be a genius to figure it out. "I know what I saw," I say, "and I'm so disgusted with myself for getting into these games with you in the first place. You bring the worst out in me, Tommy."

He shakes his head, and I nod mine.

"Yes, you do. You're toxic. *We* are toxic whenever we're near each other. You might be good with using people to score points, but I'm not."

Something like genuine regret flashes in his eyes, but it's so brief that I question if I saw it in the first place.

Probably not.

With nothing else to say, I turn my back on him and start to walk away.

"I want to talk to you! I never said you could walk away from me, Hellion."

I spin back around and face him for the final time, tears pooling, no matter how hard I fight them back. "You didn't need to, Tommy. Because I just fucking did."

ELEVEN

TOMMY

UNKNOWN NUMBER

So, last night, this really weird thing happened. My friend left the bar without saying goodbye, which is completely out of character. While she keeps telling me she's fine, I know her well enough to guess that she is far from okay. I also think that you had something to do with her sharp exit.

This is Darcy, BTW. I got your number from my husband's phone.

I pause my spin session and read through the text I just received on my new iPhone.

ME

Were you expecting a response to this? Because all I see is a bunch of statements, no questions.

Hi, BTW, Darcy. I hope you're having a great day.

If three little dots could look furious, I'm pretty sure that's exactly what I'm witnessing right now as they frantically pop up and disappear while she types out a response.

UNKNOWN NUMBER

> I guessed you would reply with that. Nothing is ever your fault, is it?

Abandoning my workout session altogether, I jump down from my spin bike and head for the water cooler set at the back of my home gym, refilling my water bottle as I chew over Darcy's observations.

Early morning workouts are for sure part of my schedule, but that's not why I've been pounding my cardio equipment for the past half hour.

I needed to take my mind off Jenna and the way she looked at me last night. I can still feel the sting of her words as they cut through me, the tone of her voice.

She meant it when she called me sick. And she's right. It was a dick move to engineer that prank with the blonde chick who was well up for it in exchange for free drinks for her and her friends all night. Timing it was easy enough; all I had to do was wait for Jenna to grab her purse and head for the bathroom—as she does at some point on every night out—and we could slip into the restroom just before she noticed.

I had zero intention of letting that girl go down on me. But despite making it clear to Jenna that she didn't touch me like that, I know Jenna didn't believe me.

And why the fuck should I care what she thinks? I'm free to be with whoever I want. I warned her not to play games, but she just wouldn't fucking listen.

Guilt snakes through me, and I push it away.

ME

If Jenna doesn't want to tell you what went down, then that's her private business to withhold. To be blunt, I can't see how the fuck it concerns you anyway. Don't you have a baby to care for?

UNKNOWN NUMBER

I have nothing but inappropriate responses for you. Most of which will likely get me arrested.

ME

For what it's worth, I did chase after her and try to calm her down. She wasn't willing to listen to me, and then she stormed off into the night.

UNKNOWN NUMBER

Oh, so you did do something wrong. Try apologizing again.

ME

We owe each other nothing.

UNKNOWN NUMBER

Wrong. She owes YOU nothing. You owe her an apology.

ME

I say this with the utmost kindness: fuck off, Darcy.

UNKNOWN NUMBER

You know, I really wanted to believe that you were different from the last name on the back of your jersey. My dad was a complete douchebag, too, but neither Jack nor I turned out to be a manipulative narcissist despite sharing his DNA. You aren't any different from Alex though, are you? There isn't a good bone in your body. What you need to ask yourself, Tommy, is, where is your dad now? Huh? I assume in some gutter somewhere, having

> burned every single bridge he ever had. I don't
> know how you can follow in his footsteps with
> a clear conscience. I wanted to believe you
> were better than that because just like Jenna, I
> look for the good in people.

Cortisol tears through my body as I read Darcy's message with trembling hands.

Throwing down my water bottle, I begin typing out an enraged response, explaining that I wouldn't know where my dad is since he turned his back on me as a child and again when I was seventeen. My fingers hammer the keyboard as I set the record straight, telling this posh little British girl exactly why I carry the last name Schneider even though, deep down, I hate it with every part of me. That the alternative of wearing my mom's last name feels just as painful, but at least this way, I can erase my dad altogether.

I don't hit Send on the message. Instead, I stare down at the words, which feel more and more empty each time I convince myself that I'm nothing like the guy who rejected me.

Every bridge I've ever had has been burned, including the one I once had with my mom.

Accepting the truth about who I really am and the trajectory of my career is hard, but telling the world—or even Jenna's best friend over a text—feels like an insurmountable challenge I will never overcome.

The world would laugh at me.

Poor little bad boy, all angry because he has daddy and mommy issues.

The more I consider how the public would react, if they even cared, the more bitterness and anger twist at my insides.

It feels like I'm backed into a corner with zero viable options other than to keep fighting and hold everyone who could ever make me feel something—only to inevitably tear me apart when they let me down—at arm's length.

Detaching myself from people is what I do best. It's what I've got inked over my heart.

It's an approach that hasn't failed me yet.

So, why is letting go of someone as toxic as Jenna Miller so fucking difficult? And why am I racing out of my apartment and grabbing my car keys so I can head over to her place right now?

None of this makes any sense.

I don't need to hand-deliver any more leggings. We have no reason to speak to each other ever again. Being strangers who casually catch sight of each other in Lloyd's after games is exactly what we should be. Jenna told me that I turn her into a person she doesn't like and … same.

Curtis Freeman can attest to that.

Sawyer called me out on it.

I'm so far removed from the player I could be; I barely recognize my own game anymore—or at least not the one I played when I was a kid.

Trouble is, I'm so lost that I don't know if I'll ever find my way back, and the answers don't lie in Jenna Miller's apartment.

That I know for sure.

MY HAND HOVERS OVER THE BRASS KNOCKER SET IN THE CENTER of Jenna's white front door.

I should've deleted her contact info right after I gave her the leggings, but that's the least of my worries right now.

The girl has a mouth on her—and I bet a slap to match.

Accepting my fate—and potentially a bruised cheek—I knock once and step back to a minimum safe distance.

It's possible she's out, maybe at practice.

Yeah, she isn't in. I convince myself she's not home, already hitting Call on the elevator when her door swings open.

On sight of me, she flares her nostrils as she stands in her doorway, dressed in the tiniest pair of black Lycra shorts and a sports bra to match.

The worst thing I could do right now is check her out, and naturally, that's exactly what I do.

She's the hottest girl I have ever seen, and immediately, I regret leaving my apartment wearing only flimsy athletic shorts and a Dri-FIT T-shirt.

They hide nothing.

"You've got some fucking gall." She folds her arms across her chest, and, fuck, this situation cannot get any worse.

In a declaration of peace, I hold my palms out in front of me. I know things are way past salvageable, but there are at least three other apartments on this floor that can potentially hear everything being said.

"I'm not here to argue," I say, voice low and calm. "I came to talk."

Jenna doesn't want to talk—that much is obvious. She pushes a manicured hand through her long, dark hair. "Go talk with your hookup."

A small laugh leaves my chest as I take a cautious step toward her. It feels like I'm feeding a wild animal and trying not to become the meal.

"That sounds a lot like the pot calling the kettle black." I try to suppress the smirk I know would only enrage her further. "Weren't you in another guy's bed the other night?"

Both shoulders bunch around her ears. "So, you did fuck her then?" She scoffs and reaches for the door, ready to slam it shut. "You make me sick."

"Wait!" I lurch forward, catching the door just before she crushes my hand in the jamb.

Jenna tries to push it shut, but I'm much stronger, even when she leans her entire weight against it.

"Leave me the fuck alone," she hisses through the narrow opening, trying to keep her voice low but vicious.

"Not going to happen."

In one motion, I'm through the door, and she's stumbling backward into her hallway, ready to come for me as I quickly close the door behind me and brace for impact.

I catch her arms above her head, holding both her wrists in one hand and quickly flipping us around, pressing her back into the door.

She fights and wriggles to break free, but unlike when I let her go last night, I'm not making the same mistake twice.

When Jenna finally realizes her efforts are futile, her face morphs from desperate to cunning. "If you don't let go of me, I'm going to scream. I could have the police here in minutes, and your career—what's left of it—would be up in smoke within the hour."

Challenge blooms low in my gut, picking up my heart rate and coursing adrenaline through every artery.

"Don't make promises you can't keep, Jenna. You've been desperate for me to make you scream since the second you laid eyes on me."

Despite her vulnerable position, I watch the way her pupils dilate, red creeping up the center of her chest.

I drop my eyes down her body, unable to suppress the blood flow as it pumps to my dick.

"Take a good look, Tommy. Soak it all in because you will never see me like this again. You'll never put your hands on me like this again."

The zip fastening up the center of her sports bra sparks my curiosity.

"Tell me something, Hellion."

I tease the zipper pull between my fingers, and her eyes blow wide. Despite her thrashing around in my grasp, she isn't going anywhere.

"Is this zip real or just for aesthetic purposes?" I pull it down over the first couple of teeth. Taunting her.

"It isn't real," she blurts out.

I quirk a doubtful brow. "Are you sure you're telling me the truth? I don't like liars."

Heat creeps up her neck, and she bites down on her bottom lip. An internal war is taking place inside this girl, and I'm devouring every second of her anguish.

"So, if I slip this down a little further"—I pull the zipper past another couple of teeth—"your tits won't spill free?"

She shakes her head vigorously. "I can guarantee you they won't."

She tips her chin up to look at me, her defiance inflating my dick, to the point of pain.

Jenna isn't the only one being tortured right now.

"I can also guarantee that if you pull that zipper down any further, I'll make sure you see the back of a jail cell tonight. Although I wouldn't be so concerned about the offense you're committing and more about the way my brother will dismember you."

Not a single word leaving her mouth is genuine.

"If you hate my touch so much, why is it that I can see your nipples?"

I pull the zipper down again, and she sucks in a sharp breath. By now, we both know it's real and not aesthetic, a bit like the magnetic pull between us.

"What if I took one of your peaked nipples into my mouth? Would you call the police on me then?"

She swallows thickly and tries to speak.

"Good," I say in response to her silence, pulling the zipper down once more. "I'm tired of hearing the incessant bullshit that spews from your pretty little mouth on the daily. Let your body do the talking for once."

With the zipper over halfway to being undone, I'm only a fraction away from setting eyes on Jenna's full chest.

My fingers tease the zipper pull once more, and I search her gaze for the green light to go further. "Tell me to stop."

She remains quiet, thighs pinching together.

One small tug, and I'm over another tooth. I drop my eyes down her body. "At this point, I guess you have two choices."

"What are they?" she whispers, voice laced with lust.

I pull the zipper over one more tooth, and the pink edges of her nipples come into view.

Christ, she's beautiful.

"Option one: let me remove your bra and have me banged up in custody. Or option two: be a good girl, quit fucking around, and let me bang you against this door."

I draw a steadying breath into my lungs as I will my teetering orgasm to hold off.

"Your move, Miller."

TWELVE

JENNA

One lift of my knee between his thighs, and Tommy Schneider would be rolling around on the floor, begging me not to call the police.

It's what I should do. What my brother and friends would be screaming at me to do. Just like in the hotel, he's forced his way into my apartment and pinned me against the door.

The seconds tick by as he waits on my decision. He knows I'm not going to knee him in the crotch, just like he knows I won't scream or try to press charges.

I want this, but also, I don't. I need him, but he repulses me, all at the same time.

Holt, Kendra, Darcy, and Collins will never understand that this situation runs way deeper than what they've seen up until this point.

He'll never stop asking me to fuck because he knows he's breaking me down. The number of times I can tell him no is limited before my willpower inevitably wanes and he can have his way.

Maybe that is what we need … to fuck and get it out of our systems. We sure as hell don't seem to be able to settle our differences through talking. I know he won't be gentle with me, and that's not what I want. What I want is this man out of my life for good, and if he happens to deliver a climax or two in the process, then no one ever has to know what we did.

We'll never speak about it again. I'll never have to speak to *him* again.

Carefully, I lift my knee, tracing it up the inside of his bare leg. His tattooed olive skin pebbles, just like mine, as I reach his apex and shift a little higher. He doesn't flinch, eyes only burning brighter with anticipation.

He releases my wrists from above my head, confidently smiling, like he knows I'm not going anywhere. "You don't want to do that, Hellion." Tommy speaks low, his voice gravelly. "If you take me out, I'll struggle to ruin your cunt, and we're both well aware of your desperation for my dick."

I drop my foot back to the ground, placing a hand in the center of his chest.

"Do you want me to destroy you, Jenna?"

My throat is so thick, so dry, that I struggle to form words.

He pulls down the zipper again, and both breasts bulge over the top of my sports bra.

At war with myself and powerless to act, I remain silent. I refuse to give him the satisfaction of a yes, but want him to know that being destroyed is exactly what I crave.

With one final tug of the zip, my top bursts open, flimsy material hanging down by my sides.

Tommy's eyes haven't left mine yet. He's likely desperate to take in my body, and I have to hand it to him—the boy possesses control where I didn't think he did.

Slowly, deliberately, he crouches down in front of me until his eyeline is level with my breasts.

Taking my left nipple into his mouth, he only tears his eyes away from mine when his tongue wraps around the small bar piercing.

I'm surprised he didn't see it through my sports bra.

Running a hand through his disheveled hair, he groans around my nipple, teasing and flicking it with expert precision. I can tell he's experienced in bed and that his reputation for being a fuckboy is no lie.

"What's wrong, Tommy?" I goad, trying not to soak my shorts from the way he works his mouth over me. "Is this the first time you've been with a real woman?"

I pull hard on his hair, practically tearing it from the roots.

He groans again at the sensation.

"Or is that you've never been with someone who can give as good as she gets?"

I'm hanging on for dear life, my fighting talk as much for my own benefit as it is for him.

Without warning, he bites down on my nipple, and I throw my head back into the door. Obviously, my neighbors didn't hear our fight in the hallway since armed police aren't breaking down my door. Although I'm confident anyone standing on the other side right now will know exactly what's going on.

"Don't play games with me, Jenna."

Tommy rises to his feet in front of me, cupping my pussy in his palm.

I pulse into his hand, soaking his skin through my shorts.

Goddammit.

His laugh sounds evil. "The way I want to shoot straight inside this tight pussy and then leave it right on the edge, desperate and needy for its own release. Your walls would quiver as they cling to thin air." He leans into me, sniffing my hair like a predator sizing up its prey. "Do your other men make you come, Hellion?"

As I shake my head, he hooks his thumbs in the waistband of his shorts, pushing them down to the floor.

My eyes divert lower.

"Holy shit," I announce, clamping my mouth shut so I don't pay him a compliment he doesn't deserve.

Tommy fists his tattooed cock. A script I can't read loops around his long, thick shaft.

"Take your shorts off, Jenna," he commands, dragging his hand from root to tip in slow, easy motions.

I can't lie; I've thought about this moment when I've used my vibrator in bed, fantasizing about what he would do. Each time, I've envisioned him tearing my clothes clean off in one brutal rip. But I couldn't be further from the truth.

He wants me to prepare myself for him.

He wants to watch as I yield to his commands like a good girl.

Reaching up on my tiptoes, I return the cocky smile he gives me so often. "If you want me, come and get me."

The growl he releases reverberates off the walls of my hallway as he slings me over his shoulder, marching us both toward my living room.

"Which room is your bedroom?" he snaps, slapping my ass hard.

I bite down on my lip, the sting borderline unbearable but delicious all the same.

"Jenna, I'm going to fuck you against that window for the entire world to see if you don't tell me where your bedroom is in the next three seconds."

He stalks toward one closed door, pushing it open to reveal my bathroom. Then he finds the closet next door.

Finally, he tries a third door and launches me onto the mattress.

I bounce once before Tommy's hovering over me, dark strands of hair falling over his feral eyes.

"Clothes. Off. Now." He punctuates each word with venom.

The frustration is killing him, and I take back some of the power as I shake my head from beneath him.

He gazes down at my Lycra-covered pussy, wet and seeping through my shorts. "Does Lululemon sell these too?"

I nod once.

With brute strength only Tommy could be capable of, he tears them apart at the seam, exposing my lacy black thong.

There's no grace or care when he sinks his fingertips into my hips, dragging my lower half up to his mouth. One lick against my soaking thong catapults my hips even higher, but he holds me in place as I writhe around on the bed.

I've never been licked through my panties before, and it's the most intense sensation—his tongue right there, tantalizingly close to my sensitive flesh, while his hot breath tickles and teases my senses.

Tommy suspends my lower half with one arm as he pulls my thong to one side, eyes hooded when he takes me in for the first time.

"Spread yourself, Jenna. I want to see both of your holes so I can decide which one I'll ruin first."

I try to pull away, but he holds me in place against his mouth, swiping a slow lick over both entrances.

Of course Tommy would be the same breed of animal in bed that he is on the ice.

"I don't do anal. I never have," I tell him, attempting to pull away again.

With his fingers, he parts me wider, exposing every part of me for his warm, wet tongue. "Ass play is my favorite, and that's what I want to do with you."

Another lick, and he spears his tongue inside my pussy.

I moan with pleasure, fisting the duvet as I hurtle toward my first orgasm from a guy since I split up with Lee.

Tommy pulls back, much to my dismay. "You're close. I can feel your walls throbbing around my tongue."

He drops my hips to the bed, and I release a squeal.

Slapping a palm over my mouth, he fists his cock at my entrance. "Are you on birth control, Jenna?"

I swipe his hand away, equally turned on and disgusted by his brutal actions. "Yes. Are you tested? Because I don't want to catch whatever you might've picked up last night."

Hooking a finger under my chin, he tips my head up roughly, steely eyes piercing mine. "I told you already, she never touched me like that, and I never put my hands on her. Your body is the only one I'm craving." He wraps his palms under my ass. "As pro athletes, we both get tested on the regular by our teams. Plus, I always wear a con …" He trails off, holding back his sentence.

I narrow my eyes at him, and with every ounce of strength I possess, I push at his chest.

He sits up, sliding a frustrated hand through his hair. "Are you going to ride my dick or waste my time? Because I want to fuck."

I crawl over him, hovering my pussy over his dick. "I like to ride when I fuck."

Tommy's fingertips dig into my hips, and I spread my knees, letting him sink me onto his impossibly hard cock. I stretch for him, spreading my knees even further.

When he's all the way inside, his jaw clenched and his eyes black, I get a proper look at his glorious naked body.

It's a work of art; his skin is a stunning canvas.

I rock over him once, and he licks his lips, bruising my skin with his tight grip.

"Faster," he demands.

Doing the opposite of what he wants, I go slower, and his jaw hangs open. I can tell that he's seconds away from coming, and I bask in the power switch.

My dominance doesn't last long when I'm back beneath him, my legs open as he holds me by the ankles. He throws his head back, pounding into me and taking what he wants.

"Squeeze my dick, Hellion." Tommy pistons into me again, dropping one leg to free his hand so he can play with my ass.

Even though my instincts tell me to pull away, my greedy body spreads my thighs wider for him. He gathers leaking arousal from us both onto his fingers, using it to lubricate my tight hole.

"Let's make this ass come at the same time as your pussy."

He teases one tattooed finger inside, pushing deeper with every stroke of his cock.

I claw at the duvet beneath me, fighting back my cries of pleasure. I'm fully aware I'm not quiet in bed when a man gets it right. And Tommy is infuriatingly good at fucking.

He doesn't get to find out how good.

I'm right there, right on the edge of losing it altogether, when he stops and pulls out, leaving me empty and confused.

"On your knees for me, Jenna."

"I don't get on my knees for anyone," I protest. "I'd rather not come at all."

He slaps my bare pussy, and I squeal when pleasure-loaded shock waves tingle my swollen clit. "Final warning: get on your knees before I put you on them myself."

I do as he asked, but not in the exact way he wanted. He wanted me to bend over doggy style. Instead, I rise up in front of him.

We're both kneeling on the bed in front of each other. Horny and desperate, wild and defiant.

"When I get on my knees for someone, it's because they're worth it." My voice is deeper than I've ever heard it before.

Tommy cocks his head to one side, reveling in our standoff. "You're playing games you don't understand again, Jenna."

I offer him a petulant shrug, pointing toward my bedroom door. "And if you don't like the rules I'm laying down, then you're more than free to leave."

THIRTEEN

TOMMY

She's against that damn bedroom door in seconds, suspended in my arms like a rag doll, taking my dick as I slam into her on repeat.

"I hope you don't have practice tomorrow because you won't be able to walk by the morning."

Small gasps fall from her throat, complementing the wet sounds her pussy makes as she takes me.

I'm punishing her for months of her bratty attitude with each thrust I unleash onto her body.

On the first orgasm, her head lolls forward, resting in the center of my chest. Her nails tear strips down my back, cutting into my shoulder blades.

Jenna Miller is at my mercy.

"T-Tommy," she cries. "I'm going to come. Again."

I pound into her harder. "Let me play with your ass."

With big blue eyes that usually hide all vulnerability, she nods her agreement, and I bring a single finger to her lips, asking her to lubricate it. The other arm keeps her in place against the door.

She takes it into her mouth, wrapping her tongue around my tattoos.

When she's finished, I do the same. The taste of her mouth is as delicious as her pussy. For a moment, I wonder what it would be like to kiss this girl, long and slow and with tongues tangling.

I don't kiss women. Ever.

Her asshole is still coated in arousal from before, and I slow my thrusts, easing my finger inside her.

"Oh my God," she moans when I gently move my finger, stroking her walls to create optimal pressure.

"If you weren't such a fucking bitch all the time, I could've been doing this in a much easier position."

I'm not sure if she chooses to ignore my gibe or if she's simply zoned out. Anal play will do that to a girl.

I stroke her again and feel a warm release around my dick, along with her tightening cunt.

"How many orgasms have you had now, Jenna?" I ask, pride swamping my voice.

With her eyes squeezed shut, she shakes her head. "I-I don't know."

My gaze falls to her full lips, an unexpected need to kiss her resurfacing.

This is the last girl I should be tempted to kiss. This isn't even respectful sex. This is a fuck to serve a purpose.

"Make my ass come, Tommy." She opens her eyes, pupils blown wider than I've ever seen them before. "I want to know what it feels like."

Anal orgasms aren't always possible, but when they do happen to a girl, they leave her a quivering mess. I think that's why I like them so much—it feeds my need to control.

"I'm not sure you deserve that from me," I whisper into the shell of her ear. "I might just leave you like this. Maybe one of your other men could show you what it's like? How about Gentry?"

I know for a fact that she hasn't even come during her latest sexual encounters. It was obvious from the way she spoke about them.

"But I barely know what I'm doing," I goad, turning her previous insults back around to haunt her. "I'm younger and inexperienced."

If a face could kill, that's the look she's giving me right now.

I press my finger deeper, and she clings on to me, carving more scratches into my back.

"The best way to make a girl scream—just like I promised you would—is to do this." I beckon my finger in a *come here* motion.

"That's fucking awesome," she grinds out, trying to spread her legs wider.

I have a difficult time keeping hold of her, but just about manage.

"What about if I do this?" I slide my finger out and then push it back in, circling the pad around her sensitive walls.

Blue eyes burn deep into my own, holding me captive for an uncomfortably long time.

"I-I think it's about to happen," she says, voice barely audible. "Do that again, and I'll come so hard."

Because I'm a nice guy and around thirty seconds from dropping her, I do precisely as she asked.

My dick is still hard and inside her pussy when her ass squeezes my finger on a guttural groan that emanates from her chest. Her pussy grows wetter around me.

I'm certain she's still coming when I pull my cock out and bring her into my chest, walking us across to her bed.

As I lay her down on the soft white duvet, her eyes flutter shut. Long, dark lashes resting against a perfect complexion. It's the first time I've observed Jenna without her harboring an agenda or hatred toward me, and I take the opportunity to examine her features more closely.

I hate that despite getting what I wanted from her body, I'm still—if not more—curious about the girl in front of me.

"Is your beauty spot real?" I ask, coming to sit beside her on the bed.

She doesn't answer; the soft rise and fall of her chest is the only response I get.

Carefully, I reach out and smooth the pad of my thumb under her left eye, checking to see if the spot smudges.

It doesn't, and she remains asleep, totally taken out, as I predicted she would be from her first anal climax.

I cast my eyes around the bright room, sunlight flooding the space.

On top of her dresser sit two images of equal size but in completely different-styled frames. One is of Jenna and Holt at what looks to be her college graduation; the other is an action shot of her saving a goal. It occurs to me that there aren't any photos of her parents. Based on the close relationship she has with her brother, I had assumed that Jenna's apartment would be plastered with happy family portraits and words of affirmation that would make me sick to my stomach.

I fucking *hate* toxic positivity.

Her place is a mess—scattered clothes all over the floor, a laundry basket overflowing with bras and workout gear. That part of her life doesn't surprise me; I figured she was disorganized from her loose nutritional plan alone.

The one I stood in back in Boston.

That thought has me carefully rising from the bed and grabbing my boxer briefs and athletic shorts from where I left them in the hallway, stepping into them before I make for her tiny kitchen just off the living space.

Her refrigerator is equally as messy as I push a box of half-eaten pizza to one side, gagging at the thought of how old it is.

What kind of athlete doesn't have preprepared meals? How can she function like this?

Inside her salad drawer, I find a borderline passable pineapple, green beans, half a butternut squash, and a bunch of other stuff that I think were once root vegetables.

Jesus Christ.

Closing the fridge door, I move to her cupboards—which aren't exactly bursting with food—and pause my internal scolding.

Is it possible that she's struggling financially?

Most of the stuff is canned or condensed with long-ago sell-by dates—bringing back memories of how Mom used to get by when she was in between jobs or had her wages delayed, only leaving Alex's child support payments to pay all of our bills. I know female pro soccer players earn a shit wage, and perhaps the absence of family portraits in her place is a clue that she doesn't have many people to lean on.

Join the fucking club.

Shutting the cupboard, I look around Jenna's small living space, a foreign sense of empathy for this girl creeping into my conscience as I push away memories of my childhood, along with thoughts of my mom.

"WHAT THE FUCK ARE YOU DOING?"

I pause on stirring the one pan I could find that was suitable to make a curry and turn around to see an unimpressed Jenna, dressed in sweats and a white Storm T-shirt.

She cocks her head to the side, arms tightly folded across her chest as she approaches me.

I look down at the spoon I'm holding and then back up at Jenna. "You live like a pig, so I'm helping you become more … human."

On a scoff, she snatches the spoon from my hand, peering over my shoulder to examine what I'm cooking.

"Where did you get all the ingredients to make that?"

She rocks back on her heels as her nose twitches at the fragrant smell rising from the butternut squash and pineapple Thai curry bubbling away behind me. There are at least three portions she can separate and store in the freezer for meals after a practice or game.

Choosing to rise above her lack of gratitude, I spin back around and stir the curry. "Everything in this pan I found in your refrigerator or cupboard. Both were unholy, by the way."

She moves across to her fridge, ripping it open in fury. "You cleaned it!"

Jenna was only asleep for a half hour, but it didn't take me long to disinfect. Neither did the cupboards. I knew me doing that would drive her wild, as would making her food.

"You act like it's an issue," I tell her. "You really do live up to the name Hellion. I've seen torture chambers that were more sanitary."

She swats me in the back, and I smirk at her from over my shoulder before turning off the burner.

"You think just because we fucked, you can move about my apartment as you please?"

Her defenses are up, and I sense she's embarrassed.

As she continues to rant at me, I begin spooning the curry into three separate containers.

"The sex wasn't even that good. For some unknown reason, I'd thought you'd be better in bed. I guess I should've listened to my instincts when I first turned you down," she laments.

Setting the pan and spoon back down on the cooling burner, I finally grant her the attention she's craving.

"You literally had to sleep off the orgasms I gave you. Don't start spouting more bullshit when I just made you some proper food."

She glares at me. "You tossed my pizza out."

"Another twenty-four hours, and it could've gotten up and walked out to the garbage truck itself!" I blow out, laughing at the state of it. At the state of her apartment.

She rains down plenty of judgment on me when she should take a long look at the way she lives her life.

"I couldn't even tell what toppings you had."

"Pepperoni," she bites. "My favorite."

I pretend to care. "If you'd eaten it, then you would definitely have been sick." I mirror her stance, crossing my arms over my chest. "Look at it this way; I just saved you from starvation *and* a severe case of food poisoning."

Jenna opens her mouth to argue, but I get there first.

"And I did all that without a single orgasm. I rocked your world and got nothing in return."

She might try to hide her horror, but I see it. I don't actually care that I didn't come since witnessing Jenna's euphoric state was satisfaction enough. Not that she needs to know that.

"I'm not fucking you again, if that's what you're after. I'm already regretting everything we did. It'll take me months to come to terms with what I let you do."

I take two steps toward her, enough so our bodies are almost touching. The hum of electricity—something I was sure would disappear after we fucked—is only more prevalent than before.

"No danger of that. It was the worst sex I'd ever had. You literally made zero effort and left it all to me. It was like fucking a sack of potatoes."

She rolls her lips together, and I'm surprised steam isn't billowing from her ears.

"Get out of my apartment, Tommy."

I came here earlier to try and make peace with this girl; instead, all we've done is fuck and fight.

Should've seen it coming.

"Leave the food to cool completely before you add it to the

freezer." I tip my chin at the front door, which is directly ahead of me at the end of the hallway. "Not that I expect you to say thank you or anything, but later today, you can expect a delivery from an organic food market I use on the regular. If you want to stop embarrassing yourself on YouTube videos, you need to feed your body better."

Just like earlier, Jenna battles with conflicting emotions as she stands motionless in front of me.

I step around her and grab my wallet and keys from the counter.

"You know I still hate you, right?" she says just as I reach her front door.

I pause with my hand on the handle, contemplating ignoring her altogether.

"Oh, I know," I say, keeping my back to her the whole time. I pull the door open. "Trouble is, now you've fallen in love with my dick."

FOURTEEN

JENNA

"If you pull any tighter on those laces, they're going to snap."
Kendra's observation is met with my hardest steely gaze.

She swallows thickly as I continue to aggressively lace up my cleats.

"Remind me not to piss you off in practice this morning." My best friend stands from the bench, propping one foot onto it so she can adjust her shin guard.

I release a maniacal groan.

"Do you plan on speaking today, or are you choosing silence?"

I groan again, only this time, the sound is similar to the one that rose up my throat when Tommy made me come for the third time yesterday.

I cannot believe I slept with him. I've been berating myself since the second I woke up in my bed to the sweet scent of curry as it filled my nostrils. He one hundred percent made that curry to piss me off and highlight how bad my eating habits were.

But, boy, can he cook.

And fuck.

And his body is—

"I'm going to fly to the moon for a few days and meet with a new alien species. Do you want me to bring anything back from the gift shop?"

Kendra interrupts my thoughts, thumbing over her shoulder toward the locker room door.

I deadpan and come to stand in front of her, still feeling a little sore, courtesy of the Blades bad boy. "Sarcasm is the lowest form of wit."

"Oh, so you are speaking today. Welcome back to reality."

She claps her hands together, and I know she's not going to let my mood—or the reasoning behind it—go.

"What's eating at you?" she asks, just as several of our team-mates exit the locker room, their cleats clattering against the hard floor.

Like a slideshow, brief images flash before my eyes—how Tommy pulled down the zipper on my sports bra, pinned me against my bedroom door, and thrust inside me so hard that I saw stars.

I pinch the side of my thigh, hard, certain I'll leave a bruise but determined to yank my brain away from the memories.

Sex with Tommy can never happen again.

"Nothing is eating at me," I bite out, trying to convince myself as much as my friend.

She quirks a doubtful brow at me. "Sure. You keep telling yourself that, and I'll keep waiting for details of what's really going on."

Ten minutes later, I'm having the worst practice session of my career. You know it's bad when you're beaten at your near post—three times in quick succession.

On a headshake, I snatch up my water bottle from behind the net, taking two large pulls before throwing it back down.

"What's the issue, Miller?" Coach Anderson approaches me,

scratching at her temple as she tries to work out what the hell she's witnessed today.

I'm playing like a stand-in goalie who just got woken from a ten-year-long coma.

I release a long sigh; I have zero answers for her—or at least reasons I can give that she'd understand.

"I think I ate something weird last night; I haven't felt well all morning."

Her eyes descend on my body.

Coach Anderson is one of the best I've worked with, and she can smell bullshit from a mile away.

"Why didn't you report how you were feeling when you arrived? This Saturday is a key game and could dictate whether we lift the shield at the end of the season. If you aren't feeling right, then I don't want you wasting precious energy in a nonessential practice."

Reaching up, I pull at the end of my high-top ponytail, frustrated at myself for telling lies. "I thought I could ride it out, but I was wrong."

She nods once, narrowing her eyes at me in question. "Do you need to see the team doctor?"

I shake my head. I do not need to see a team doctor because there's zero wrong with me, other than my state of distress over what I let Tommy Schneider do to me.

"Well, maybe you should skip out on the end of this session," Coach suggests, pointing toward the main building. "Grab a warm shower and head home to relax. Get some decent nutrition on board too."

I practically scowl at the two remaining containers of curry sitting in my freezer.

"Oh, and, Miller?" Coach calls out to me as I turn on my heel and head toward the locker rooms.

"Yes, Coach?"

She bends down, retrieving the water bottle I forgot.

I take it from her with a smile and wait for her to speak.

"I need to talk to you about next season and how I see the team shaping up. I planned to pull you to one side after this session, but now I'm thinking we'll hold off until after Saturday's game."

I bite down on my bottom lip, genuinely unsure what she wants to discuss. Surely, my nutritional habits haven't gotten back to her ...

"Is everything okay?" I ask, impatient to know if I should be worried.

Coach's expression turns soft. "Everything is fine. There's nothing to worry about. I'll have someone in admin fire a meeting request to you, and we can catch up and talk."

THE RAIN BEATS DOWN AGAINST THE ROOF OF MY CAR WHEN I make a run for it across the parking lot.

With my training bag hanging off my shoulder and icy-cold rain soaking through my hoodie, I dig around in the pocket of my sweatpants for my car key.

"Nice practice."

Rainwater drips from the end of my nose when I spin around and come face-to-face with the last person I wanted—or needed—to see.

"Why are you here? Don't you have more episodes of *Hell's Kitchen* to record?" I reply in a trembling tone. I can feel the chill as rain saturates my clothes, but it's the spike in adrenaline that leaves my hands shaking.

Beneath the hood of his black raincoat, I can barely make out his smirk, although I know it's there.

Tommy takes a few steps toward me until we're only a few

feet away. Practice is just wrapping up, so we're the only ones in the parking lot.

"I like what you did there ..." Tommy edges even closer, and it's then I can see the darkness in his eyes. Water cascades off the edge of his hood as he leans forward, demanding that I look at him. "But I'm not the hellion around here."

Grumbling, I finally locate my car key and hit Unlock.

I spin back around and yank my driver's door open, only for a large palm to wrap around the top of the doorframe, holding it in place.

I ignore him and throw my training bag on the back seat.

"Move out of the way, or I'll slam the door shut on your fingers," I say, dumping myself in the driver's seat and pulling on the door with all my strength.

It doesn't budge, and Tommy's drenched and ominous figure continues to loom over me.

"You're getting my car wet!" I raise my voice, trying to slam my door shut once more.

Tommy inspects my white Ford Focus, which has seen better days. "How long did you save up for this beauty?"

Slowly, I close my eyes, hoping if I will it hard enough, then he'll be gone when I finally reopen them.

"I don't know why you're here or how you even found out I had practice today, but please, just go."

Still holding my door in one strong palm, Tommy reaches down and pulls on a lever next to my steering wheel. My hood pops up.

"What the fuck are you doing?"

He just shrugs, water now collecting at the ends of his thick, dark lashes. "I want to talk to you."

"And I want to go." I try the door again, hoping I can catch him off guard.

Tommy only grips the door tighter this time, chuckling to

himself as he does. "You can't drive anywhere with your hood open; it's dangerous."

As I drop my forehead to my steering wheel, I let my frustration get the better of me. "I don't want to talk to you. I don't even want to look at you."

Suddenly, my driver's door closes, quickly followed by a small thud and then the passenger door opening as Tommy climbs inside. With my head down and forehead still pressed against the steering wheel, I swivel my eyes to look at him. He's so tall that his head brushes the ceiling.

He pushes back his hood, and I narrow my gaze at him.

"You're dripping everywhere."

Tommy's eyes sparkle with mischief.

I hold up a hand. "Don't even think about referencing yesterday because I never want to think—let alone talk—about it ever again."

Like none of this comes as a surprise to him, he points to my steering wheel. "Crank the engine."

I drop my shoulders and stare out of the windshield, only to notice my hood is now back in place. That must've been what he was doing when I was groaning against my steering wheel.

Feeling like resistance is futile, I start the engine, and Madonna's "Holiday" immediately comes from the speakers.

To my surprise, Tommy doesn't berate me for my taste in music as he buckles himself in and I do the same.

"Where are we going?" I ask, turning down the volume.

He motions toward the parking lot exit. "I got an Uber here, and the ride wasn't even a three-star. So, you're taking me home. We can talk on the drive there."

I scoff and turn off the engine. "Are you for real?"

"Deadly, Jenna. I came to watch your practice—which, by the way, is published on your team's website—and now I want to head home."

I could wring this guy's fucking neck. The audacity rolls from him in waves.

"I'm not taking you home or talking to you. Yesterday was a huge mistake."

He clicks his tongue. "A huge mistake you'll definitely be making with me again." He points toward the door where the players emerge from, and a couple of my teammates start filtering out. "And one you'll have to explain away to Kendra in the next couple of minutes if we don't get out of here."

Reluctantly, I start the engine and shift into drive, pulling out of the lot and onto the main road.

"You're going the wrong way. I live in the nice part of town."

How the fuck did this happen? This morning, I vowed never to make eye contact with Tommy Schneider ever again. Yet by lunchtime, I'm giving the fucker a ride home.

"You can get the bus in a second," I bite out, doing a U-turn in the road.

We head in the opposite direction, and Tommy tells me to take a left.

I stay silent, focusing on getting the ride over with as fast as possible.

"Are you sore?"

My foot slides off the accelerator, and I hit the brakes sharply when we approach a stoplight.

"Excuse me?" I reply, staring straight out the windshield.

"Your pussy, Jenna. Are you sore after yesterday?"

His voice is heady and thick, just like it was when he pinned me against my bedroom door, and I squeeze my thighs together. This guy is several years younger than me. He has no right to be this skilled at turning me on. Especially when I hate everything about him.

This time, I choose to give him eye contact. "No. I barely noticed you were inside."

On a deep laugh, Tommy throws his head back into the seat.

The stoplight is still on red when Tommy leans toward me. The scent of his breath transports me back to my bedroom, where he dominated my body, leaving me breathless and comatose.

He pauses only an inch from my lips and breathes out slowly.

Instinctively, my tongue swipes across my bottom lip.

His eyes track the action, and he sits back in his chair. Satisfied with himself. "Yeah, that's what I thought."

A flush of warmth paints my cheeks as, mercifully, the light turns green. I hit the accelerator, and my car wheels spin against the wet road.

Fucking prick.

FIFTEEN

TOMMY

"No way! Did you see that hit?!" My friend Jackson vibrated with excitement on the couch next to me.

We were watching the game between the Philadelphia Bolts and the New York Blades, and Alex Schneider had just Kronwalled the Bolts forward, Kyle James, for the second time in the same period.

Leaping from the couch, Jackson pointed toward the TV as James lay crumpled in a heap on the ice. "Do you think Schneider killed him?!"

Right at that moment, the Bolts captain dropped his gloves, making a beeline for Schneider.

It was a bad idea on the captain's behalf. No one could overpower Alex Schneider—whether it was an on ice hit or a full-on tilt, otherwise known as a straight hockey fight.

The Bolts captain lasted all of thirty seconds before he hit the ice himself after Schneider landed an uppercut to the underside of his jaw. I leaned forward on my elbows as Jackson continued to cheer at the TV. Meanwhile, all I could think was how awesome the Blades enforcer was. What it must feel like to be that feared, that powerful. To be the one no one wanted to mess with in the league.

One of the refs finally pulled Schneider off his latest victim, and Jackson came back to sit alongside me on the couch.

I could already predict what he was going to say. The thought was written all over my friend's face.

He chewed on the inside of his cheek for a second as we both watched Alex skate toward the penalty box. Something that was a part of his game routine.

"Are you sure that you aren't related to him?" Jackson nodded toward Schneider, and I watched as he threw his stick against the plexiglass in anger, multiple Philly fans jeering him while he continued to wind them up.

Jackson wasn't the only one on our peewee team who had talked about my likeness to the Blades defenseman. The older I got, the more obvious it was. We shared the same everything physically. Hell, I even skated the same way as him.

I pressed my lips into a thin line, remembering everything Mom had told me about my father and how he'd died in Afghanistan. I knew the chances of Alex Schneider being my dad were crazy low, but a part of me hoped the living legend was my biological father.

No chance. Shit like that only happens in the movies.

"I told you," I replied to Jackson, "my dad died years ago."

"Jackson, you have got to stop making up ridiculous stories like that." Jackson's mom walked into the living room with a couple of sandwiches and Cokes and set them down on the coffee table in front of us.

She propped her hands on her hips and gave me an empathetic smile that I hated. They had way more money than Mom, and their house was bigger and in a nicer part of town. It was like she only allowed her son to be my friend because she pitied me or some shit like that.

My best friend sat back on the couch, crossing his arms over his chest in frustration. *"I'm not the only one saying it, Mom. Everyone at school and on the team can see the similarities."*

She turned to look at the TV and then back at me. "And I'm certain that if there was even the slightest ounce of truth in what you're saying, then Tommy's mom would've let her son know. There are many people on this earth who look alike without sharing a shred of DNA."

With that, she turned and left the room.

Jackson reached forward and picked up his plate, immediately tucking into his sandwich.

I didn't feel hungry, but I also didn't want to go home and be around Mom's latest boyfriend. He was an asshole, and I hated him.

I snatched up the can of Coke and opened it, taking a large pull before setting it back down.

"I think you should ask him yourself," Jackson said quietly. "Track him down and where he lives and go ask him if he knows who you are."

A burst of my laughter filled the room. It was the craziest idea I'd ever heard. "Are you for real?"

He nodded his head. "Deadly."

I pointed to the center of my chest. "I'm twelve years old. How the hell am I supposed to get on a flight to New York?"

Jackson winced. "Yeah, that's true."

"And how would I find out his address?" I continued. "Celebrities like that don't give away where they live."

Jackson looked more confident with his response as he said, "That part would be easy. Alex Schneider loves the media." Dipping into the pocket of his jeans, he opened up the defenseman's social media profile, one I'd looked at a ton. He scrolled down a couple of times, stopping when he found a picture of him standing outside a large complex with two supermodels hanging off him. "A hundred dollars says that's where he lives. Everyone knows that's NHL player territory."

I could see the logic in what Jackson was saying, but I still had my doubts as he locked his cell and slid it back into his pocket.

"Let's just watch the game," I suggested, feeling frustrated that I'd probably never find out the truth.

I had to believe what my mom had said. I just found it strange that despite her telling me it was a onetime thing with my biological dad, she didn't have a single photo of him to show me.

Jackson turned back to the game as the Philly powerplay wrapped up and Schneider rejoined the ice.

It must've been five minutes before either of us spoke again, even though our thoughts were louder than the noise in the hockey arena.

"You'll never stop wondering—you know that, don't you?" Jackson broke the silence.

The shrug I gave him was indifferent. I was trying not to let it show that this whole conversation had bothered me.

"Whatever," I breathed out, grabbing my can of Coke and taking another large gulp. "If he is my dad, then he clearly doesn't give a damn about finding me, so why should I?"

THE MEMORY OF THAT AFTERNOON WITH MY FORMER BEST friend, Jackson, had never been so vivid as it played out in my dream.

Lying in bed for way longer than usual—since at this time in the morning, I'd normally be in my home gym—I couldn't help but wonder where Jackson was now. I heard he had taken a job as a PE teacher since he had always been sports crazy. He was a good friend that I had until I turned eighteen and left for college, and after that, we lost touch.

I grew apart from a lot of people back in my hometown in

Minneapolis. No one else from my team was drafted into the league, and all my teammates either quit hockey and eventually settled down with families or fell off the face of the earth entirely.

Rolling my lips together, I internally smirk at thoughts of where my dad is today. Shortly after I confronted him, he went totally dark himself. I don't know how much of that was to do with me, and honestly, I wish I could say I didn't care.

They say that losing a parent is the worst thing that can happen to a kid, and I don't doubt it is. Losing a parent when they're still walking this earth though? Now, that's a whole new level of pain. The fact that they know their own flesh and blood is out there but don't care enough to make an effort cuts like a blunt knife, no matter which way you try and spin the reality of their rejection. Or how you try and justify that their absence is for the best.

I don't buy into that kind of bullshit—the school of thought that dictates that you're better off without toxicity in your life, no matter who they are to you.

The only way a person is better off is when they get the chance to avenge the wrongdoing. I saw my dad for who he really was that day—a heartless prick who didn't care about anyone but himself. Yet it was me who still got rejected. It was me who got the apartment door slammed in my face when he got bored of our conversation and kicked me out onto the Brooklyn streets.

Truthfully, I shouldn't care where he is right now or what gutter he's probably lying in. But I do. Because all I want is another thirty minutes in his company. A half hour where the roles are reversed and he's the one sitting on the end of *my* couch, in *my* fancy fucking apartment, listening to *me* lecture and castigate, making him feel like the worthless piece of shit he really is.

Voicing the thoughts I should've said when I was seventeen

would make me feel a whole lot better. Having the chance to reject his love would purge our poisonous relationship from my veins forever.

When my phone receives a text, I reach over and pick it up, half expecting it to be from Mom. Her attempts to contact me usually increase around my birthday, and as I turn twenty-four today, she'll no doubt send me the usual blanket message.

HELLION

My car smells of wet dog this morning, and given that I don't have a pet, I can only conclude it's the stench you left behind the other day.

This is way better than a generic birthday message.

ME

How do you have my number, Jenna?

HELLION

It was detailed on the order receipt for my leggings.

Satisfaction curls inside me. She wants me again.

ME

That's stalkerish behavior.

HELLION

So, I'll assume you went ahead and deleted my number, like I'd asked you to?

ME

Of course not. I hate it when girls play hard to get. Especially when they don't mean it. You wanted me to keep your number, and you know it.

I can see it now: you lying in bed each night, holding your phone as you will it to ring with a booty call from yours truly.

As I roll out of bed and head toward my en suite, I chuckle at my last text, knowing it will rile the shit out of her.

HELLION

The only thing I'm holding is my nose when I climb into my car. I need you to pay for a full detail. The smell isn't fading.

ME

The car is worth less than the cost of a full detail. How about I buy you a new one?

HELLION

I would rather never drive again.

ME

Tell me, have you ever expressed gratitude for anything in your life, or are you a bitch around the clock?

HELLION

I'm grateful to people who are worth my thanks.

ME

How was the curry?

HELLION

Fucking terrible. I gagged on the first mouthful.

Standing fully naked in front of my bathroom mirror, I open the Camera app and take a quick shot of me posing.

ME

picture attached It won't be long before you're gagging on something else.

HELLION

Never again. Ever.

ME

I somehow doubt that. You also said you'd never speak to me again, but here you are, texting me.

HELLION

Because my car stinks!

ME

That's bullshit, and you know it.

If you want to come by later, we can fuck after I get back from practice.

HELLION

Find some other victim to torment and lose my number.

ME

I'll see you around 7 p.m. then.

HELLION

Fuck off.

SIXTEEN

TOMMY

"Take a seat, Tommy." Adrian Carney, otherwise known as the New York Blades GM—and pretty much the only person on the team who's ever liked me—points to a soft black leather chair set on the opposite side of his desk.

He straightens his tie and pulls off his glasses, and I flop down, drawing a full breath into my lungs after an intense practice session. Since I received the written warning, I'm not idiot enough to know that if I want to stay on the team, then I need to step up my performance. Even if there was nothing wrong with my game in the first place.

Adrian rolls his lips together, lifting his eyes from the desk in front of him to mine.

I sit back in my chair and spread my legs, folding my arms in a protective stance.

"Curtis Freeman called you a dangerous thug on social media last night. He went on a long ramble about how you should be ejected from the league and stripped of your contract with us."

When I was called up to his office ten minutes ago, I'm not sure exactly what I expected the GM to say. But it wasn't that.

I clear my throat, my pulse picking up at the potential repercussions that could rain down on my career. Pretty much the entire hockey community will side with Curtis Freeman after what went down. Despite multiple protests from our PR team, I no longer have social media accounts since I fucking hate them and all the dirty laundry society is hell-bent to air online. I wash my shit in private.

"I haven't been made aware of any statement he put out," I reply, never more grateful for living offline.

Adrian shakes his head, making full eye contact with me. "That's because the post was taken down within seconds of it going live—and I mean seconds. I don't know if his agent got ahold of it or if he had second thoughts, but let's just say, limited screenshots are doing the rounds, which our PR team is working to have removed where possible."

Feeling like he's skating around the real reason he called me into his office, I scratch at my chin. "So, why am I here, talking to you?"

Adrian Carney is one of the most confident guys I've ever met. He makes a decision and runs with it, no matter what anyone says. When he did a deal with the Detroit Sting to trade me here, there were a ton of people fighting it. I half expected the deal to fall through, but it didn't. Right now though, as he drums his fingers on the dark wooden desk in front of him, I know whatever is going to leave his mouth next is not in my favor.

My left foot bounces in anticipation as he opens his mouth, looks at me again, and then averts his gaze.

"The post might've been removed, but we, as a team, cannot ignore the truth in what Freeman had to say. I feel like it would be remiss of us as an organization not to respond in some way. The league isn't taking action against you on this occasion, but that doesn't mean to say we can turn a blind eye to your continued poor conduct."

I nod my head, already knowing exactly where this is going.

"You want to go further than just the written warning you origi-nally handed out."

A sharp knock sounds on the GM's door before Coach Morgan steps into the room and quickly takes a seat next to me. He knows I had a great practice, but you wouldn't believe it with the way he can barely acknowledge my existence.

Like a petulant child, I throw my head back toward the ceiling and groan. "Can someone just come the fuck out with it so I can go home and punch something?"

The next voice belongs to Coach. "While we will include you on the roster for the next five games, your ice time will be limited, if at all."

My jaw hangs open. "Five games?!"

Coach Morgan looks across at the GM for support.

"Are you fucking kidding me?" I exclaim, pushing my chair out and standing.

The GM holds up a calming hand. "Sit down, Tommy."

His condescending tone, like he's trying to pacify a toddler having a tantrum, only enrages me further.

I point at my chest, heat flaming into my cheeks. "I just put in the shift of my life out there, and now you're telling me I have to sit out five games because some baby can't take a beating for being a fucking brat to me?!" I scoff at my GM. "I thought you were tougher than to yield to my haters. And you ..." I turn to Coach. "You need me on the first line, and you know it."

My outburst is met with silence for what feels like an age.

Finally, Coach speaks as I pace the room like some kind of bull, hands shoved into the pockets of my gray sweats.

"I want to try out alternative lines too. The guys on the team see you as a loose cannon. Moreover, you can't be a valuable asset to me if you aren't a team player. You're spending more and more time in the box when you're paid to be on the ice."

I pause on my pacing and stalk toward him, and all the while, he maintains a stoic expression. I might not particularly like

Coach, but I'll give him one thing—the guy isn't intimidated by shit.

"Give me a chance." I hold up a single finger in front of him. "One more chance."

"Chance at what, Tommy?" Adrian asks. "I've got a stack of complaints about you from your teammates. Rebuilding relationships with them is going to require a lot more than 'one more chance.' "

Dropping my finger, I dump myself back down into the black leather seat, bracing my elbows on my knees. "You used to support me. Back when I got traded here, you said I was what the team needed, and at the start of preseason, you told me to give you 'more of the same.' " Just like Adrian did a second earlier, I quote his words back to him.

His face softens the slightest fraction. "I know I did, Tommy. But Coach Morgan is right on this occasion; the Blades are at risk of regaining the reputation they fought hard to shake off after what your ..." He pauses and looks off to the side.

"What my dad did?" I finish for him. "You're referring to the hit he put on Zach Evans several seasons back, aren't you?" My voice is incredulous. "I'm way more skilled than Alex ever was, way more valuable."

Adrian doesn't respond initially, instead rising from his chair. He looms over me, both palms planted firmly on his desk. "Son, I don't know what kind of relationship you have with your father, and I don't need to know either. But let me tell you something. I believe in the enforcer—you know I've always felt that there is a place for them in this league. What I don't believe in is the kind of shit Alex Schneider used to hand out to the opposition." He rises to his full height, steely gaze still locked on me. "That shit you pulled in the penalty box after the fight with Curtis Freeman stunk of your father's attitude. You're an enforcer, not a killer."

Emotions sting my senses, and I bite the inside of my cheek

so hard that I can taste the metallic sensation as it trickles down my throat. "I'm better than him."

The voice sounds foreign, and I look across at Coach to see if the response belonged to him or me. In truth, I know it was my own.

My GM just nods his head softly and turns his attention to Coach. "The five-match restriction still applies." He then refocuses back on me. "I backed your trade when no one else would, and I need you to prove to me that my faith in you wasn't misplaced."

"I'm the better Schneider." I repeat my sentiment.

"Words are cheap, Tommy." He thumbs behind him to nothing. "I've got a bunch of players wanting to know when I'm going to trade you. Another minor infraction, whether it be on the ice or in the locker room, and best believe I'm going to start making calls to your agent to discuss your imminent departure."

Like a sitting duck, I nod once and push up to stand. Done with the conversation and this entire fucking team.

"Jenna Miller ..." Coach says, stopping me in my tracks, and I spin a one-eighty and come back to face him.

I swear to God, if she has had a hand in any of this, I'll lose my shit completely.

"What about her?" I ask, keeping my tone light.

Coach quirks an obvious brow, like I should know exactly what he's insinuating. "Did the altercation with Freeman have anything to do with Jenna Miller?"

I cast my eyes to Adrian, who looks on, waiting for me to answer Coach's question.

"No. I haven't spoken to her in a while." It's a lie, and I know it. I spoke with her two days ago on my birthday, when she declined my invitation to come over and fuck.

Of its own accord, my dick twitches in my pants.

Jesus Christ, this isn't the time to get horny over thoughts of my Hellion, naked and sprawled out beneath me.

"You sure about that?" Coach pushes me further.

I throw my arms out to the sides. "Why does it matter to you? I told you I haven't seen her. Freeman was giving me shit over the game, and Jenna Miller isn't that important. She fucked a veteran hockey player who's past his best and then decided to spread shit about me." A wry smile pulls at my lips. "Trust me when I say that she won't be doing that again."

Coach probably thinks I'm referring to her talking about me when, actually, I'm referring to her climbing into bed with any guy other than me.

She might hate my guts, but her body is dying for me to put my hands on it again.

Only me.

"Good. Keep it that way," Coach replies, pulling his baseball cap off and swiveling it forward. He nods at the office door. "Go ahead and join the others for conditioning. I've got a few things I need to discuss with Adrian."

I look at my GM, feeling like I lost my only ally.

"I don't know any other way to be. You knew what you were getting when you signed me." My words are wrapped in frustration.

He runs his tongue across his bottom lip, considering an appropriate response. "Stay out of trouble and in control of your temper, and we won't have a problem, Tommy."

SEVENTEEN

JENNA

"No, but seriously, that punch made it halfway down the pitch!" Darcy rockets her arm forward, almost catching Collins square in the nose. "I was convinced that ball was going straight into the back of your net." She takes a sip of her cosmo, eyes wide with excitement. "But in the blink of an eye, you cleared it *and* turned it into the best counterattack move I've seen in modern-day soccer." She shakes her head and takes another sip of her drink. "I mean football."

With a rare pint of IPA in one hand, I stand, staring at my cute, petite British friend. "Modern-day soccer?"

Darcy just shrugs. "It sounded like I knew what I was talking about, adding that part on."

From behind, Archer approaches, wrapping his arms around her waist. He sets a kiss on top of her head and gazes around our small group of friends. Every time one of my girlfriends interacts with their man, it's like a sharp sting of something shoots through my veins. It's only brief, but it's there, and it doesn't get any less painful.

Sometimes, I hate myself for feeling that way. I should be

happy for Kendra, Collins, and Darcy as they gather around me, wearing rings that sparkle and reflect the happiness and contentment they've found in their lives. But to suppress my own sadness would be unnatural or maybe inhumane. I have feelings and needs myself, and I long for a man to wrap his arms around my waist from behind, even if I'll never let it show how deep that desire runs.

Kendra nudges me in the shoulder. "What are you thinking about? I feel like you've been more absent than present lately."

Buying myself a second to gather my thoughts, I take a sip of beer. "I'm not sure if I completely agree with that. I just kept a clean sheet, and we're one win away from the shield."

"Off the soccer pitch, I mean," she counters, eyes turning from playful to more concerned. "I feel like if we weren't a part of the same team, then I wouldn't see you nearly as much as I'd like." Kendra turns around and sets her water glass down on the bar behind her. "And that worries me because you're my best friend. You were there for me when everything went down with my shitty ex and when I moved to this city and had no one."

A lump forms in my throat as Darcy, Collins, and Archer talk between themselves.

"We'll never lose touch, Kendra. You're my number one girl." I set my glass down beside hers and take my best friend into my arms. "I rarely promise anyone anything, but I'm promising you this now: we're together forever. You can trust me on that."

To my surprise, she sniffles into my hair, her breath tickling my neck as she speaks quietly. "I'm pregnant."

I pull back, my hands braced on her shoulders. "You're what?" I heard Kendra clearly the first time around. I just want her to say it again because I know how much this means to my friend.

"I'm pregnant," she says, rosy stains painting her cheeks. "I took a test this morning, and I'm definitely pregnant."

My eyes rove the bar for her husband and find him staring straight at his wife from across the room, a broad smile spread across his face.

"Does he know?" I ask, turning back to Kendra.

She shakes her head. "No. With our match this morning and then the hockey game straight afterward, we've barely had time to talk. I took a pee test because my period hadn't started straightaway, and I'm ordinarily like clockwork. Jack had already left for the rink."

I'm practically vibrating on her behalf. "I bet you can't wait to get home and tell him."

Her smile widens. "We're going to have a July baby! Only …" She trails off and looks down to the floor. "That puts my due date right in the middle of the season. Not ideal, I know."

With my finger under her chin, I tip Kendra's face up to look at me. "Having this baby is the most important moment in your life. I know how much you have both wanted this, and soccer can wait. The team can wait."

Kendra's eyes shine beneath the bar lighting. "I'm so fucking happy, but I'm going to keep it quiet until I get a chance to tell Jack. Then we'll decide when we want to break the news."

I nod and pull my friend back into a hug.

"What did Coach want to see you about after the game?" she asks, picking her water glass back up and taking a sip.

I tap the side of my nose and wink. The way I want to spill my secret to Kendra because she will undoubtedly go crazy on my behalf, even if I know that I have to keep quiet for now. The entire team was aware that Hollie Browne would be stepping down from her role as captain at the end of this season since she's reaching the twilight of her career. What I never expected was to be called up to take her place. It's a dream come true, along with a bump in salary that I desperately need.

"I can't actually tell you right now," I reply on a wince.

Like a child, Kendra drops her shoulders. "For real?" she whines.

I offer her another wink, hoping that will satisfy her. "The whole team will find out soon enough."

Silence falls between us as Kendra stands there, studying my face for clues.

"Aside from both the Blades and the Storm winning today, do you know what's taken tonight from an eight to a full ten out of ten?" Collins breaks the silence, flicking her mid-length pink hair to the side.

"Pray tell," I reply, equally amused and enraptured by anything and everything this girl has to say.

She raises a single brow and looks between Kendra and me. "The absence of one Tommy Schneider."

The brief mention of his name fires off a surge of goose bumps as they break out over my skin.

"No snarky comments or cocky smirks. Just a bunch of friends having a great night, like the old times." Darcy joins our conversation when Archer returns to a small group of his teammates.

She props a hand on her hip. "I'm convinced, even at five months old, Emily hates him. She threw her teething ring on the floor when he joined the team on the bench tonight."

"You should've been at the game earlier," Collins adds, gaze floating from Kendra to me. "The look on his face when the Jumbotron focused in on him, it was a sight to behold. He was seething at being benched for multiple games."

"He shouldn't be a first-rate arsehole then." Darcy snorts. "He's definitely getting traded before the March deadline." She downs the rest of her cosmo in one, enjoying a child-free night with her husband and friends. "Although I'm not convinced he'll find another team."

"Why isn't he here tonight?" I ask casually, brushing off comments about Tommy getting traded.

I haven't spoken to him since our last text exchange, where I told him my car stank and it needed detailing. The truth is, it did smell, just not badly. I swear his cologne has permeated my seats, and I hate that. The best place for Tommy is on the other side of the country and as far away from me as possible.

I don't trust him, but more than that, I don't trust *myself* around him.

"Probably licking his ego wounds." Kendra rolls her eyes.

"The team was way more cohesive without him on the ice. If they play like that again for the next few games, I'm certain the GM will put him on the trade list," Collins adds. "The only reason he made it to New York in the first place was because of the GM insisting. Sawyer tells me he's even turning his back on the guy. I don't think Curtis Freeman taking to social media helped either."

My heart rate picks up to a wild pace. "Wait. What do you mean?"

I assumed Tommy was being punished for something he had done in practice. The Blades haven't made an official statement about why Tommy was benched, and frankly, him being repri-manded isn't exactly news.

Collins tips her head to one side, surprised that I'm not aware. "A couple of days ago, Curtis Freeman took to his socials with a scathing three-paragraph post, calling for Tommy to be canceled from ice hockey, like his dad basically was. He said he was a danger to the sport or some shit like that. The post was taken down really fast, but naturally, screenshots were taken. Sawyer thinks it was Freeman's frustration bubbling over when the league deemed no action needed to be taken for the way Tommy had beaten him up in their last game, but the Blades have obviously responded with a punishment of their own." She blows out a long breath. "I can't say I blame them for benching him, someone had to do something."

My throat runs dry. Maybe that's why Tommy hasn't been in

touch for the past few days. It sounds like he has bigger fish to fry than antagonizing me.

Or maybe he just grew tired of our antics.

Discomfort settles in the pit of my stomach as my girls continue to speculate on how long the Blades enforcer has before he's shipped out altogether.

"You know what?" I finally speak up after losing track of time. I don't make eye contact as I adjust my handbag on my shoulder and feel a vibration. "I'm going to head out."

The first person I make eye contact with is Kendra. Running out on her when she just dropped the biggest news of her life makes me feel like a shitty friend.

"I'll text you when I get home," I tell her.

She nods once, and Darcy laces her hand through mine. We've grown way closer since last year, when I stayed over at her place one night and she told me all about the secret pregnancy with Archer.

"Do you need a ride home?" she asks. "Archer isn't drinking, and I'm sure he'd run you back to your place."

I shake my head immediately. Thoughts of a ten-minute walk in the cold November air grows more appealing with each passing second. I need to clear my head.

"No, it's fine. I'm fine," I lie, just as my phone vibrates again. "Let him stay and celebrate a hard-earned shutout. The entire walk home is lit, and I have a can of three-year-old pepper spray in my bag that I'm dying to use."

Collins snorts a laugh, and Kendra rolls her eyes. These girls know that leaving bars alone—or with strange guys—isn't unusual for me.

"Did you get a booty call or something?" Collins chuckles.

Heat rises from my toes to the tips of my ears as I scramble for an answer. In the end, nothing materializes, and I conclude my silence is probably the best option since telling them I can't stop thinking about the most hated guy in Brooklyn—or his tattooed cock—likely wouldn't land well.

Collins raises her glass in my direction. "Jen is getting dicked down tonight. Let's all say our goodbyes and wish her a pleasure-filled evening."

EIGHTEEN

TOMMY

D runk texting is probably the worst idea I've had all year. That's what enters my head as I hit Send on a second message to Jenna.

ME

> Did you fuck Curtis Freeman and then use his phone to post on social media about me?

> You did, didn't you?

Tossing back another bourbon in a seedy bar on the opposite side of town from my apartment, I raise a finger at the bartender, who strolls across with the bottle, ready to refill my glass. Either he recognizes me and has wisely chosen to keep his mouth shut or he knows nothing about hockey.

When he tips the spout toward my glass, I wrap an unsteady hand around the bottle neck.

"Just leave the whole thing here and put it on my tab." I slur out the demand.

Whichever part of my conscience remains sober knows that I'm going to regret this decision tomorrow. Trouble is, I can't find it in me to care tonight.

Throughout my hockey career, the one thing I've always done right is look after my body, but tonight, I'm punishing it.

The bartender shrugs and walks away, and I refill my glass, setting the bottle down with a thud before downing the shot. The liquor burns as it glides down into my stomach, strong enough to numb some of the anger I still feel from the game earlier.

It was fucking humiliating to be sat on that bench, all padded up, knowing that Coach had zero intention of calling my name. The smirk on my captain's face said it all, along with the rest of the team. They got exactly what they wanted, and so did Curtis Freeman.

And the kicker? The team actually played well tonight.

I huff out a laugh into the darkened bar; only the bartender and another guy a couple of tables away are witnesses to my spiral. It's like the entire team waited until I got dropped and then all came together to put in their best performance of the season against one of the league favorites, Colorado.

They want me out of the team, out of Brooklyn, out of hockey altogether.

HELLION

Yeah, that's right. I fucked a guy just so I could get ahold of his phone and screw you over.

With numbing lips and clumsy fingers, I snatch up my phone and type out a response.

ME

You have a history of fucking players and throwing me under the bus. Well, congratulations because I think you just put the final nail in my coffin.

HELLION

I don't care about you enough to go to all that effort. Sorry to break it to you.

A slow smile creeps across my lips.

> **ME**
>
> Where are you?

HELLION

Heading home. It's been a day.

> **ME**
>
> I thought you'd be out celebrating. You just won a key game and actually played pretty well from what I saw.

HELLION

Stop being nice. It doesn't suit you.

My tentative smile grows more obvious.

> **ME**
>
> I'm in your shitty part of town. Come have a drink with me.

HELLION

I can't share a drink with my enemies. It doesn't sit well with my conscience.

> **ME**
>
> Why not? I've got half a bottle of bourbon remaining and a sticky booth reserved in a seedy bar.

HELLION

You already drank half a bottle of liquor?!

> **ME**
>
> Not quite, but if you don't join me, I'll likely finish the entire thing myself. I don't drink often, and it might not end well …

HELLION

And now you're blackmailing me with your safety.

Is it working?

HELLION

FFS. Give me the address.

I'VE NO IDEA HOW MUCH TIME HAS PASSED—OR HOW MANY MORE drinks I've taken on board—when Jenna dumps herself down opposite me in the booth.

My vision might be a little hazy and my brain slower to process regular thoughts, but fuck me, is she beautiful.

Especially when she's mad, like she is right now.

I draw my bottom lip between my teeth, turning my empty glass around on the table.

Jenna reaches across and inspects the bottle, a disapproving groan floating across the table, along with her perfume. "You drank another quarter while I was on my way over here?"

Pinching my thumb and forefinger together, I can't help an intoxicated chuckle. "Only a little more."

Rolling her eyes, she snatches my glass and pulls the bottle toward her, removing the cork and filling it to the brim.

She tosses it back in one and—Jesus fucking Christ—doesn't even flinch when she slams the glass down, swiping the back of her hand across her mouth.

My jaw is agape when she refills the glass and sinks another shot.

Her silky, dark hair—which is down and around her shoulders—shines red beneath the neon sign attached to the wall above the booth.

"Why are you drinking yourself silly?" she asks in an agitated tone.

I go to swipe the glass back, but her excellent goalie reflexes, combined with my inhibited ones, has me coming up empty.

"Aside from practices, I'll likely not play for another four games. I figured, why not use the rest period and have a little fun?"

Her gaze roves around the bar before it lands back on me. "You call this fun? Jesus, you're more miserable than I first thought."

I try for the glass once more and fail.

"Do your precious girlfriends know we fucked yet?"

She deadpans, "No one knows what happened, and that's the way I plan to keep it."

I lean forward on my elbows, pinning her in place with my stare. "And have you fucked anyone else since me?"

My question was intended to sound hot and inviting, but instead, it came off as borderline desperate.

Jenna smirks at the upper hand I just gave her, leaning across the table until her breath fans my face.

"What if I told you that I was on my way over to a guy's place right when I got your text?"

I sit back, dragging my flat palms across the table. Jenna can't resist sneaking a peek at my tattoos.

"I'd say, that pleases me greatly. You blew off one guy so you could blow me instead."

She scoffs, but it isn't hostile.

Jenna Miller loves giving me shit. Which is just as well since I'm incapable of being any other way around people. Whether I find them hot or not.

"Listen, I know you're drunk and everything …" She reaches across the table and presses her pointer finger against my temple, and I feel that shit everywhere. "But it's high time you start listening to me when I say that I'm never going to sleep with you again. Ever."

"You could just suck my—"

"I could just do nothing," she cuts me off, releasing her finger and sitting back in the booth.

Like a game of footsie in high school, I wrap my leg around hers, and when she pulls back, I hook my foot around the back of her calf, making it more difficult for her to move away.

To my delight, she doesn't fight for long, but I don't miss the rise and fall of her chest beneath the V-neck sweater she's wearing.

Seconds, maybe even minutes, pass between us as the jukebox in the corner of the room switches to Meat Loaf's "Bat Out of Hell."

Jenna presses her lips into a thin line, but it isn't enough to suppress the giggle that rises up her throat. I've never heard her laugh like that in front of me, and in a three-second window, I see a different side to this girl. A little like when she fell asleep right after I fucked her brains out.

"We're bad for each other, Tommy. You know that; I know that. There's way too much toxicity between us."

The alcohol thrumming through my body feels like it's starting to fade in response to the direction this conversation has turned.

"I only want to fuck you, Jenna. Not marry you."

Is it possible for a person to look partly turned on and offended at the same time? Judging by the look on Jenna's face, maybe.

"Despite myself, I was actually considering coming back to your place tonight. But you had to go and spoil it by being an asshole all over again."

I shrug, totally confused. "What did I say wrong?"

This time, her scoff is hostile. "You! Assuming that I'd ever want anything from you, let alone your cold, empty heart." Her eyes scan my body with disdain. "If you even have a heart, that is."

"I've got a heart," I tell her, hooking my foot even tighter around her calf.

"Then why don't you have any friends or even a shred of evidence that anyone likes you?"

My trademark smirk falls into place effortlessly. "Because people let you down, so why take a chance on shitty relationships when you can live your life free from emotional risk? The only person you can rely on one hundred percent is yourself."

Her eyes grow wide, and I swear I see understanding in them.

"That's a really sad way to exist, Tommy. Really fucking sad," she volleys back without empathy. Not that I need any from her.

"Other than your fake-ass friends, I don't see you making waves socially."

Her mouth pops open. "I might not have a ton of people around me, but those I do, it's because I care for them. I'd do anything for my girls and brother." Jenna points at her chest. "Maybe if you stopped punching good people, you'd start to enjoy their company."

I ignore her gibe and home in on something that's been playing in my mind since that day in her apartment. "What about your parents? You've mentioned the love you have for your brother so much that I actually feel nauseous, but you never mention your mom and dad."

I've always considered Jenna to be a guarded person; maybe that's why we have this unexplainable affinity. Her walls have never been higher than right now though.

"I don't get along with my parents that well."

It's more information than I thought she would give me, and instinct urges me to push further.

"Let me guess …" I click my tongue and sit back in the booth, eyes still directly on her. "Holt is the perfect offspring who can do no wrong, and you're … well, you're the black sheep who lives in your sibling's shadow?"

Jenna presses her calf into my foot, extending my leg with a look of malice in her eyes. "Fuck off, Tommy."

I snort a laugh and pull my foot back toward me, Jenna's resistance no match for my strength. "I'd say I'm medium to hot with the accuracy of my guess."

"I don't want to talk about it," she bites back, finally freeing her leg and sitting up straighter in the booth.

"See, that's where I think you're lying. I think you do want to talk about it," I retort.

She drums her manicured fingernails against the sticky table, resting her chin in her other palm. A mischievous glint appears in her eyes, and I can tell it's time to retreat from my inquisition.

"Since you're so interested in talking about family, how about you tell me a little about your parents and why I never see them at games? I thought your dad would be all over that shit. Alex Schneider always did like the limelight. He'd be proud of your five-match ban."

"I'm not banned!" I announce, anger lacing my tone. "Coach and the GM want to make an example of me so they can keep the haters happy."

Jenna quirks a brow. "Oh, and you definitely have haters, Tommy. That's one thing you have for sure." She clears her throat. "Anyway, back to your dad."

I've never regretted starting a conversation so much in my life.

"There's nothing to say." I shrug. "I see him from time to time, but we aren't tight, and that's my decision. Like I said, I don't get close to anyone."

"Your mom?"

"Same," I rush out, desperate to shut this exchange down. "We have limited contact."

She isn't convinced, but I couldn't give a shit. I'm just grateful for the silence that's descended between us.

After a few beats, Jenna opens her mouth but then clamps it shut again.

"Whatever you're going to ask next, the answer is no," I confidently say.

She wets her lips, pupils dilating as her eyes burn with a need I haven't seen since I unzipped her sports bra.

"That's too bad," she eventually says. "Because despite the fact that I hate your guts, the truth is, I do kind of love your dick, and I was about to ask if I could see it again."

NINETEEN

JENNA

"Stay really fucking still."

Because Tommy couldn't wait to get me into his bedroom, I'm sitting on his white marble island, my lower half completely naked and exposed.

"What the fuck are you doing?" I ask when his hand disappears between my thighs.

All he does is smirk, and I roll my eyes.

"If you aren't going to tell me, then I'm not sticking around to find out." I go to slide off the island.

Tommy's jaw tics, one hand moving from the counter next to me and resting on the top of my thigh. Thick, dark hair falls over his deep brown eyes, and even if I still wanted to, moving is no longer an option.

I'm paralyzed by this man. That, and too fucking stupid to walk away when I know all he can give me is a night filled with orgasms, coupled with the heavy weight of regret the next morning.

I take the opportunity to study his bare chest and tattoos more carefully as he stands in front of me, wearing only a pair of black boxer briefs that hug his perfect hockey thighs.

There's still a hint of bourbon on his breath, but given the size of this guy, it doesn't surprise me that he's back in control of his senses. That, combined with the thirty-minute Uber ride we took in silence.

As Tommy's lips ghost over mine, it's not lost on me that we've never kissed, although I've thought multiple times that he was going to.

"What do you want me to do, Jenna?" he asks, so fucking sure of himself that it makes me sick.

I look up into his eyes. We're nose to nose.

"I'd like you to do anything because right now, I'm really fucking bored."

His lips tip into a wicked smile, leaving me in no doubt that he's right in his element and I'm right where he wants me.

"Before you interrupted me, I was going to finger your pussy. But given that all that leaves your mouth is bullshit I can't stand, I'm thinking I'll stuff my cock in it and give us all a fucking rest."

My breathing is ragged, my words barely a whisper. "Is that what you did with the blonde chick? You silenced her with your dick?"

He's already told me that she never touched his dick. Still, I'm not about to let what he did go. He doesn't get any free passes from me.

Tommy brings his hand from between my thighs to play with my hair. He hasn't touched my pussy even though it contracts like I'm on my third climax.

He wraps a piece of my hair around his tattooed finger, and I swallow hard, wondering what's going to leave his mouth next.

"How many times do I need to tell you that she didn't suck my dick?" He tugs on the strand, pulling my head to one side and exposing my neck. He ghosts his lips over my soft skin. It's a possessive move, and I hate myself for loving it. "How did it feel, Jenna? Thinking I was with another girl."

I know what he's referring to—that day in Rise Up, when I casually disclosed my one-night stand from the night before.

"I felt nothing," I lie.

"Final chance before I fill this bullshitting mouth."

My lips tingle with anticipation. I've never been especially bothered about giving a guy head, but I know going down on Tommy will be good.

"All I felt was hatred and not an ounce of anything else," I lie again.

He drops my hair and finds the waistband of his boxers, pushing them to the floor in a single motion. I'm the perfect height to be entered.

"So, if I pushed inside another woman like this"—with one hand around his thick shaft, Tommy eases himself inside me—"you wouldn't give a fuck that it wasn't you?"

Lost for words, I shake my head, tears pricking at the corners of my eyes in response to the way he stretches me out.

I forgot how big he actually was.

When I look down between us, the tattoo scribed around his dick disappears completely, and then he's seated all the way inside.

He doesn't move, and neither do I.

"Why the fuck can't I get you out of my life?" Tommy eventually speaks.

It's the first real show of vulnerability I've witnessed. There have been fleeting moments, where I saw softness or hurt in his eyes, but these are the first words he's spoken outside of his usual hardened character.

"I think this might be the first thing we agree on," I reply, just as Tommy makes his first stroke inside me. "I never want to see you again after this."

He glides into me again, and goose bumps break out down my spine.

"At least not until the next time we fuck, Jenna."

I shake my head, deep pressure already building inside me. "I hate it each time you enter me."

Tommy's hands come to the V-neck on the sweater I'm still wearing. In one motion, he tears the material clean apart.

I'd ask him what the hell I'm supposed to wear home if I cared enough.

His eyes fall to the lacy black bra I'm wearing, the dark color a complete contrast to my flushed skin. "We fuck because we're the same person, you and I."

That's the craziest statement I've ever heard, and the sarcastic laugh that emanates from my chest reflects my thoughts.

"We are," he continues, taking a single finger into his mouth and then offering it over to me.

Like the weak-willed woman I am, I open my mouth and swirl my tongue around it, tasting what it would be like to kiss him.

"You're a wild child, Jenna Miller. You've also been through some shit—I can tell."

He's too close to me, in body and mind.

Pulling away, I brace my palms behind me and open my legs wider. "Just get on with it and fuck me, Tommy. I thought twenty-three-year-old boys were full of energy."

"Twenty-four," he corrects, leaning over me and running his tongue up my sternum, stopping when he reaches my pulse point.

He's fucking me with such purpose, with languid strokes that have my pussy gripping him tight. How the guy hasn't already blown inside me, I'll never know.

"How did you celebrate your birthday?" I ask, fighting the urge to scream his name and give him the satisfaction.

The smile that tips up his lips is nothing short of devilish. "Like this—by fucking the girl I've been lusting after for longer than she deserves."

Wrapping a strong arm around my back, Tommy pulls my body back into his and then proceeds to fuck me hard and fast, his skin glowing with a thin sheen of perspiration that's hot as fuck.

"It's your birthday today?"

"Not anymore, and stop talking, Jenna," he demands. "I want you to come all over my cock, not ask me a thousand questions."

I double down. "Happy belated birthday, asswipe."

Tommy immediately grinds to a halt. "What did you call me?"

In a condescending manner, I reach up and cup the side of his cheek. I meant for it to be anything but intimate, but the way his eyes fall to my lips leaves me questioning, once again, if we'll kiss.

"I'm not going to kiss you," I say. "Don't fucking panic."

His attention hasn't left my mouth.

He runs his thumb along my lower lip, pressing it into my teeth. While it doesn't hurt, it's definitely an action typical of Tommy.

"Do you kiss guys when you go home with them?" he asks, reverting back to fucking me at a slow, torturous pace.

"No. But sometimes, I'm left with no choice."

When his hand wraps around my throat, fire burns in his eyes. I'm certain he's pissed at me, and I'm not afraid to acknowledge a seed of fear as it takes root.

"You're telling me the last time a guy kissed you, it was without your consent?"

I swallow and feel the column of my throat pressing against his palm.

"Don't get all high and mighty. Did you forget the times you burst into my apartment and hotel room?"

Something akin to regret forms on his features.

Or maybe that's just wishful thinking on my part.

"You might think of me as an asshole, Jenna. For what it's

worth, I already know I am. What I'm not though is abusive. I've known cruel people, and I'll never be like them."

I could scoff and remind him of his behavior on the ice, although we both know this conversation has nothing to do with hockey.

"So, let's agree on a safe word since we both know you like to be punished, and I need to know how far I can push this body." He brings his finger to my temple, a little like I did in the bar. "I'm betting it's stronger than you think."

Tommy quickens his strokes, squeezing his hand around my throat with each motion. "When your pussy is burning from my thrusts, say the word *cobra*, and I'll know to go easy."

I'm an experienced woman when it comes to the bedroom, but even I know that I should be running for the hills right now. I've never done anything like this before, and it should intimidate the fuck out of me. If this were happening with any other guy, I'd freak out.

Instead, my body trembles with anticipation.

Tommy tightens his grip around my throat. "I know you love this because it's what I love, and I know you want to play because I'm desperate to start the game." He thrusts into me harder. "Tell me it's what you want. Blink once if you do."

For the briefest moment, I'm motionless. And then I blink, my response automatic, almost like my subconscious demanded it.

The chiseled god standing between my legs doesn't breathe another word, his face stoic and focused when he takes my pussy way deeper than ever before.

I thought he'd fucked my brains out in my apartment. I was wrong.

With each thrust, he punishes me like I know he's been desperate to do. He fucks like he hates me but handles my body with the perfect balance of respect.

Is this guy really twenty-four, or is he lying to the world?

"Is your cunt burning yet, Hellion?" he grits out, perspiration now dripping down his skin. "Or do you want some more?"

"More." My single plea ignites a fire in his eyes as he hauls me into his arms and marches us into his bedroom.

I barely get a chance to take in my surroundings when I'm launched onto his bed, bouncing once and releasing a squeal.

"Ass up and on your hands and knees," he demands.

I'm tempted to argue back in the same way I did the first time we fucked.

Only now, I know what he wants to do, and—much to my surprise—I want to get my ass pounded.

He slaps it hard, the crack echoing around his room, and I fall from my hands to my elbows.

"Cobra?" he asks.

I shake my head, white-hot pleasure racing through my system and driving me back to my hands. "Again."

"I'll give you more later."

A protest is on my lips when my ass cheeks are spread open, and I feel Tommy's hot, wet tongue swipe from one hole to the next.

"Nice and bare. Just how I like it," he growls. "And so fucking sweet."

He pierces my asshole with his tongue, driving it deep inside, and I fall to my elbows once more, burying my face into the soft gray duvet.

"Spread your thighs wider, Jenna."

Fresh out of protests, I do as he asked, lurching forward when he smacks my swollen clit.

"For an older girl, you've got a fucking awesome cunt."

I could wrap my hand around his throat right about now; instead, I turn my head to face him. "Cobra."

He pauses on opening the drawer to his nightstand. "The fuck?"

"Cobra," I repeat. "I reserve the right to use the word not just when you're going too far physically, but when I've had enough of your attitude as well. Being a prick is a deadass turnoff." I quirk a brow at him. "Just ask the other guys I've been with."

He grinds his teeth, snatching the lube from the drawer and coming to stand behind me.

"Do you want to stop playing, Jenna? Or do you want me to fill your ass?"

Every single muscle contracts beneath the weight of his filthy words.

"Make a choice," he commands.

I hate myself more than I do Tommy right now. "I want you to fuck my ass."

He cups his left hand around his ear, his hard cock long and daunting. "So I'm not accused of going against your wishes, can you repeat that for me?"

I swallow, resentment, trepidation, and excitement taking over. "I want you to fuck my ass."

Popping the cap on the lube bottle, he kneels directly behind me, coating his shaft with smooth strokes of his hand.

Next, he moves to my asshole, spending a good amount of time teasing and preparing my entrance. That alone is enough to make me come, and I dig my fingernails into the duvet.

As he positions himself behind me, Tommy traces a soft finger down my spine, causing me to shiver.

He pauses over my asshole, and then he enters me slowly, expertly.

"Don't collapse on me." His voice is softer when he wraps an arm around my waist, holding my body in the position he wants.

"I—I can't take any more." I shake my head.

"I'm only halfway inside you."

Panic lances through me, and I go to pull away. His arm circles me tighter.

"You can take me, Jenna. You want to take me too."

He's right. I do.

"Exhale and relax your body. It's going to be so fucking good, I swear to God."

I push all the air out of my lungs, and my shoulders drop. Tommy moves further inside. There's no pain or resistance, just a delicious burn that promises the best orgasm of my life.

"I hate it when you're right, but I hate it even more when you pretend to be kind to me."

When he pushes all the way inside, his cock grows even harder, and I release a lust-filled moan.

His hips are totally still when he runs his finger down my spine once again, only taking his first stroke when another finger pushes inside my pussy.

"You took the words right out of my mouth." His voice is full of victory.

I'm too full, too horny to care, and I back into his cock, wanting him even deeper.

"That's it. You know what you want."

We fuck. Hard, slow, our joint moans and gasps filling the room. I'm lost in a completely different world, barely able to recall my own name but still capable of screaming his.

On the first orgasm, I know he isn't nearly done with me, pumping his fingers and cock so relentlessly. The safe word sits right at the tip of my tongue.

Tommy retracts his fingers from my pussy and unloops his arm, spreading my ass wide.

"How mad do you think Holt would be if he could see us right now?" he jests. "His precious sister taking her enemy's cock so deep in her ass."

I groan out a, "Fuck you," and it only makes him harder.

"You're damaged goods now, Jenna. *My* damaged goods."

His possessive statement is his final undoing, and hot jets shoot straight inside me.

"Fuuuuck." Tommy whimpers out the word, still moving inside me and pulling every last drop from his dick.

He's hot and sticky and so fucking perfect as he holds himself over me, running his tongue across my shoulder blades.

I, on the other hand, only feel nauseous, sick to my stomach over my lack of willpower.

"Give me a second, and we'll go again. You can ride me this time," he says, pulling up to a stand and slipping out of my ass.

The sensation is odd, but not horrible, unlike how the rest of me feels.

I roll onto my back, sleepy but not as comatose as the first time.

"I need to leave." It's a quick statement, delivered with venom.

He takes a step back, running a palm over his mouth. "Are you for real?"

Just like every time I'm with a guy, I rush out of his bedroom and grab my clothes, not caring that my sweater is hanging completely open when I pull it on like a cardigan.

Tommy stalks after me, completely naked and leaving me second-guessing my decision to leave.

I push away temptation and look him dead in the eyes, padding toward him with a single finger out in front of me.

"You fucked me to prove a point. This is all about my brother, isn't it?"

He just shrugs, annoyance creasing between his brow. "Tell yourself what you want. Repeat whatever words help you sleep at night."

Anger rages inside me. "You're fucking me as a middle finger to my brother, aren't you? When you said it outside of Rise Up, I thought you were being cruel, but now I think you're being serious."

When his trademark smirk fails to emerge like I predicted, I'm left a little confused.

Tommy steps so close that my finger presses into his sternum.

He points toward his front door, my boots and jacket in a heap beside it. "I couldn't care less about your brother." He shakes his head at me. "I don't know how many chances you think you're going to get with me, Jenna. But you walk out of that door, and I'll never fuck you again. I won't even so much as *look* at you because you'll be dead to me."

"A plan with no drawbacks." The lie tumbles from my cocky lips.

He retracts his finger and forms a fist, jaw ticcing, heat pooling in his face. "Then be on your motherfucking way, Hellion. There's plenty more where you came from."

TWENTY

JENNA

H*ow I got my fingertips on that strike will forever remain a mystery to me.*

That's my exact thought as I stand beneath the jet stream of my postgame shower and replay the final three minutes of the last game of the regular season.

Maybe it was good timing on my part? I have a good leap on me, thanks to my obsession with plyometric training, or maybe the Orlando Waves center forward didn't put as much power as she usually does behind the shot. She could've scuffed the ground before she connected with the ball.

Either way, I made the fucking save, and we take home the shield for the first time in our team's history. It's seismic, life-changing, and I get to captain a league-winning team next season.

As I squeeze the shampoo from the tips of my hair, it feels like the smile I'm wearing has been absent for way too long.

"Babe, your cell keeps ringing over and over." Kendra's bright voice cuts through the billowing steam in my shower stall.

Reaching over the door, I grab my towel and wrap it around my chest.

"It's Holt," she confirms when I open the door and step into the changing area. "He wants to be the first to congratulate you."

Her smile is as wide as my own when she hands me my phone and blows me a kiss before pushing through the door into the locker room.

"All right, superstar." I don't know how my brother can tell I'm listening when I put the phone to my ear, and he immediately starts speaking. "That save was wild, and it's all over social media."

My stomach churns with a mixture of excitement and nerves. While our sport gets some exposure online, it's rare for it to trend like Holt is suggesting.

I snag another fluffy white towel from a hook next to the mirrors and begin drying my hair, tucking the phone between my ear and shoulder to free up both hands.

"By 'all over social media,' I assume you mean it's been covered by a couple of news outlets, and our former neighbor shared it to his Facebook?" I say, trying to play it cool.

Holt just snorts out a laugh. "You never were good with having the attention on you, Jen. I think it's fair to say that there are a few more than just a couple of news channels reporting on the game. Orion Hardman just went really bold—claiming your winning save was one of the best of all time."

I practically choke on my own tongue.

"Umm … come again? You mean *the* Orion Hardman? The same Orion Hardman who captained London Villa to three separate Champions League titles as well as England to World Cup victory?"

Even though I can't see him, I know my brother well enough to recognize when he's smiling, and right now, I have no doubt.

"Yes. That Orion Hardman. The English goalkeeper you still have plastered on your bedroom ceiling back in Mom's house."

Immediately, my smile falters. The game wrapped up well over an hour ago, yet still no word from my parents. Dad—I never really expect much from him. I doubt he'd even show to my own wedding. I guess I always hold out some hope that Mom watches my games. She says she does when we speak on occasion, but normally, that's when I call on her birthday, or vice versa.

Today was the biggest day of my career. Bigger than any World Cup game. Winning the shield has been at the top of my bucket list forever.

"She said she's going to call you later tonight."

Like he can read my mind, Holt's voice pulls me back from a spiral.

Grabbing my shampoo, conditioner, and body wash, I zip them into my wash bag.

"No offense, but I've heard that promise from her a few times."

"She hasn't been well," he replies on a breath. "She caught that flu virus that's been going around and has been out of action for weeks."

"I'm sorry to hear that," I reply. "Still, it doesn't account for the other twenty-seven years of my life."

I sound bitter in my retort, and that's something I've always tried not to be—bitter or resentful toward Holt. I know he doesn't deserve my attitude; it's not his fault that she calls him weekly. He didn't ask to be put in this position.

"Why don't you call her?" he suggests, which does kind of piss me off.

When I push through into the locker room, there's only our current captain, Hollie Browne, remaining as she packs up her kit bag and silently motions toward the exit.

I give her a thumbs-up, confirming I'll meet everyone in the players' lounge before we head out for celebratory drinks.

Tonight is going to be messy, and I'm all the way here for it. Fuck knows I need to let my hair down.

Again, my stomach knots. Ordinarily, a night like this would end with me falling for another guy's charm and empty promises before jumping into bed with him.

It hasn't been all that long—less than a week, in fact—since Tommy told me to be on my "motherfucking way" after I freaked out on him.

All I need is one hot night with a guy to fuck the memory of the Blades bad boy out of my system.

"Isn't it supposed to be the other way around? It seems a bit fucking odd for me to call her so she can congratulate me," I finally reply to Holt as I dump myself down on the bench and put him on speaker so I can quickly get ready. I'll do my makeup in the taxi into town.

"Why don't you come back to Mom's with me for the holidays? It might be a good chance to get closer to her again."

My second knee-length boot hits the floor with a thud.

"Holt," I say in an exasperated tone, "I love you more than life, but you cannot be serious when you suggest a couple of nights' stay back home in Nebraska, singing carols and eating turkey, will solve a lifetime of parental issues."

He hums softly, and I can tell he's grasping at straws on my behalf.

"I just don't want you to feel hurt or like you don't belong, Jen. You are always welcome back home, and you know that."

Shoving my Storm hoodie into my bag harder than I need to, I fight back tears as I recall the last time Mom and I spoke. It was maybe three months ago, and it ended in a fight between us, where she hung up the call. I'd told her that living in Brooklyn was heavy-going financially, and she suggested that it was time for me to grow up and get a proper job that would pay better.

That cut deep.

Holt has never earned a ton of money. As fly-half for his team, he typically earns better than most of his teammates. Still, it's hardly an NHL salary. Yet I never once heard her question Holt about his choice in career, and that was what I called her out on when we spoke. She didn't want to hear it and told me I should either get a different job or quit complaining altogether.

Mom doesn't believe in women playing sports. I could tell from the passive-aggressive comments she mumbled over it "not being very feminine." And once, when I was in high school and one of my friends took a cleat to the eyebrow that needed stitches, she insinuated to my friend's actual face that her boyfriend would probably dump her for being way too manly.

I never told Holt any of that since I couldn't see how it would improve my relationship with Mom. We simply aren't on the same wavelength, and she's stuck with outdated views steeped in misogyny. If I thought she'd listen, I'd educate her and help her see how fundamental sports was to women and younger girls.

Picking up my bag, I throw it over my shoulder and then grab my cell from the bench, bringing it to my ear.

I'd love to be really honest with my brother and tell him that despite his efforts and concerns, I was lonely, and I couldn't feel any more cast out of my family if I tried.

But that would be me wallowing in a pity party that wouldn't change anything between me or my parents. All it would do is put my brother under pressure when he already carries so much on his shoulders. I refuse to let negativity taint my relationship with him. And I refuse to hold on to bitterness that I didn't get the relationship with my mom that I'd desperately wanted as a younger girl.

"You're right." Holt speaks softly. "Mom should be the one to call you, and when I end this conversation, I'm going to tell her to pick up the damn phone and contact her only daughter." His voice is filled with emotion—a blend of frustration, sorrow, and awe. "I'm so fucking proud of you, Jen. You slayed out there today, and when I come over to see you at Christmas, we're heading out for beers and chicken wings."

I release a single burst of laughter as I swing the locker room door open and head for the player's lounge.

"I'm down for the beer and wings, but please don't contact Mom. Your phone call is enough for me."

I pause at the door to the lounge and watch Kendra at the bar, handing drinks out to the team. Her rosy cheeks are more prominent as she takes a sip of her soda and clinks her glass with Coach. She and Jack haven't announced the pregnancy yet, but I hear they plan to soon.

"Are you celebrating tonight?" Holt asks while I stare through the window set in the top half of the door.

"Is it going to get dark tonight? Naturally," I answer.

Something like a rumble echoes from my brother's throat. "Okay, well, have fun and all that, but—"

"Don't go home with strange men?" I finish for him. "You're so transparent, Holt."

He chuckles at that, knowing I'm right. "Speaking of guys, has Tommy Schneider been staying away?"

I practically pass out on the spot, grabbing hold of the door handle to keep me steady. I guess part of me hoped that Holt had forgotten all about his run-in with Tommy back in January. He's barely mentioned him since.

I swallow thickly and pull the door open, music and voices instantly hitting me. It's deliberate on my part since all I want is to end this conversation right now.

"I've seen him around when I've gone to watch Blades games, but, yeah, I think he got the message when you threatened to end his hockey career if he ever bothered me again."

Jesus Christ, I'm a terrible liar.

When Holt doesn't respond, I check my phone just in case we got disconnected.

"He's probably going to get traded soon anyway," I continue.

Finally, Holt speaks, and I breathe a sigh of relief. If he could see my flushed cheeks, he'd instantly know I was lying. To be honest, I can't be sure he's buying my bullshit right now.

"Stay away from him, Jen. You know I never interfere with

your life because who the fuck am I to get involved? But that guy …" He trails off, and I can practically hear his molars grinding. "He's bad fucking news. Men like him wouldn't know how to treat a woman right if they had a decency chip planted into their brain. He's a prick. Plain and simple."

As Holt finishes up his warning, Kendra approaches me with a beer, and I take it from her.

She cocks her head to the side, studying me carefully. I know my expression is the complete opposite of the one I was wearing in the shower, and that's not something I can hide from my best friend.

"I need to go," I tell Holt. "Kendra just handed me a beer, and the girls are waiting for me to finish it so we can head into town."

"You heard what I said, right, Jen?" Holt presses me for at least an acknowledgment.

I take a small sip of beer and catch Kendra's concerned gaze.

"I heard," is all I say, shifting from one foot to the next.

Holt makes something akin to an agreeable noise, and my shoulders drop from around my ears. "All right, sis. Go have fun, and I'll catch up with you soon."

When I disconnect the call, I can feel a pair of brown eyes boring into my skull. Kendra is on the warpath.

"You're hiding something from me, Jenna, and I want to know what it is."

I'm scrambling for something, anything, to satisfy her and throw her off the scent of Tommy. And while I know I technically should keep this to myself until the team officially makes an announcement, it's the only plausible alibi I can think of on the spot.

I pocket my phone and look up at her, plastering on a faux smile.

"Can you keep a secret?" I ask, knowing full well she can. Kendra is a vault.

She steps closer, one brow quirked. "Spill."

"Well, tonight, we aren't just celebrating the shield."

Her eyes grow wide. "We aren't?"

I shake my head, and my real grin returns. "Nope. Tonight, we can secretly celebrate my recent appointment as your new captain for next season."

TWENTY-ONE

JENNA

"I'm part delighted, part fearful that as of next season, you will be my boss." Kendra's ambivalence is reflected on her face when she takes a sip of soda and leans against the pool table.

We've been out for several hours, and I've lost count of how many drinks I've had. Still, I'm pretty much in control of my senses, if not a little wobbly on my legs.

Leaning forward on my pool cue, I size up my next shot, closing one eye to focus on a purple number 4 ball.

I miss in spectacular fashion, not even coming close to sinking the ball, and I drop my head down against the green felt lining the top of the table.

If Kendra hadn't made it as a pro soccer player, I'm sure she could've made a living from this sport instead. She's been kicking my ass for the past fifteen minutes.

"You look like you could use a little help there."

A deep voice I don't recognize speaks from behind me, and I look up to find my best friend already on her way to the restroom. I haven't taken in the source of the voice, but judging by the way Kendra just made herself scarce, I'm guessing whoever is standing behind me is hot.

Goose bumps shimmer down my arms, fired off by a mixture of excitement and dread. I want to have fun with guys, just like I've always done. Although I can't deny the shift inside me, and I know that my reluctance to hook up is down to the bad-boy hockey player I shouldn't be thinking about at all, let alone right now.

With the pool cue still in my hand, I slowly rise from the table and turn to face the owner of the deep, flirtatious voice.

Ugh.

He's just my type. I'd pin him as a similar age to me, with a sweet and sexy smile that reaches his ears. Floppy, dark hair contrasts with his bright blue eyes, and while he isn't tattooed, he is broad and tall—at least six feet.

He takes in my outfit, his eyes ascending from my knee-high black boots to my dark blue jeans before finally landing on my crisp white button-down blouse that is partially open and skimming the top of my cleavage.

I look hot tonight; I can't deny it. I applied a touch of makeup in the taxi but left my hair to air-dry naturally since I'm one of those lucky people who likes their hair when I don't bother to style it. I rarely need to use straightening irons.

"You're Jenna Miller, right?"

His confident question shocks me. I don't think any stranger has ever instantly recognized me like I'm some kind of celebrity.

I look off to the side and bite my bottom lip. "That's a little presumptuous, don't you think?"

He smiles wider. "Knowing your name is presumptuous?"

I shake my head and switch the cue from one hand to the other, leaning my ass against the pool table behind me. I feel like I'm failing miserably at flirting.

"No. It's presumptuous to think that I'd confirm my identity to a strange man."

Taking a small step toward me, he seems to appreciate my response and respects my boundaries, and I feel my shoulders relax a little as a result.

"I watched your game earlier," he confirms, taking another tentative step so I can smell his cologne. It's strong and spicy, and he's wearing way too much. "I know I'm not exactly famous, but I used to play semi-pro soccer in England before I ruptured my ACL and came out of the sport altogether. That save you pulled off today was legendary."

He has a soft Southern accent that I usually adore, but it's not really his voice I'm hearing, and that frustrates the shit out of me. If it wouldn't make me look like the biggest weirdo, I'd slap myself across the face to break from my Tommy Schneider thoughts.

He motions to the cue I'm holding. "I'm also pretty good at pool if you want me to give you some pointers?"

"Learning how to play pool is not high up on my priority list."

The nameless guy scrubs a rough hand across his mouth. "You can just tell me to fuck off if you'd like."

It's my perfect opportunity to break free and head home for the night or at least make an escape to the bar for another drink.

But for what purpose? And why should I? The Jenna from a few weeks ago wouldn't have hesitated to flirt like crazy with this guy, who is obviously into me. Sure, he might've gone a little heavy on the cologne, but he's at least being inventive with trying to pick me up. Most men have already promised the world in bed by now and given me the full ick.

For a brief second, I let my gaze rove the length of his body. He, too, is wearing a white shirt and blue jeans.

"We match," I tell him, pointing to my own outfit.

My observation must spur him on because he moves closer to me—one more inch, and he'll be pressing into my body.

I fight the urge to step back, even though I couldn't with the pool table set right behind me.

"My name's Ethan. Nice to meet you, Jenna."

THE WOBBLY LEGS I HAD EARLIER IN THE NIGHT WOULD collapse underneath me if it wasn't for Ethan's strong arm holding me up.

The last thing I can remember is Kendra leaving to head home hours ago and then Ethan guiding me to the bar. The rest is history.

"I'm supposed to be a pro athlete," I slur out into the night sky as Ethan continues walking us both back to my place. At least, I think that's where he's taking us. I gave him my address and handed him the key to my apartment.

When we turn a corner, my apartment building comes into view, and I heave a sigh of relief. I should recognize these streets, but everything about this night has passed by in a blur.

"I wasn't supposed to get this drunk," I tell Ethan when he holds on to me with one arm and uses the fob attached to my key ring to enter the building.

"We'll take the elevator," he confirms, hitting the button and falling back into an awkward silence.

This guy was full of talk earlier tonight, helping me refine my pool skills and laughing at everything I had to say.

"You bought me waaaaay too many drinks." I chuckle and then burp as we enter the elevator, and I squint against the bright lights overhead. "I never drink this much."

Ethan remains silent, and for the first time tonight, I feel less than safe in his presence. He has ahold of my bag, which means I can't make use of the pepper spray Holt got me as a stocking stuffer one Christmas.

The elevator pings, and the doors slide open onto my floor.

"I think I have it from here," I say, summoning my soberest voice and attempting to pull away from his grasp.

He doesn't let me go, instead walking us out of the elevator and coming to an abrupt halt that has me almost tumbling to the floor.

"I said … I can take it from here. Thank you for walking me home, Ethan."

My heart sinks when he still doesn't release his hold on me, and suddenly, I'm fearing the worst. If he was concerned about me getting home safely, then he already made sure of that. So, what other reason does he have to keep hold of me?

A rush of adrenaline surges through me, fight-or-flight instincts kicking in and cutting through my alcohol-fueled haze. It's still not enough for me to break free from this guy I barely know.

You were a fucking idiot to leave with him, Jenna. You should've gone home with Kendra.

"She asked you to let go of her, Ethan. Twice."

At the sound of Tommy's voice, my head shoots up from where my eyes were trained on the floor.

Dressed in all black and with a hot-as-fuck black baseball cap turned backward, Tommy pushes off my doorjamb and stalks toward us.

"Holy shit …" Ethan announces. "Y-you're Tommy Schneider, the Blades defenseman."

Tommy doesn't even bother to acknowledge Ethan, and I know exactly what's coming, even before the crack of Tommy's knuckles against Ethan's nose rings in my ears.

"What were you planning to do with my girl once you got her back to her apartment?!" Tommy bites out.

My hazy brain tries to piece his sentence together.

Wait … did he just refer to me as—

"Jesus fucking Christ, I think you broke my nose!" Ethan

interrupts my slow thoughts, blood dripping from his hand to the floor as he tries to stem the flow.

With one firm hand to his chest, Tommy pushes him back into the far wall, leaving Ethan with no escape.

"It's okay, Tommy." I quickly soothe, stumbling toward them both. "It's okay," I repeat, placing a hand on his shoulder as he towers over Ethan with a murderous expression that has me convinced he's about to commit a felony.

At the touch of my palm, his shoulders drop an inch, although it isn't enough to calm him entirely.

"When a girl tells you to let her go, that's exactly what you do. There's a difference between playing around and trying to take advantage of someone who's intoxicated."

Ethan's eyes grow wide, and I expect him to deny any malicious intent toward me. I didn't pick up on any dangerous vibes from this guy, I'm normally hot on that shit.

"We'd been flirting all night, and Jenna wanted me just as much as I did her. I had no idea she had a boyfriend."

His words shock me, a cold reality punching me right in the gut. He planned to try and fuck me—or at least press for more. I didn't even kiss this guy, and while I would describe my behavior as very friendly, it wasn't especially flirtatious since the guy dressed in black and pinning Ethan against the wall was all I could think about all night.

I've zero idea what the time is, but I'm sure my neighbors are sleeping. It's just as well since the growl that Tommy releases is enough to shake the building at its foundation.

"It doesn't matter what she told you earlier in the night. She clearly changed her mind. If I hadn't been here, waiting for her to come home, then ..." Tommy pulls a deep breath into his lungs, his voice shaking. "Then fuck knows what you would've done?!"

He rears his fist back again, and I squeeze his shoulder, reassuring him that I'm okay.

"Just let him go, Tommy." I look at Ethan then, narrowing my eyes in warning. "Ethan isn't going to speak a word about this or ever return to my apartment. Are you?"

Without any hesitation, he shakes his head quickly while still pinching the bridge of his bloody nose. "Nothing. You have my word on that."

I still can't be sure of what Ethan planned to do once we got to the other side of my apartment door; all I know is that, for once, I've never been so relieved to see Tommy's face.

And as that realization sinks in, another feeling hits me immediately after.

Safety.

The kind of security only my brother has ever brought me. When Holt was around, I knew everything would be okay. And right now, I can't deny that same reassurance as it radiates from Tommy and wraps around me in the kind of hug Archer, Sawyer, and Jack always give their girls.

"Go home, take a cold shower, and think about how you can continue your sorry life with more dignity and respect." Tommy releases Ethan, who instantly slips out from underneath his arm and heads straight for the stairs, not bothering to wait for the elevator.

It must be ten seconds before we hear the main building door slam shut behind Ethan and another couple of beats before Tommy finally turns to look at me, red staining his left knuckles.

I keep my eyes down on his hands, wrapping my arms around my middle to comfort myself. Tears bleed from my eyes as I squeeze them shut and fight my emotions down with everything I have.

"Look at me, Jenna."

I shake my head, embarrassment and shame curling inside my stomach. I feel sick, and it has nothing to do with the alcohol. "Just go, Tommy. Thank you for tonight, but please, just go."

When he turns his back on me and makes for the stairs, I

realize he isn't going to fight me tonight. He's practicing what he just preached to Ethan a few minutes earlier and respecting my boundaries.

But instead of the relief that washed through me when Ethan disappeared, panic is all I can feel as the distance between us increases.

When his foot hits the third step, I'm powerless to prevent my plea. "Wait."

Tommy stops in his tracks but keeps his back to me, both hands shoved into the pockets of his black jeans.

"What do you want from me, Jenna?"

If I didn't know it was Tommy speaking, I wouldn't recognize his voice. It sounds broken and weak. A little like my resolve to keep away from him.

Wrapping my arms tighter around my middle, I rock back on my heels. Another tear hits my cheek, sliding down to my chin.

"I-I ... I don't know what to say to you." And it's the truth; I don't. All I know is, I don't want him to take another step away.

Tommy releases long, slow breaths, turning his face slightly so I can see the tension in his jaw.

"If you want me to stay with you tonight, then I'm going to need you to tell me that. You're drunk, and ordinarily, you hate my guts. Plus, the last time I was here, you threatened to call the police on me."

The tension between us is so thick. Regardless, I'm tempted to laugh at the memory of him bursting into my apartment and volleying back and forth with me.

Tommy might be brutal in the way that he goes after what he wants, but he has never made me feel like Ethan just did. There's good in the boy standing in front of me.

"Okay, well, I can't stay here all night, waiting on your response. I have to head for an away series tomorrow, and I need to get some sleep." He huffs out a laugh. "I'll need all the energy I can get to warm the bench."

As he takes another step away, unease kicks up my heart rate. "Stay."

Tommy immediately turns around to face me, deep brown eyes falling to my protective and vulnerable stance. "And what do you want from me if I do?"

I swallow thickly, arms dropping to my sides as I ball my hands into fists. My nails cut into fleshy palms while I battle to push out words I never thought I'd say to the boy standing in front of me, "I ... I just want you next to me."

TWENTY-TWO

TOMMY

Jenna's sofa bed is the modern world's answer to medieval torture; I'm convinced of it.

And speaking of medieval, so is her skillet. I've wasted three pancakes since the nonstick is basically nonexistent.

This girl has zero interest in domestic tasks, and that was only evidenced further when I snuck out of her bedroom after she immediately fell asleep and figured out that the sofa actually doubled as a bed, only to find a red thong shoved down the back of one of the cushions.

That's … not how I pictured seeing Jenna's underwear again, although at least they were clean.

When I finally have four passable pancakes and a partially crystallized tube of maple syrup, I snag the two mugs of black coffee I brewed a few minutes earlier and head for Jenna's bedroom door.

It's still closed with no sign of movement on the other side.

Depressing the handle with my elbow since I don't have any free hands, I'm surprised to find Jenna sitting up in bed, scrolling on her phone.

She's still dressed in the white Blades T-shirt I handed to her last night. The partially ripped collar hangs over one of her shoulders, and her hair is a disheveled mess. She hasn't bothered to remove the makeup she was wearing last night, and I'm thankful that my hands are full right now, or I'd be tempted to wipe the black mascara smeared under her left eye.

I'll be completely honest; I can count on a single hand the number of times I've been scared in my life. Once when I was eleven, and a group of friends and I decided to play a game of chicken with cars on our street. Another time when I went cliff diving with the same group of friends a couple of years later on a school trip. The final time was when my dad kicked me out of his apartment and I realized that I was, in fact, alone in the world.

Last night though? I think that was the first time I was genuinely scared on behalf of someone else. Sure, Mom has had her fair share of asshole boyfriends, who I wanted to beat to a pulp when they broke her heart or left her for another woman. But Ethan? He was another brand of dangerous, and Jenna was at the top of his hit list. When I pulled back her duvet and helped her into bed, I could tell she was more sober than when she'd walked out of the elevator, pinned in that sick bastard's grasp. But that was only because she'd just had the wake-up call of her life. I'm painfully aware—unfortunately for me—that Jenna isn't shy to go home with guys, and honestly, when I was mad at her in the past, it wasn't because I was judging her choices. She has every right to do what she wants. With whom she wants to do it.

It just sucks to think of her willingly giving herself to someone other than me, and that's a bittersweet pill to swallow.

Last night was anything but consensual though, and if I hadn't showed up at her apartment and waited for her to come home when she didn't answer the door, then ... I don't even want to think about what could've happened to her.

And the really fucking weird thing about all of this? When my knuckles connected with Ethan's nose, all I could see was her goddamn brother and his face in the final second before I punched him.

In that moment, when Holt had fallen back into the table behind him, I knew I'd overstepped, even if I didn't—and wouldn't—admit it to myself. Holt had shown no sign of assaulting me, and he had every right to defend his sister when I gave her shit and told her she looked like it too.

At the time, it felt like the most important hit of my life— defending my honor and ego against a girl who'd humiliated me and told all her fucking friends how she blew off my advances.

That punch had been anything *but* significant, along with the words that left my mouth that night.

To be honest, none of my punches before last night had really carried any meaning. They were superficial and a projection of the man I—and the rest of the universe—is determined to see.

"Are you going to stand in the doorway all day and stare at me, or actually hand over those pancakes?"

Jenna sets her phone down on the white duvet, and she sits up taller in bed, resting her head against the dark green headboard behind her.

I begin walking toward her, smiling the whole way over to her bedside. "Generally speaking, people are a little more grateful when someone brings them breakfast in bed."

As I set the plate of pancakes in front of her, along with a cup of coffee on her nightstand, she looks up at me with her blue eyes and takes the maple syrup from my hand.

"Did you ... sleep in my bed last night?"

I'm wearing only my black jeans and nothing on top, and I'm sure she can see my skin as it pebbles at the thought of sharing a bed with this girl.

Hate sex is one thing. Climbing under her duvet and spending the night is an entirely different concept. Something I never ever do.

"You mean, did we fuck?" I ask, taking a seat at the end of her bed. "My name isn't Ethan."

Jenna drops her eyes to the pancakes in her lap, shame coloring her features.

Yeah, I don't fucking like that.

"Hey …" I reach across and hook my pointer finger under her chin. Her glassy eyes connect with mine. "You'd best not be thinking what I think you are right now."

"Are you trying to control my thoughts now as well, Tommy?" Jenna's voice doesn't match her words. It bears no malice or resentment, only uncertainty and a vulnerability, which makes me even more thankful that I waited for her to return home last night.

"Don't be a fucking brat, Hellion." I shake my head at her, lips curling into a cocky grin. "You're hungover to shit and wasting four perfectly good pancakes I just had to fight with your crappy skillet to make. You're in no position to give me back talk."

She quirks a brow at me, my finger still hooked under her chin when I inch a little closer.

Jenna draws her knees up to give me space, and like the fucking magnets we are, there's zero resistance to my approach.

"If you have even one single, tiny thought that anything about last night was your fault—or of your own making—then I want you to listen to me very fucking carefully."

She drops her eyes to her breakfast again, and since I figure the pancakes are already cold, I slip them off her lap and onto the side table beside her coffee. Next, I set my own coffee mug down and take the maple syrup from her hand, setting that on the floor beside the bed.

When she looks at me again with big eyes, framed by thick lashes, all I can think about is kissing away any invasive thoughts this girl might have. She might hate my guts, and I might find her insufferable ninety-nine percent of the time. Yet, despite all the toxicity that has passed between us, Jenna Miller is the kind of person who deserves good things.

Bad people do not belong in her life. And if they are, then that has nothing to do with her and everything to do with them crossing boundaries into a world where they don't belong.

"What's the matter?" Jenna leans forward, one soft palm coming to rest on my shoulder.

My heart rate slows to a more gentle pace, although my invasive thoughts remain.

She was right when she said that I was bad for her because I don't belong in here, in her world.

"I ..." Like an out-of-body experience, my own voice doesn't feel like it's mine when I begin speaking. "I need to get home and pack for Colorado. The team plane leaves in three hours."

Jenna cocks her head to one side, eyes narrowing slightly. "Now, I want to know what *you're* hiding."

My overpowering need to protect you from bad people.

"My annoyance over you wasting the breakfast in bed I made," is what actually leaves my lips.

She scans my face, and my stomach coils under the weight of her gaze. "You're just one big act, aren't you?"

Every muscle in my body mirrors the tension in my stomach, and I shift my hand from under her chin to grasp it between my thumb and forefinger. I'm holding her tighter than I want, but I'm so fucking tense that it's impossible to ease my grip.

"Am I hurting you?" my subconscious asks on my behalf.

"No." Jenna's voice is soft and breathy as she edges a little closer to me. "But I do want you to tell me why you suddenly need to leave. Was it something I said?"

My tongue runs across my bottom lip. We're still an arm's length apart, although it feels like I'm pressing her up against the wall again.

"Normally, you can't wait to see the back of me," I playfully counter. "Did I say something to make you like me all of a sudden?"

I'm waiting for her to slip into banter mode and tell me that nothing's changed between us. That she still hates my guts this morning as much as she did the last time we saw each other.

Come on, Hellion. Play the game.

Her face doesn't change, and neither does the softness behind her eyes.

"You can talk to me, you know? I know I'm probably the last person you ever thought would say that to you, but somehow, I feel like I might also be the first. You don't have to keep pretending that you're someone you're not or maybe don't want to be."

Before I know it, I'm closing more distance between us, and my hand is sliding from her chin to the back of her head, pulling Jenna's mouth closer to my own.

Other than this girl right in front of me, I can't remember the last time I kissed someone or was even remotely tempted to share something deeply intimate like this.

Fuck.

Her breathing is rapid and ragged, eyes centered solely on my lips.

"Cobra." My subconscious played no part in what I just said. It was purposeful and protective, and … fuck … I'm already regretful.

Jenna drops her hand from my shoulder and pulls back, just like I expected her to the second our safe word left my lips. After all, that's exactly the effect I wanted it to have. It's what it's designed to do.

What it isn't meant for is to cause hurt, and that's precisely what I see creased into the lines across Jenna's forehead.

"Yeah …" she breathes out with a cutting edge to her tone, almost like normal service has resumed between us. And I should be relieved that it has. "Perhaps you should head home now."

She motions to the door with her hand, and my own falls to the nape of her neck—a silent plea for her not to push me away.

At this point, hell only knows where my brain is at. I'm so fucking confused, so fucking conflicted and torn. None of this is familiar to me. Jenna's absolutely right; she is the first person to truly invite me to open up to her. In my adult life anyway.

"Jenna, I …" My sentence fails under the heavy weight of scrambled thoughts.

Reaching behind her neck, Jenna places a palm over the back of my hand, wrapping her fingers around the edges of my own.

I can feel her touch all the way to my toes, and more goose bumps erupt across my skin.

"Let go of me, Tommy."

My hand drops to the pillow behind her, eyes still fixed on hers.

I don't want to leave, even though I'm going to miss my flight and land myself in more shit with the team if I don't head out now.

"I'll be gone for eight days," I tell her. "Keep your door locked and the dead bolt on at all times."

"You don't get to tell me what to do, Tommy."

I know I don't, but that doesn't change the fact that I will. Especially when it comes to Jenna's safety and sickos like Ethan.

Sensing that she's about to ask me to leave for a second time, I rise from the bed and make for the door, harboring a shred of hope that she'll ask me to stay, like she did last night.

It feels wrong for us to part like this. I don't want to go on bad terms. Not after what she's been through.

I pause just as I reach her door and turn to look at her. She hasn't taken her eyes off me the whole time.

"In case you were wondering, I stopped by last night to apol-

ogize for kicking you out of my apartment the last time we …
yeah."

Jenna goes to say something, but I get there first, raising a
hand in front of me.

"I also wanted to congratulate you on the game and that save
you'd pulled off." I can't help the smile as it tugs at my lips.
"Sure, Orlando's center forward connected with the ground
before the ball, but still, the shot was bending away from you
when you made contact. It was a wild strike and an even better
stop. You've got serious talent. Even if you feed your body like
shit."

On a headshake that feels like it's made to mask her
emotions, Jenna scoffs softly at me. "Thanks, asswipe. I'm sure
you'll need to lie down after that display of kindness."

I want to laugh so hard, and I bite the inside of my cheek to
stop myself.

Jenna flicks a hand out in front of her, reaching for the
pancakes and picking them up. "Now, be on your motherfucking
way. I've got cold and distinctly average pancakes to annihilate."

TWENTY-THREE

TOMMY

We're destroying Colorado, dismantling their defense and outplaying them on every inch of the ice.

The team player in me should be happy to see the Blades dominate strong opposition and especially on an away series.

Fuck. That.

With every goal and shutout the Blades secure, it feels like any reason or previous justification the GM might have had for keeping me gradually fades into nothing.

I should consider my place on the bench a privilege compared to my incoming fate—aka the farm team in Connecticut or the trade list by March.

And who the fuck is going to want me? While I'm warming this plank of goddamn wood beneath my ass, I'm not out there, proving to other teams that I'm worth taking a chance on.

"Penny for your thoughts." Sawyer takes a seat next to me at the next line change.

He's so fucking annoying, mainly because there's actually very little to dislike about him. At least Jack and Archer give me a reason to hate their guts. This guy is as pure as the freshly driven snow.

He's also got over ten years of life and playing experience on me, which means I should probably listen to what he has to say. I can sense that he wants me to.

Twisting my hands in my lap, I turn my neck and deliberately look the other way.

"I doubt I'll get called back onto the ice, so that means I have all the time in the world for your response."

I continue to ignore him, closing my eyes and swallowing thickly. It's been five days since Jenna asked me to open up to her, and suddenly, after years of no one apparently giving a shit, there are two people trying to coax me into talking.

"Hoping that the burger joint I used to work at back home might still have a job for me." I tag on a sarcastic laugh to the end of my statement.

Maybe Sawyer will think I'm joking when I'm really not.

He clears his throat and takes a second, which feels like a fucking lifetime.

"It isn't too late, you know? When the GM sealed the deal and traded you here, I got to sit in on some of the post-deal discussions between him and Coach. Call it captain privileges." He chuckles. "Anyway … when I initially found out you were headed for the team, I was pissed off with the GM, convinced that he'd just made the biggest mistake of his career."

I turn to look at my teammate, one unimpressed brow raised in question. "I'd say you were right, wouldn't you?" I drop my eyes to the bench beneath me.

Sawyer just shrugs, doubtful and dismissive of my self-flagellation. "I'd say I will be if you carry on the way you are."

"I've tried everything I fucking can," I tell him, just as Jack sinks the puck, putting us three goals ahead in the third.

Sawyer stands to bump fists with him as he skates past the boards. I remain seated, head down and anything but happy for my asshole of a captain.

When Sawyer takes a seat next to me again, he motions

toward Jack. "You see, that's what I'm talking about. You should've been up on your feet for the team regardless of how fucking shit you're feeling about your own game."

He's only stating the obvious. As if I haven't already worked that one out.

"They hate me, and there's nothing I can do to fix that."

My veteran teammate releases a frustrated grumble, chewing on the corner of his mouth shield. "That's your default setting talking. If you had the same faith in other people as you do in your own hockey ability, then we wouldn't even be having this conversation." He turns to look at me then, eyes boring into my own. "Stop waiting for something to go wrong in relationships and start giving them the benefit of the doubt."

"Says the guy who's happily married with a perfect family bubble." I drop my head between my shoulders, shame creeping up my spine. "Shit. I'm sorry, man. I know your first wife passed away. I shouldn't have—"

Sawyer raises a hand to halt my apology, and when I swivel my head to look at him, he's actually smiling directly at me.

He should be so fucking pissed at what I just said; he has every right to be.

"Seriously, Tommy, you're fine. I've had way worse said to me over the years, trust me. In fact, I'm kind of glad you did say it, to be honest."

I throw him a puzzled look before he continues talking.

"You overstepped with what you said and immediately apologized. I haven't seen that from you before, and I know, for a fact, that your teammates haven't either. Beneath the bravado and dickhead attitude you bring, there's actually a good person in there. I've thought it for a while, and I've been praying you would turn your attitude around before it's too late. Now I feel like I need to step in because, clearly, you aren't going to change your ways."

He points to the center of his chest, and I'm ready to leap over the boards and make a run for it.

"Can I ask you something?"

I get the feeling he's going to whether I want him to or not.

"Shoot," I reply, eyes pinned ahead.

Sawyer pulls his mouth shield away and begins chewing on his bottom lip instead.

Fuck, this isn't good.

"What's the deal with you and Alex? I get this is none of my goddamn business, and you can tell me to go take a fucking leap if you want, but … what's the deal?"

I shrug and watch the game as it plays out the final two minutes. "I don't get why you're asking. It's just a regular father-son relationship."

Sawyer shakes his head. "Nah, what I have with my son is a regular father-son relationship. Why isn't he here? Alex was an asshole through and through, but one thing he did love was hockey. So, why isn't he here, cheering on his son? You're a carbon copy of him, and I figured his ego would love that."

"I'm nothing like him." Just like that time with Jenna, my subconscious controls my mouth. My words are cold and callous and serve as a window to the truth of why Alex Schneider is never seen at his son's games.

Only the noise in the arena sits between us for what feels like an eternity.

"He isn't really your dad, is he?"

My eyes snap to Sawyer. "Are you calling me a liar?"

He shakes his head slowly, one hand raised in surrender. "No. You're jumping to conclusions and assuming the worst in people again. What I'm saying is, he isn't actually a dad. He didn't take on responsibility for you, did he? You might wear his name and possess his DNA, but that's as far as your connection runs."

I'm ready to empty the contents of my stomach out onto the floor beneath me.

"You're wrong," I lie. "He just has a lot going on in his life, and with the way his career ended, he doesn't love hockey anymore." I blow out a breath. "And I can't say that I blame him. He was cast out of the NHL for doing his job on the ice."

"He nearly killed someone." Sawyer's voice is incredulous. "And why are you defending him when you don't really mean a word you're saying?"

Yeah, why are you defending him, Tommy?

I look up at the Jumbotron, desperate for the game to end and the buzzer to save me. Thirty seconds feels like the longest time.

"And why are you trying to be him, Tommy? Trying to fool everyone into thinking that you're the same beyond the way you skate and look?"

The final question from Sawyer hits me like the punch I threw at Ethan that night.

"You have no idea what you're talking about," I bite out. "I'm more talented than he could ever be. My name will be remembered long after my career is finished."

At this point, I'm spouting shit and contradicting myself at every turn. Sawyer has me wrapped around his finger and cornered like a wild animal being hunted.

He just chuckles at that. Although it's dark and not at all amused. "You want to know how you're going to save your career and stay on the team?"

I don't respond.

"Accept the fact that you are nothing like your estranged dad and everything like the Tommy Williams you used to be."

I guess it wasn't hard to find my former last name—the press reported my name change when I signed for Detroit.

"I'm done talking now," I croak out. Swiping the fastest hand across my eyes.

Jesus Christ, I hope nobody caught that shit on camera.

Sawyer rests a strong palm on my shoulder just as the buzzer finally fucking goes.

"Yeah, Tommy, I know you are. Just ... give what I said some thought instead, okay?"

TWENTY-FOUR

JENNA

I'm portioning out pasta into separate containers ahead of the playoff games we have this week when my cell lights up with a text from Tommy.

ASSWIPE

> So ... apparently, you're nice enough to make captain now?

I haven't heard from him at all on his away series, but that doesn't mean that I didn't watch the Blades games.

ME

> That only just got announced on the Storm's website ... you really are my real-life stalker.

ASSWIPE

> It passes the time.

ME

> Did you text me for a reason or just to annoy me again?

ASSWIPE

Actually, I wanted to say congrats on getting the captaincy. I guess this means you'll be sticking around Brooklyn then …

Setting the containers into my freezer, I find myself over-thinking Tommy's last text. Why does he care where I am? And when did I ever give the impression that I'd be moving away from Brooklyn? I decide to ignore his comment and change the subject.

ME

Where are you right now?

ASSWIPE

On a flight home. We land in an hour. Where are you?

ME

In my kitchen.

ASSWIPE

Eating more out-of-date takeout?

ME

No. I just made pasta dishes for this week's pregame meals.

ASSWIPE

Show me the evidence, or I won't believe you.

Stepping across to the freezer, I pull the door open and snap a photo of the containers.

ME

picture attached

ASSWIPE

Such a good girl.

It feels like every hair on my body stands on end.

ME

> Don't patronize me. Believe it or not, at twenty-seven, I have made my own food before you forced your way into my life.

ASSWIPE

> No one forced anyone, Jenna.

ME

> That's not how I recall it.

ASSWIPE

> Okay then, if you're so keen to get rid of me from your life, don't reply to this text. If I don't hear anything back after an hour, I'll delete your number, and aside from the odd time we see each other after games, you'll never see or hear from me again. Because that's what you want, right?

My hairs are still standing on end, but this time, it's for a very different reason.

I shouldn't reply; in fact, I should block his contact altogether and do exactly what Holt advised.

But do my brother and friends really know this guy? Or do they only see what he lets people see? I'm not even sure Tommy sees himself as a good person. And a part of me thinks his last message wasn't sent to play a game with me; rather, it was an honest opportunity for me to get out.

I should reply.

But I can't.

What would I say to him if I did?

In the end, all I do is stare at our text conversation before I close out the thread altogether and lock the screen.

Motivated by nothing but pure, unadulterated frustration, I toss my phone across the room, and it silently lands on the soft cushions on my sofa.

The sofa he slept on that night he rescued me from Ethan. He could've crawled into bed with me and asked for sex, and I would've given it to him, no questions asked.

I *wanted* to sleep with him again that night. I'd be lying to myself if I said I didn't. It's why I asked him to stay and not leave; it's what I was hoping for when he lay beside me on the bed until I slipped into a deep sleep.

For the next half hour, I busy myself around the apartment, cleaning every surface and tidying away every item of clothing I can find.

It's not enough to distract my brain or to stop me from clock-watching.

There's twenty-five minutes remaining in Tommy's window, and then he'll step away forever.

I'm halfway to my bedroom with another stack of freshly laundered clothes when my phone starts vibrating between the cushions.

I drop the clothes on the floor and scramble to answer it without checking who is calling. "Hello?!"

"Jesus. You sound like you're running sprint drills or something," Kendra replies on a half laugh.

Disappointment passes through me, followed by a sharp pang of guilt for being anything other than happy to hear my best friend's voice.

She sounds joyful, and she has every right to be too—married to the man of her dreams with their first child due in the new year.

"Sorry," I reply, walking over to pick up my clothes before dropping them onto my bed and collapsing onto the mattress beside them. "I was doing some housework and didn't want to miss the call."

I'm met with silence initially and then another chuckle from my friend.

"Housework?! Okay, we both know you don't do housework. Have you got your mom coming over to stay?"

While Kendra knows I don't see my mom often and that my dad is a dick, she doesn't know the whole picture with my family. Her family is tight, and so is Jack's. A little like my apparent inability to bag a caring man, my lack of decent relatives also feels like a sob story I'd rather not share.

"How can I help thee?" I ask, changing the subject quickly.

For once, Kendra doesn't fight me to answer her question as I hear her move about.

"So, Jack and I are thinking of announcing the pregnancy to everyone all at once. I'm still not twelve weeks, but unlike Darcy, I can't wait another second to share."

I go to respond, but she carries on, her excitement becoming increasingly obvious.

"We were thinking of throwing a house party at our place next week. The guys play on Friday night so we could hold it on Saturday. It could double as a celebration for you getting the captaincy too."

Pulling back the phone, I check the time.

Twenty minutes until Tommy's window closes.

Placing a flat palm against my forehead, I can feel the stress headache as it builds behind my eyes.

"I don't want me getting captain to overshadow your news. Seriously, let's just focus on your announcement."

"But—" Kendra tries to protest, but I cut her off abruptly.

"But nothing. I was thinking of having a small celebration at my apartment at some point after the playoffs are finished. Hollie is still the captain right now, and I don't want to step on her toes."

Kendra goes quiet. She usually does when she knows I'm right.

"Why are you so grumpy?" Her next question is not what I was expecting. "You just ticked off two major goals in your career, and you sound anything but delighted about it."

This is one of the reasons why I like Kendra, Collins, and

Darcy so much—they aren't afraid to speak the truth. I've met my fair share of people with an alternative agenda to last me a lifetime.

"I'm not grumpy," I attempt to deny, checking the time once again.

"You are," she volleys back, only sounding more and more determined. "I've felt like something has been going on with you for a while now, so tell me, is it to do with Holt?"

The temptation to lie is so great. I'm not a liar though, and Kendra doesn't deserve to be deceived.

That's not what good friendships are built on.

Maybe it's the fact that I now have a little over fifteen minutes to save whatever it is I have with Tommy that drives me to be truthful. I don't know. But when I close my eyes and let the words come, so does a sense of relief.

"It has to do with Tommy," I tell her quietly.

Any background noise on Kendra's end immediately stops.

"Tommy?" Her voice is cold and cutting. "What the fuck has he done now?"

I press my palm harder into my forehead, almost like I'm pushing the thoughts out of my brain and into the open. "He hasn't done anything wrong."

There are a few beats of nothing before Kendra speaks again.

"I'm confused, Jen. If he hasn't done anything wrong, then what is the problem?"

Opening my eyes, I stare up at my white ceiling, the outdated textured pattern the previous tenant left blurring with wetness.

"Jen?" Kendra gently presses me for more information.

"I … I don't really know what to say." My voice is equally as soft.

"Can I ask you something then?"

I nod my head in an empty room, but despite my best friend not being able to see it, she continues with her question.

"Has something been going on with you two?"

I spent weeks dreading the thought of anyone finding out about me sleeping with Tommy, for fear of how my friends and Holt would react.

Yet, as Kendra finishes up her question, all I feel is more relief.

"I've been sleeping with him."

To my total surprise, Kendra chuckles. "I figured something was going on. You two might hate each other's guts, but you can't deny the insane level of sexual tension between you both."

The relief I was feeling earlier vanishes in an instant. I'm back where I was before—feeling like I'm out on an island when it comes to guys and my friends. How the hell am I supposed to explain that what I have with Tommy feels like more than just sex, even if it was never supposed to be more than a quick fuck to satisfy an itch.

All I know is, I can't let my heart get involved with a boy who is bound to break it.

"Is he good in bed?"

Any response I could potentially form sticks in my throat.

"Jen …" Kendra's voice is back to soft, her concern evident just from the way she says my name.

"I know you think he's a complete asshole," I whisper, finally finding my voice again. "But I think we might have him all wrong."

"Oh shit."

"What?" I reply, thinking her response is unrelated to our conversation.

"Have you caught feelings for him?"

I bolt up to a seated position on the bed, crossing my legs underneath me. "Just because I think he might not be all bad after all doesn't mean I'm falling in love with the guy."

"I never said you were falling for him," she quickly counters.

She's right; she didn't. It's not enough to lower my defenses though.

"You basically insinuated it with what you said." I push a hand through my hair and clear the emotion from my throat. "All I'm saying is, I've spent some time with him away from the hockey rink and other people, and … he isn't the person he makes himself out to be."

Kendra stays quiet, and I swallow thickly.

"Say something," I whisper.

She pulls in a breath and releases it slowly. "I guess it's my turn to not know what to say."

"You think I'm being an idiot, don't you?"

Kendra puffs out another breath, and images of the punch Tommy landed on Holt flash in front of me.

Of course she thinks I'm a fool.

"We've built our friendship on total transparency, right?"

"Yes," I confirm.

"Well, in the spirit of keeping that alive, I'll be really honest with you right now."

It feels like all the oxygen in the room has been sucked out as I fight to inflate my lungs.

"Tommy reminds me of my ex, Tyler. Sure, Tyler was never so explicit with his assholery, but he sure shares a lot of Tommy's characteristics. He's cold and calculating and always looking to gain the upper hand over you. Tyler and Tommy are selfish men who care about only one thing—themselves. Why do you think Tommy is sleeping with you?"

I can sense her question is rhetorical, and I don't reply.

"Because you turned him down last season and now he sees fucking you and fucking with you as interchangeable. This is all a conquest to him. *You* are nothing but a conquest to him. And probably a massive *fuck you* to your brother too." She pauses for a breath and then speaks much lower. "Don't fall for his games, Jen. How many times did you tell me to sack Tyler and find someone I deserved to be with? Countless. So, now, here I am, telling you the exact same thing. You fucked him and scratched that itch. Don't let him get in your head and mess with you. He isn't boyfriend material, but there is a guy out there who would kill to be with y—"

"There's no one out there for me," I bite out. Tears now flow freely down my cheeks. "Trust me when I say, I've looked and held out hope for Mr. Right, who would wrap his arms around me and tell me I was the only girl for him. It's time I faced facts and accepted that I'm going to be on the shelf forever, and that's how I'm trying to live my life—in acceptance. If I continue hoping my dream man will suddenly show up and sweep me off my feet, then I'll just keep on hurting myself over and over."

I can feel my stomach churn as a sob breaks free from my throat.

"Jen, please don't cry," Kendra pleads.

We're not really girls who cry, so when we do, the other knows and feels the pain.

With the corner of my hoodie sleeve, I wipe roughly at my eyes, feeling the material chafe my sensitive skin.

"Do you know how hard it is to watch my friends all get married and have babies? I don't want to sound like that person who isn't happy for her friends because I am and I always will be."

"I know, Jen."

The confession continues to tumble from me in a landslide of emotion.

"But at some point, you have to reach a conclusion where you accept that you aren't desired because you're nothing but undesirable. You start to look in the mirror and think, *What's wrong with me? Where did I go wrong? Is it because I have a resting bitch face, or did I do something in another life that has left me with a big red flag above my head that only the opposite sex can see?* Maybe that's why Lee backed off our relationship —because he could see I wasn't long-term material and there were better options out there for him than me."

"I didn't mean to upset you with what I said." Kendra sounds full of regret and sorrow, and I feel the same emotions too. Deep in the pit of my gut.

Unloading on my friend like this when all she called about was her pregnancy announcement party was unfair and selfish.

"I'm going to come over and see you right now."

I shake my head to no one. "You don't need to do that. Jack will be home soon and hasn't seen you in over a week."

"Doesn't matter," she immediately counters. "I'm going to come over, and we'll eat ourselves silly and watch all the movies you want. You need me tonight, and I need you, friend."

When I pull the phone away from my ear, the final minute on Tommy's window expires, and more regret and sadness overwhelm my senses.

I could really use a friendly face tonight.

"Okay," I eventually reply, uncrossing my legs and drawing my knees toward my chest. "Bring some wine too."

TWENTY-FIVE

JENNA

"I'm sorry, but nonalcoholic wine is gross and totally counterintuitive if you ask me."

After my meltdown earlier, I'm trying to be as upbeat as possible since I don't want Kendra to harbor any guilt for what she said to me over the phone.

Swirling the clear, gross liquid around in my glass, I set it down on the coffee table in front of me and kick my feet up to rest them next to my drink.

In all honesty, Kendra is probably right about Tommy. Not that he's as bad as Tyler—not many people are as callous and cruel as he is. However, she was right when she said that Tommy wasn't boyfriend material. Although it's not like I ever thought he would be.

"Can I ask you something?" Kendra holds a hand out in front of her as she sits beside me on the couch. Dressed in one of Jack's Blades sweaters and blue jeans, you'd never know she was pregnant, aside from her rosy cheeks and thicker hair. "And please don't answer if you're not comfortable talking about it again."

I roll my lips together and nod once.

"What did you want to get out of sleeping with Tommy?"

It's a great question and one I know I'll struggle to answer.

Picking up my fake wine, I take a small sip and slide the glass back onto the table.

"I think you hit the nail on the head when you said it was a fuck to scratch an itch. He wanted me and wouldn't let it drop because he knew I wanted him too."

My friend tips her head to the side as she studies me. "How many times did you sleep together?"

"Twice."

She seems surprised by that.

"What?" I ask.

She just shrugs. "With the way you were talking about him on the phone, I figured you'd met up way more than that."

I side-eye her. "We did a lot of talking, and that night when we won the shield …" I trail off, wanting to explain what happened and how Tommy stepped in, but I'm struggling to find the right words to essentially tell my friend that I was about to be assaulted—or that it was very likely.

"That night we won the shield …" Kendra picks up my sentence, encouragement in her voice.

I'm ready to tell her everything when there's a knock at my front door, and Kendra springs from the couch, already heading to answer it.

"Ah, thank Christ. That'll be the pizza!"

Still thinking over her question about Tommy, I pick up my wine again and knock the rest of it back.

"Umm … what are you doing here?" Kendra's faint voice snags my attention.

If it was the pizza delivery guy standing at my door, I'm pretty sure she wouldn't be questioning why.

"I need to speak with Jenna." A deep voice I'll never mistake has my heart rate kicking up, and I drag my feet off the table and stand, heading straight for my hallway.

Tommy's tall figure looms over Kendra as he stares down at her with annoyed eyes, but as soon as I come into view, he pins all of his attention on me.

I feel like a shy schoolgirl as I lean against my white wall. Dressed in black sweatpants and a white cropped T-shirt with an old stain down the front, I feel anything but glamourous.

"Hey," is all Tommy says, his eyes tracking to the messy bun atop my head.

At least this time, I guess I don't have mascara smeared under my eye.

"Hey," I reply.

Jesus, this is awkward.

When Kendra spins on her heel to face me, I can tell she has already made up her mind to leave. She's barely been here twenty minutes.

"I was just leaving, wasn't I, babe?" she confirms, floating past me and into my open plan living area. "And I'll cancel the pizza, if you like?"

My eyes flick to Tommy's and he smirks knowingly at me.

Caught red-handed.

"Sure, thanks," I absentmindedly reply to Kendra.

Tommy and I remain fixed on each other. The only move he makes is to reach above his head and take a firm grip of the doorjamb.

He looks tense and stressed out and completely at war in his head.

I feel the same.

"What are you doing here?" I ask quietly.

Tommy only smiles, the kind of grin I haven't seen before. It's not cocky or clever. It's more inviting than that. More genuine and warm. "That's exactly what Kendra just asked me. Do you finish each other's sentences too?"

I deadpan as I push off the wall, "I'm not in the mood to play games, Tommy."

Tommy's trademark smirk reemerges just as Kendra does too.

She kisses me once on the cheek. "I'll call you tomorrow, okay?"

I don't know why I feel emotional when she smiles at me sweetly, but I do.

"Yeah, sure," I reply, just as she spins and walks past Tommy on a wave.

As she disappears downstairs, Tommy enters my apartment, closing the door behind him with a click.

"I want to talk to you, Jenna. No games."

I nod my head once when he comes to stand directly in front of me and then loop my arms around my middle.

"What more is there to say, Tommy? The hour window you gave me expired, and I didn't text you back."

He frowns. "Are you being serious?"

I don't know what I'm being.

"You gave me a way out, and I took it." I no doubt sound about as convincing as I look.

Tommy reaches forward, wrapping his hands around my arms to unloop them. He keeps ahold of one of my forearms as I drop them to my sides.

I look down at the connection. "I don't understand why you're here."

He says nothing more and simply guides me into my living space, and we take a seat on my couch.

Tommy cocks a brow at my empty wineglass.

I shrug a quick shoulder and anxiously mess with my hair. Something about this interaction feels different. *He* feels different.

"It was nonalcoholic and actually really gross," I explain, trying to keep the conversation light.

He chuckles at that, shifting a little closer so our thighs are touching. I'm guessing he came straight here from the airport since he's dressed in Blades training gear, although I don't see his bags anywhere. Maybe he drove to my place and left them in his car.

"I'm going to level with you, Jenna." Tommy turns to face me fully, resting his arm along the back of the couch behind me.

He could easily pull me into his body, and I'd happily let him. There's an intensity in his dark eyes tonight, and I conclude that's what feels different about him, along with the softness in his voice.

"Go ahead," I tentatively reply.

Tommy takes his eyes off mine and focuses his attention on the arm currently resting along the couch cushion. He looks deep in thought, and I give him some time to find the right words.

He twists his lips to the side, a small frown creasing his brow. "When you didn't text me back earlier, I was really disappointed because I'd figured you would."

I pull back slightly, irked at his assumption. "Why is everything you do all a game?"

Tommy looks at me then. "What do you mean?"

More annoyance bubbles inside me. "The ultimatum you gave me—it was a test to see if I'd bite and message you back, wasn't it?"

Jesus, Kendra was absolutely right. He just wants to fuck with my head.

Frustrated and irritated with myself, I shift an inch away from him, but Tommy wraps his hand around my forearm again, and I feel the buzz of adrenaline pulse through my body.

"I think you should leave," I say, shrugging off his hand and standing from the couch.

Tommy rises to his full height, towering over me. His cologne is the perfect blend of spice and clean.

My mouth waters with attraction, and I swallow thickly.

He doesn't make to leave as I asked. All he does is stare down into my eyes.

"I want you to leave," I reaffirm, lifting an arm and pointing in the direction of my front door. "Once bitten, twice shy. I won't be a participant in your mind games anymore."

With a clenched jaw, Tommy makes no sign of moving. "We really are the same in so many ways, Hellion."

I shake my head at him, still pointing toward the door. "No, we aren't. Kendra knows we've slept together. She warned me you were just doing it to mess with my head after I turned you down, but I defended you tonight. I told her I could see the good in you, the conflict when you tried to act like the asshole you always are."

I redirect my outstretched arm and press a finger into the center of his sternum. "You say that you're disappointed I didn't text you back? Well, I'm disappointed I was even tempted to reply in the first place." I press my finger even harder into his chest. I know it isn't hurting him, although inflicting physical pain was never my intention. I want him to feel the weight of my words and hear me when I end whatever fucked-up shit we have going on between us.

Right here, right now.

"I'm done with you, Tommy. Finished."

My words slice through the air like a sharp knife through melting butter. And then …

Silence.

Tommy doesn't move or speak.

All I can hear is the traffic below us.

All I can feel is the soft beat of his heart.

All I can smell is the addictive cologne he wears that I'm certain I'll never smell again.

All I can see is goddamn wetness as it coats and blurs my vision.

I drop my gaze and focus on the finger that's still pressed into his body.

"Jenna …"

"Don't say my name," I scold. "I prefer it when you call me Hellion."

"Jenna," he repeats, reaching up to pull my finger away from his chest. He interlaces our fingers, dropping our joined hands down between us.

More tears emerge, and I use my free hand to swipe at them.

"I'm not playing games, Jenna." Tommy's rough thumb wipes under my eye, pausing over my beauty spot.

I'm powerless to stop myself from looking at him. While he isn't crying, I see so much emotion in his gaze. So much concern.

"Stop calling me Jenna." I try one more time to regain some control.

Dropping his head down, he rests his forehead against mine, and I squeeze my eyes shut.

"I swear to God, Tommy, if you're fucking with me and you're about to burst out laughing and leave, I'll … I'll …"

"You'll what?" He releases a slow, easy breath, which fans my face. "Call the police? Have me locked up for emotional manipulation? Or will you demand I buy you a whole new wardrobe this time?"

I'm tempted to laugh at the memory of me haphazardly adding Lululemon leggings into his shopping cart. Instead, I draw my bottom lip between my teeth and bite down hard.

"Because I will if that's what it takes. I'll empty my accounts and serve a lifetime behind bars."

Butterflies shimmer down my spine. "If that's what it takes to what?" My voice is weak when he hooks his pointer finger under my chin, tipping my mouth up to his.

How I'm still standing is a mystery that will likely never be solved. Bones aren't supposed to melt like this and still function.

Our mouths have never been this close as we swallow down each other's exhales.

Tommy wets his lips, and I watch the column of his throat work.

"If that's what it takes to spend one more night with you. Give me tonight, and I'll prove why you were right to let me stay. I'll prove that your instincts were right when you stopped me from walking away that night I punched Ethan."

He edges even closer to my mouth until we're practically kissing.

"I'll prove why you were right to defend me to Kendra and why, despite the way I want to hold you at arm's length and recount the times you turned me down, I'll never be able to stop coming back to you. We aren't enemies, Hellion. We're fucking magnets."

We eyeball each other. A final standoff of wills.

"I'm waiting for you to tell me *cobra* again," I whisper.

He just shakes his head on a smile that I feel against my own mouth. "Not a motherfucking chance."

And then … he's kissing me.

It's everything I expected and knew he was capable of as our tongues collide with reckless abandon. I can't be sure whose whimpers fill the room as we explore each other's mouths for the first time.

I don't know when he last kissed a woman. It could be weeks, months, or even years. Still, I'd never be able to tell since he's so perfect at it, so brutal yet so precise with the way he massages his tongue against mine.

I'm so caught up in him, in his kiss, that I don't notice when he releases my hair until it's hanging around my shoulders.

Tommy unlaces his fingers from mine, cupping the sides of my face between his warm palms.

He breaks from the kiss, and I'm already desperate for more. I want him everywhere.

"Can I stay tonight, Jenna? Give me a chance to prove that your instincts were right about me."

He asks the question like I still might be having doubts. I don't care if he's the greatest con artist to ever walk the earth. *No one* can fake a kiss like that.

Blood pumps through my body, fire singeing every nerve ending.

"And what happens after tonight?" I ask between ragged breaths.

Tommy brushes his thumbs underneath my eyes, setting a kiss against my forehead. "That's entirely your call. No one hour windows and no pressure. You give me tonight, and in return, I'll give you space to decide if you want me to remain in your life."

TWENTY-SIX

TOMMY

M y arms tremble as I carry Jenna into her bedroom and kick the door shut behind us. She has her legs wrapped around my waist and her mouth clamped firmly against my own.

I was nervous to kiss her and not just because of fear that she could reject me. I can't remember the last time I kissed a girl, and that's the God's honest truth. With sex, I'm confident of my abilities, but with kissing, I've genuinely no idea if I'm any good.

Jenna has always teased me for being younger, and the last thing I wanted was to show myself up as inexperienced.

Truthfully, tonight, I haven't got a fucking clue what I'm doing. I might as well be marooned on a desert island with no map or supplies. I'm completely out of my depth. Still, there was no chance that I was driving straight home from the airport. I'd never gotten through security faster and never made a twenty-five-minute car ride in fifteen minutes either.

I wasn't lying when I said that I expected her to text me back. I'd felt sure the day I left for our away series that she was feeling the kinds of feelings that I was. A kind of attraction that runs way deeper than lust.

For the final hour of our return flight home, all I could think about was Jenna getting all dressed up to go out with her girl-friends, only to end up in another dude's bed. I knew she'd be tempted to go searching for affection in an empty hookup because we're the same. It's what I've always done with women. If I'm going through shit in my head, I'm more likely to bag a girl and bring her back to my place for some fun.

Jenna might act like the playgirl—easygoing and not after commitment. That's not who she is though, and I can see that in her eyes. I can feel it in the way she kisses me back.

When she appeared at the end of her hallway tonight, I couldn't miss the redness around her eyes. She'd been crying, and I guessed that was why Kendra had come over to keep her company.

I fucking hated to see her upset, but realizing that my worst nightmare of her sleeping with another man hadn't come true, and instead, she was curled up on the sofa with fake wine, only spurred me to push the boundaries and refuse to leave her place when she repeatedly asked me to go.

This girl might think that *I'm* the one playing games, but right now, the only one fooling themselves is her. She wanted to text me back, and I honestly thought I could walk away if she didn't.

I was wrong.

I can't walk away; I could barely spend eight nights before I lost my goddamn mind over who she might be jumping into bed with, letting them touch her body. The only hands that should be on her skin are mine.

Laying her on the bed beneath me, I swipe a pile of folded clothes on the floor and crawl over her body, caging her in with my arms. We're both fully dressed, but that's okay. I've got way more I want to prove to her tonight than just how well I can fuck her.

I don't know what we are to each other, and frankly, defining us isn't my priority. Jenna Miller needs to see the real me. The person I buried so many years ago that I'm struggling to remember what he looks like. I know she can see him behind the bravado, and I know I'll lose her forever if I don't at least try and reconnect with who I was before I "lost" my parents.

"What's happening in here, Tommy?" Jenna taps my temple softly.

Fuck me, she's beautiful like this. No makeup, pieces of dark hair scattered around her face. It would be so easy to kiss her again and then fuck her raw until the sun rises and I have to show up for practice. But avoiding her question would get us nowhere, and I'm tired of being an asshole to this girl. I know she doesn't deserve it. She had every right to hate me for what I did to her brother, although I can't say that entitlement stretched to me hating on her too. Jenna was right to turn me down last season. She valued her self-worth and didn't want to get caught up with the Blades bad boy, who only looked at her like a piece of ass he couldn't wait to conquer.

I squeeze my eyes shut at the memories, along with the recollection of what Sawyer said to me on the bench the other day. He spoke a lot of truths I couldn't deny. Or at least maybe didn't want to anymore. Especially not to the girl patiently waiting on me for an answer.

My voice is thick and hoarse, almost gravelly, when I reply, "So much, Jenna. I wish I could lay it all out for you in a few short sentences."

She presses her head into the duvet as her eyes analyze my face. "Why do you need to summarize your thoughts so succinctly? I've got the time to listen."

I can feel the coil of tension as it twists and contorts in my stomach. How the fuck am I supposed to open up to someone after years of hiding beneath layers of bullshit?

"I'm lonely too." Jenna's whispered confession is the hardest punch I've ever taken, and her words hang between us, unrequited as they wait for me to add my own.

As I open my mouth, I'm unsure if I'll speak or puke, my stomach contracting, to the point of pain.

"But you have friends and family," I tell her, twirling a piece of her hair around one of my fingers.

Jenna shrugs a shoulder. "Just because I don't look lonely doesn't mean I'm not."

"And just because I pretend I don't care about anything doesn't mean I don't," I whisper back, appreciating how smooth her hair is against the rough pads of my fingers.

"Tell me something you care about, Tommy," Jenna says, draping one arm over my shoulder so she can run her fingertips along the shaved hairline at the nape of my neck.

The sensation feels soothing, and instinctively, my eyelids flutter closed.

"I care about being wanted." My arms tremble again as I hold my weight above the girl who seems to have mastered the art of infiltration, pulling me apart from the inside out. "And I care about what certain people think of me."

Jenna moves her hand up the back of my head, gently stroking her fingers through my longer hair. "Like whom?"

I'm back to feeling nauseous, fighting the urge to get up and run while I still can. Something stronger keeps me here though, pinned to her mattress with my eyes fixated on her blue irises. "My teammates and coach," I reply, swallowing past the lump in my throat. "My mom."

Dropping my head down, I brush my lips across her mouth. "You."

Jenna's breath catches in her throat, but she doesn't say anything in response.

"I don't want you to hate me, Jenna."

She shakes her head. "I mean, I did. But I don't anymore.

I'm mixed up over how I feel about you, but I definitely don't hate you, Tommy."

I know she's confused over me. Who wouldn't be after the way I've acted?

"I shouldn't have punched your brother, and for that, I'm sorry. He was defending your honor, and for what it's worth, I'd have done the same if I had a sister."

Jenna rolls her lips together, nodding her head once in acknowledgment. I've got zero idea what happens after tonight, but whatever transpires between us, it feels good to get that out in the open. Being a good person feels good.

"No, you're right. He didn't deserve it," Jenna confirms on a sly smile. "And right after we left the bar and went back to my place that night, Holt told me never to go within a hundred feet of you again." She laughs darkly. "As you can tell, I always listen to my brother."

I smile down at her. "Holt would fucking murder me if he knew what I planned to do with his sister tonight."

I don't know if it's my imagination playing tricks, but I swear to God I feel her body radiate heat from beneath me.

"What do you have in mind? Taking my ass and making me scream so he can hear over in France?" She laughs nervously.

I pause for just a second before I shake my head and run my thumb across her plump bottom lip. "No, Jenna. That's not what I want to do with you tonight."

Pushing off the bed, I stand in front of her and undress until I'm fully naked.

Jenna lifts her hips up, and I peel her sweats down her legs, taking her soaked thong along with them.

She sits up and removes her T-shirt and then unclips her bra and tosses them both on the heap of clothes beside my feet.

We're both bare and silent.

Comfortable to observe and absorb the shifting dynamic between us.

Taking my cock into my left hand, I pump myself a couple of times, the tip instantly shining with hot arousal.

God, I want her so badly.

Jenna's about to flip onto her hands and knees for me when I stop her with a firm hand on her upper thigh.

"No. I don't want you like that tonight."

She pauses, and I crawl back over her sweet body.

"I told you I want to prove myself to you, and that's what I'm going to do."

TWENTY-SEVEN

JENNA

Tommy tracks my movements as I drag my body into the center of my king-size bed.

"Are you trying to escape?" he teases, smiling down from where he's hovering above me, braced on one elbow and gripping his thick cock in the other hand.

Even if I wanted to run, I couldn't, and it has nothing to do with the way he has me boxed in. I'm practically paralyzed, every muscle liquefying each time his eyes burn into me.

"I'm used to you being a brutal asshole." I cast my eyes down to where he's slowly pumping himself between my legs, pre-cum leaking from his dick and onto my duvet.

Tommy strokes himself again, spreading his palm over the head this time. I can tell it feels good when he does it, his blown pupils only growing wider.

"What kind of sex do you like, Jenna?"

His simple question pools in my core, and I spread my thighs wider.

Tommy takes advantage, settling down between them. One thrust of his pelvis, and he'll enter me with ease.

"If you could design the perfect night with a guy, what would it look like?"

My body might be on fire, but my cheeks still flush hotter. I don't need to think about the answer to that question since I've fantasized about Mr. Right so often that I could write a full-blown novel about him. Regardless, admitting to a boy—especially one I've hated for so long—about my true desires in bed feels like I'm stepping into a whole new vulnerable world with him.

Tommy notches himself at my dripping entrance.

"Let me tell you what I think you want from a guy." He pushes just the head inside me and pauses on a steadying breath. "I think you want your man to throw you around the bedroom on occasion, but take it slow with you on the daily."

Tommy's tattooed hand ascends my upper thigh, wrapping around my hip. I'm not petite, but his handspan dwarfs every part of my body, and I love the dominant way it feels.

He pushes inside another inch, and I spread wider, partly to accommodate his size and partly because I'm powerless to resist his advances.

I can't be sure where I am in the maze that is Tommy Schneider, although I'm not looking for the exit.

"You want a boyfriend who will mark your body and claim you as his in private and then wrap his arms around your waist for everyone to witness."

When he pushes another inch inside, overwhelm slams into me like a ten-ton truck.

Tommy observes the flush of crimson that spreads from my cheeks all the way down to my chest.

"I'm right, aren't I?" His smile is cocky, voice self-assured.

I wish I had the fight to deny him like I have so many times before. It would be safer to lie and tell him that he's way off the mark.

I spread my thighs wider, and his smile turns warm.

"Good fucking girl."

Now fully seated inside my pussy, Tommy swallows thickly as he shifts his hand from my hip and takes his full weight on both forearms.

"Reach down and feel us," he commands, dipping his chin to where we're joined.

I slide a hand between our bodies, and my duvet is soaked from us both.

Tommy pulls out slightly, and I smooth my fingers along his slick shaft, trailing a course toward his balls. They're coiled so tight; I've no idea how he hasn't blown already.

"Is that why you aren't moving?" I ask.

He closes his eyes on a headshake, lips trembling with amusement. "You think I'm going to blow my load before I've even started?" He opens his eyes and looks straight at me. They're almost black. "You'd never let me live it down."

I massage his balls in my palm, using my own release to intensify his pleasure.

Tommy groans into my darkened bedroom, unable to stop himself from pushing all the way back inside.

"You might think you have me all worked out …" I whisper from beneath him, now massaging his dick each time he pulls out on slow strokes.

Tommy drops his head into the crook of my neck, setting open-mouthed kisses along my collarbone.

I can barely form words, but I'm determined to have my say too.

"And maybe you do know me better than I first gave you credit for." My fingers are dripping and only getting wetter each time Tommy slides out of me. "But I'm certain that I know what you want too."

"Tell me," Tommy rasps against my sensitive flesh, sucking hard just below my ear.

I push through the pain, more desperate to let him mark me than I am to pull away from the sting.

"I think you want a girl you can leave in your bed at the ass crack of dawn and race home so you can climb back under the sheets with her after morning skate."

Tommy hums against my neck, moving steadily toward my pulse point. "Keep going, Hellion."

When he slides a hand under my pelvis, tilting it to hit a different spot, I gush all over us both.

"I'm going to come," I whisper.

"I said, keep going," he repeats, continuing to mark my throat.

Another stroke, and I climax, gripping his dick within my walls.

"Tell me what else I want, Jenna. Please." Tommy's voice is a plea, desperate for me to speak, while he fights back his own high so he can hear the words.

It feels like we can only be honest while he fucks me in this way. Like being this vulnerable with our bodies has somehow opened the gateway to the truths we're longing to share.

This, right here, is two people being transparent after years of closure, and it's scary as fuck for us both.

"Jenna," Tommy bites out, growing impatient with my silence. "Please, keep going."

When I squeeze his balls softly, he whimpers and moves his lips to my mouth.

"If you don't level with me in the next thirty seconds, I'll never fuck you like this again," he threatens on a smile that reveals the lie lurking behind his statement.

I smile back and squeeze him again. "You really care what I think about you, don't you?"

He licks into me, gliding his tongue across the roof of my mouth. I shudder at the sensation, which only kicks up the intensity of our sex.

"Look who's playing games now," he teases.

"I think …" I release his balls and trail my pointer finger toward his ass, stopping when Tommy pulls back from my mouth, eyes wide with lust.

I wait for him to give me the safe word, although it doesn't arrive.

Pressing my slick finger against his tight hole, I edge only a centimeter inside him. It's enough to shoot blood to his dick, and he grows even harder inside me.

With my other hand, I palm the back of his head and bring his mouth back down to mine.

"I think you like to play with a girl's ass, but really, your ultimate fantasy is to be dominated." I slide another centimeter inside, and Tommy moans into my mouth.

"Trouble is," I continue, "you've never found anyone who could work that out." I slide my finger out and then press back in a little further.

Tommy spreads his knees for me on a guttural groan, and I come all over his dick.

"Finger my ass while I fuck you, Jenna."

Tommy begins moving faster inside me, and I gently return the favor.

"Has anyone ever done this to you before?" I ask.

He shakes his head, our teeth clashing on a frenzied kiss. "No. Only you. I would only ever let you do this to me."

Slowly, I move deeper. I'd love to tell him that this is a first for me, too, but … playgirl, I guess. It's true that I've never had anal sex before Tommy since I never felt the desire to let them take my ass, but I have slept with some kinky guys.

I push further inside him, and it doesn't take me long to find the walnut-shaped gland I know will blow his mind.

Tommy stiffens above me when I circle his prostate.

I palm his left cheek and look him straight in the eyes when I see, for the very first time, the real Tommy. Pure vulnerability reflects back as he fights with himself—two personalities warring to break free.

"It's okay; I got you," I tell him. "Give me the real Tommy and let the other go."

He presses his forehead into mine, scrunching his eyes tightly. "I swear to God, if you break me, Jenna …"

We both know that he isn't talking about physical pain.

"I have zero agenda with you." I attempt to soothe his anxiety. "But I do need you to relax for me."

Tommy's shoulders drop an inch.

"More," I tell him, swiping my thumb under his left eye, like he does so often with me.

He studies my face for a beat and then exhales a long breath that uncoils every muscle in his body.

"Atta boy," I praise, circling his prostate once more.

Tommy seals his mouth over mine, now framing my face with both hands.

On every thrust of his pelvis and stroke of my finger, he whimpers a different pleasure-filled statement. "Goddammit, Jenna. What the fuck are you doing to me?"

I come again, and Tommy reaches down and hooks my right leg into the crook of his elbow. We aren't fucking any longer, and we both know it too.

"Helping you prove what you promised to me. You're showing me the real you."

"And it feels so fucking good," he rasps. "*You* feel so fucking good."

"Do you want me to make you come now?" I ask, soaking up my control.

Tommy nods once. "What does it feel like—to come like this?"

I laugh into his mouth. "I'm not a dude. I wouldn't know. It might knock you out for the night though."

"Do it," he commands. "Show me."

I move my finger in a downward motion and then revert to a circular stroke.

"Fuuuuck." He tosses his head toward the ceiling. "I ... I can feel two orgasms building."

He thrusts into my pussy so hard that I shift up the bed.

"Hand yourself over, Tommy."

He spreads his knees wider, and I massage him, pulling out briefly to gather our joint arousal before I'm diving back inside.

"Jenna." He calls my name, and, Jesus Christ, that sounds fucking good.

"Jenna," he repeats, shaking his head with pupils so wide that his eyes are fully black now. "I'm coming so fucking hard, Jenna. Y-you're amazing."

I feel his ass contract around my finger, and a second later, Tommy spills his hot cum deep inside my pussy.

I don't think I'd be human if I didn't come at the sight of this brutish, tattooed guy falling apart under my touch.

"Me too," I softly reply. "All over your huge cock."

Tommy's body is wired with pleasure, shaking and shuddering above me. It's the best sex of my life—and undoubtedly, his too. It's us both stepping over into a world we didn't think we were capable of entering.

It's ... perfection.

When he's emptied everything he has, Tommy drops his head against my chest, still holding himself on one arm so he doesn't crush me.

He's fighting to stay awake, and I stroke the tiny hairs at the nape of his neck.

"Thank you ..." he slurs, raising his head so he can watch me.

He looks like he did that time in the seedy bar. But this time, he's drunk for an entirely different reason.

"For what?" I ask him, feeling his release leak out of me.

Tommy pulls out and then reaches down between us, gathering his cum and pushing it back inside my pussy.

He exhales a slow, satiated breath and kisses between my breasts. "For giving me this chance and letting me stay with you tonight."

TWENTY-EIGHT

JENNA

I might be a pro athlete who works out almost daily, but that doesn't prevent the full-body aches that hit me when I stir from a deep sleep and roll onto my back.

Tommy and I went at it all night, and it was ... mind-blowing. I'd never had so much sex, and I'd never ... been fucked in the kinds of positions he took me in. The man is a machine in bed, and I'm not mad about it, not one damn bit.

There isn't a single second about last night that I'd change, although there are unanswered questions I want to ask him this morning. Like the brief reference he made to his mom and the comment about his coach and teammates. I know, deep down, Tommy cares about what they think, and I want to help him earn the respect I know he deserves from the rest of the team.

He earned so much from me last night.

"Tommy," I whisper into my dark bedroom, the blackout blinds I installed a few months back keeping out the rising sun. "I think you might've actually broken me." I chuckle, draping an arm across the other side of my bed.

I'm only met with a soft duvet, and I immediately bolt up, still naked with marks littered across my breasts. I know there are more along my neckline—I can feel the faint sting of them, even now.

There's no light filtering in from under my bedroom door and no sound or movement coming from the rest of my apartment.

Did he have early morning skate and didn't tell me?

Perhaps he wrote a note before he left.

Pushing back the duvet, I slip into an oversize Storm training top and shove my feet into my fluffy white slippers, the chilly fall air now evident in my old apartment building, which doesn't have the greatest furnace.

When I pull my bedroom door open, there's no sign of life when I flick on the main light in my living space, and everything is just as we left it when Tommy carried me into my bedroom.

Did I dream this entire thing?

I turn on my heel and head for my phone, ready to text him and check I'm not going crazy when a message from Kendra lights up the screen.

KENDRA

> This is your reminder to use protection. That boy looked like you were his last meal, and I get the slightest inclination that you plan to go at it all night.

> Seriously though, babe, he actually shocked me tonight. Maybe you were right when you said that he isn't the bad person we thought he was. Turning up at your place and wanting to talk things out? That's not the Tommy Schneider I thought I knew …

Both her messages were sent last night.

He really was here, and we really did go at it all night if I didn't check my phone once.

Taking a seat at the foot of my bed, I wince at the dull ache between my legs. Under different circumstances and if he were still here, I'd definitely welcome the reminder of how hard we fucked, but I can't deny the cloud of dread as it settles above me.

The first call I make to Tommy immediately connects with his voicemail, and I hang up, more unease washing a wave through my gut.

He promised he'd prove he was different. Was it all just a play so he could fuck me all night and then toss me in the trash, like he'd once said?

Holding my cell in one hand, I bring the other to the side of my neck and then stand in front of my dresser mirror, the light from my living space enough to reveal the marks he made.

Humiliation rips through me, and I hit Call on his number again, anticipating that all I'll get is his voicemail.

This time, his phone rings, and I hold my breath, praying he'll pick up and explain he snuck out to grab us some breakfast.

His voice never comes, only the same recorded message to leave my name and number.

Now, I'm pissed. Convinced he's definitely fucked me over.

As the woman continues talking, I wait for the beep so I can give him a piece of my mind. None of this makes any sense—the way he kissed me, looked at me, opened up and lowered his walls to let me in.

Last night felt so genuine.

"Tommy ..." I finally begin speaking, my voice a mixture of pained and agitated. "I woke up around five minutes ago, but you aren't here, and you didn't leave a note. I don't know ..." I trail off, struggling to find the right words. I swallow hard and sit back down on my bed. "I don't know what's happened or if you planned to just do what we did and then leave without a word, but if you did, just know that's a really shitty move." My voice cracks, and I pinch my bare thigh. Hard. "If all of last night was a game after all, then you can be sure that this is the last time you'll hear my voice. But if something happened and you need my help, then just please, call me back, okay?"

"HELLO?" I RASP INTO MY PHONE, HITTING STOP ON THE treadmill and pulling in a deep breath.

After I waited around for an hour for Tommy to call or text me back, I gave up and came to the gym.

We have a playoff game tomorrow, and technically, I shouldn't be working my body this hard, but I needed to blow off steam, and this was the only way I could get out of my own head.

"Jen, why are you answering your phone all out of breath?" Holt's cringe-loaded voice replies.

With the treadmill belt now completely stopped, I take the pace up to a slow walk and connect the call to my earbuds, beginning a cooldown while I speak to my brother.

"I promise you I'm not getting it on," I tell him, earning a side-eye from a woman a couple of treadmills down from me. "I'm at the gym, on the treadmill."

"Thank Christ," Holt replies and then pauses. "Wait, you're working out with a big playoff game tomorrow? Shouldn't you be keeping things light today?"

A lump sticks in my throat. For my entire life, the only man who has shown up repeatedly and ever given a shit about my welfare is my brother. When I'm this upset, I don't usually answer his calls, for fear of making him worry. I should've checked who was calling before I picked up my phone.

"What's the matter?" he presses, and I know he isn't going to let this drop.

Giving up on my cooldown, I pray that the buildup of lactic acid isn't too bad tomorrow and grab my towel and water bottle from the holder.

"I don't even know where to begin," I tell him, pushing into the women's changing room, which is, mercifully, empty.

"I always find the best place to start is at the beginning." He chuckles, and I hear a chair scrape along the floor.

"Where are you?" I ask.

"At home."

I shake my head and take a seat on the bench. "But you don't have any hard floors at your place."

"We were talking about you, Jenna." Holt brushes my observation off, and my mind wanders to last night.

The safest option would be to tell my brother about what happened with Tommy but replace his name with a random guy's. I'm done with trying to defend Tommy though; he deserves to be ousted for the bullshit he pulled.

Setting my towel, phone, and bottle down on the bench, I begin unlacing my sneakers.

"I need you to promise me that you won't go crazy when I tell you."

A deep rumble vibrates down the line. "How about I save you the trouble and go ahead and tell you what I think has been going on?"

Blood drains from my face, and I sit up straight on the bench. "Okay."

I hear Holt shift and take a sip of a drink before he continues, "If I said the name Tommy Schneider, would I be along the right lines?"

I'm pacing the changing room before I can register what I'm doing.

"Perhaps."

Another rumble, but this one is louder.

"What's going on, Jen? I got the impression you were keeping something from me the night you won the shield, but I didn't push it since, despite being your brother, your love life is none of my business." He clears his throat, voice turning deathly serious. "But if there's one thing I can't fucking stand, it's men who treat women badly. And judging by the tone in your voice and the fact that you're kicking the shit out of yourself on the cardio machines, I'm guessing Tommy has been about as good to you as I predicted."

I drop my head between my shoulders, determined not to cry. Tommy doesn't deserve my tears.

"We've been sleeping together," I confirm.

Holt blows out a long, hard breath. "Keep going."

Images of last night—Tommy's smile and the way he held me as we fell asleep—flash through my mind in a carousel of heartache.

"At first, we were messing around. Hooking up to scratch an itch, you know?" I bite down on my bottom lip.

My brother doesn't know what I mean because he only sleeps with girls he's dating.

And right now, that seems like the smartest approach.

"The sex didn't mean anything, and I spent most of my time frustrated at myself for letting him in my bed. Then ..." I walk back over to the bench and dump myself down.

"Then it wasn't just for fun anymore?" Holt's soft voice asks.

I shake my head to no one. "No, it wasn't. Or at least it wasn't for me anyway. I started to see a different side to him, and Tommy started to chase me. He turned up at my apartment last night after I basically decided, for the final time, that I couldn't keep sleeping with him." My heart sinks an inch in my chest.

"Anyway," I continue, "last night, he told me some stuff, and like the idiot I am, I believed him when he said he wasn't the asshole everyone thought he was. We shared a night, which was ..." I scuff the floor with my sneaker, tears falling to the ends of my lashes. "It was the kind of night I'd never thought I'd have with a guy. It felt like we were ..." My voice fails when I try to finish my sentence.

There's a stretch of silence, one we both need to gather our thoughts.

"This morning, I woke up, and he was gone," I continue. "No note, no phone call or text. And what's worse, he isn't answering mine."

A sob splutters out of me just as the same woman on the treadmill pushes through the door before she registers me crying and turns on her heel.

The door slams behind her, leaving me alone again.

"I'm going to fucking murder him." Holt's voice reminds me of Tommy's when he pinned Ethan against the wall outside my apartment.

Panic floods my insides. "No." I shake my head. "This is my fault. You, Kendra, Darcy, Collins—you all told me to keep away from him. I didn't listen, and I have to deal with the consequences of that now."

Not bothering to shower, I shove my used towel down the laundry chute and grab my bottle, phone, and bag, throwing it over one shoulder.

"You don't need to murder him because I've finally woken up and I'm never going to go there again. I told him on voicemail this morning that he'd never hear my voice after I hung up, and he won't."

When I reach the changing room door, I grip the handle so tight that my knuckles turn white. A small part of me hates myself for thinking this, but it's time I faced facts and woke up to everyone else's reality. The Jenna from last season was right, as were her instincts to turn Tommy down the first time.

"He's just like his dad, Holt. Only worse."

TWENTY-NINE

TOMMY

"Yeah, seven at our place. Kendra and I are going to cook for everyone, so make sure you bring empty stomachs and nothing else."

Stepping into the locker room before practice, I ignore the conversation going on between Jack, Sawyer, Emmett and Archer and head straight for my bench, dumping my kit bag down with a thud.

"Why do I get the feeling there's a surprise lined up for us on Saturday night?" I hear Archer ask.

"I'll be there, but I'll be alone," Emmett adds, wincing and scratching at the back of his neck. "And probably not for the whole night. I'm sorry."

I turn my back to the rest of the room and begin stripping down to my underwear.

"Holy SHIT."

Jack's raised voice causes me to partially turn around to face him, although I wish I hadn't since he's standing there, pointing at me. Jaw agape, eyes bugged out.

Archer's, Sawyer's and Emmett's expressions aren't any

different, and as I scan the rest of the locker room, I realize I have the attention of most of the guys.

Archer reaches behind him, pointing to his back. "Jesus Christ, Tommy. Did you have a fight with a bear last night?"

Jack snickers from beside him, edging closer to get a better look. His lips tip up when he registers the marks. "That's no bear, Archer. They're fingernail tracks."

"Holy HELL," Emmett declares, stepping forward to get a better view.

Turning back to face my bench fully, I snatch up my Dri-FIT top and pull it overhead.

"I mean, I thought Sawyer was into kinky shit … but … fucking wow." My captain continues talking, much to my annoyance.

With my top half now covered so they can't see the marks Jenna left on my torso, I take a step toward my teammates, offering a glare to all those eavesdropping. They get back to their own conversations.

"How about you mind your own business?" I tell all four of them, centering my attention mainly on Jack and Archer.

Sawyer shifts closer to me, placing a palm on my shoulder.

I fight the urge to shrug it off and cross my arms instead.

"Just ignore these three." He thumbs to his teammates. "They'll do anything to get under a guy's skin."

"That's what she said." Archer snickers, causing Emmett and Jack to fall about laughing.

On a raised brow, I look between them, quietly waiting for them to get it the fuck together.

"You act like you're a virgin who just got out of college," I tell Jack when he finally stops laughing. "Hardly captain behavior."

At this point, I'm out to rile him up. Jack Morgan is captaincy material through and through, and we all know it. Even if I don't want to admit it out loud.

I tip my chin at Archer. "And you need my ass for shutouts, so how about showing me a little respect?"

He scoffs at that. "Respect? You haven't shown an ounce of that since you got traded here last season."

Emmett hums his agreement, and I throw him a look.

Respect.

Something I failed to show Jenna when I snuck out of her apartment at five a.m.

I know I've fucked up. Big time.

When Jenna fell asleep in the early hours, I desperately wanted to stay with her, wake up, and then take her for breakfast at Rise Up—the café where we randomly bumped into each other that time. That's what I should've done, and I know it. Instead, I freaked the fuck out and snuck out of her bed, grabbing my clothes, phone, wallet, and keys on the way.

And when she called me and I listened to her voicemail? I didn't know what to say. She's right; it was a shitty move. But something tells me that my inner fear of getting close to another human being isn't going to wash with her.

Jenna deserves a man who will go all in, with zero fear of getting hurt. She doesn't want or need a guy who can't push past his own rejection issues and tell her what he truly wants. I promised that I'd prove myself to her, and I've gone ahead and done exactly that.

I'm an asshole who knows that he doesn't deserve her.

My teammates might be pointing to the scratches she left on my back, but in truth, they could never see her deepest marks.

I've got feelings for Jenna Miller. And I haven't got a fucking clue what to do with them.

Archer is still waiting on my response when I turn back to my bench and continue getting ready for practice. I'm done with games and trying to gain the upper hand in verbal duals.

It's fucking exhausting.

"Tommy ..." Sawyer's calming voice filters over my shoulder.

I can sense he's standing directly behind me, although I ignore him.

"Slow down, buddy. You're going to damage something, ripping at your pads like that." He rests another palm on my shoulder, trying to steady my temper as I continue getting ready.

He probably thinks I'm mad at my teammates. He's wrong. I'm only mad at myself.

"They weren't trying to humiliate you." Sawyer continues talking.

On a deep exhale, I spin around to face him, half dressed for practice. "I couldn't care less what they think," I lie, taking another metaphorical punch to the gut in the process. I told Jenna who I cared about, and that definitely included my teammates.

Sawyer's brows knit together; he's not buying a word of what I say.

I cast a quick glance around the locker room, which is slowly emptying as the guys head out to the ice.

Ten seconds later, we're practically alone.

Sawyer doesn't bother to move or show any sign of heading for the rink; his attention is locked in on me.

I pick up my training jersey and throw it overhead.

"Which begs the question ..." I lift a brow at my former captain. "Why do you give a shit about me?"

Sawyer props his hands on his hips, kind of how I imagine he would with his teenage son. He's reaching the end of his patience.

"Does your particularly bad mood have to do with the scratches on your back, or were you really in a bear fight?"

Right at that moment, the locker room door opens, and Coach Morgan walks in.

I deflate, knowing being late on the ice won't go over well

when I'm already on a warning. Friday's game is my first one off suspension, and I'm already fucking things up.

Although the look on Coach's face isn't mad; it's more empathetic.

"Bryce"—Coach thumbs over his shoulder toward the door he just came through—"can you give me a second with Schneider?"

Like the perfect team player Sawyer is, he nods once and drops his hand from my shoulder, exiting and leaving me and Coach on opposite sides of the room.

Coach blows out a long breath and sets his iPad down on an empty section of the bench. He takes a seat next to it and rests his elbows on his knees.

He looks torn up over his thoughts—or maybe whatever is about to leave his mouth next.

An icy-cold trickle chases a path down my spine.

Coach points to my section of the bench, lifting his gaze to look at me. There's only sincerity in his eyes, and that kicks up my trepidation.

"Take a seat, Tommy. My staff is running the first part of practice so I can speak with you."

I do as he asked and wait for Coach to elaborate. Whatever he's about to say can't be good. Coach rarely hands practice over to his team—and only under serious circumstances.

"I swear I arrived on time for practice, Coach." I begin talking, the nervous silence proving too much for me to take. I need my place on the team, and I'll be goddamned if I lose it because I got held up, talking in the locker room.

He shakes his head, running a palm over the scruff of his jaw. "It isn't to do with practice."

My mouth runs dry. "What is this about?" I ask, mentally cycling through the events of my life the past few days.

Jenna.

Fuck. Did something happen to her?

Coach twists his hands together in front of him. "Does the name Ethan Hadley sound familiar to you?"

At first, the name means nothing to me … and then … my eyes grow wide as I take in Coach's concerned gaze.

He takes my expression as confirmation that I've heard of him.

"He's a former semi-pro soccer player with a decent following on social media."

My heart hits the fucking floor.

"Anyway, around a half hour ago, he made a post, claiming you had beaten him up on a night out and included images of his broken and bloody nose. He states that the attack was unprovoked and over an undisclosed girl he was innocently walking home after she drank too much."

If my stick was next to me right now, I'd launch it against a wall since I won't be needing it any longer. My career is as good as fucking over.

Leaning back, I can't help the wry smile as it traces my lips. It's effectively my word against his. I know there isn't any CCTV footage outside Jenna's apartment door—I already checked. No one is going to take my word—one that's already tarnished with a bad rep—over an "innocent" member of the public's. Why Ethan waited until now to post, I have zero idea. Perhaps he was hoping to catch our PR team or my agent off guard. Or maybe he sat in his rage and finally decided he'd go for the jugular.

And there's no way I can expect Jenna to rescue me with the truth; she already hates my guts. Plus, coming forward and speaking out would effectively unearth all that's been going on between us. She wants me to get out of her life, not get more entangled in it.

"Is it true?" Coach's voice is quiet and guarded. He knows my future with the Blades is resting on a knife edge.

I stand from the bench, thrusting a hand through my hair. "No." I quickly deny it and then stop. "Well, kind of."

Coach pushes out a frustrated breath. "Which one is it, Tommy? Yes or fucking no?"

I throw my arms out to the sides. "Neither!" I announce. "What he's reporting happened a while back, and he's twisted the story to make me look like the perpetrator."

Coach stands and walks across to me, both hands propped on his hips. "Our team is trying to get the post taken down, and your agent has been blowing up your phone for the past half hour because right now, you look every bit the guilty party. Why would the guy lie, Tommy?"

I switched my phone off after I listened to Jenna's voicemail.

"I hit him for a good fucking reason," I explain, my voice shaking with rage.

"Why?" Coach presses. "I need more than that from you, Tommy. The GM is ready to put you on waivers."

What strikes me most in all of this is the way Coach Morgan sounds desperate for my alibi, almost like he's pleading with me to give him something plausible. My entire time with the Blades has been a battle with him and his doubts over me as a player. But that's not what I'm witnessing in this moment.

"I thought this would be your perfect excuse to ship me out," I tell him straight, my voice devoid of sarcasm.

Coach looks off to the side and then back at me again, and I'm relieved he isn't provoked by my question. I'm genuinely looking for an answer because I need to know if he really is an ally.

"You might be a first-rate asshole at times, Tommy, but I already told you that you're a gifted player. Plus ..." He trails off, pausing for thought. "Sawyer has asked me to give you a second chance. I don't know what you guys have discussed, and I get that he isn't our captain anymore, but that doesn't mean that I don't respect his opinion."

He steps toward me, close enough so our interaction feels more personal. "I might have retired a few seasons back, but that doesn't mean I've forgotten what it's like to play with the weight of the world resting on your shoulders. I know your place on this team means something to you. And I want you to keep it and make a proper go of your career as a Blades defenseman. If you weren't worth it, Sawyer wouldn't have come to me, and I wouldn't be harboring this gut feeling."

"Gut feeling?" I question.

Coach nods his head once. "That you're ten times the man your dad is."

I drop my head to hide my eyes, blinking rapidly to clear my vision.

"I hit Ethan because he didn't have good intentions with the girl he was walking home. She'd asked him to let go of her, and he didn't." With my emotions under control, I finally lift my head and pin Coach with a look that cannot be misinterpreted. "I know a predator when I see one, and he is the really bad kind. I wanted to make sure he was clear never to come near the girl again, and I thought he'd gotten the message when I told him to straighten out his life."

Coach just stares back at me.

"You have to believe me," I add. "I swear to God, I'm telling the truth."

"And the girl? Who was she?" Coach asks.

My gaze is back on the floor. "I can't say. That's her private business to tell, and I doubt she wants anything to do with me or this situation."

Coach clears his throat. "I can respect that, Tommy. And for what it's worth, I think that's noble of you to keep her confidence."

More emotions sting my senses. "So, what happens now?" I ask.

"Look at me, Tommy."

I shake my head, eyes still fixed on the floor. "Not right now, Coach."

"Tommy," he repeats, only earning another headshake from me.

"I need you to head home while we try and get this PR nightmare under control. Speak with your agent and take some advice. I'll talk with the GM. We have to tread really fucking lightly here; if we accuse Ethan Hadley of lying or, at best, twisting the story, then we could make the situation way worse."

"I can't play, can I?" I ask.

"Tommy …"

"Just"—I hold up a hand, refusing to lift my head—"confirm what I already know. I can't play this Friday, can I?"

Silence descends on the room before Coach finally speaks. "No, Tommy. Right now, the team needs you to stay away."

THIRTY

JENNA

The soccer season has been long and grueling, so I guess if I could find one positive about losing today's playoff game against Milwaukee, it's that my body will finally get a rest.

My mind, on the other hand … well, that's working overtime. To the point where I can't focus on anything other than the voice in my head, telling me to step in and do something.

Tommy's career is all but done if I don't speak up and set the record straight about what happened with Ethan. I can't believe that bastard went back on his word about keeping quiet and spouted so much crap on social media. I was convinced he was lying when he said he once played semi-pro soccer since I'd never heard of an Ethan Hadley, but turns out, he did. And he's using his modest platform to try and bring down a good person.

Only … is Tommy a good person?

He's like the ultimate version of Jekyll and Hyde. One second, he's rescuing me from the clutches of a creep, and the next, he's walking out of my apartment after promising to prove me wrong about who he is.

I'm confused and going back and forth over what to do. Does Tommy even want my help? He's the kind of guy who doesn't thank anyone for coming to his aid. Every battle is his own to fight and win.

Sounds kind of familiar when I think about it …

"So, I ended up flying to the moon, and I got you a key chain from the gift shop." Kendra lowers her voice so only I can hear her.

Collins and Darcy continue to talk about Emily and all the gifts Archer has bought his baby daughter for Christmas. Knowing Archer, I'm sure they could be working through the list for a while.

Half expecting to find the answer to Tommy's predicament in the bottom of my glass, I toss back the rest of my beer and set my empty back on the bar. It's been a while since we went out as a group of girls, and I feel bad for not being as engaged as I should be.

"Does your silence have something to do with Mr. Schneider?" Kendra leans in closer to me, and I rest an elbow on the bar.

Glancing up, I catch Darcy as she studies my expression with concern, and Collins breaks off from talking.

Now sitting in complete silence, I drop my eyes to the floor, wondering why the fuck I chose to wear strappy black sandals in the middle of fall.

"Don't be down, babe. You did an amazing job, winning the shield." Darcy's singsong voice tries—and fails—to lift my mood.

"It doesn't really have to do with the playoffs," I reply, lifting my gaze to my friends. "Or even soccer, to be honest."

Darcy's eyes flick to Kendra, and immediately, I know I can't keep hiding what's going on from them.

"How much have you had to drink?" I ask, pointing at Collins's and Darcy's glasses. I've been so absent tonight; I can't remember if this is their first or fifth drink.

Now looking more concerned, Darcy lifts herself onto a barstool behind her and sets her half-empty cocktail glass down.

"This is our second, but I'm thinking that we should be ordering a third," Collins chimes in, already lifting a finger to distract a bartender's attention.

It's a quiet night in Lloyd's, and I'm grateful for the relaxed atmosphere because I feel anything but.

"I'd say that's a good idea," Kendra agrees, pointing to a Mai Tai on the menu. She knows it's my favorite cocktail.

Collins clears her throat and pulls up a stool next to Darcy. "Okay, hit us with it, Miller."

I turn to look at Kendra as I deliver the bomb. "I've been sleeping with Tommy."

The gasp Darcy releases pulls my attention straight to her and Collins, who looks equally as shocked. I guess Tommy and I really did do a good job of hiding our hookups.

"And the guy who's claiming Tommy hit him in an unprovoked attack ... let's just say, that punch wasn't unwarranted."

Kendra's eyes flare wide since this is news to her too.

"I don't know what question to ask you first." Collins breaks the short silence between our group. "I thought you hated Tommy?"

I nod once and immediately grab my Mai Tai after the bartender sets it down. "I do hate him," I reply, taking a long sip.

"But you're sleeping with him?" Darcy questions. "Are we talking about a hate-fuck arrangement here? Because don't get me wrong; he's hot and everything. But I can't imagine a situation where anyone could like that arsehole."

Something about the way she says that in her refined British accent pulls my lips into a wry smile, as do the memories of Tommy pinning me against several walls. I can still feel the ghost of his full, soft lips as they skated across my collarbone. He is an arsehole—as Darcy put it—but he's one who's left a lasting impression on me.

"Jenna?" Darcy brings me back into the room, and I shake off my trance.

"I …" My throat runs dry, and I take another sip of cocktail. "I don't know what to say." I shrug a shoulder and set down my glass. "And I guess the details don't matter much now anyway since whatever we had is over." The disappointed inflection in my voice is unmissable and completely unintentional too.

Collins sits forward on her stool, rolling her lips together in thought. I can't tell if she's disappointed in me for going there with a guy everyone cannot stand. I guess, to them, there's plenty of other guys I could be sleeping with and none who are dicks to their husbands.

"How long was it going on for?"

"For a while," I reply uneasily. "He was the one who'd instigated it, and I …" I trail off again, struggling to find the right words tonight.

"And you enjoyed every fucking second?" Collins finishes my sentence.

I can't deny that she's a hundred percent correct. The smile and wink she gives tells me she couldn't care less about me getting with Tommy, and I breathe an inward sigh of relief.

"No comment," I volley back, suppressing a smile.

"And what did you mean when you said the punch that Ethan guy took wasn't exactly unwarranted?"

My growing smile flattens in response to Kendra's question.

"I mean, he deserved it," I clarify.

Collins quirks a brow, followed by Darcy.

"Jenna?" Kendra's soft palm wraps around my upper arm. "Jenna? What's the matter?"

As dampness stings my eyes, I bite the inside of my cheek. I wasn't expecting to get emotional, but here we are. Apparently, crying is my new favorite hobby.

"The 'attack' Ethan is talking about online was in defense because Ethan tried to …"

"Tried to *what*?" Collins's voice could cut through solid steel, and I swallow hard.

I inhale a huge breath and allow my brain to go back over a night I would rather forget. "So, this guy, Ethan, was walking me home because I had gotten really drunk the night we won the shield." I turn to look at Kendra, anticipating that she'll connect the dots since she was there too.

"Wait …" she responds, already halfway to working everything out. "The guy you were playing pool with is the same guy making these claims?" She props her hands on her hips, the smallest bump starting to show through her blue bodycon dress. Ethan never introduced himself to Kendra since she was heading home within minutes of him approaching me. "I really wish that I'd stuck around." Guilt and anger flood her features. "God, Jen. I'm so fucking sorry. In the two minutes I was around him I was convinced that he was genuine. I'm such a fucking idiot."

I reach out and take her hand in mine, letting her know it's okay.

"I don't think his intentions were solely to walk me to my door that night. I think he planned to do more."

"Holy hell." Collins shakes her head, rage now flowing from every pore. "And Tommy was there, wasn't he? Waiting outside your door."

I just look at her through glassy eyes; nothing more needs to be said.

"Oh fuck, Jenna. I'm so sorry." Darcy slides off her stool, wrapping her arms around me. "Tommy hit him to protect you, didn't he?"

I drop my head into the crook of her neck, sobbing quietly. "It was so fucked up, Darce. I don't know what I'd have done if Tommy hadn't been standing outside my door. I'm such a fucking idiot for trusting a guy I barely knew to walk me home."

Two more pairs of arms wrap around my shoulders, warmth from my girlfriends heating and soothing my soul.

"And that bastard has the audacity to claim that Tommy assaulted *him*," Kendra bites out.

Lifting my head from Darcy's shoulder, I cast my eyes around my closest friends. "Tommy lost his shit and pinned Ethan against a wall when he wouldn't let go of me. So much of that night is a daze because I was really inebriated and it's like my brain never wants to think about what could've happened if Tommy hadn't been waiting for me."

Collins nods once. Of all my friends, I think she can relate to what I've been through the most. She's spent a lot of her adult life alone, and I know she's run into her fair share of asshole men.

"Were you expecting to see Tommy that night?" she asks.

I shake my head and then look at Darcy. "No, I wasn't. And you were right when you said that we were just hate-fucking. It's like … I'd sleep with him and then not only hate him for pursuing me, but I'd hate myself for wanting it with him too. We're like magnets that should repel each other, not be drawn in, no matter where we are. Tommy was waiting outside my door because he wanted to talk after the last fight we got into."

Kendra tucks a piece of stray hair behind my ear. "And what happened after Ethan left?"

Another tear tumbles from the ends of my lashes. "I asked him to stay with me."

Collins looks almost mad again. "Did Tommy try and sleep with you while you were drunk?"

"No." I look her straight in the eyes. "He made sure I got into bed safely and slept on my pullout in the living area."

Kendra winces, and somehow, I manage a soft snort of laughter. She hates that sofa bed and calls it the devil. When she split with Tyler and her apartment was condemned, she had to endure a week on it.

"No one is going to believe Tommy's version of events." I speak quietly to all three of my friends. "Not unless I set the record straight. Trouble is, the last time I saw Tommy, he bailed on me after a night together that was …" I trail off again, another lump forming in my throat. "After a night that was so much more than just two people hooking up," I finish. "I'm mad at Tommy right now for hurting me, but I can't let his career get torn apart over something he didn't do. He's already on a warning with the Blades."

Kendra, Collins, and Darcy all look between them.

"I think you should say something to Jon," Darcy says, earning agreeable nods from the other two. "As the coach, he can go to the GM directly. This isn't just about hockey and careers. Ethan is going to press charges against Tommy."

As Darcy finishes speaking, my cell buzzes in my shoulder bag, and I unzip it and pull it out.

HOLT

> Looks like you won't need to worry about that prick Schneider any longer. The Blades just announced that he's fully dropped from the team, pending a full investigation into the attack he put on Ethan Hadley. Karma will always find you.

Locking my phone, I drop it back into my bag, clear on what I need to do.

"Darce …"

"Yeah?"

"Is there any chance you can get Jon on the phone right now?"

THIRTY-ONE

JENNA

"Oh my good bloody God. I'm going to be an auntie!"

Darcy defies gravity, launching herself across Jack and Kendra's living area and into her sister-in-law's arms. I'm not sure who's more excited over the pregnancy—Darcy or the rest of her family. Felicity—Jack and Darcy's mom—releases a high-pitched squeak that could call ships into dock. Jon—aka Coach Morgan—clears his throat, fighting back an onslaught of emotion.

"Do you ever wish you had parents like Jon and Felicity?" Collins points toward the Morgan huddle of love.

Collins is a closed book when it comes to her past, but I know her parents died when she was younger, and she's never had a close bond with her blood family.

I shrug a single shoulder and set my water down. I've been drinking way too much lately and need to cool it, even in the offseason.

"I'd like to think Holt would react in a similar way if I announced a pregnancy."

Collins casts me a side-eye. "Have you heard anything from

Tommy lately? Sawyer tells me he's not permitted to practice either."

I shake my head. It's been two days since I made a statement to Coach Morgan, setting out exactly what had happened that night. He said he'd make it his priority to see Tommy back in the team. Still, there hasn't been any word from the Blades, and Tommy has gone dark on us all. I can't be sure he's even in town right now.

"Sawyer tried to call him last night, but he didn't get an answer. He's worried about Tommy." I can hear Collins speak, but I don't process her words.

"I haven't told anyone what happened, Jen." Collins takes my hand in her soft palm and squeezes gently. "Are you doing okay? You've been through a lot. There are people you can speak to if you need to talk about what happened with Ethan."

I shake my head again. "I have a feeling if Tommy hadn't been there, then I would need way more help." My voice fails a little on the final word. "I just hope my version of events is enough to vindicate Tommy. He doesn't deserve to have his career cut short, like his dad."

"You did the right thing, babe," Collins confirms. "Even if he bailed on you the morning after, like a complete A-hole."

We watch on from the open plan kitchen as Jack passes around early scan photos he and Kendra got because they couldn't wait to see their baby. I'm so fucking happy for them both. Kendra is glowing, and Jack looks like he could take on the world with his smile alone.

I think that's the beauty in a true friendship—no matter how much shit you have going on in your own life, seeing your best friend realize a dream in their life can fill your own with joy.

"He's a complex person," I reply to Collins. "He's closed off because he's damaged and confused." My response was intended to be an explanation, but it sounds more defensive than that.

She turns to face me fully as I turn my back on the rest of the room. The entire Blades team is here—minus Tommy—and I want my conversation with Collins to be private.

"He made a comment about his mom and caring what she thinks of him," I continue. "Something tells me we aren't the only ones wishing we had a different deal with parents."

She takes a sip of her drink, swallowing slowly. "From what I hear about Alex Schneider, I can't imagine life has been all peachy for Thomas."

I go to reply, but she continues, "That said, we all get dealt a bad hand in life from time to time. Doesn't mean we can treat people badly and use them, like he has done with you."

Her statement sticks in my throat, making me want to gag. She's effectively validated my fear that Tommy only wanted sex to prove a point that he could bed me. And I fell for it.

"You really think that?" I ask, hoping she'll change her assumption.

Both brows rise into her hairline as she shifts her weight from one foot to the other. "Listen, Jen. Aside from my own dad and the men on Kendra's and Darcy's arms, I've only ever met one decent man—the one I now call my husband. The vast majority seem to think it's their God-given right to behave like the world—and all women—owe them something. When in fact …" She pauses her rant, cocking her head to the side.

Collins isn't looking at me any longer as her gaze travels behind me.

"What's the matter?" I ask, noticing her brown eyes as they grow wider.

"Jenna."

At first, I think I'm dreaming when Tommy's voice filters over my shoulder.

"Look at me, Jenna."

The second time he speaks, I know for sure he's here, and I turn to face him.

God, he looks amazing. So good that it pisses me off. An

asshole has zero right to be this handsome. He's unshaven and wearing all black, his dark hair messy and falling over intense eyes.

Even though there's a party going on, everyone has fallen silent as they watch on. It's something I've noticed when it comes to Tommy—when he enters a room, people stop and take note. At first, I thought it was out of fear for what he might do or say next. Now, I'm thinking it has more to do with his presence. I've never met a guy like him before, and I'm betting that's the same for the vast majority of people he comes into contact with.

Tommy's eyes briefly dart around the room and then fall back on my face. His gaze is soft and kind, almost pleading.

"What are you doing here?" I ask, my voice low and gravelly.

He just offers me a cocky grin. "I got invited to the party, and you know how much I love to socialize."

Despite myself, I can't help a smile. "I told you on voicemail that you'd never hear my voice again. You have zero right to be talking to me."

Out of the corner of my eye, I see Collins move away, offering us some privacy. The rest of the room takes that as their cue to go back to their conversations.

"I know you did." Tommy takes a small step toward me, and I feel every muscle tighten. His cologne is evident, and it transports me back to the last night we shared. "But you see, the thing is, Hellion … I don't think I can live without the sound of your annoying voice in my life. The way it grates on me is addictive, and I love the fucking punishment."

I can't be sure if I'm breathing any longer when he moves even closer. The only breath I can feel is his.

"Or without my hands on you." He continues edging closer to me, and I feel Tommy's palm as heat permeates the thin material of my black dress, wrapping around my right hip.

He casts his eyes down my body and then back to my lips.

"But most of all … I don't think I can bear another second without telling you how fucking sorry I am for hurting you."

It would be so easy to accept his apology and demand he take me back to his place for another night together. That's not who I am though, and he'll have to work way harder to earn my time.

"Why did you leave me like that?" I ask. "You said you wanted to prove yourself, and then you went right ahead and cemented everything I'd originally thought when I met you."

"What were your initial thoughts, Jenna?" he asks.

My ears beat with the adrenaline pumping through my body. "That it's dangerous to have you in my life. That you're the kind of guy who takes care of number one and couldn't give a crap about anyone else. You take what you want and never give out second chances." I swallow hard. "People who don't offer second chances scare the shit out of me."

"Why's that?" He replies, studying me carefully.

Perhaps he wasn't expecting me to go down this route, and to be honest, neither was I.

I try to pull away from his grasp, but he keeps me in place, and I don't fight harder.

"Because people who live their life with a lack of compassion for others generally have little for themselves too. Living life without making mistakes is impossible and a one-way ticket to loneliness." I motion between us. "For example, if I lived my life without compassion, then I'd never have spoken to you again after the incident with Holt." I hold up a hand. "Now, giving out third, fourth, and fifth chances? That's where I start to make a fool of myself. And I'm not allowing you to humiliate me again, Tommy."

His face contorts with anguish. I know a lot of what I said is the truth. He doesn't need to confirm it.

"You're right about showing compassion. I'm terrible at it—to others but mainly toward myself. What drove me to leave the other morning was out of fear."

He blows out a long breath and casts his gaze around the room. With the way we're standing so close and he's holding my hip, it's obvious that we're involved. Not that I can find it within me to care. This is a safe space with people who aren't about to spread bullshit and rumors online.

"Keep talking ..." I implore, determined for this man to show his cards.

He chews his bottom lip for a second. "I was convinced you were going to tell me you regretted sleeping together again." A crease forms between his brows. "And I didn't think I could cope with hearing your rejection again. Not with the way you made me ..."

His palm squeezes my hip tighter, and I can see the way he's shutting down.

My hope for him to open up dissolves.

"Can we get out of here and talk? I've got so much I want to say."

I really want to leave with him, especially since I want to talk as much as he does. This time, it's fear holding me back. That, and my reluctance to split on one of the biggest nights of my best friend's life.

I shake my head. "I can't leave my friend during her pregnancy announcement party. She always has my back, and I can't let her down again."

When Tommy's lips ghost the shell of my ear, my core tightens and tingles.

"And I can't leave you here and walk away again. What you did for me—the statement you made about Ethan—no one has ever looked out for me like that. But you did, Jenna. Even when I didn't deserve it and even after my third, fourth, and fifth chance, you still stepped forward. With your version of events, my attorney was able to apply pressure, and Ethan retracted his claims against me. I think you just saved my hockey career and my reputation." He huffs a sarcastic laugh. "What was left of my reputation."

"I want another hour to celebrate with Kendra and her family," I reply, just as Jack approaches from behind Tommy.

Jack holds a bottle of ice-cold beer out in front of him, and initially, I think he's offering it to me. But then he taps Tommy on the shoulder.

"The rule for tonight's party stipulates that all guests—apart from my pregnant wife—need to have an alcoholic drink either in their hand or next to them." He offers the beer to Tommy, who takes it. "You have neither."

Tommy stares down at the brown bottle in his hand and then back up at his captain, shock painted across his face.

The golden retriever smile I know so well, but has never been directed at his defenseman, spreads across Jack's face.

"I don't know all the details because it's none of my business, but as the captain, I am privy to certain information before the rest of the team is. Jon told me what Ethan Hadley purported wasn't the truth and that you had good reason to punch that fucker. Word is, it was to protect someone who needed it."

Jack's eyes travel to mine, warmth and understanding in them. I guess the hand Tommy has on my hip likely gives away who the vulnerable person he was defending could be.

"The announcement has been done, and the party will start winding down soon. Kend is flat on her back ..."

Jack's eyes grow wide, and I blow out a laugh.

"I mean ... when I say flat on her back, I'm referring to exhaustion." Amusement pulls at his lips. "Although she'll probably be flat—"

"Yeah, yeah. We get the picture, Morgan," Tommy interjects, lifting his beer and smirking. "Thanks for the beer, but I'm driving." Tommy sets the bottle down beside him, his eyes sparkling as they drop down the length of my outfit. "Besides"—

his thumb begins drawing circles on my hip—"I need to take my girl home and work on earning a sixth chance with her."

THIRTY-TWO

TOMMY

I feel like I'm fifteen again, staring at a girl sitting next to me while I have no clue what to do with myself. All I know is, I want to spend more than only a night with Jenna, but more than that, I want her to want me in her bed for more than just sex.

"Are we heading back to your place or my place?" I ask, gripping my steering wheel tight, hoping it will temper the cringe as it rips through me. Jesus, it's like I've never spoken to the opposite sex before.

It's the first time Jenna has been in my car—or one of them —and she inspects my Corvette Z06 carefully. I've never much been into cars, but the second I laid eyes on this supercar, I figured it would make a great signing treat to myself.

"I didn't think orange cars would be your thing." She smiles over at me.

Other than the streetlights lining Jack and Kendra's block, the entire sky is pitch-black, and a shadow casts across Jenna's profile as she looks at me.

"You're right," I reply with a smirk, gripping my steering wheel even tighter. "Ordinarily, they aren't. This color was the only one on offer, and I needed to save money. The signing bonus from the Blades was shitty."

She rolls her eyes, and I crank the engine to life.

"So, are we heading to your place or ..." I begin repeating my previous question but trail off when I notice what's got her distracted.

She shrugs and begins searching through the most recent playlists saved in the entertainment system. The second she scrolls to Black Sabbath's "Paranoid," her finger hovers over the track.

"That's a personal favorite," I say, heat starting to warm my car through and pinken her cheeks.

She crosses her legs, the fitted black dress she wore to the party tonight rising higher on her perfect thighs. I can't deny that I can still feel the animosity between us, but it's gradually being devoured with an attraction that runs way deeper than lust. It's formed in understanding and respect—a currency that means so much to us both as human beings.

Jenna hits play.

"The lyrics to this song"—she turns to face me in the black leather bucket seat—"it's like they were written with you in mind."

Not saying a word, but keeping my eyes pinned on hers, I hit the electric recline button on the side of my seat.

"Why don't you come sit in my lap while we listen to it?" I suggest.

The corner of Jenna's upper lip tips up. I can sense she really wants to accept my offer, but isn't ready to forgive me just yet. I can't say I blame her. The second her apartment door closed behind me that morning, I regretted my decision to leave.

"All right ..." I blow out a breath and slide my seat back even further. "How about I sit in your lap?"

She snorts a laugh, and the sound lights me up like the fucking Rockefeller Center Christmas Tree. I wasn't sure I'd ever get a chance to speak with her again after the voicemail she left me, let alone hear her laugh.

"Tommy, you're six foot five. I'm shocked you can even fit in this car, let alone climb into my lap."

I tap my knee. "Best you come sit in mine then, yeah?"

She tussles with herself a little more, and I give her a second before she releases her safety belt and does as I asked.

I was half hard the second I laid eyes on her in Jack and Kendra's apartment. And now that she's perched in my lap, my arms wrapped around her waist from behind, I'm fighting with everything I have not to go off in my pants.

Her hair and perfume smell insane, making my mouth water. This girl is way out of my league, and I know it.

"Does Holt know you made a statement, clearing my name?" I ask, burying my face into the hairs at the back of her neck.

She sucks in a sharp breath, releasing it slowly. "No. Last I heard from him was via text. He said that karma had finally been served since you'd been dropped from the team."

I move her hair to one side, pushing it over her left shoulder and exposing the sensitive pebbled flesh at the nape of her neck. "You're a special person, Jenna, and I meant what I said earlier—no one has ever stood up for me in the way you did. You could've let my career burn and kept your mouth shut."

She turns her head to the side, watching me as I run my tongue from the base of her neck to just below her right ear.

"I want more with you."

My declaration hangs in the silence of my car. I drove here tonight, determined to bring Jenna Miller back into my life. Did I expect to ask her for more than that? No. But this girl is like magic, drawing inner thoughts and feelings from me without uttering a word.

I take her hand in mine, intertwining our fingers together in her lap.

"You've always wanted a man to wrap his arms around you, no?"

She nods once, shallow puffs of breath steaming my windshield. The streets are busy tonight, but my windows are tinted, granting us all the privacy we need.

"When was the last time you had a boyfriend, Jenna?" My voice is just as breathy, my heart working overtime to pump oxygen to vital organs. I've never felt so lightheaded.

"A while ago," she replies.

I kiss the underside of her jaw. "I've never had a girlfriend. Ever."

She nods like this isn't news to her.

"But I want to try with you. My heart hasn't left me with another choice. I think it set out hating you because, deep down, you've had this hold over it, and that's not something that's ever happened. Not with any other girl."

Casually, I trail my other hand across her upper thigh, stopping when I reach the high split in her dress, and I dip my fingers beneath the material. Her skin is soft and hot, reacting with every inch I take toward her apex.

When I reach her pussy, her flimsy excuse for a thong is already drenched, and I part my thighs wider, taking her thighs wider too.

"I get it if you don't want to put a label on us yet. Maybe it's too soon, or maybe you're still pissed at me for everything I've done."

I push my fingers beneath her panties and slide two through her. "But at least let me touch you and take you out like you're mine."

I enter her with a single finger, and she throws her head back into my shoulder, moaning toward the roof of my car.

Pride swells in my chest. *I did that to her.*

"Tommy, if you hurt me one more fucking time, I will unleash my brother on you."

I'd laugh if I didn't think she was serious. Holt Miller is a fucking fly-half tank.

Withdrawing my finger slowly, I push it back inside her, and she moans again. Then I add a second and pump her carefully. I know she'll make a mess of us both and likely my seat.

Good.

Leaning forward, I whisper into the shell of her ear, smiling the whole time, "With the way I'm starting to feel about you, Jenna, I'll annihilate myself before your brother even gets a look in. You're fully under my skin, penetrating my bones."

"You see ..." She sucks in a sharp breath and releases it when I curl my fingers and find her front wall. "This is the Tommy I like—the one who makes me feel special."

When I withdraw my fingers and bring them to my mouth to taste, Jenna turns in my lap to watch the way I lick her clean from my hand.

"Let me take you back to my place tonight. You can stay all day tomorrow. I might be back on the team, but we don't have a practice."

"I hate spending all day in bed," she replies, running her finger across my bottom lip. "I like to be active."

"Okay," I reply. Pushing my fingers back inside her heat. "We can do something tomorrow, but only if you agree to this one thing."

She looks suspicious, and my heart rate picks up.

"Agree to date me," I say quietly. "Before I let myself go any further with you, I need to know that you won't mess around with other guys." I close my eyes and wish away thoughts of Jenna in another man's bed. "Date me and give me one last chance to be the man I know I can be for you."

I stroke inside her pussy, and she pins her bottom lip between her teeth as she clamps her thighs around my hand, slowly coming all over my fingers.

"I'm mad with myself each time I give in to you, Tommy. You don't deserve any more pieces of me."

I nod and massage her swollen clit with the pad of my thumb. "I know I don't," I whisper. "But you also saw the real me the other night, and I want to show you more of him. Only you, Jenna. He's desperate to share his bed and bring you morning coffee."

I can see the way she melts at my words, along with a flicker of hesitancy as my girl battles inside her head.

"Let's go back to your place," I suggest, hooking a finger under her chin before pressing my lips against hers. "Your place, your bed, your rules."

She kisses me back, and hope blooms in my chest.

"Okay," Jenna whispers against my mouth. "I'll give you one more chance."

I smile like I just won the fucking lotto or something.

"But," she scolds, holding up a finger between us, "I need more time to think about what I want between us." Her face softens, eyes darting between mine. "I like you—a lot. I can't lie and say that I don't, despite everything that has gone down. But I'll be dammed if I roll over and let you call all the shots when I'm still waiting for you to show me exactly why I keep letting you back into my life."

With one more kiss against her lips, I retract my hand and lick her from my finger for a second time.

"You just got yourself a deal, Miss Miller."

THIRTY-THREE

TOMMY

I've kept Jenna awake all night, and I have zero regrets over it too. I want her constantly aching and exhausted—it's the only testament I'll accept when it comes to me sliding inside her tight body.

When I roll my hips into her again, she falls apart beneath me, pink flushing the apples of her cheeks.

Her soft moan is more of a whimper as the rising sun seeps into her room, drenching us both in an orange glow that looks so fucking beautiful against her skin.

"Eyes on me." I hold my weight above her on one arm and motion between my eyes.

Still drunk on lust, she gazes into them.

"I'm still here, in your apartment. I'm still inside you, and I have no intention of letting up anytime soon. I'm not going anywhere, Jenna."

Her warm palms wrap around the nape of my neck, pulling me down for a kiss.

"If you leave me like that again, then you'd better watch out. Next time, it will be something way worse by your door than surf 'n' turf."

I smooth my tongue across her bottom lip, dipping inside to massage against hers. "I'm starting to question who the bad one in this relationship is. I might carry the rep, but I think you deserve the accolade."

Jenna pulls back, dropping one of her hands back to the mattress.

Still inside her, I sit up on my haunches and bring her body with me. I've never fucked a girl in the lotus position before. To be honest, I've never done most of what I do with Jenna. I'm flying without a safety net with little to no clue what the fuck I'm doing.

And it all feels so fucking good.

"Did I go too far?" I ask, pressing my forehead against hers. "When I said relationship?"

She loops her palm back around my neck, and I set a kiss on the underside of her chin.

"Don't go silent on me, Hellion," I plead. Like a fucking simp. "I got carried away after the night we just shared, and I know you need some time to process everything."

Jenna spreads her legs wider, taking me deeper into her pussy. "I don't know how to answer that question, Tommy." She closes her eyes for a brief moment, and I can tell she's deep in thought. "After I split with Lee and for what feels like an eternity, all I've ever wanted is to have what my girlfriends have—a man who loves and cares for me and a chance to start a family of my own."

If it wasn't for the mattress beneath us, I'd fall through the damn floor.

"But now? Is that not what you want?" The tremor in my voice is unmistakable.

After everything, she's going to reject me. Us. All over again. Maybe the playgirl lifestyle is for her, and I've misjudged this entire thing between us.

Jenna shakes her head, squeezing the back of my neck. "It's not that. I still want all of those things. It's just ..."

"You don't want them with a guy like me?"

I'm fully aware that I don't know what I want in my own life. Having a girlfriend has never been at the top of my priority list, never mind starting a family. But the idea of Jenna not envisioning herself doing that with me evokes a kind of nausea I never want to feel again.

"I want to spend time with you, Tommy." Her fingertips brush through the clipped hair at the back of my head. "I want us to start over and find out what it is that keeps driving us back together. I share and have feelings for you too. But I'm scared that you'll hurt me."

I'm desperate to fill her head with affirmations and reassurance that her fears won't happen. Something tells me that those words will come across as empty. She doesn't need lip service. She needs something more tangible. To feel my vulnerability.

I press my forehead against hers again and release a steadying breath, knowing that while this may be the hardest thing I've ever done, it's the strongest move I can make right now.

"My dad ... Alex," I begin, nausea creeping back up my throat, "he wanted nothing to do with me. From the second I was born to the present day."

Jenna's eyes hold nothing but understanding. "I know, Tommy. Despite the name you wear on your back."

The thought of someone—anyone—knowing the truth behind my father's rejection has always filled me with the deepest sense of foreboding. So, why is it only relief flooding my insides?

"How did you find out?"

We aren't fucking anymore, but I'm still hard and inside my girl. I wrap my arms around her shoulders, pulling her body closer to mine. Her warmth acts like a balm.

"I didn't. I worked it out."

I smirk against her lips. "Am I that transparent?"

She just grins back. "A little bit, yeah. You aren't as dark and mysterious to me as maybe you think you are. I do have one question."

"Shoot," I reply.

"Why do you play under his name? Back when you were younger, you played under Williams. I'm guessing that was your mom's name."

I'm desperate to turn this conversation and focus on the fact that she looked me up. Instead, I opt to keep it centered on me and the uncomfortable truths I know she needs to learn about my life.

"When I was seventeen, I took a trip from my home in Minnesota to Brooklyn. I'd always had this feeling that my dad wasn't who my mom claimed he was—a soldier in the US Army who died on a tour in Afghanistan. The older I got, the less likely that story became."

I pause for a breath, and Jenna cups my cheek in her hand. I know this is exactly what she needs from me.

"I looked like Alex Schneider, skated like him. And the more time that passed, the more convinced my friends and teammates were that we were related. As a teenager, I thought their theories sounded crazy. But the more times I asked Mom if I was his son, the less convincing her denial became. That was when I finally saved up enough money from a job I was working at to get a flight to Brooklyn. Alex didn't exactly make where he lived a secret since he was constantly pictured with girls as he took them back to his apartment."

"What happened?" Jenna asks quietly, her heart breaking on my behalf.

"I showed up and gave my name to the security guard on shift. As I stood there, waiting for him to call Alex, I was convinced I'd be turned away. Maybe even laughed at. But when

I was told to head upstairs, a spark of hope ignited that maybe—just fucking maybe—I was right to travel all that way and hold out hope that my dad wasn't dead and he was actually a hockey player. One I'd looked up to for his presence on the ice. I thought maybe he wasn't the asshole people had made him out to be in the sport and in his personal life, that he was actually decent. I hoped that I was some kind of secret baby my mom had hidden from him, and now we were about to reunite, and my whole life was about to change."

Silence descends between us until I finally speak again. It doesn't feel like my voice belongs to me any longer.

"What I found was both what I'd hoped for and my worst fear. He was my dad—he confirmed it. But he had known all about me. He'd basically been paying my mom inflated child support payments, and he'd had her sign an NDA to keep quiet about him being the father since he wanted zero association with her and me. He told me he never wanted a family and looked at me like I was a fucking disease."

"Tommy ... I don't even know what to say."

Placing my hands over hers, I close my eyes and sit with my reality. I feel different than I did a few minutes ago, having shared my secret with the one person I could only ever imagine telling. The weight feels lighter, easier to digest.

It feels like I might be fully falling for Jenna Miller.

"You don't need to say anything, Hellion. Just having you here, listening to me without judgment, is everything I need."

She nods lightly. "You played under his name to spite him, didn't you?"

I smile because it's like she's in my head, pulling the strings and controlling me. Even if I wanted to keep something from her, I don't think I could.

"I changed my name and owned who I was—a Schneider who loves to fight and is good at it too. If Alex didn't want to acknowledge my existence, then he could watch as I buried his legacy underneath my own." I puff out my chest. "I know I'm a better player than he ever was. And I know it hurts his massive ego each time I put a shift in on the ice."

"But, Tommy," she whispers, "you aren't a Schneider. If you were, you wouldn't have come back to me. I wouldn't be here, in this bed, with you. I might not know your dad personally, but any man who rejects their own flesh and blood is no person I would ever allow into my life."

The first tear runs a warm track down my cheek, and Jenna swipes it away.

"What about your mom? You once told me that you cared what she thought of you, but that's all I got."

A pain I only ever feel when I think about my mom curls inside my gut.

"My mom, Helen, wasn't always the best parent. But she was never cruel. Alex had her over a barrel with money and the NDA. I don't think he paid her a fortune, but it was enough to keep our heads above water and food on the table. When I found out the truth, I was so twisted with anger and betrayal. She lied to me for all those years," I bite out. "Her own son." Another tear emerges, and I swipe it away in frustration. "If it were me, I would've chosen the truth over his money. No matter how desperate things got financially, I'd have chosen integrity."

My girl presses her lips together, a softness forming in her blue eyes. "Remember when we spoke about compassion? People make mistakes, Tommy. You, me, everyone. I'm guessing she was fairly young when she had you, judging by Alex's age."

I nod, falling a little harder each time Jenna speaks. "Why are you so infuriatingly wise?"

She shrugs nonchalantly. "It's a gift I wear with pride and save to use exclusively on you. I'm not saying you should open the door back up to her fully, but I am suggesting that you think it over a little. Don't burn every bridge in your life, even the ones that need a little maintenance and repair."

I just look at her, taking her in carefully. Every feature on her face, especially the beauty spot beneath her left eye.

"Where did it all go wrong with your parents?"

Jenna's previously soft expression hardens a fraction. It's a defense mechanism I recognize all too well.

"The story there is very different from yours. But I do understand what it feels like to be rejected. I also know what it's like to have an asshole father; mine wasn't Alex, but he was a selfish prick who hurt my family. My mom and I ..." She pauses and swallows hard. "We just don't get along. We're two different people who don't align. Not in our interests or values. My family is my brother, and I'm good with that."

Before I can think, I'm kissing the bridge of her nose.

"Your brother won't always be your only family. A woman like you deserves a man who will give her the world. And I think the only reason it took you a little longer to find him was because all the other guys, including your ex, knew they couldn't match up to you. Women like you intimidate some men."

"You talk like my search for Mr. Right is over?" she asks.

I move my hips below her, and she moans a little.

"I mean, I know I have a big ego, but I'm starting to think I might fit the bill."

THIRTY-FOUR

JENNA

When I push through the door of Rise Up a week later, I'm immediately met with the familiar sound of the bells above the door—letting Ed, the owner, know he has a customer—along with three inquisitive faces in the form of Kendra, Darcy, and Collins. Emily is sitting at the head of the table in a high chair. A rattle in one hand and a chew ring in the other.

Since Tommy turned up at Jack and Kendra's that night and then we went back to my place and I had the best sex of my life, I have been unusually quiet. Normally, they get a rundown of nights I spend with guys, but with Tommy, they've heard nothing.

As I take a seat opposite Collins—Kendra and Darcy flanking me on either side—Collins slides a cup of steaming coffee across to me, quickly followed by a still-warm brownie.

"I assume you're hoping for information by inviting me to our favorite café and buying me my favorite baked goods?"

Darcy lifts a shoulder, pulling her adorable daughter into her lap. "We can neither confirm nor deny such behavior." She leans forward, and Emily looks up at her mom with the most adorable eyes that remind me of her dad. "Give us the deets. We aren't leaving until we get the complete story of what happened when you left with Mr. Schneider."

Kendra empties a sachet of sweetener into her coffee, stirring it into her drink. "The soccer season is over, and we have all the time in the world."

"I know what I want to know." Collins rests her chin in her palm, pinning me in place with her brown-eyed stare. "Did you screw him hard?"

Darcy's eyes flare wide before she drops them to her daughter.

Collins rolls her lips together, looking half regretful. "See it as extending her vocabulary early."

We all briefly laugh before Collins refocuses her attention back on me. "So?"

I take a sip of coffee and set my cup back down on the table in front of me. "I really like him. Despite myself and everything that has previously gone down between us, I really like him."

Darcy's squeal is enough to turn a few heads from tables seated around us. "So, I assume you're dating?"

Butterflies flutter through my stomach. I'm not sure I've even processed the fact that Tommy wants to date. He isn't the dating kind, and that makes me equal parts excited to be the first girl he's ever wanted that with, but also fearful that things could blow up in my face.

"He wants to give it a try, and I'm …" I trail off and look between my girls, Emily listening intently too. Bless her heart. "I'm hesitant to get hurt."

Because it's the offseason and she knows she can, Kendra adds another sweetener to her coffee, tapping the packet against the side of her cup. "I might be tripping out, and I can't actually believe I'm about to say this, but … I think you'd be crazy to walk away from each other."

"Agreed," Collins simply adds.

"Seconded," Darcy announces. A small giggle bubbles from Emily.

"Wait." I hold up a hand. "You guys couldn't stand the sight of Tommy not all that long ago. I know he punched Ethan, but he'd also punched my brother who, by the way, still hates his guts."

This time, Collins clasps both hands under her chin as she leans even further toward me. "I know what I've said before. However, I've also learned in this life that it's okay to pivot on my opinions. Boys who aren't serious about you don't look at you the way Tommy did that night at Kendra and Jack's party." She leans back in her chair. "Trust me, I've dated enough bull-shitters to identify the down bad ones. Some guys tell you what you want to hear, while others show you with their eyes. And eyes don't lie, Jen."

I cast a quick glance at Kendra. Of all my friends, she is the one who knows the full extent of my feelings on what I want in my future. And as close as our quartet is, I know she would never repeat our conversations without my permission.

"If I give us a chance and he hurts me, I'll lose faith in finding the one altogether."

She nods lightly, staring down into her cup of coffee. "I get that, Jen." She lifts her eyes and slides her hand toward mine, intertwining our fingers. "I think Collins is right. If you walk away, then you'll always wonder what could've been. I have to be honest and say that I'm struggling to comprehend that the Tommy Schneider we witnessed at the party is the same one who had hit your brother back in January. Jack is feeling the same way too." She squeezes my hand. "You can't tell me that his transformation doesn't have anything to do with the way he feels about my best friend."

More butterflies flutter around in my belly, spreading all the way to the tips of my toes. Tommy and the boys have been on an away series for the past few days, and I've missed him. A lot.

"I think I just need some time. And to talk to Holt. He's coming over later this month for the holidays, and I figure then will be a good time." I shift in my seat. Memories of the hit Tommy landed on Holt's jaw still eat away at me in the depths of my gut. "It might be a good time for Holt to meet Tommy." I glance around at my friends. "Properly."

"You didn't tell Holt about the Ethan thing?" Collins asks.

I shake my head. She doesn't get why, but she doesn't have a brother and especially not one like Holt.

"Holt would be in custody right now, and Ethan would be pushing up daisies. That's the kind of news I'll break to him when I can physically lock him in my apartment until the steam stops billowing from his ears."

Collins just snorts a laugh.

"Give Tommy a chance, Jen. And don't worry about seeking your brother's approval. If the guy you want is decent, then he'll eventually accept him." Darcy winks at me as she unclips the strap on her nursing top and Emily latches on.

That girl is a natural-born mother with an incredible mind. She recently got appointed to senior editor at the high-end fashion magazine she works at, *Glide*, making her the youngest to ever secure that position. Even while still on maternity leave, she's earning promotions. Unsurprisingly.

I'm about to reply when my phone interrupts me, and I pull it out of my pocket.

TOMMY

Fuck, I miss you. I just had to say that.

ME

You're turning soft.

TOMMY

Yes, I am. But only for you. Only ever for you.

More butterflies ...

ME

I'm sitting in Rise Up with the girls, and that's not what they tell me. I think you're in danger of making some friends.

TOMMY

It's seriously disturbing. As you know, I'm rooming with Jack again. He actually invited me down to the bar for a drink last night.

I know I'm smiling on the outside as well as the inside.

ME

And did you go?

TOMMY

Yes.

ME

And? Jesus, Tommy, it's like pulling teeth here.

TOMMY

Socializing isn't as painful as I first anticipated.

ME

I'm actually rolling my eyes right now.

TOMMY

I wish I could be there to see you do that. You have pretty eyes.

ME

Can I ask you something?

TOMMY

Is it about you coming over to my place so we can fuck all night when I get back? Because yes. The answer is yes.

ME

That wasn't what I was going to ask.

TOMMY

Irrelevant. It's happening.

ME

Now that we might actually like each other a little bit, do you still plan on calling me Hellion?

TOMMY

There was more than just a single reason why you acquired that nickname.

A throat clears from beside me, and I look up to find Darcy reading over my shoulder. She's practically vibrating in her seat.

"This reminds me of when Archer and I started seeing each other. It was so freaking romantic! Only you guys have come full circle. When you get married and if you have babies, you will be able to tell them all about how you first hated their daddy." She chuckles and points to herself. "And then their unofficial aunties can verify your story and confirm that he was, in the beginning, a complete and total douchebag. A true story of redemption."

I smile and type out a reply to Tommy.

ME

What were the other contributing factors?

TOMMY

Now, that would be telling. I can't give away all my secrets until you agree to go on a date with me.

ME

Good relationships aren't built on secrets. Tell me.

TOMMY

Demons are known to harass and persistently torture. And since that's all you did to me, despite not even trying, I knew the nickname fit you perfectly.

That, and ... holy shit, have you seen you in bed?!

I squeeze my thighs together underneath the table.

"Having fun there, babe?" Collins asks on a raised brow.

I drop my phone, a hot flush radiating across my cheeks. "Shit. I'm sorry. I—"

"Got a little sidetracked?" Kendra asks on a smile.

"Exactly that," I reply, picking up my phone.

ME

> I'm with the girls, so I have to go. I'll see you later … maybe.

TOMMY

> What plans do you have today?

ME

> Not much. Probably the gym, and then I might head to that wholesale foods store you always order from.

TOMMY

> Feeding your body well. Good girl. You'll need all the energy you can muster for tonight.

ME

> I said I might see you later.

TOMMY

> You can see me right now if you'd like. Turn around.

Slowly, I turn in my chair.

There, with his dark blue Blades hoodie pulled up and over his head, Tommy stands in the window decorated with string lights and wreaths.

My mouth waters.

He drops his eyes from mine and back down to his cell.

TOMMY

> We got an early flight home and Archer told me where you'd be with the girls.

ME

So it appears.

TOMMY

Come on a date with me, Hellion.

THIRTY-FIVE

TOMMY

"Full transparency." I stop just in front of Jenna, throwing ice onto her black jeans.

She looks down at the wet patches forming where the ice melts, her hands propped on her hips in disgust.

"You're way better at skating than I thought you would be."

Reaching up, she cups my cheek in one of her palms. She's wearing black gloves since I took her home to get wrapped up before driving us to the ice rink under the Brooklyn Bridge, for what I'm convinced is my first official date with a girl.

"Tommy, ever the cocky one. I went skating with my brother and his friends a ton. If I wasn't playing soccer, I'd probably be playing hockey." She smirks up at me, rosy cheeks only heating further when I bring my mouth closer to hers. "I wanted to be a goalie so I could boss asshole defensemen and women around."

I point at myself. "But assholes can still be endearing, no?"

She taps her chin in thought. "I'm thinking I can make an exception for you."

My stomach flips at her words, and as she turns around to skate away from me, I wrap my arms around her waist, resting my chin on her shoulder.

Even beneath the layers of clothing separating us, I'm sure I feel her heart rate pick up. The puffs of air she exhales in the darkening night sky for sure become bigger and more frequent.

"This is what you want, right, Jenna? To feel safe and wanted in your man's arms?"

I know a picture of us can't go any further than my own phone gallery, especially given Jenna's brother doesn't know about us, and announcing I have a girlfriend I don't officially have as a first social media post might be taking things a step too far. Still, I pull my phone from my pocket, opening the camera to selfie mode.

Jenna turns her head over her shoulder, our lips close, breaths mingling. "What are you doing?"

"Making you another curry," I sarcastically reply.

She rolls her eyes at me, and I snap the first picture of us. It seems fitting that the first photo we take is one where she's irritated with me.

"Can we take another?" I ask, turning her around to face me.

She rests her arms over my shoulders, and it's all the excuse I need to press my mouth against hers and take another picture of us kissing.

"What if someone recognizes you?" she whispers into my mouth. "I mean, I'm hardly famous, but someone is bound to notice you."

"Do you care?" I ask her. "Because I don't give a flying fuck."

She shakes her head. "No, I don't care what anyone here thinks. But I do think I should talk to Holt."

"What are you going to tell him? That I'm your man?"

She looks up at me, two big pools of blue that make me want to submerge myself in her forever.

Jesus Christ.

"Because I want to be," I clarify, just in case she hasn't gotten the message yet.

Her eyes drop to the center of my chest. "I know … I know you do, Tommy."

I tip her chin up to look at me. "Tell me what else is holding you back from giving us a shot. Is it Holt? I'll set the record straight between us, I promise."

She shakes her head again. "The Holt thing is tricky, but only because he is a protective brother."

"Tell me what else I need to do, Jenna."

Running her tongue across her bottom lip, she looks off to the side and then back at me. The string lights set up all around the rink burst into life and twinkle in her eyes as darkness continues to fall.

"I want you to keep showing me Tommy Williams. Because that's the boy holding my chin. He's the one you've buried inside you." Her palm comes to my chest again. "The tattoo over your heart—what does it mean?"

Hearing Jenna call me by my mom's name, coupled with her direct question, knocks me off guard, and I drop my eyes to her glove. "The scissors and thread?"

She nods subtly. "Of all your tattoos, that's the one that stands out to me. It has to have meaning."

"God, Jesus." I close my eyes. "How do you know all the questions to ask me?"

"I think because of all the people you've met in your life, I'm the first one that you want to open up to."

I kiss her, so fucking hard, lifting her up so she wraps her legs around my waist. Sure, there's a chance she could slice my leg open with a blade, but it'd be worth it to hold her like this.

She's right. So fucking right.

"It was my first tattoo."

Jenna cups the back of my neck in her palms, and I skate over to the side, setting her down on the boards and stepping between her legs.

"Sir, I'm afraid we don't allow people to sit—"

The guy working the rink stops dead in his tracks when I growl at him. He isn't disturbing this moment with my girl.

"Never mind. As you were." He waves me off, eyes flared wide.

"I shouldn't find your assholery sexy," Jenna sighs. "But in this moment, I do."

I take one of her hands and place it back over my heart.

"It was the first tattoo I ever got. Right after everything went down with Alex and he kicked me out of his apartment, I had time to kill before my flight home. So, I got my first tat. It symbolizes cutting ties."

Jenna stares at my chest, almost like she's trying to see it through my clothes. "Like cutting your mom and dad out of your life?"

That wasn't what I was going to say, although she's not wrong.

"Cutting ties with my feelings. I felt like it was a crime to care about people or that it was easier to just walk away from emotions and any kind of relationship. The hurt I felt toward my parents twisted me up good, Jen. It still does."

"That's a long time to hold so much anger in your heart, Tommy."

"Do you not feel bitter toward your parents for favoring your brother over you?"

Her dark hair is almost as black as the beanie she's wearing. But none of Jenna is dark. She's a wild child, for sure, but her soul is as pure as freshly Zamboni'd ice.

"What's the point of holding on to anger or bitterness? Just let it go and concentrate on the people in your life who bring you joy and safety. If they don't make you feel good about yourself, then they aren't worth a second more of your energy."

She presses her forehead against mine, looking me square in the eyes. "And, yep, you can take that as a compliment. I wouldn't be here with you if I didn't want to be."

Like I'm a fucking teenager or something, my cock strains against the zipper of my jeans. "Spend the night with me. Come back to my place. We can watch movies, and I'll cook for you. I'm addicted to spending time with you because you make me feel so good."

"That depends." She grins.

Cupping the back of her head in my palm, I run my lips across hers. "On what?"

"If that annoyingly delicious curry you made me is still on the menu. I haven't stopped thinking about it since I finished the last of it from my freezer."

"I can teach you how to make it, if you'd like?"

She pulls back, scrunching up her nose. "I hate cooking. It's a means to an end for me."

"Ah yes," I jest. "You prefer moldy, horrible takeout pizza that's likely to give you food poisoning."

She looks genuinely hurt at my dig. "Actually, I have been eating way better since I met you."

I inch forward so my hard cock presses into her jean-covered center, and I swear to God, I feel her grow wet for me. "What are you trying to tell me, Jen? That I'm having a positive impact on your life?" My words are dripping with bravado, although I mean every one of them.

"You definitely are when it comes to my nutritional plan."

"Mmhmm," I hum against her lips. "Speaking of nutrition …"

"Oh my God …" she quietly croons when I press myself into her a little more.

I'm fighting with everything I have to keep this interaction PG since there are a couple of families still on the rink.

"I think it's high time I ate." I drop my eyes to her pussy, now convinced she's soaking. "And my girl is on the menu tonight."

She bites down on her bottom lip.

"Along with butternut squash curry," I add, pulling a giggle from her.

"Okay," she answers after a couple of beats. "I'll come home with you."

I light up like a fucking preteen when he sees his date at the school dance.

Jenna jumps down off the side and taps me on the shoulder. "Don't get too carried away, Tommy. I'm only using you for your culinary skills."

THIRTY-SIX

JENNA

I've made a lot of assumptions about Tommy over the months I've known him. But one assumption I didn't make? How hands-on he can be with a girl.

From the second he wrapped his arms around my waist at the outdoor rink he took me to after we left Rise Up, I don't think there's been a full minute where he hasn't found a way to hold a part of my body.

It's like he knows that physical touch is my love language. And I'm starting to think it might be his too.

Tommy was right when he said that we were essentially the same person. Only now, I can find fewer reasons to refute his claim. I don't want to refute it anymore.

Taking me by the hand, he leads me out of the elevator and into his apartment, scanning the door lock with his key fob. The last time I was here, I hightailed it out of there after having another meltdown over sleeping with him. That night didn't end well, but it feels like so much has shifted between us since.

The man standing in front of me, removing my beanie and taking my coat, is not the same person he was back then.

Scratch that thought. He was always this person. It's just now he's allowing me to see all of him.

Privilege over being the person he's opening up to runs through my veins, inflating my heart as he pulls me into his warm body. Tommy is the only guy I know who is just as hot without an inch of effort to his appearance as he is in a tux. I've always been painfully attracted to his physique and looks. And now that I can see the person beneath the tattoos and muscles? Let's just say that he'd better not hurt me.

Uncertainty overtakes my thoughts as he looks down at me. Only the lamp in the corner of his living space illuminates his face. I can tell he's trying to work out what's going on in my head. Good luck to him since I can't figure out my own emotions. They feel scrambled. All I know is that I want to be here tonight, in his company.

"I know I said I'd make you food, and I promise I will. But right now, I really want you, Jenna."

He drags his hand down my side, gripping my hip in his palm and pressing me further into his body. I could feel how hard he was back at the rink, and now he's like steel.

"I want to do so many things to this tight body. Take it apart in ways you never thought possible. Unravel you so you're hanging on my next move ..." He licks into my mouth on a possessive growl. "I'm falling for you, Jenna. I've never loved a girl, but I know I could love you. You're my Hellion and my angel. My torturer and my sanctuary. You pull the impossible from me—love. An admission of who I am. Peace."

My eyes glaze over. In all the time I was dating Lee, he never told me that he was falling for me. No man has ever uttered such honesty.

As I gaze up at him, he strokes his tattooed fingers lightly down the column of my throat.

"I want to sleep with you so badly, but I can't. Not tonight."

A crease forms between his brows. "Why not?"

I'm twenty-seven, and I shouldn't get so embarrassed over being on my period.

"I'm … it's that time of the month and …" I trail off, dropping my eyes down my body.

Tommy just grins down at me, running his fingers through the length of my hair. "I'm not great with girl code, but I think you're trying to tell me that you're on your period."

I pin my bottom lip between my teeth. "Why do I feel like I just got my first cycle and I need to ask for a ride so I can buy tampons from the store?"

Tommy kisses the bridge of my nose. "And why are you the cutest fucking thing I've ever laid my eyes on? I don't care if you're bleeding." He pauses for a second. "Unless you do?"

"I don't care," I whisper. "But pretty much every guy I've ever been with did."

Something akin to a grumble vibrates in his chest before he crosses both arms over it and removes his hoodie and shirt in one motion, leaving him in only his jeans.

"I never want you to even think, let alone talk about, another man. The only cock you'll ever ride is mine."

He pulls at the hem of my sweater, and I lift my arms overhead.

"Goddamn, Jenna." Tossing my clothes across his apartment, he drops his eyes down my half-dressed body, biting on his fist as he does. "Get in my bed and fucking stay there until I tell you that you can leave."

I'm over his shoulder before he's even finished his sentence.

When he kicks his bedroom door closed with a thud and tosses me onto his mattress, we're drenched in darkness. All I can hear is the zipper on his pants as he undoes it and his belt buckle rattling when he pushes his pants to the floor.

I'm throbbing with need, scrambling to find the button on my own jeans when he stops me.

"Get on your hands and knees."

All I can picture is how he'll take me slowly, just like he did the last time we spent the night together.

I thought that was what I wanted this time around. But as a lustful fire burns in his eyes, I know Tommy wants to unleash.

He pulls down my jeans and period panties, not caring about the streaks of blood they leave on the inside of my thighs. If anything, the sight only fuels his desire.

I do as he asked and get on all fours on his bed.

"I might ruin your white bedsheets," I tell him, feeling just as turned on as he looks. "And I apologize for that in advance."

Now totally naked, Tommy hovers on his knees directly behind me, the mattress dipping with his weight. The city lights create the softest glow, and I see the way his hard cock shines with desperation.

"I don't need your apologies, Hellion," he growls at me. "I need your cunt. Drop your face to the mattress and stick this fine ass in the air for me."

He smacks my ass hard, and I jerk forward, collapsing my face into the sheets.

"Do you remember our safe word?"

I nod once.

"Good."

With one more crack of his palm against my ass, he plunges his tongue into my pussy, licking me ferociously.

"So fucking gorgeous," he croons, moving to my asshole.

I knew it wouldn't take him long to tease my ass, anal is his favorite kind of sex.

"Can you be on your period all the time?"

I twist my head around to look at him. "Not with the cramps that accompany it."

In response, Tommy runs his warm palm along my lower back, still eating me out so good. "Want me to take it slow?"

I narrow my eyes at him. "I want you to take me harder than you ever have. Coming hard actually helps me with the pain."

Tommy's lips are tinged with red when he pulls back, licking them clean. He's all cocky and sexy and … holy shit … pushing inside me with the hardest dick I've ever felt.

"Your pussy is so pretty like this, Jenna. And knowing that I'm the only man who has fucked you like this, the only man you've ever let see you in this way?" He shakes his head and passes his fingers over my clit, bringing them to his mouth to taste. "I'm equal parts feral and honored."

With his other hand, he moves my knees wider, spreading me out for him so I'm just how he wants me.

The cramps in my lower back give way to a needy pulsation as I grip his cock tightly.

Tommy pulls out and slams back into me, drawing moans from us both.

"Harder," I demand.

He wraps my long hair around his fist, guiding my head back toward him. The next thrust has me seeing stars as I stare up at the ceiling. I'm impaled on his cock and ruining his bedsheets, and I've never been so fucking horny.

"Does that feel good, Jenna?" He groans out his question, snapping his hips back into me once more.

I just moan into the room—the only response I'm capable of giving him right now.

"Fuck it. I need to see you." Still inside me, Tommy reaches across to his bedside lamp. "Shit, baby," he announces, his voice filled with humor. "I'm covered in you."

Fueled by embarrassment, I pull off him and go to climb off the bed, but Tommy grabs my left ankle, dragging me back beneath him.

"Where are you going?"

My face must be as red as his dick. I chance a glance at his lower half; he keeps himself well-trimmed, and that only makes the mess I've made more obvious.

Not saying another word, Tommy lifts my leg into the crook

of his elbow, spreading me wider for him. Now on top, he sinks back inside my pussy, his eyes never leaving mine as he does.

"Paint me, Hellion. Come all over me."

I tighten to the point of pain. It feels like I'm crushing his cock, and Tommy only grinds deeper inside in response.

"Tell me something," he says between deep thrusts that push me to the very brink of ecstasy. "I get to take you out and buy you cocoa at the rink. Then you let me take you back to my place, where we do things together that we've never done with anyone else before. At what point can I call you mine?" His deep gaze burns into me. "I need you to write me a list of all the things you need me to do, so you'll give me a chance as your boyfriend."

I wrap my legs around his ass, pushing him deeper inside me.

"I've told you … just keep doing what you're doing. Keep being this version of the man I know you are. Keep letting kindness and compassion win, and I promise you will find your happy place in life. Maybe even with me by your side."

I'm so desperate to tell him that we can make us official right this second. But I hold back again. I know Collins, Kendra, and Darcy would be screaming at me to just go for it.

Tommy reaches between us, eyes glittering with hope and possession. He brings his covered fingers to his mouth, sucking me from them, one by one. "Is that a promise?"

Just like he wanted me to, I unravel all over his cock, melting into the mattress while he fucks me hard.

"I'll wait for you," he declares. "For as long as you need, I'll wait."

THIRTY-SEVEN

TOMMY

Even though Jenna still hasn't given the green light for me to officially date her, the past ten days of my life have never been so easy. Or drama-free.

"That has to be some kind of record," Archer comments, pulling off his pads as we all get ready for the showers.

We just nailed Philly to the wall, and my goalie is in a particularly good mood, having secured yet another shutout.

I take a seat on the bench and start unlacing my skates. I've no idea what he's referring to, but I hope he's about to thank me for putting in my best performance of the season so far—maybe even since I signed for the Blades. Archer might have made the shutout, but no one was getting through our defensive line. I was on fucking fire tonight.

My goalie shakes his head, tossing his jersey into the wash bag set in the center of the locker room. "A whole game and not one punch thrown. I'm starting to think Philly lost that game through shock more than our own performance."

From beside Archer, Jack snorts a laugh. It isn't designed to antagonize or berate me. It's friendly. "How does it feel?" he asks me.

"How does what feel, Cap?" I reply, head down and focused on my skates.

"To be growing all soft?" he clarifies.

I lift my head up and smirk at him. "I've got zero idea what you're referring to."

With a towel wrapped around his waist, Jack folds his arms over his chest, eyeing me carefully. He's all golden retriever. If there's one thing I've learned about Jack Morgan since I moved to Brooklyn, the guy loves it when there's a love story blooming.

"You know exactly what I'm talking about. Let's just say, Kendra announcing that she's pregnant wasn't the only surprise revealed that night."

Emmett sidles up next to Jack, a broad grin across his face. Over the past few weeks, he's been more forthcoming in conversation in the locker room and generally looks more relaxed than I've ever seen him before. I don't know why that is, but I like it. I like Emmett to be honest, he's a good guy and a great player and I want to get to know him better. "When they left your place, Tommy and Jenna definitely didn't hate-fuck. Oh no, it was slow and passionate."

For the first time in my life, I blush in front of my teammates. Dropping my head, I stand from the bench and start working on my pads. "How about you all focus on your own relationships?" The second the words leave my mouth, I know I fucked up.

"Wait." Archer cups his hand around his ear, pretending like he can't believe what he just heard. "Did someone say relationships?!"

Jack claps his hands together, full fucking love-guru mode activated.

I roll my eyes and blush a-fucking-gain.

"Do you looooove Jenna Miller?" Jack dances over to me like a ballerina, a smile popping the dimple in his cheek. "She's got you wrapped around her little finger; I could tell by the puppy-dog eyes you gave her at my place."

"We aren't dating," I confirm, not bothering to deny that I have feelings for her since it would be a lie.

But do I love Jenna? I think there's a fair chance I'm heading that way. And when I reach my final destination, I'll likely crash and burn when the feeling isn't reciprocated. Either way, I know I'll never want to leave.

"But you want to date her?" From nowhere, Sawyer joins the conversation, and suddenly, I'm surrounded by four hockey players.

"I'm not discussing my love life with you," I bite out, fighting against a tidal wave of intrigue.

"It's okay." Archer shrugs a shoulder, casting his eyes around our group. "I can get my bulletins from Darce. Jenna is keeping the girls updated."

And just like that, I'm now the one desperate for information. "Wait, what?"

Archer rolls his jaw around, satisfied he now has me hooked.

He isn't wrong.

"Jenna apparently told the girls that you want to date her," Archer replies, drawing an excited gasp from Jack and a raised brow from Sawyer and Emmett.

I smirk, but it isn't for the benefit of my teammates; it's more to myself. Jenna is talking to her girlfriends about me. While I know absolutely nothing about dating and relationships, I do know that when a girl is caught up over a guy, she generally turns to her friends for advice.

Yeah, she's into me.

And because my girl obviously doesn't mind others knowing where we're at, I decide what's the harm in talking to a few guys about matters of the heart?

"Jesus Christ, this is fucking weird for me," I announce, pushing a hand through my sweat-soaked hair.

Sawyer looks confused. "You mean talking to people about emotions or just talking to people in general?"

I can't help but laugh at my own expense.

"Oh my God." Jack points at the center of my chest. "Did I just witness Tommy Schneider laugh?"

"You sure did, Jack. I'm still processing the phenomenon myself," Emmett replies.

"Fuck off," I volley back.

"Annnd normal service has resumed," Archer quickly counters.

I fight back another laugh and reset my focus on Jenna. "I won't bore you with the details, but—"

"No. Please go ahead and bore us with the details. We want to know it all, from start to finish." Jack steps forward.

Sawyer drops his head between his shoulders. "I say this with the greatest respect for my captain. But, please, shut the hell up, Jon, and let the guy speak."

I offer Sawyer a thankful look.

"Jon?" Jack's head darts to Sawyer. "My name is Jack."

Sawyer just grins at him. "Sorry about that. I got the two of you mixed up for a second. You're like the same person."

Jack narrows his eyes at him, and, yep, I laugh again. What I've also come to learn is that while Coach Morgan may be Jack's stepdad, they're also like two peas in a pod, and this winds the hell out of my captain.

Handy to know.

"So, yeah, I have feelings for Jenna." I cut to the chase. "I'm in unknown territory because I've never been remotely interested in a girl before. Trouble is, we didn't get off on the right foot with each other, and now I'm trying to make up for being an asshole. We might've started out hating each other, but that changed over time. We've been meeting up ..." I pause and rephrase to something more accurate. "Well, I've been showing up at her apartment because I can't seem to stay away."

I run a hand down my face, parting my fingers to eye my teammates, who stand, waiting patiently for me to continue.

"Up until I met Jenna, every person I'd ever known had been convinced I was an asshole." I huff out a breath and flick my eyes to Sawyer. Bar Jenna, he's the closest anyone has ever come to seeing beneath my bullshit. "I get why she hated me since I'd punched her brother and treated her like shit, but I think I know why I did."

"Why?" Archer asks quietly.

I shake my head, remembering the way I told her that she was too old to interest younger guys like me. "Because she intimidated me, and conversely, I seemed to have zero effect on her. She stood up to my gibes." I scratch at the back of my neck. "Planted surf 'n' turf in my hotel room late at night so I'd stand in it when I got up and tried to work out what the fuck the smell was."

"What?!" Jack bursts out.

I wince. "When we were in Boston, I kind of slid her dinner into her lap. The same surf 'n' turf I then stood in later that night."

I look around at the four of them, all red-faced.

"Go ahead. Laugh." I motion around the group.

Raucous laughter fills the locker room.

I wait a few beats for them to gather themselves. Like fucking kindergarteners.

"For a long while, it was back and forth like that. We'd fuck, and then she'd flee, hating herself for being with me, but equally unable to say no." I look down at the floor. "I was the same."

When I lift my head, Jack and Archer are exchanging a glance.

"What?" I ask.

Jack waves my question off. "It's just your reference to fucking and fleeing. Archer used to do that when he was a playboy."

Jack might be dismissing the phrase, but it isn't totally irrelevant, and I know it.

"I think that's why Jenna intimidates me." I swallow and think about the real possibility that she could decide I'm not worth the risk and move on to someone else. I wouldn't blame her if she did. I'm not exactly boyfriend material.

Even though I know I could be with her.

"She's uber confident and sure of herself in bed. She's fucking fine to look at and super smart in general. Add in that she's a pro soccer player and about to be captain." I swallow hard. "I don't stand a goddamn chance, do I? Jenna was convinced that I was playing a game with her heart and head, but …" I smile to myself, knowing I've been outplayed in every way possible. "She was playing me all along. Even if neither of us knew it."

Sawyer claps a hand on my shoulder, squeezing it in his palm, and I blink several times. What is it about this guy that stirs something deep inside of me?

I look up at him, not caring that he can probably see the emotions I'm feeling. This guy is a true father, the blueprint of how you should treat a son. Between him and Collins, Ezra is a lucky little dude.

Jenna was right again when she said that if I stopped acting like an asshole and actually gave people a chance, I might see the good in them.

Right here, in the Blades' locker room, I feel myself fall for her a little harder.

"I'm royally fucked," I say, dropping my head and pinching the bridge of my nose. "My feelings are getting stronger for her, even when she isn't around or trying."

Jack clears his throat, stepping toward me as Sawyer takes a pace back.

"You aren't fucked, buddy. You're just on your way to the greatest fucking redemption I've ever witnessed." He casts his hand around the room. "Every guy in here can see and appreciate the work ethic you're putting in for the team. You swallowed your pride and got on with being the player we knew you could be." He edges even closer, dropping his voice to keep our conversation private. "And on a personal note, my respect for you soared when you did what you did to protect Jenna from that fucker."

He doesn't say Ethan's name, and he doesn't need to.

"I can tell the depths of your feelings just by the way you look at her."

I simply nod at him, right as the locker room door pushes open and Coach Morgan walks in.

He scans the room, and his search finally ends when he lands on me, standing alongside my teammates. His face warms the second he takes in my surroundings, and then he quickly resets his demeanor, thumbing over his shoulder. "Grab a shower, Schneider. I need to talk with you in my office."

THIRTY-EIGHT

JENNA

I can't remember the last time I slept in my own bed.

Okay, that might be an exaggeration given it was only last week, but still, I've been waking up at Tommy's more often than not.

The Blades just got back from another away series in Texas, and I decided to surprise him by showing up at his place in the dead of night. Dressed in a raincoat and barely anything else.

"What do you have planned for today, Jenna?" Tommy releases a contended sigh, planting kisses along my collarbone. "It's a crying fucking shame that you don't like lazing around in bed because I could help fill in your free time."

Beneath his duvet, I curl my toes, desperate for him to enter me. The skimpy outfit I wore had the desired effect, and I was railed to within an inch of my life all night, but somehow, I still want more.

"I could be convinced to stay in bed a little longer, if the offer's on the table," I reply with a giggle.

Tommy's dark hair brushes over my forehead as he hovers over my body, bringing his lips to mine. "Last night was the first time that you showed up at my apartment. Normally, it's me doing the chasing." He licks along my bottom lip, a promise of what's to come. "So, yeah, I'd say you're a shoo-in for more playtime in my bedroom."

Naked and needy for him to slide back inside me, I clamp my legs around his ass, guiding his hips toward my entrance. I know Tommy's hard—he's always hard for me.

Initially, he lets me have my way, pushing maybe an inch of his dick into my pussy. I feel sore and overstimulated from the way he fucked me without mercy the second he clapped eyes on the tiny black underwear lurking beneath my raincoat. But then he stops sliding inside.

I double down and squeeze my thighs tighter. "Make me come, Tommy," I plead. "Make me scream like only you can."

He gazes down at me, his jaw clenching as so many thoughts race through his mind.

Reaching up, I run my fingers through his soft bedhead.

"Is it only me, Jenna?"

I throw him a puzzled look; I haven't slept with anyone else in a while, and he knows this.

He presses his forehead against mine, closing his eyes. He looks pained … or maybe more perplexed. He needs an answer from me about us. He wants to make us official, and I need to start communicating where my head is at.

Truthfully, I wouldn't be here, in his bed, begging him to fuck me, if I wasn't all the way involved with Tommy or if I didn't see a future with him. I might have a history of casual sex with guys, but I make a hard pass if I think they have potential feelings and I'm about to hurt someone.

I look down my body to where we're connected and then back up at Tommy. The more I see of this man, the more I'm convinced of the boyfriend I know he can be. He's cleaned up his act on and off the ice. He cooks for me and treats me like a fucking queen. He's so perfect. My girls say it, and my heart agrees. I just need to convince my brain that it's okay to take a risk on the boy I, once upon a time, couldn't even look at. The boy who hurt my brother.

Twisting a piece of his hair around my finger, I wait for him to lift his head and look at me. I want him to see the sincerity in what I'm saying. "You know I only want you."

Tommy squeezes his eyes shut. "Are you talking about me being the only guy who gets to sleep with you or the only guy who gets to call you his? Because there's a huge difference between the two, Jen. And while I want both, it's the latter I'm burning to be."

"Why do we have to put a label on us?" I ask.

I know he's hurting and likely frustrated, but he doesn't let it affect the way he speaks or treats me. I'm not trying to test him or play games. And I don't miss the patience he repeatedly shows me. He knows he has a long way to go to earn my trust. And I wasn't full of bullshit when I left that voicemail, telling him he would never hear my voice again.

"I just want to be certain that when we fully commit to each other, the past won't come back to bite us. We might've met each other over a year ago, but I feel like we only started getting to know each other more recently. I'm learning all about you, Tommy."

He slides in a little deeper, satisfied with my response. "If heaven and hell came together and made a living being, then they would be exactly like you."

"So you keep reminding me." I chuckle and then gasp when he pushes all the way inside.

Tommy reaches above my head and grabs hold of his headboard, rolling his hips into me slowly.

"Since I'm learning all about you, specifically my favorite body part of yours ..." I begin.

Tommy grins down at me, teasing my nipple piercing with his other hand. "Go on ..."

Like the needy bitch I am, I spread my thighs even wider for him.

"The script tattooed around your cock—whenever I see it, it's usually buried deep inside me within seconds, so I never get a chance to read what it says."

Tommy releases the headboard, bringing his hand to the side of my face as he grinds into me again. "What it says is irrelevant because it's no longer my truth."

I immediately reply, pressing a hand to the center of his chest. "*Everything* about you—past, present, and future—is relevant to me. Don't hide from me, Tommy."

The second I finish my sentence, Tommy has me in his arms, carrying me over to a chair which is set in the corner of his room. He sits down first and then lowers me onto his dick. We're facing each other and he's deep inside me, burying his face between my breasts.

This position is a favorite of mine, and he knows it. Briefly, I wonder if this is a distraction tactic on his behalf, but he proves me wrong when he starts talking again.

"It's written in Italian. I've always had this fascination with Italy. The food, drink, the people." He smiles. "The fact that their country is shaped like a kicking boot."

"You see"—I glide my palm across his smooth pecs—"I'm learning all about you."

"But what it says isn't something I believe anymore, Jenna. Some of the tattoos I have on my body never meant anything other than I liked how they looked. Others I put there to remind me never to trust a single person." He kisses my shoulder. "And never to trust love."

"Is that what the tattoo says?" I ask. "*Never trust love?*"

Tommy hooks his finger under my chin, asking me to look at him. "Yes. But like I told you, I don't believe in it anymore. I was nineteen when I got that done, and I never could've predicted the turn my life would take a few years later."

I shake my head. Confused. "Right now, you might as well be speaking in Italian."

Tommy presses his mouth against mine, passion flowing from him and flooding my insides. "It's hard to doubt love when you feel the way I do for you. All-encompassing, life-changing." He sighs against my lips. "So much fucking love."

I'm sitting in his lap, waiting for my brain to spin out and scream at me to run. To declare that this is too much and too dangerous and this whole thing is going to end in the biggest car crash.

I wait for the images of Tommy hitting Holt to come sailing back into my mind or the way he made me cry in Lloyd's. The ways we tried to fuck each other over in the early days.

Not one of those images materializes. Only peace. All I can see is Tommy in front of me.

He takes my hand and kisses each one of my fingers in turn. "I'm so fucking scared. I love you, and I'm so fucking scared about what that means for me if you walk away and decide that there's too much history between us. That we're irreparable and I've hurt you too many times. I know I'm not the safest bet when it comes to boyfriends, and I know when your brother finds out that I pushed my way back into your life, he'll want to murder me, but I have to tell you. I can't hold it in anymore because it's who I am now. And you know what?" He places my palm over his heart, and I watch as the scissors and thread disappear beneath my hand. "You put me back together. I think you might've fixed me. So, while—for once in my life—I'm not ashamed to admit that I'm terrified, I am so thankful to you for helping me see light. The tattoos on my body no longer reflect who I am, but serve as a reminder of the person I never want to be again. Even if you turn away and decide I'm not the guy for you, I know I'll never go back to the bitter man I was before I met you."

"Tommy I—"

"Shh …" Tommy sets a single finger against my lips. "It's okay, Jenna. You don't need to say a thing. Let's just live in this moment. Let me have my time with my girl."

My throat is thick, and my palms are sweaty as Tommy continues to move beneath me. There's no way that we're just fucking anymore. His breathing, his eyes, and his actions have turned into something way deeper. And I move with him, taking a risk with my own feelings while I let him pull me in.

Ringing filters from another room in Tommy's apartment, cutting through the moment between us.

"Wait, what's that?" I say, looping my hands around the nape of his neck.

Tommy's brow creases as he listens. "Did you swipe my card and order more leggings when I wasn't looking?"

I smirk and shake my head at him. "No. But that isn't a bad idea."

He rolls his eyes when the ringing doesn't stop, and I reluctantly climb off his lap.

Tommy stands and pulls on some athletic shorts, handing me his oversize training top to wear.

It smells of him as I pull it on, and for the briefest second, I catch his eyes as they ascend the length of my body, pausing when he sees his initials stamped across my chest.

He leans down, setting a kiss over them. "Stay here for me. I'll go and see what they want."

THIRTY-NINE

TOMMY

Because I don't do takeouts and my social calendar isn't exactly stacked, I know that whoever is requesting permission to access my floor is likely someone I don't see on the regular.

Security only ever dials my internal phone when they have a visitor standing in front of them in the lobby.

Maybe it's Jack, Archer, Sawyer or maybe even Emmett stopping by to kick back and relax or work out in my home gym —which they have freely admitted is ten times better than their own, just by the pictures I showed them the other day.

After Coach called me into his office following the Philly game and confirmed that my official warning had been rescinded and that they had zero intention of dropping me from the roster, my life feels a world away from where it was six months ago. Even three months ago.

All I need is the girl in my bedroom to make it official between us, and I'll be golden.

"Hi," I simply say when I pick up the receiver.

"Good morning, Mr. Schneider," a deep and very official-sounding male voice greets me.

I've been living in this apartment since I signed with the Blades, but I have made zero effort to get to know the doorman or security stationed down in the lobby. Jenna would know this guy by name. Hell, she'd probably even share a pizza with him.

"How are you?" I blurt out awkwardly.

There's a pause on the line. It's brief but pronounced, and I cringe at how weird that just sounded.

"I'm, err ... very well. Thank you for asking, Mr. Schneider."

"You can just call me Tommy." I continue my ramble.

Another pause.

"Tommy," he says, "I have a visitor down here in the lobby who is requesting access to your floor. He tells me he's family and you are expecting him. However, as he doesn't have a temporary code, which only you can provide to guests, I wanted to be sure that we should go ahead and allow him up."

I heard a total of two words in that sentence—*he* and *family*.

A cold shiver chases down my spine, and I grip the handset tighter.

"Did the visitor give a name?" I ask cautiously.

"He did. Alex Schneider. I have verified his identity. Do I have your permission to allow him access to your apartment door, Tommy?"

All over again, it's like I'm standing by my dad's front door, bending down to untie the laces on my battered sneakers.

"Sir?" The security guard yanks me back to reality.

"Yes. Send him up, but please provide him with a onetime-only access code."

"No problem. And sorry to disturb your morning."

When the call cuts, I replace the handset and stalk back into my bedroom, ready to get Jenna out of my apartment. I have no idea why Alex is here, but I don't want him to set eyes on her. Beyond my teammates and her friends, the next person to find out about whatever we are should be Holt.

Steam filters from under my en suite door, quickly followed by Jenna's happy humming, and my heart swells and drops at the same time.

She's in the shower, and there's no time to get her out.

Grabbing a Dri-FIT from my dresser, I throw it on and quickly smooth my bedhead, pausing and taking a second to center myself.

I shouldn't have let him upstairs. He has no right to be here.

By the time I reach the door, the smart doorbell is already ringing, and I pause for another second, drawing a deep breath into my lungs.

I've imagined this moment a lot since I was unceremoniously kicked out of his apartment at seventeen. Pent-up anger, hatred, and bitterness indulged my fantasies, to the point where I'd dream about a day similar to this one, where I finally got a chance at retribution.

But as I pull my door open, I'm not greeted with the same man who laughed in my face and humiliated me, all while playing his PlayStation.

From when I was a young kid and all the way through to the moment I opened this door, the image I've carried of Alex Schneider has been one of strength, brutality, and superiority. Everything I've tried to emulate throughout my career.

That's not what's staring back at me. This is a shadow of the man I had pinned to my bedroom ceiling when I was twelve years old. He's a walking, breathing version of consequence and what happens when you burn every bridge you've ever had and tread all over those you've ever known.

Alex Schneider is his own retribution.

"Son."

That's all he says from my doorway. His voice is soft, a stark contrast to the rough edges of his beard. His hair is still dark, like mine, but I can tell he's dyeing it, unlike Coach Morgan, who is a year younger than Alex and embracing his salt-and-pepper hair.

And while Alex's clothes are obviously designer, his overall outfit screams of a man trying to project an image far more glamourous than the lines in his face reveal.

His red eyes tell me he's traveled a distance to be here.

I drop my eyes down the length of his body, cocking my head to the side when I take in his dark sneakers. It's almost Christmas, and winter has fully set in outside. I'd expect this guy to be wearing weather-appropriate boots and a coat, not a tan leather jacket that's seen better days, along with his battered and rain-soaked sneakers.

Like a vampire, he's waiting for me to invite him in, and I step to the side, offering him just enough room to squeeze past me and into the vast expanse of my open plan living area. From memory, my place is not unlike Alex's, and I fight the urge to remind him that what goes around eventually comes around.

When he drops his black leather bag onto my gray tiled floor with a thud, I thank myself for being a neat freak. Just like I did when Jenna showed up unannounced last night, I look like I have my shit together, even if the truth couldn't be more opposite.

To hide the tremors in my hands, I shove them into the pockets of my shorts and stride across to my corner couch, smiling that I don't even own a gaming console anymore.

Throwing myself down on the couch in a faux casual manner, I cast a quick glance toward the hallway leading to my bedroom. Jenna generally takes the longest showers in history, but there's no way Alex will be gone by the time she's out. He came here with a purpose. I can tell by the way he sits down on the chair opposite me, crossing his leg over at the knee.

I point to his sneakers. "You're leaving marks on my polished floor."

Alex casts his gaze to them, shrugging a single shoulder. "You didn't ask me to remove them."

Jesus. It's like witnessing myself twenty years from now. And I don't like what I see. The internal battle my father is having to speak respectfully with his own flesh and blood is not the person I want to be. He knows he has no right to be here, and I suspect he's surprised I allowed him past security. Still, his vulnerable position isn't enough to totally eradicate the smarmy, cocky attitude imprinted on his soul.

Mom had to deal with this man. Whether she liked it or not, she needed his financial support in order to feed and clothe me.

I bite down on my bottom lip, a wave of emotion stinging the back of my eyes.

Maybe she denied my true father's identity because she knew nothing good could come of me knowing him.

When I first walked away from her, the phone calls were frequent, and my voicemail was often full. But as the years have passed and time has worn on, her attempts to make contact have lessened. I guess she would know I'm doing okay from media reports.

But how is *she* doing? She didn't even send her regular text on my last birthday.

Alex's eyes rove around my apartment. "Did you buy this place yourself, or is the rental built into your terms?"

I lean forward, bracing my elbows on my knees as I take him in. "After all this time and everything that's gone down between us, that's the first question you ask me?"

He runs a rough palm over his mouth. Like me, he's covered in tattoos. Although he hasn't maintained them, and they look faded.

"What do you want me to say, Tommy?" He slaps his thigh with frustration.

I return the shoulder shrug he gave me earlier. "I wasn't particularly bothered about hearing from you at all. You're the one who showed up here, so I figured you had something important to say."

"Well, I do," he counters.

I motion to the space between us. "Go ahead then. The floor is yours." I sit back on the couch, checking once over my shoulder. Really, I'm looking for signs of Jenna, but I play it off as checking the clock set on the wall behind me. "I have an appointment I need to be at in a half hour, so best make it quick."

Alex clears his throat, his unease at my dismissive tone evident.

"I actually came here to apologize. I've …" He trails off, shifting in the chair for a second. "I've had a few health issues lately, and it's brought it home that life is fragile and not guaranteed, and I wanted to reach out and tell you that."

I nod appreciatively, my heart beating clean through my chest. Like a swan on a lake, I appear centered and calm. Underneath, I'm frantic, my mind trying to work out if his words are genuine.

"I watched your game against Philly and then your away series in Miami." He raises his brows. "Your game style—it reminds me of my own. It's nice to see that the enforcer hasn't totally died a death in the league."

Twelve-year-old Tommy would be screaming with excitement and blushing at the compliment. Seventeen-year-old Tommy would think he was right on track with his aim to be the best Schneider to ever grace the league. Present-day Tommy feels sick to his stomach at the thought of ever wanting to be like the man sitting in front of him.

"I'm nothing like you. On or off the ice." My voice is quiet but solid, and I mean every word.

Alex huffs out a doubtful laugh. "Son, you have fifty percent of my DNA. Of course you're like me."

I shake my head and think about my captain and Coach Morgan. Jack doesn't share a shred of DNA with his stepdad, yet they are essentially the same person. I know next to nothing about Jack's father, but I do know he's alive, and he never comes to his son's games.

If I had a son, I'd be all over his career. Involved in every aspect of his life.

I'd want to be like Sawyer.

"I used to believe that," I reply, lifting my head to look at him. "Not so much now."

He looks like he's fighting with his temper, and I maintain my silence and eye contact with him. It's easier if he shows his true colors now rather than in ten minutes when I eventually ask him to leave.

Alex Schneider has nothing for me. Nothing good anyway. He's here because he feels sorry for himself. Maybe the health story is true, and he has had a wake-up call. I don't much care. He didn't care when he treated me like a piece of shit that he just stepped in on the sidewalk.

Rage builds inside me, turning my knuckles white as I dig my fingernails into the soft flesh on my palms.

I want to cut him down and stick the knife in a little deeper when I'm done.

"All right ..." Alex cracks his jaw. "Since you don't care for small talk or anything nice I have to say, I might as well take the direct approach."

I remain silent, fighting internal trembles as they vibrate through my bones. I've no clue what's going to leave his mouth next, but I'm pretty sure I won't like it.

"I have medical bills I need to pay. My liver has been playing me up for a while now, and let's just say, my insurance company wasn't the most understanding when they learned about the life-style I'd been living the past ten years."

Fuck.

"I ended up approaching some not-so-savory loan people to help me fund the medical care I needed, and you'll be pleased to know that I'm living the good life and feeling a lot better." He smiles like that's the best news I've ever heard.

"Trouble is"—he winces, almost sarcastically—"now they want their money back, plus some pretty steep interest."

I roll my eyes toward the ceiling. "And you haven't got the money to pay them?"

"Bingo!" he declares, snapping his fingers. He leans forward on his elbows, mimicking and mocking the way I did the same a couple of minutes earlier. "So, tell me, *son*, is this place a rental, or do you own the deed? Because these loan sharks are *really* interested to know." He leans back, satisfaction rolling from him. "You play under the same name as me. They know you have money. They figure that you don't want to see your old man back in the hospital."

My fists ball even tighter. Images of me putting him back in a hospital bed myself flash in my mind as the red mist descends.

There's no way I'm paying off his debts, and he probably knows it. He's just trying his luck at threatening me with the fear of filthy scum showing up at my door.

What Alex Schneider has failed to realize is, the scum's already here. And he's sitting right in front of me now.

Once bitten, twice shy.

I'm ready to launch. Anger burns in my muscles, coiling them for a strike.

No one threatens me. No one.

Especially not with my girl in the other room.

Jenna.

"Because people who live their life with a lack of compassion for others generally have little for themselves too. Living life without making mistakes is impossible and a one-way ticket to loneliness."

The words she once said douse the flames burning through me. My fists are still coiled, adrenaline raging through every part of my body.

But it's enough. Her sentiment is enough to remind me of the person I want to be for her. For us. For me. She needs to see the real Tommy, not the twisted-up one.

And that's the type of person I want to be.

When I stand from the couch, Alex's eyes track my movements. I can feel them burn into the back of my head as I make my way to the front door and calmly twist the handle.

Pulling the door open, I motion toward the hallway. "I'm sorry to hear of your health and financial issues, Alex. Hopefully, you can turn your luck around, but I'm not in a position to be able to help."

He flies from the chair, snatching up his bag before he's right in my face. I can smell the liquor on his breath.

"You can't even help your old man out?" he sneers, looking down the length of my body. "The league says that you're a rotten piece of shit, destined for the farm team, and now I see why! You're no Schneider, and I'm ashamed that you wear my name."

I just smile at him and flick my eyes to the open doorway. "Keep watching my games, Dad. Because next season, your name will be a distant memory. Last week, I put in a request to play under Williams."

On a scoff, he stalks through the door, and still wearing the same smile, I calmly close it behind him.

"You're going to play under Williams?"

I turn on my heel to see Jenna. Wrapped in a fluffy white towel, she looks at me with soft eyes, waiting for my reply.

I nod my head as I walk toward my girl, wrapping my arms around her waist when I reach her. "Yeah, Hellion, I did. I figured it was time for a change."

Dampness coats her eyes, and I palm the back of her head, pressing a gentle kiss against her temple.

"I heard it all. Everything he said to you and everything you said to him. I'm so fucking proud of the way you handled that piece of trash."

My heart races. "He won't bother me again. I promise."

"Us."

I pull back at her single-worded response. "What?"

"Us," she repeats with a bright smile. "He won't bother *us* again." She wraps her arms around my waist as I tower over her. "I'd already decided this in the shower, but now I'm a thousand percent sure of it. I want to take the next step with you. And I want us to tell my brother together. It's time to build some bridges, Tommy."

FORTY

————

TOMMY

"You have to be the only person I know who would want to come to the beach at the height of winter," I whisper into Jenna's ear as she looks out over the horizon.

The moon reflects off the water, glowing against her cheeks.

She scrunches up her nose. "I don't care much for the sun. I'm a fall and winter girl myself."

I look around us. We're the only crazy people for miles, buried under thick winter coats and sitting on a single plaid blanket, eating sandwiches.

It's been a few days since Jenna and I made it official, and tomorrow, her brother arrives for the holidays. When I asked Jenna where she wanted me to take her for our second date, expecting her to suggest the movies or a cutesy restaurant downtown, I probably shouldn't have been shocked when she told me Coney Island.

I've never been here, but I have to admit, she was right about the spectacular light displays.

"You're like a magpie or something," I tell her, reaching across the blanket and interlacing our fingers as we both sit, staring out at the ocean.

"What?!" She bursts out laughing. "Why do I remind you of some random bird?"

I don't immediately answer, taking the time to appreciate the way she giggles in my presence. Seeing the relaxed side of Jenna is relatively new to me. And while I love every part of her personality, even moments when she scorns at me, seeing my girlfriend light up like this is something special.

"Magpies like bright and shiny things," I reply. "They're attracted to sparkles."

"You know that's a myth, right?" she volleys back.

"Myth or not," I cast my hand out across the shining ocean and then around me at the twinkling lights. "The sentiment is still the same, and I'm willing to bet that Christmas is one of your favorite times of the year."

Beneath the dark sky, I see the way she blushes as she says, "Maybe."

I release a sigh, kicking some sand out with my boot.

"Oh, don't be such a Scrooge!" she announces, pressing her palm into the center of my chest.

I collapse onto my back, and she hovers over me.

Her hair falls around us both, shielding us from some of the biting wind that has turned the tip of her nose pink.

"How was practice today?" she asks. "Are you feeling ready for the big game against the Scorpions?"

We're nowhere near the end of the season, but Saturday's home game against one of our oldest rivals is paramount.

"All the guys are feeling the pressure. Especially Archer. If he can keep their forward, Jessie Callaghan, at bay, then we have a shot at coming away with the W."

She nods her head in understanding. I fucking love that Jenna is into hockey and sports.

Reaching up, I slowly pull at the zipper on her coat, memories of the way I teased her with her sports bra roaring back to life.

She blushes and places her hand over mine. "When we get back to my place. It's way too fucking cold out here for sex."

Looping my arms around her back, I roll us over until I'm on top. "I love you. So fucking much. These past few weeks, even the past few days ... they've been some of my best, and I just want you to know that."

"I know, and I'm having the best time." She kisses the tip of my nose, and I can't help but whimper, already desperate to leave and get her in bed. "Have you spoken to your mom?"

I shake my head, a knot forming in my stomach. "No. I left her a voicemail, asking her to call me back. I haven't heard anything since."

Jenna doesn't take her eyes from mine. "Give her time. I bet she's still in shock and wondering what to say when she calls you back."

So much of me hopes Jenna is right. It was a standard recorded message rather than my mom's voice, which makes me worry that she changed her phone number since she last tried to contact me.

"I asked her to come watch our game against the Scorpions. I figured it would be a chance for her to meet my girlfriend, and if your brother doesn't murder me when we tell him about us on Christmas Day, I want you to wear my jersey. With the name I'll be playing under next season."

Jenna cups my face in her gloved palm, concern flooding her eyes.

"What?" I ask. "I thought that was standard practice—for a player's girl to wear their name."

"Yeah, it is," she replies. "But that's not what's worrying me."

I breathe a sigh of relief.

Jesus, who are you, and what have you done with tough Tommy? Now you're practically having a breakdown over a girl's facial expressions.

"Your mom," she continues. "How will she afford the airline ticket to get here? Travel at this time of year is especially expensive."

I smirk down at her. "I don't know if you're aware, but I'm kind of a big deal, and I earn around seven million dollars a year, plus add-ons. I have her airfare covered."

She swats me in the chest. "Why do you always have to be so cocky?!"

"Because you drive me wild and it's my natural defense mechanism," I retort. "Plus, I still think you love the old Tommy just a little bit." I squeeze my thumb and forefinger together, my shoulders vibrating with laughter.

Jenna stays silent.

Shit. I said too much.

She shuffles out from beneath me and stands up, flicking her long hair from her collar.

"Jen, I'm not trying to push you into saying it back. I just ..."

She steps forward as I rise to my knees. Placing a hand on my shoulder, she sets a kiss against my lips. "I know you aren't trying to push me. I just need to use the bathroom and call my brother to let him know that I can get him from the airport."

With that, she begins walking toward a bar across the street from the beach, and I'm left wondering why the fuck I can't control my mouth every time I'm around this girl.

Reaching into my pocket, I pull out my phone to check for a reply from Mom but come up empty-handed.

I'm about to repocket my phone when a group message flashes across my screen, and I click on the notification.

JACK

Welcome to the world's greatest group chat, Tommy.

JACK RENAMED THE GROUP CHAT: TOMMY'S
TURNED INTO A SIMP.

ARCHER

He's with Jenna right now—I can feel it.

ME

I don't want to know what you're feeling, if it's
all the same to you.

SAWYER

So, Tommy is the latest victim of Jack's group
chat. Don't worry, buddy; last season, he
changed the name to something like Stop
Boning My Sister when he witnessed dressing-
room sex between Archer and Darcy.

JACK

I just vomited at the memory.

ARCHER

Christ. That was the hottest sex of my life.

JACK

I actually might hate you.

ARCHER

But your sister doesn't, does she?

ME

If this is what it's like, making friends with
teammates, then I think I'll pass.

SAWYER

This is precisely what it's like.

ARCHER

So, come on then, Tommy. Tell us, are you
with Jenna right now?

ME

Yep. We're on a date, but it's cold as fuck, and
I want to go home ...

With my girlfriend. Obviously.

ARCHER

Why go home when you can bang in public?
As I once told Jack and Sawyer, there's this
Acer tree in the Japanese Gardens. I haven't
taken Darcy there yet, but it's really romantic.

JACK

IF YOU FUCK MY SISTER AT ONE OF YOUR
FORMER PLAYBOY SPOTS, I WILL SHOVE
MY STICK WHERE THE SUN DOESN'T
SHINE.

ME

What the fuck is this group chat?

SAWYER

It's unhinged and disturbing. I've tried to leave
multiple times, but Jack just adds me back in.
I fear the same fate may be bestowed on
you too.

JACK

No one appreciates me around here. Or the
hard work I put into our friendships.

ARCHER

I appreciate your sister.

JACK

You're a father now, Archer. Grow up.

Anyway, I'm actually messaging you all for a
purpose. The game against the Scorpions on
Saturday. When we secure the W, I think we
should all go out and celebrate. Former
Scorpions Captain, Zach Evans, is coming to
Brooklyn to watch the game with his family.
Between him, Jensen Jones, and Jon, we'll
have three Scorpions legends present to
watch their former team burn. *evil face*

SAWYER

Ooof. That's a bit presumptive. I mean, I have every faith in our team but ... Jessie Callaghan and Curtis Freeman. Both are having crazy good seasons.

JACK

Nah, Tommy's got Jessie and Curtis covered, right?

I look up and see Jenna strolling back toward me. She's all smiles and rosy cheeks.

Sitting down next to me on the blanket, she places a hand on my shoulder and whispers into my ear, "I'm getting there, Tommy. I promise."

If I wasn't wrapped in layers of clothing, I swear my heart would burst straight through my chest.

ME

Sorry, you'll have to clarify. Jessie and Curtis who?

FORTY-ONE

JENNA

Christmas Day

TOMMY

I'm about to leave my place. Just finished cleaning ahead of Mom arriving tomorrow.

ME

There is literally nothing left to clean. Your entire apartment squeaks when you touch any surface.

TOMMY

Want to know something about your new boyfriend?

ME

Um, yes. Always.

TOMMY

I clean when I'm nervous.

ME

So, you're nervous all the time?

TOMMY

You know I'm rarely nervous. But when I am, the cleaning increases. It's like my own version of ASMR or something. It's therapeutic. Controlling.

ME

Well, in that case, can you be nervous more often when you're at my place?

TOMMY

Oh, I will be. In around a half hour when I walk through your door and come face-to-face with your six-foot-five brother.

ME

You realize you are also that tall?

TOMMY

True. I can take him.

ME

DO NOT PUNCH MY BROTHER.

AGAIN.

TOMMY

Was the timing of my joke still a bit too soon?

ME

It will never be appropriate.

TOMMY

But what if he punches me when he finds out his archnemesis is dating his baby sister?

ME

Holt doesn't have enemies.

TOMMY

He really is the golden boy of rugby, isn't he?

ME

Rugby's golden boy ... yes. Golden boy elsewhere? Not always. Holt has some skeletons in his closet. We all do.

TOMMY

True that, Hellion.

ME

Are you still bringing dessert with you? Holt and I just finished our entrées, so that will be perfect timing.

TOMMY

Dessert for you and Holt is in hand. My dessert is already there.

ME

I am not having sexual relations with you while my brother is staying here.

TOMMY

I cannot believe he's sleeping on that sofa bed for four nights. He's crazy. One night, and I needed to call an emergency chiropractor.

ME

Go complain to those who decided to pay female pro soccer players next to nothing.

TOMMY

Oh, I will. I'm going to join social media for that reason alone. My first post will be how gross I think it is. You girls work so damn hard.

ME

Flattery will get you everywhere.

TOMMY

Even between your thighs tonight?

ME

Don't push it, Tommy.

TOMMY

I love it when you're mean to me. It just makes me want to fuck you harder.

"Jen," Holt announces from behind me, "do not tell me, now that all the stores are closed, that we have no dessert on Christmas Day."

Setting my phone down on the foldable table we're using as a makeshift dinner table for today, I rise from the chair and come to sit at one of the barstools facing my tiny kitchen.

My brother looks happy, healthy, and in better shape than I've seen him in a long time, maybe even ever. I hope that the happy part will stick around after I tell him that we do, in fact, have a dessert and it is, in fact, being hand-delivered by his favorite person.

"We have dessert," I reply.

He looks around, scratching at the back of his neck. Just like Tommy, Holt in my apartment is kind of comical. Like a giant moving around a doll's house. Everything is so tiny in my one-bed, and Holt is huge in every way possible. As a fly-half, he also has to be agile and the brains of the team, the playmaker literally calling the shots.

"Is it a magical dessert that's suddenly going to appear, or should I make one up? You actually have proper food in your fridge for once, so I could definitely put something together."

Picking up my wineglass, I smile around the rim. The only reason I have proper food these days is thanks to the boy due to arrive anytime.

I take a sip and set the glass back down on the breakfast bar, making a split-second decision that now is as good of a time as any to tell Holt about Tommy. Waiting until he walks through the door might not be my best move.

I clear my throat. "Actually, can I talk to you about something?"

Holt narrows his eyes at me playfully, undoing another button on his white dress shirt. "If it's about how high you run the heating in this place, then sure."

Sliding off the stool and grabbing my wine, I walk across to the couch and take a seat, tucking one leg beneath me. "My cheap-ass landlord finally replaced the furnace. He didn't relish the idea of being sued for freezing his tenants to death."

Holt huffs out a laugh and flops down into the chair on my left. "No. He's going to boil them and their visitors instead."

Glancing quickly at my watch, I know Tommy could arrive at any second. With the way he drives and with hardly any traffic on the roads today, I know it won't take him a half hour to get here—fifteen minutes, tops.

I flick my eyes up to Holt, who's busy typing something on his phone before he sets it down on the coffee table in front of him and gives me his full attention.

"I know you were joking about dessert magically appearing, but …" I tuck some hair behind my ear, fidgeting. "It actually will. Any minute now."

Holt cocks his head to the side in question.

"My boyfriend is bringing it over to eat with us."

I feel my entire body flush with heat as Holt's jaw pops open.

"You didn't tell me you were seeing someone, Jen."

He looks mildly hurt, and that's the last thing I wanted. He's going to be even more upset when he discovers who my mystery guy is.

"I wanted to wait until I could tell you in the flesh."

It's like Holt puts all the pieces together in the time it takes me to sip my wine. He must know that Tommy never got traded in the end, although he's never once mentioned anything to me since he messaged me about it. And he's right to be shocked about me keeping secrets. We never do. Not unless we suspect the other might hate what we have to say.

When my smart doorbell sounds, I genuinely don't think the timing could be worse.

Holt leaps from his chair and storms toward my hallway, swallowing up the distance to my front door in three large strides.

He slides the dead bolt and yanks the door open, practically pulling it from its hinges.

Like the ultimate face-off, Tommy stands on the other side of the door, holding the pecan and maple pie he promised he'd make me since it's my favorite dessert of all time.

I rush to catch up to Holt as Tommy takes a single step back.

Holt's dark brown eyes are black, painted with fury. "What the fuck is he doing here, Jenna?" He drops his attention to the pie in Tommy's hands. "And why is he here with our favorite dessert?"

Dropping my face into my hands, I exhale a slow breath. "Holt, this is Tommy. My boyfriend."

"I know who he is," Holt bites out. "The last time I met him, he insulted my sister for telling him to take a hike and almost broke my jaw."

In retreat, Tommy takes another small step away from Holt, one hand coming up in front of him. "I came here today to talk. I want to set the records straight between us."

Holt's shoulders drop a quarter of an inch from where they were bunched around his ears. He turns his head to look at me, a brief flash of hurt passing over his features. "Why are you mixed up with this asshole? You are worth so much more than him."

Back when I first met Tommy, Holt's statement—while only coming from a place of care and protection for me—would double as a red rag to a bull for my boyfriend. But as I look up at Tommy, I see hurt on his face, too, and my heart sinks into my stomach.

"Can we at least all go inside so we don't run the risk of making a scene out here?" I suggest. "Every neighbor is at home today, and they're probably already listening."

Holt crosses his arms over his chest, one challenging brow raised. "The only person incapable of controlling their temper around here is him." He nods his head at Tommy.

I place my hand on Holt's upper arm. He's so used to protecting me, although he doesn't need to in this moment. I can't say that I blame him. I'd do the exact same thing if this was over a girl who had a history of hurting him and me.

"Hear him out, Holt. Please."

When he steps to one side, I breathe a sigh of relief. Holt's hands slide into his pockets, and Tommy takes a couple of strides into my apartment, closing the door behind him. He hasn't taken his eyes off mine, and when I reach across and take the pie from his arms, I feel the way he brushes his fingers against mine. He wants to reassure me that everything is going to be okay.

Turning on my heel, I make for the kitchen and set the pie on the breakfast bar, a wave of emotion crashing into me when silence descends on the apartment. The boys aren't exchanging a word, and I have no clue how to fix this.

A few months ago, the thought of alienating my brother over a guy was unthinkable. Unfathomable. Holt and I are a team, and we always will be. But today, the thought of losing either of the men standing in my hallway from my life consumes me with fear.

The fear sits there, manifesting in the pit of my gut until I can no longer stand the aching pressure, and I head back up the hallway, stalking toward them both.

Holt's eyes flare wide at the sight of me—and Tommy's aren't dissimilar.

"I need you to give Tommy a chance, Holt. I know what happened back in January was wrong, but he isn't the piece of trash you think he is."

Tommy swipes a palm across his jawline. I can see the wheels turning in his head on what to say.

A couple of beats pass before Holt shrugs his shoulders, exasperated. "Well, if the dude's changed and he's somehow become a good person for my baby sister, then I'm certainly not hearing anything from him to prove it."

"Words are cheap." Tommy's deep voice cuts through the tension. He motions to my brother with his hand. "I could stand here, in my girl's apartment on Christmas Day, and tell you all the ways I'm sorry for what I did that night back in January. That I'm sorry for hurting her on multiple occasions and for being the biggest asshole on planet Earth." Tommy drops his eyes to the floor, scuffing it lightly with his sneaker. He shakes his head, and I can tell it's from memories of himself. "A few words aren't going to cut it though, are they?" He centers his attention solely on my brother.

Holt frowns. "Probably not, no."

Tommy nods his head lightly, like he knew that fact all along. "Good. I'm glad they wouldn't—because they wouldn't for me if I had a sibling and their new partner had behaved in the ways I have." Tommy presses his palms together in a prayer-like manner as he edges toward my brother, eyes boring deep into Holt's. "So, let me *show you* how much I love Jenna. I know we don't have much time before you return to Europe, but give me a chance and watch the way I worship the ground that she walks on. I have zero excuses other than I've not had the easiest life, but neither has Jenna, and I know shit has been tough for you too."

I watch the way Holt swallows thickly. My brother is a sensitive guy, playing in a sport that demands nothing but respect between teammates and from the opposition. He's listening to Tommy, and I'm so damn proud of them both right now.

Pride is a difficult pill to swallow, as is bitterness.

"Your sister has changed my life; even if she didn't realize she was doing it, she was. Sometimes, we're so blinded by our own agenda that we forget to stop and listen to other people and admit when we're wrong. I was wrong to lash out at you that day, Holt. I let my ego get the better of me. All I'm asking you to do is watch me as I build the bridges that only I am responsible for burning."

Tommy turns to look at me, reaching out and taking one of my hands in his. He intertwines our fingers, and suddenly, I'm having *really* inappropriate thoughts involving sports bras, zippers, and this very hallway we're standing in.

"Jenna told me that pecan pie is her favorite and it's yours too." Tommy smirks down at me. "And since she hates cooking, I figured I could stop by and bring you one I'd made."

Holt stands motionless. He wasn't expecting any of that from Tommy. It takes him a good few seconds to reply, and I'd trade anything to know his thoughts.

"Sure. Let's go eat," he finally confirms. "Why not?"

Holt spins on his heel to make for the kitchen when Tommy lands a hand on his shoulder, asking him to wait a second.

My brother turns back to him.

"Jenna tells me that you don't leave Brooklyn for another couple of days and that you like a bit of hockey." He reaches into his back pocket. "When I was younger, my mom always said that ice-level seats beat any corporate-box bullshit you could buy." Fetching out three tickets, he holds them out to Holt. "So, I went ahead and secured three seats for our home game against the Scorpions. The third one is for my mom, Helen. She will be there, and I know she'd really like to meet you." He smiles at me, the corners of his eyes crinkling with warmth. "She's practically vibrating to meet the woman I love."

Holt's large hand wraps around the tickets. I haven't seen paper tickets in a long while, and I love that Tommy got them for us.

Rolling his lips together, Holt stares down at the seat row and number. "These are hot property." He lifts his head to Tommy. "Sure. Count me in."

FORTY-TWO

TOMMY

"Holy HELL!" Emmett announces as we take to the ice for the first period following the warm-up.

Archer slides alongside us. "I have never, in the history of playing for this team, seen an arena this full or heard it this noisy."

"It's like the goddamn colosseum or something," I muse, gazing around.

Archer's right; I've never seen the arena like this. Not during fights, not at any game I've played in or spectated.

The hairs on the back of my neck stand on end, and adrenaline races through my body. This game is huge—a chance for old rivals to make a statement against each other in a fixture that promises to be significant in the race for the playoffs.

Archer nods his head across the ice, the corner of his lip tipping up. If he thinks I haven't seen her yet, then he's wrong. In a crowd of over twenty thousand, I could spin until I'm dizzy and still point her out.

The game's about to start, and I absolutely don't have time, but fuck it. Heading straight toward the plexiglass she's sitting behind, flanked by my mom and Holt, I reach the edge and come to a stop, throwing up ice onto the board.

Our dates to the outdoor ice rink and the beach never made it onto the internet but given that she's wearing a jersey with *Williams* stamped across her back, there's a chance that some of the crowd will connect the dots and remember my former last name. I don't plan on making a big deal or a formal statement about reverting back to *Williams*. My silence will speak all the words that need to be said—I'm done with Alex and with the Schneider last name. My "dad's" legacy can die quietly while I build the life I've always wanted.

The life I deserve.

With no one sitting in front of them, I flip a gloved hand toward me, smiling at my mom as Jenna stands from her seat and takes the couple of steps down. I can't be sure if the arena has genuinely fallen quieter or if I'm zoning out the background noise, but all I can focus on is the dark-haired beauty wearing the jersey I got her specifically for tonight.

With a physical barrier between us, it would be impossible to hold a conversation. Not that I need to open my mouth to say everything I need.

In her sneakers and me in my skates, I tower over Jenna as she looks up at me, eyes sparkling with curiosity.

Tucking my stick under my arm, I twist my gloved finger around, and she does as I asked.

I form a heart with my hands and press it against the plexiglass, right over the name on Jenna's back.

When the crowd bursts into cheers and whoops, I know their reduced noise wasn't coincidental or because I was filtering them out. They had eyes on us both, and now they know how I feel about the goalie and new captain of the New York Storm.

But just to clarify for anyone still unclear, I push off the boards and skate back a few feet, waiting for Jenna to turn around and face me. When she does, I blow her a kiss, followed by a wink.

Yeah. She's my Hellion. And I'm going to love her every goddamn day of my life.

JESSIE CALLAGHAN, PROLIFIC FORWARD FOR THE SCORPIONS, IS having a wild ride tonight.

In my back fucking pocket.

He's barely seen the puck, let alone touched it. Emmett, Sawyer, and the rest of our defensemen have matched my performance.

Archer could probably head home for the third period if he wanted to, he's had next to nothing to do for the first thirty-eight minutes of the game.

Meanwhile, Jack has been kept busy, netting two in the first period and narrowly missing a third when his shot bounced off the inside pipe.

It's been all about the Blades tonight, and I couldn't be fucking happier.

Another failed Scorpions attack hands us an opportunity to counter, and as the puck spills from the boards and across the ice to me, I let Archer know I have it covered and collect it onto my stick.

It's amazing what happens when you're looking for the next sequence in play and not for an excuse to fight. Everything is just so much clearer, including the opening I can take toward goal. I had strict instructions tonight from Coach to stay in my lane and not leave any part of our defensive line exposed, but this opportunity to push forward and get a third goal before the buzzer is too tempting to pass up.

The chance to be the hero and not the villain for once is right there, taunting me in the form of three red posts and a bunch of Scorpions players, who are parting like the ocean for me to skate through.

I know I have the speed and the skill set, and I want to prove to my team, the league, Jenna, and every other person watching that regardless of whatever name I wear on my back, I'm nothing like the person I worked so hard to emulate.

I'm fucking *me*.

Skipping past the Scorpions center is easy enough, throwing him a simple deke that leaves him stranded.

And then I'm across center ice, heading into territory I rarely travel—without the use of my fists, that is—my eyes fixed on the task at hand. I can see Jack in my peripheral vision, and I get a flash of Coach as he watches on from the bench. He's got his hands in the pockets of his black dress pants. Good. He isn't waving them around, asking me to stop.

I can't remember the last time I lit the lamp outside of practice, and it feels almost poetic to do it in front of my girl, her family, and my mom, who traveled to be here today.

The Scorpions goalie is probably their weakest link since Jensen Jones retired a couple of seasons back, and it's right at that moment, when I catch the whites of their goalie's eyes, that I'm certain he fears an incoming shot from me. I might be quick across the ice, but my shot is arguably more impressive. Back in high school, I was called The Hammer, and it had nothing to do with fighting.

Confidence swells inside me as I barrel toward the goal, moving the puck from one side of my stick to the other.

Jack knows I'm planning to go it alone and does me a favor, moving into a position that draws their defenseman away from me as he makes the impossible choice between following Jack to intercept a pass or heading straight for me.

I'm clear and in space, through on goal and sizing up when to take the shot.

The home crowd is sensing Scorpion blood, and I'm feeding off of their energy, winding back to find the top shelf when a last-minute call echoes across the rink.

"Cobra." It's high-pitched, and I swear to God, it sounds like Jenna's voice.

When I hear it for a second time, I'm convinced it can only be in my head, and I take another stride, resetting myself before winding back to take the shot.

It never comes.

The shot.

The puck doesn't travel toward the top-right shelf, and the lamp doesn't light.

In fact, I don't see anything, as everything goes so fucking black. I'd be sure this was all a dream if it wasn't for the searing hot pain traveling down the back of my neck.

Seconds ago, the crowd could sense blood, but all I can do is taste it.

All I can hear is the incessant ringing in my ears before it gives way to Jenna's frantic screams.

This isn't right.

Since we've been together, I've only ever dreamed about Jenna smiling. I've seen and heard enough of her tears to last me a lifetime.

"Tommy!"

The wail penetrates my subconscious once more. I can feel myself reaching out for her. At least, I'm trying to, but it doesn't feel like I'm inside my own body. The pain reminds me that I am, but the rest of reality feels so fucking far away.

So fucking dark.

"Callaghan, I need you to move away. Now!" Another voice, more official, hauls me back into the room.

"I'll step back when I know that a fellow player is going to be okay! What the fuck have you done, Curtis? What the fuck have you done?!"

"Tommy." A male voice I fully recognize speaks softly to me. "Tommy, it's Sawyer. I don't know if you can hear me, but I want you to know that you're going to be okay. You took a hit, and we can't move you, so we're waiting on the medics right now."

A warm, rough palm presses against my own, tempering some of the pain.

I try to nod my head, desperate to let him know that I can hear him, even if I can't form the words. But the second I try to move my neck, pain like I've never felt before in my life ricochets throughout my entire body.

"No. Don't try and move, Tommy. Just …" Sawyer trails off, and I feel the hand as it squeezes mine tighter. "JESUS FUCKING CHRIST, CAN WE GET THE MOTHERFUCKING MEDICS HERE ALREADY?!" I hear Sawyer bellow. Panic lancing through his shaking voice.

Sawyer is the king of cool, the guy everyone wants around them in a bind. He doesn't break; he doesn't waver. He's the dad we all hope to have in our lives, in any way possible. So, when I hear the pure terror in his words, I know that whatever just happened isn't good.

I know that it's entirely possible that my career—maybe even my life—will never be the same again.

FORTY-THREE

JENNA

People race around this place, looking all busy and important, yet no one seems to be able to give me any answers.

Is my boyfriend going to be okay?

That's all I want to know—seven words that form one of the easiest questions I've ever asked. But with the way nurses and doctors are dodging me right now, you would think that I wanted to understand the meaning of life.

I just want to see and speak to Tommy.

My face flops into my hands once more as I lean forward on the uncomfortably hard plastic chair in this godforsaken waiting room.

"How long have we been here exactly?" I ask Holt.

"Maybe two hours," he replies, pocketing his phone and standing just as Helen pushes through the door with two trays of coffees.

She begins handing them out—one each for Holt, Sawyer, Archer, and Jack. She then approaches me with the cappuccino I ordered but can barely think about drinking.

I take it from her and feel the warmth as it radiates through the takeout cup and into my palms.

"Try and at least drink something, Jenna." Her voice is soothing and caring as she places a hand on my knee. "The doctor will update us when he has a clear picture of where Tommy is at."

Her Midwestern accent is way more noticeable than Tommy's. From what Tommy has told me, she has spent most of her life as an assistant stylist in a hairdresser just outside of Minneapolis.

She's a caring person and a far cry from Alex, I can see that in her demeanor and the way she winds her gold cross pendant around her fingers. She told me earlier that when Tommy turned his back and left home shortly after he tracked down Alex, she turned to the church to help her deal with the rejection and pain.

I'm personally not religious—never have been. But I respect anything that helps people deal with the shit in their lives. We all need to find our strength from somewhere.

I blow out a long breath and take a small sip of coffee.

"I just don't understand how a CT scan can take so long. They said Tommy was an emergency case when we got here."

The blood covering his face when they bundled him into the ambulance and sped off to the hospital was the last thing I saw of him. Sawyer is pretty sure he has a fractured arm, multiple lacerations to the face, and possibly a broken ankle, too, judging by the unnatural angle it was in when Tommy was lying on the ice.

But it's the damage to his head, neck, and spine that's the real worry circulating around this room. No one wants to talk about the way Tommy fell or the hit Curtis Freeman put on him. Well, almost no one. Before Darcy took off for home to get back for Emily, she looked me straight in the eyes, telling me how the hit was like a replay of the one Zach Evans took at the hands of Alex. The only difference was, Zach collided with the plexiglass before he hit the ice. Curtis, on the other hand, dropped his shoulder in a premeditated hit at speed, and Tommy went flying over his body, somersaulting in the air before landing on his head.

The way I'd screamed his name when I saw Curtis set off across the ice. It was obvious he only had one thing on his mind. His face was twisted with anger. He was determined to halt Tommy's attack. I never thought a guy like Curtis was vengeful, but he wanted to put Tommy in his place for the beating he'd handed out earlier in the season. Instead, he put him in the hospital.

"The silence is killing me," Jack announces, flying up from his chair as he begins pacing the room. "He has to be okay ..." He pauses his sentence and then continues pacing. "It's Tommy, for fuck's sake. He's basically indestructible."

Sawyer pushes a distressed hand through his hair. He got the best view of Tommy's injuries before the medics entered the ice and crowded the space. "That hit ... it was like nothing I'd ever seen before."

I look at Jack, who looks back at me. We're both thinking the same thing. Zach Evans pulled through with broken bones and a bad concussion, and Tommy can do the same.

"He's going to be just fine, Jenna." Helen knocks her cup against mine.

She can't be much older than Jon Morgan, which would put her in her mid-forties.

"It's just the longer we go without hearing anything from the doctors, the more I feel like there's something really wrong with him." I chew on my bottom lip and set my coffee on the side table to my right. "What if he never plays hockey again?"

Helen dismisses my concerns with the wave of her hand. She's barely spent any time with her boy since she arrived in Brooklyn. She must be reeling inside with worry, but much like her son, she doesn't let her fear show.

Tommy has spent so much time focused on the ways he's just

like his father when, in a short space of time, I can already see how similar he is to his mom. Her short, dark hair is cropped into a bob style with long bangs and dark brown eyes. Tommy definitely got his height from Alex since Helen is petite and slight in build, but her broad smile and full lips remind me so much of my boyfriend. It's hard for me to admit, but Helen radiates a kind of warmth and kindness I've never seen in my own mom. I wonder if that's always been the case or if the mistakes she's made along the way have shaped her into a more compassionate person.

Whatever past events in life got her to this point, I feel like Tommy was right to extend an olive branch.

"I can't picture a day where my Tommy isn't playing hockey," she whispers. "It's all he's ever known. All he ever wanted when he was a boy."

I pick up my coffee and turn the takeout cup around in my hands. "What was he like when he was younger?"

She just smiles, more warmth glowing on her cheeks. "He was inquisitive and fiercely independent. But he had a lot of friends at school. He was one of the popular kids." She chuckles. "Especially with the girls."

I nod along, laughing quietly. "Oh, I can imagine. And what Tommy wants, Tommy gets."

Helen looks a little uncomfortable at that, and I wait to see if she'll say anything more.

"When Tommy makes a decision, no one can stop him. He made the choice to board that plane to New York and find his dad … and when he came home, he was never the same. He moved out and into temporary accommodation shortly after he turned eighteen and then went off to college after he was drafted to play for Detroit."

"He told me he was deeply hurt that you didn't tell him the truth about who his father was," I say.

She drops her eyes to the floor. "I was pinned between a rock and a hard place. I found out I was pregnant with Tommy after a wild night at a bachelorette party in St. Paul. We'd wound up at some bar where the Blades were drinking, and the rest is history."

She turns to look at me. There's no denying her beauty. I can see why she was—and maybe still is—a hit with men.

"Alex told me we'd exchange numbers and it wouldn't just be a onetime thing. I really liked him, and I was so damn young, not even legal to drink." She snorts a soft laugh. "When I found out I was pregnant, I got in contact with him, and that's when I saw the ugly side of that man. He wanted nothing to do with Tommy or me, and he paid me off to keep my silence. It wasn't a whole lot more than the legal amount, but I was short on cash, and I just knew Alex wasn't the type of father that Tommy needed in his life. I hoped I would eventually meet someone who would be a good father figure to him." She clicks her tongue. "I guess I'm just bad at finding decent men, full stop."

This time, I reach across and place a hand on Helen's knee, and I look up and smile at Holt. He's watching us both from across the other side of the room.

"Yeah, that's it. I'm going to spontaneously combust if I don't get some answers in the next thirty seconds." Jack stalks toward the door right as it opens inward, and he grinds to an abrupt stop.

Relief floods my veins when the doctor we initially spoke to on arrival walks into the center of the room, closely followed by Coach Morgan, Jensen Jones and Emmett Richards.

The doctor tucks his pen into the top pocket of his white jacket and takes a seat on the coffee table.

Holt, Archer, Sawyer, and Emmett all come to sit on our side of the room so they can hear what the doctor has to say.

Jack tips his chin at Emmett. "Thanks for coming, man. I know you have a lot of shit going on at home right now, but Tommy will appreciate you showing up for him."

Emmett looks as concerned as I feel, pulling off his backward cap and turning it around in his hands. "I know what it's like to suffer a serious injury that has the potential to change the shape of your career and life. I wouldn't want to be anywhere else than in here with my teammates."

Emmett casts his eyes around the hospital like this place is all too familiar to him, and I see a flicker of sadness in his eyes. From what I know about the veteran Blades defenseman, he largely keeps to himself, but there's been the odd story in the press about his marriage and how it's allegedly on the rocks. When he comes out to Lloyd's for postgame drinks, he's often the first player to leave and head home since his wife has never been keen on socializing with the team or their families.

When the doctor clears his throat and begins to speak, every pair of eyes in this room is laser-focused on him.

"Mr. Schneider—"

"Williams," Jack interjects. "He plays under Schneider currently, but he's in the process of changing his last name. Schneider has no place inside these four walls. I should know what it feels like to carry the name of an asshole father." He huffs out an angry breath.

Helen's head whips up to me. Obviously, Tommy never told her his plans for next season.

I nod once at her, and she smiles so big that I'm pretty sure I just witnessed all this woman's dreams come true at once.

"I appreciate what you're saying, Mr. Morgan, but for now, I have to address him as the name he was admitted under."

"Call him Tommy then." Jack shakes his head, crouching down and bouncing on his heels.

I can tell he's really struggling right now.

The doctor casts his eyes around our group. "We had to place Tommy into a medically induced coma, having sought permission from his lawyer, who doubles as his appointed health-care proxy."

"Oh Jesus." Helen's hands fly up, covering her face.

"From what I understand and from revisiting the game tape, the impact of the hit catapulted Tommy over the opposing player's shoulder, causing Tommy's helmet to shift significantly. This left part of his skull exposed, which, unfortunately, took the brunt of the landing, along with his neck." He scratches at his jaw. "I've seen a thousand head injuries in my time, and this one is really unlucky. The CT scan reveals that the trauma sustained to his skull resulted in swelling of the brain. This swelling needed to be immediately addressed to minimize the risk of further damage. To achieve that, we reduce its activity and essentially slow it down. Placing the patient into a coma is the most effective way to do this."

Tears begin to fall down my cheeks.

This really isn't good.

"In terms of other injuries sustained," the doctor continues, almost like he's reading from a grocery list, "there is a serious fracture to his left elbow, which will need to be pinned. Stitches have already been placed in his upper and bottom lip. He has a badly twisted, but not broken, right ankle, and I suspect he has two broken fingers to his left hand. We can splint those."

"Fuck me." Jack shakes his head.

Straight after the game—which the Blades won comfortably —Archer, Sawyer, and Jack flew from the ice to be here. I think they were hoping that they would be helping their friend home in the morning.

I think we were all kidding ourselves.

"But, of course, it's the head injury that continues to concern us the most. All we can do is monitor the swelling on his brain and then gradually reduce the drugs to wake him back up. Hopefully, there won't be any lasting damage to his brain. We were happy with what the scans were showing in that regard, although we can never be certain. He was in an incredible amount of pain when he was brought into the emergency room. I'm surprised he was still partially conscious."

"I'm not," Archer puffs out. "And when he wakes up and you get a chance to speak with him, you'll understand what I mean," he tells the doctor, drawing a few muted laughs from us all.

The doctor stands and makes for the door. "I'm sorry I can't bring you any more in the way of updates, but I will check back in with you as soon as we complete an MRI and Tommy is moved to a room that can accept visitors."

With that, he walks through the door and closes it softly behind him.

"Curtis fucking Freeman needs the book thrown at him," Archer bites out.

Sawyer shakes his head. "Curtis has a clean record. The worst he'll get is a game penalty."

As frustrating as it is, Sawyer's right. Curtis wanted to take Tommy out, maybe even cause him harm. But this is hockey, and I'm pretty sure he never intended to hospitalize him. The way Tommy fell was sheer bad luck, as the doctor explained.

"This whole thing makes me sick to my stomach." Jensen shoves his hands into the pockets of his dress pants, eyes flicking up to Jon. "The best-case scenario is that Tommy is out for the rest of the season and on crutches for a long while."

"The worst-case scenario is, he'll never play hockey again." Archer pulls at his hair.

"No," I quickly correct him. "The worst-case scenario is when he wakes up, there's damage beyond his ability to pick up a stick and skate."

Holt comes to stand in front of me, reaching down and taking my hand in his. He has ahold of my car keys in the other. "Come on, Jen. I'll drive you and Helen back to your apartment so you can get a shower and a little rest. There isn't much more we can do right now."

"I can't leave him," I whisper, standing and throwing my arms around my brother's neck.

I need Holt to make this all okay. Just like he's always done.

"He saved me, Holt. He saved me from being attacked back when I was convinced he was a bad guy. But he turned everything around and showed me who he really is. And now ..." I bury my face into his chest. "And now he could change all over again. I need him to be okay. He *has* to be okay."

Holt runs a palm down my hair, cupping the back of my head in his huge hand. "Look at me, Jen."

I pull back a few inches and stare up at him.

"I promise you that nothing is going to happen to Tommy. There are too many people in this room willing him to pull through and live a long, happy, and healthy life." He rests his chin on top of my head, releasing a slow, calming breath that infiltrates my own panic. "Me included."

FORTY-FOUR

JENNA

"At what point can we expect him to fully wake up?" Sitting next to Tommy's bedside, the place where I've been planted for the past five days since the hit, I repeat the same question to his doctor I've asked over and over again.

He adjusts the oxygen mask on Tommy's face and then walks across to a tray table, picking up Tommy's medical file and taking down multiple notes.

"It's hard to say, Miss Miller. But Tommy is a strong athlete and is already showing signs that he doesn't need the oxygen mask. He's responded well to being removed from the ventilator. Better than I anticipated, in fact."

That's the best news I've received since I walked into this hospital, and I pull out my phone to text Helen the update. She's back at Tommy's place, cleaning.

Like mother, like son.

I set my phone down on the edge of Tommy's mattress and ask the doctor just as he turns to leave the room, "Is there anything more I can do to help?"

I focus back on Tommy. He looks so peaceful despite the fight his body has been—and still is—going through.

"With the increased leg and facial movements we've seen over the past forty-eight hours, I would suggest that Tommy's consciousness is becoming more aware. While he cannot see anything, he may be able to hear you. Lots of patients have reported this when they've fully woken from a coma. To reorient him, you may want to speak with him directly and remind him that you and his family and friends are all here."

So, basically, I need to keep doing everything I have been since he was put into the ambulance.

I offer the doctor an acknowledging smile as he turns to leave.

When the door closes behind him, all I'm left with is silence and incessant beeping from the machines that have helped keep my boyfriend alive. I'm grateful to every person and piece of equipment that has played its role, but I know there's only so much medicine can do. Now it's down to Tommy to wake up and confirm what the scans have all shown.

That there is no significant sign of brain damage.

My phone lights up with an incoming message, and I click into it, expecting a reply from Helen.

COLLINS

Jenna, since I know you'll be nowhere else but at his bedside right now, I need you to tell your boyfriend something …

I actually went to the gym today. That's right. I did exercise. I'm that stressed out over all of this. So, for the love of God and to save myself from having to go through that ordeal ever again, can he please wake the fuck up now and be okay? TIA.

I snort a laugh to myself.

"Tommy," I whisper, squeezing his good hand gently, "Collins is exercising—she's that twisted up over you. So, you should know that's how much you are loved around here."

I wait for a response or sign that he's heard me, but nothing comes. I know he can hear, and I know the doctor is expecting him to wake at any time.

Keeping his oxygen mask in place, I lean forward and kiss his cheek. I'm surprised he hasn't developed sores from where I've kissed him that often.

"Please, please wake up, Tommy. I miss you. So fucking much."

Picking up my phone, I open YouTube and search for a song I haven't yet played him. "Paranoid" by Black Sabbath.

"I meant what I said that day in your car," I tell him. "The lyrics of this song will always remind me of you. But not in the way I know you now. They're who you were when I met you."

I stand from his bed and pick up his comb, parting his hair to one side and styling it in the way I know he likes best.

Setting the comb down, I retake my seat next to him, along with his hand.

He still looks so peaceful, the gentle rise and fall of his chest letting me know that big heart of his is still going strong.

ME

I told him, Collins. He hasn't laughed yet, but I'm sure he will when he wakes up. That, and he'll probably offer you a monthly pass to his home gym. Just to irritate you.

COLLINS

At this point, I'll sign up for the whole fucking year if it means Tommy can ask me himself.

KENDRA

The boys are heading over to the hospital straight after practice. Jack is determined that if he isn't awake by the time they get there, then he's going to put onion paste in Tommy's hair gel.

> **DARCY**
>
> And I'll force him to come shopping with me. I know how much he loves the mall. And people.

> **COLLINS**
>
> Yeah, that's actually way worse than going to the gym.
>
> WAKE UP, TOMMY!

A knock on the door makes me jump, and I spin around to see Holt as he walks into the room. He was due to leave Brooklyn right after the game and head home to see Mom for the new year. But he decided to stay here and support me. Truthfully, I needed him, and he knew it.

He casts his eyes down at my phone as it finishes up playing Black Sabbath. "That was one of my favorite tunes when I was younger."

I tip my head at Tommy, closing out of YouTube and setting my phone down so I can take Tommy's hand in both of mine.

"The doctor said that speaking to him as he begins to wake can help with familiarization of his surroundings. I remember when I got in his car once, that song was in his playlist. He told me it was one of his favorites."

Holt takes the seat facing me and next to Tommy's bedside. "Can I ask you something?"

I nod my head once.

"Back when we first got here and the doctor told us about the coma, you said that Tommy had saved you from something really bad happening."

I glance at Holt and then back at Tommy, tears starting to form in my eyes. "I did."

Holt sits forward in the chair, setting a hand on my forearm. "I'm going to be really honest with you, Jenna."

My heart sinks at the way he says that, and I close my eyes

tightly. The last thing I need is for Holt to tell me that I'm an idiot for getting myself into stupid situations.

"I trusted the guy to walk me home, and I thought that was all he was going to do. Believe me when I tell you that I've already berated myself enough over what happened."

Holt pulls back, shock painting his face. "Jenna, are you kidding me right now? I would never blame you for what happened. The only person who needs to take a look at themselves is the guy who tried to attack you." He puffs out a slow breath and sits back again. "Was it the same guy who claimed Tommy had punched him in an unprovoked attack? Ethan was his name, right?"

I don't respond, allowing my silence to confirm it.

"Yes. And before you ask, I did make a statement to help set the record straight, and I did let the police know what happened too. I knew you were waiting and praying for Tommy to be traded away from New York. Truthfully, I was dreading it. So, I stepped up to defend justice and what was right. I think that was the catalyst between me and Tommy. It was a wake-up call for us both—realizing how much we meant to each other regardless of all the pain we'd caused."

Holt looks at Tommy for a second. There's distress in his features but also gratitude, and I know it's because of what Tommy did for me. My brother doesn't need to know all the details of what went down that night.

"You wanted to be really honest with me?" I remind Holt of what he said earlier.

"Yeah," he replies, clicking his tongue, "I did."

"Tell me what you were going to say," I press.

Holt looks unsure.

"Please," I say.

He shifts in his chair and glances at my boyfriend again. "When you first told me that Tommy had saved you from an attack, I was worried that you felt like you owed him something. Or that you could have your feelings confused over him."

I go to shut that shit straight down, but Holt gets there first.

"And I'm glad I didn't say that to you at the time because …" He drops his eyes to my hands, wrapped around Tommy's. "I know now that you aren't mixed up over him at all."

He smiles like he's having a private joke with himself or possibly like that feeling is familiar to him. I want to ask what that's about but decide that now isn't the right time.

"You love him, don't you, Jen?"

I couldn't be surer of anything in my entire life.

"Yes," I whisper, picking Tommy's hand up and kissing his tattooed knuckles. "I do. I only wish I'd stopped fucking around and returned the words before he took the hit."

Another tear slides down my cheek, splashing onto Tommy's hand. I don't bother to wipe it away. I know Tommy wouldn't want me to.

Holt stands from his chair, leaning down to set a soft kiss into my hair. "Then tell him now. The doctors have said he'll likely be listening. So, go ahead, sis. Tell your man that you love him."

As the door closes behind Holt, I'm left, once again, with only the beeps of Tommy's machines, and I tip my head toward the ceiling, making a silent plea to fate.

Please, let him be okay.

"Jenna."

I practically give myself whiplash when Tommy whispers my name.

"Tommy!" I whisper-hiss. "Tommy, tell me I'm not hearing things."

With the hand and wrist that's in plaster, Tommy reaches up to try and remove his mask.

"No. No, baby. You need to keep that on."

On a wince, he removes it anyway, and I'm too relieved to be mad at him.

"You need to put it back on," I repeat.

Tommy's eyes are barely open as he tries to absorb his surroundings. I can see the confusion in his eyes, but I take solace in the fact that he's already said my name.

"Where the fuck am I?" He slurs his words, but I can make out what he's asking.

"In the hospital," I reply. "You took a bad hit, and you're just waking up."

"I had crazy dreams."

I blow out a soft laugh and lean forward, setting a chaste kiss against his dry lips.

I want to offer him a drink, but I know I'm not allowed to do that. "Do you want me to wet your lips and call the nurse?"

I'm not sure if he understood what I said, and I go to pick up the cup of water set on the table next to his bed.

"No," Tommy groans.

"What do you need?"

"You. To feel you."

Leaning forward, I brush another kiss across his mouth. Blowing softly against his lips. "That's all you're getting for now."

He smiles like he already knows.

I go to hit Call on the button next to his bed, but he squeezes the one hand that's still wrapped around his.

"Zach Evans."

I cock my head to one side. He's definitely confused, but I decide to play along.

"What about him, Tommy?"

He rolls his lips together, squeezing his eyes shut, like he's trying to find words. "In my dream."

"You dreamed about Zach Evans?"

Since he's still in a neck brace, Tommy can't nod. "Yes, and a table."

I lean forward and run my hand through his hair. "You have had some crazy dreams."

Tommy takes a deep breath, fighting to push out a sentence. "He told me I would be okay."

I squeeze his hand. "And he was right. You are, and you will be."

When Tommy closes his eyes and drifts into a sleep, I replace his oxygen mask and hit Call next to his bed.

But before I pick up my phone to text everyone and let them know he's awake, something settles over me.

Was Tommy dreaming?

My gaze scans the room, searching for clues that Tommy's dream was real.

Rounding the bed, I come to a full stop when I set my eyes on the low table we haven't used on the other side of Tommy's bed.

A puck sits alone. It has the Scorpions logo in the center, along with words and a name scrawled underneath.

GET WELL SOON, TOMMY.
—ZACH EVANS

"Holy shit," I whisper to myself, turning the puck around in my hands.

A small tap rattles against the glass of Tommy's door, and I spin around, expecting it to be his medical team.

It isn't.

Zach Evans, dressed in a black Scorpions cap and jacket, stands on the other side of the door.

He smiles through the glass at Tommy and then gives me a quick salute before he's gone.

I knew he was in town to watch the game, but I had no idea

he was still in Brooklyn or how he got a chance to visit Tommy. I guess Coach Morgan or Jack could've signed him in, anticipating that he wanted to privately reach out to my boyfriend. I guess if there's anyone who would understand what he is going through, then it's Zach.

Another bridge rebuilt, Tommy.

When the doctor arrives and pushes through the door, I tell him that Tommy is now awake and set the puck down on the mattress next to his hand, retaking my usual spot beside him.

Leaning forward, I know he's in a deep sleep, but I'm certain he can hear me better than ever before.

"You weren't dreaming, Tommy. Zach Evans was really here. He left you a Scorpions puck and wishes you well."

As the doctor steps away to make some notes on his vitals, I lean a little closer to his ear, just to be sure he knows the score.

"You want to know something else?"

I watch the way his lips tip up into his trademark cocky smile —an expression I wouldn't change for the world. He can hear and understand me just fine, and I know he can sense what I'm about to tell him too.

I place my palm over my favorite tattoo of his and let way overdue words tumble from my lips. "I love you. So fucking much."

EPILOGUE
TOMMY

August

JACK

I need updates.

SAWYER CHANGED THE NAME OF THE GROUP
TO: JACK MORGAN IS INTOLERABLE.

JACK

What a way to speak about your captain.

SAWYER

Former captain. I retired, remember?

ARCHER

Are you in the Caribbean yet?

SAWYER

Nope. Just about to leave for the airport.

JACK

Jetting off where he wants, when he wants.

SAWYER

You bet I am. I've waited a long time for this.

JACK

I can't believe you're officially retired from the game. Are you sure you haven't got another season in those legs?

SAWYER

With the way I'm having to keep up with Ezra's motocross obsession, I barely have any time—or energy—left to spare.

ME

But what a way to round off a career—winning the playoffs and lifting the Cup. It doesn't get any better than that.

Actually, no, it really does.

ARCHER

Speaking of ... why are you texting us and not balls deep in Jenna?

ME

Sawyer, you were right. I regret being added into this group chat, and I'm not sure how to get out of it now.

SAWYER

There is no way out. I've seen supermax penitentiaries easier to break out of than this group chat.

JACK

Quit whinging and tell me if you asked Jenna yet.

ME

If I had, then you'd know.

ARCHER

If you want my best advice, then you'll run away together and get married in secret. It's way easier.

JACK

Easier when you're scared shitless of being taken out by her brother. Tommy has more class than that. He doesn't bang teammates' sisters.

ME

Did you read that, boys? Cap here thinks I have class.

ARCHER

Economy class.

ME

Wait until I'm back on the ice this season. You'll wonder how you ever kept a shutout in game seven.

EMMETT

Because he had me in the starting line. *flexes muscles*

ME

You weren't bad for an old man, I guess.

P.S. Welcome to the group chat of doom, Emmett. A place where hockey players are forced to socialize for an eternity. And on occasion, look at pictures of Archer's naked chest.

EMMETT

I get enough of that shit in the locker room. I'm only here for the gossip.

SAWYER

Well, three of us are married with children. And the other is about to get engaged, if he would get off his phone. There isn't much gossip going down in here. Trust me.

EMMETT

Damn. And here I am, newly single and hoping to spice up my life. Maybe I should join the rookies' group chat.

JACK

Don't listen to Sawyer. Allllll the gossip goes down in here. I might be a new dad to a princess. But that doesn't mean I can't keep up with what's going down.

ARCHER

Actually, that reminds me. I booked us for that dad-and-daughter event you want to go to next week. I said you'd bring scones.

JACK

That works perfectly. Esme and I are baking this afternoon, so I'll add cherry scones to the menu.

SAWYER

Esme is a month old ...

JACK

And?

ME

And she can barely support her own head, let alone whip up a mixture.

JACK

She's supervising Daddy.

Selfie of Jack crouched behind Esme's bassinet. A mass of bright blonde hair and big blue eyes staring at the camera.

ARCHER

I'm off to find your sister. I need to get her pregnant again.

JACK HAS REMOVED ARCHER FROM THE GROUP CHAT.

"I swear, you boys are worse than women."

Jenna's shadow looms over me from behind, and I pocket my phone and lean back on one elbow.

"Jack's the ringleader. I've been roped in against my will."

She looks doubtful, and I pull at the hem of her oversize white T-shirt. "Come sit with me."

It's a warm seventy-nine degrees in Brooklyn Bridge Park today, and I remove my backward cap, placing it on Jenna's head.

"How did practice go?"

She takes a seat on the plaid blanket next to me, but not in the position I wanted.

"Nah," I tell her, pointing between my spread thighs. "Come sit here."

She rolls her eyes and comes to sit between my legs. I rest my chin on her shoulder and feel the afternoon breeze that whips through her freshly showered hair. Her familiar scent fills my nose. Reminding me of home.

A minute, maybe two, passes between us before she turns her head to look at me. "Do you still have the picture we took when we came here to skate?"

I smile. "I actually saved it as my phone's background this morning, just after you left my bed to go and kick ass on the field."

She chuckles, and I wrap my arms around her waist.

"Can we take another? I feel like we should take one under Brooklyn Bridge each year," she suggests.

Pulling out my phone, I seal my mouth over hers and snap the picture.

"When you talk about taking a photo every year, it almost sounds like you might want to be around me for a while longer." My trembling fingers tuck a piece of stray hair behind her ear. "Do you think you could stand me for years to come?"

She scrunches up her nose. "Yeah, that's a fair point actually. Holt told me I should remain cautious of you."

I pull back, shocked. "Are you serious?"

Throwing her head back onto my shoulder, she laughs toward the clear blue sky. Despite recovering from multiple broken bones and a head injury, I think this has been the best summer of my life. Sure, I didn't get to be on the ice when we won the Cup; instead, I went one better than that—I was a real part of a team. And I had my mom and girlfriend by my side throughout my rehabilitation. I know there's still some way to go before I'll be game fit again, but that doesn't matter. That's just time and dedication, and nothing about that scares me.

"No!" She continues giggling to herself. "Holt is probably more in love with you than I am."

My mouth is back over hers as she turns in my arms and straddles me.

"This is a family picnic spot, Miss Miller. And you're threatening to make me hard in public."

She throws her arms over my shoulders, running her fingertips through my hair. Just like the first time Jenna touched me, all my senses are alive with anticipation. I know a lot of people talk about how true love fills their heart with happiness. Jenna Miller started mine beating.

She turns back around so she's sitting between my thighs again, and we both look out over the water, enjoying the relative silence since the park is pretty peaceful for a sunny day.

"I once told this tattoo artist that I wasn't like other people." I dip one hand into my jeans pocket, sensing this is the moment I've been waiting for.

"You aren't like other people, Tommy. I've never met anyone like you before."

With one hand, I reach around her waist and interlace our fingers.

"The thing is, Hellion, when I said that back then, it was

because I didn't want to be like other people. I wanted to be different for the sake of being unique. I wanted to be a lone wolf because that was the safest option for me to take. I thought that was me being brave and infallible when, actually"—I turn the diamond ring around in my palm—"it wasn't what I wanted at all."

Jenna twists her neck to study me carefully. "And now you're happier?"

I bob my head from side-to-side, pretending like my life isn't fully perfect with her in it. I never heard from Alex—or his loan sharks—after I closed my apartment door on him. I guess that not all bridges are meant to be repaired, and I'm good with the peace that thought brings me, along with his permanent absence from my life. "Getting there, I think."

If she can't feel the fast thump of my heart as it beats against my ribs, then I'll be surprised. Jenna has no clue I'm about to propose to her. The only people who do know are our friends, her brother, and my mom. And I only told the boys last night, for fear that Jack would never shut up, asking when I would pop the question.

Now all I'll have to deal with is a coach trying to organize the shit out of our day if she says yes.

Jesus, please say yes.

"What's missing?" she asks. "A vacation to Italy so we can gorge on amazing food and drink wine in Lake Garda?"

I bob my head again, a wry smile pulling at my lips. "You're half correct with your guess."

She releases a long sigh. "I think we should head there in your bye week in February. Just say fuck it and board a flight. The soccer season will be over, and it'll be the only chance we get."

"That sounds like the best idea you've ever had."

Still holding the ring, I release her left hand and slowly slide the ring onto the tip of her engagement finger.

A small gasp leaves her lips when she feels what I'm doing.

"But how about instead of just going on vacation to Lake Garda"—I push the ring down to her knuckle and stop, pleased when I realize it's going to fit perfectly—"I make you my wife while we're there? Just you and me and any friends and family you want to invite."

"Tommy ..." She looks down at our hands.

I know she can't see the ring I picked out yet because my fingers are blocking the view.

With my free hand, I pull my cap from her head and set it on the blanket beside us.

"Marry me, Jenna. Let me be the man to wrap his arms around your waist each night. Let me fill your life with all the love and happiness you've ever dreamed of because there is no one on this earth who deserves it more than you. I believe in love and friendship and good people because of you, and I never want to stop exploring the very depths of your heart and soul in the hopes that, one day, I'll be half the person you are."

I hover the ring on her knuckle, waiting for a response.

When the first tear falls and runs a track down my hand, a memory unlocks from the time I spent in the hospital. I know these are her tears of joy and not sadness, and I let it trickle over my skin.

"I never thought I'd say this ..." She sniffles, turning her head to look at me.

I press my forehead against hers, closing my eyes as I do. "Never say what, Jenna?"

"I'm so happy you punched my brother and made me hate you."

We both release a laugh, our breaths mingling when I cover her wet lips with my own.

"Hating you only made me more intrigued with the person you were, and that fueled my need to know more, no matter how many times I convinced myself that I should run."

She looks down at our hands, and I uncover the ring. It's a marquise cut stone, set on a simple white gold band. It's elegant, classy, and stylish, just like the girl I'm desperate to marry.

"But I never ran because you wouldn't let me. And for that, I say thank you."

She pushes the ring past her knuckle, and a happy sob breaks free from her chest. "Yes, Tommy. I'll marry you."

Flopping back on the blanket, I bring her down with me, and she turns in my arms, giggling as I roll us over until I'm on top of her.

She casts her eyes at the ring and then around the park. "There could be families around, remember?"

I smooth the pad of my thumb over her beauty spot. "I promise to keep it PG, Mrs. Williams."

"Okay," she whispers. "Be a good boy for me now. And after that, I want you to take me back home and remind me just how bad you can be."

THE END

ALSO BY RUTH STILLING

Seattle Scorpions

Boarded Hearts

Frozen Over

Dead Rinker

Ruled Out

The Blade Kings

Perfect Deke

Total Shutdown

Shots Fired

Full Tilt

Within Range

The Rules of Rink

Fair Game

Code Violation

Break in Play

Close Quarters

ACKNOWLEDGMENTS

My Husband: Thank you for holding my hand and being a rock in my life. It's hard to find people you can truly trust and count on and I'm so lucky to have married a person who is exactly that. You have been there for me since the day I met you, and throughout my writing journey. Tommy and Jenna's story was one of the hardest I've written, but their characters and strength inspire me, just as you do, every day.

My Dad: With every book I write, I thank myself for having you in my life. There's no way I could've written this one without you. And now I'm planning a fifth in the series, all because you believed in me, my writing and give me the courage to chase my dreams and write the characters that truly sit within my heart.

My little boy: You are the strongest person I know. Truly. This book is for you, and I know that Tommy would find great inspiration in your character. Keeping shining, H.

My Beta Team: With every book I think it, and this time is no exception—I don't know where I would be without you and your guidance. You are the best group of women—smart, funny, passionate about reading and romance stories, and just all-round amazing people. Thank you for working with me on *Full Tilt*.

Nay: I'm just going to leave this here: thank you. You know how deep those two words run for me, along with the love I hold in my heart for you and our friendship.

Erica: My wonderful PA and friend. You keep me on

schedule and make my life and work so much fun. I think it's fair to say that I'd be lost without you.

Kayla: I know you have been waiting—so very patiently—for Tommy's book. Well here it is, in all its toxic, enemies to lovers, redemption story glory. Thank you for your countless voice notes and words of encouragement. You mean the world to me.

Jenny: Aka, the virtual arms that wrap around me. It's true when they say that some people are meant to be in your life for a season, while others are here for a reason. You are here for a reason, and I truly hope we can be friends for a lifetime. I've learned so much from you, and from across a whole entire ocean, you are a shining light, even on the dimmest of days. I'm forever grateful that I found you, friend. And I'm forever grateful for our friendship.

To the Bookstagram community: The love you have for my books will never fail to blow me away, and I'm truly so excited to share Tommy and Jenna's story with you. This was such fun to write—especially the banter—and I cannot wait to hear all your thoughts on my baddest boy yet, Tommy! Thank you for all of the beautiful edits and words you have shared in the buildup to release. You are all phenomenal!

To all my readers: Thank you. Thank you for picking up my books. I know life is busy and with so much going on in the world I feel very privileged that you spent the time reading my words. I am nothing without my readers and the love that you show for my characters. I know they—especially Jon—are delighted that you chose to spend a few hours immersed in their world. I hope Tommy and Jenna's story is everything you want, and more. With all my love, Ruth x

ABOUT THE AUTHOR

Ruth Stilling is an avid romance reader turned writer. Having spent many years reading about and dreaming of her ideal book boyfriend, she finally decided to create her own and to share them with the rest of the world.

Living in a small town in Derbyshire, England, Ruth is an introvert by nature and spends much of her time talking with her equally book-crazy friends from across the globe.

When she isn't writing your next book boyfriend, Ruth enjoys watching all kinds of sports and is an Aston Villa and Derby County fan. The outdoors is a real favorite, and if the British weather were kinder, she would spend all her time writing outside.

Ruth is a wife to her best friend and number one cheerleader, whom she married in 2015, and a mom to her beautiful son, who has shown her a new perspective on life—enjoy and celebrate who you are as a person and cherish those who are there for you through rain and shine.

Ruth is incredibly excited to share Perfect Deke, the first installment in her second generation series, The Blade Kings!

You can follow Ruth and keep up to date with what's coming next via Instagram and TikTok by searching @authorruthstilling